something
only we know

ALSO BY KATE LONG

The Bad Mother's Handbook
Swallowing Grandma
Queen Mum
The Daughter Game
Mothers & Daughters
Before She Was Mine
Bad Mothers United

kate long

something only we know

**SIMON &
SCHUSTER**

London · New York · Sydney · Toronto · New Delhi

A CBS COMPANY

First published in Great Britain by Simon & Schuster UK Ltd, 2015
A CBS COMPANY
Copyright © Kate Long 2015

1 3 5 7 9 10 8 6 4 2

Simon & Schuster UK Ltd
1st Floor
222 Gray's Inn Road
London WC1X 8HB

www.simonandschuster.co.uk

Simon & Schuster Australia, Sydney
Simon & Schuster India, New Delhi

A CIP catalogue record for this book is available from the British Library

PB ISBN: 978-1-47112-892-9
EBOOK ISBN: 978-1-47112-893-6

Typeset by Hewer Text UK Ltd, Edinbrugh
Printed and bound in Great Britain by CPI Group (UK) Ltd, Croydon CR0 4YY

For Amanda

PROLOGUE

To get to The Poacher you park on one side of the canal, then walk across. As kids, Helen and I used to skip along the top of the lock gates to reach the far bank, while Mum and Dad always took the sturdier option of the footbridge. Obviously now I'm grown up I ought to make straight for the bridge, no question. But I'm still seriously tempted by the lock gate route.

I do love this pub. It's part of our family history. It's where we came to celebrate Mum getting her receptionist's job, and Dad landing his first major haulage contract, and when I heard I'd got into St Thom's High, and the day my A level results came through. They brought me here for Sunday lunch the weekend before I went to uni; I was wearing this flimsy gypsy top and I remember a guy off one of the narrowboats wolf-whistling me. One time I spotted a kingfisher in a tree by the toilet block and Helen missed it because she was arguing with Mum, and after-wards she wouldn't believe me, which is typical.

Hel's currently stopped halfway along the bridge. First it was to empty out a stone in her shoe; now she's leaning over as if to study the water and the clouds of tiny flies hovering above its surface on this hot June day. Her red hair falls down, hiding her face, and in her white maxi dress she's like some Victorian painting of a ruined maid contemplating suicide.

'Get a move on,' I say, coming up alongside her. She swings round and flashes a look at me. I don't care. This is my day, and besides, unlike Mum and Dad, I'm immune to her moods. For once she can do what I want.

'Yes, come on, girls,' calls Mum from the pub doorway. She's trying to sound cheery, like a mother on an ordinary, carefree family outing.

I give Hel a slight shove and she detaches herself from the railing and drifts over to the courtyard. Already one or two people at the picnic tables are looking in her direction. A man winding the handle at the lock gate stops to stare.

Inside the saloon it's gloomy after the bright sunshine. 'Table for four,' Dad says to the bar lady. 'We've booked. Crossley. One p.m.'

'It's my daughter's birthday,' adds Mum unnecessarily.

'Mum,' I say.

'Twenty-three today!'

'No one's *interested*.'

But she only grins at me because she's happy to be out, happy that we're here together to share a nice meal in a normal family style. Which is so not what we did on Helen's birthday. Hel's thirtieth was marked by a shop-bought pavlova with a single candle pushed into the centre. The meringue proved impossible to slice, crumbs exploded everywhere, and the whole cake kind of deflated so all anyone got was a plate of soggy mess. It was what she'd asked for, though.

We're given a table by the window. The light's streaming in, making my sister's hair look as though it's on fire, a glorious pre-Raphaelite cascade. The little girl at the table next door nudges her mother and whispers, 'Who's that?' The mother shrugs. The child's father keeps flicking his eyes towards us, to Helen's long, slim neck, her slender arms, her heart-shaped face.

Then we start with the fussing. Hel can't read the swirly print on the menu, there's nothing here she fancies, haven't they heard of steaming, she has a headache coming on. She turns the laminated sheet over and over. *We could have had a perfectly nice meal at home*, she vibes across the table at me.

My day, my choice, Helen.

Another great sigh, then she swivels in her seat to inspect the window and the countryside beyond. God knows what she's expecting to see. An escape route, maybe? Might she leap up, wrench the latch open and clamber across the sill?

'I need the toilet,' she says.

No she doesn't.

Mum half-stands so Helen can squeeze past her. At the same moment a waiter appears, a boy of about seventeen with bum-fluff on his chin. Mum tells him we're not ready. 'I am,' I say. 'I could eat this bar mat I'm so hungry.' But I'm wasting my breath.

We wait for what seems like a long time. I notice the little girl at the table next to us has slid her hair bobble up her arm and is pinging it repeatedly against her skin; I can see the red mark from here. If I were her mum I'd be worried about that. The waiter walks by with a huge ice cream dessert and I follow it with my eyes till it's out of sight round the corner. Dad checks his watch, then goes to fetch a copy of the *Shropshire Herald* from the bar.

3

Eventually Mum says, 'I think I'll just nip to the loo myself, freshen up.'

For a while I read the back of the newspaper where Dad's folded it over, assessing the layout of the page and the balance of the articles. The *Herald*'s always got a chatty feel to it, upbeat and reassuring. *This county's great*, it tells its readers. *You're lucky to live here*. A story catches my eye about a young farmer who's trekked across a desert and raised a stack of money for WaterAid. There's a photo of him smiling in a floppy canvas hat. He looks nice. The slightly bewildered pitch of his eyebrows reminds me a bit of Helen's boyfriend, Ned. I wonder about pointing this out to Dad. Then I happen to clock the expression of the barmaid who I think is also the pub manager. She's clearly cheesed off with us for taking so long.

'Hey, I'll round them up, shall I?' I say to Dad, pushing my chair away.

He gives me a tired smile. His hair's started to thin lately, I've noticed, and the buttons on his shirt are straining across his belly. I don't like to think about him getting old.

When I open the door to the Ladies', Helen's bowed over the sink and Mum's standing next to her, stroking her shoulder.

'They're waiting to take our order,' I say.

'Yes, you go, we're on our way,' Mum replies.

I don't move an inch. 'Stir yourself, sis.'

'That's right, sweetheart, come along.' Mum pulls at her arm so that Helen's slim frame leans briefly against her bosom. Hel bears it for about two seconds, then wrenches herself free and pushes past me to the exit.

Finally we're all at the table reciting our orders – roasts for Mum and me, lasagne for Dad, fishcake starter as a main for Hel – and I know I ought to try and relax. The food's on its way and what happens after that's not my problem. It's really not. I want to enjoy myself. I want just one meal to be special and pleasant and untainted by angst. But Helen's mouth is set in a determined line and her eyes are wide and anxious. Above the lace neckline of her dress, her collarbone stands out, betraying the clenched way she's holding her body. I know that even though she's officially recovered, even after all these years, she still finds eating in public a trial. I get that. It's not her fault. It's probably always going to be hard for her. So why did Mum insist she came? Why couldn't we leave her at home as she wanted? For a moment I imagine asking this out loud, and hear in my head Mum's inevitable response: *Because she's your sister.*

'You look nice, anyway,' says Mum, nodding at my new top, a cerise scoop neck that I chose because it makes the most of my boobs. 'And your hair, you suit it bobbed, and darker. It's smart. More officey.'

'Thanks.'

'Doesn't Jenny look nice, Don?'

Dad nods.

'I ought to. It's my birthday.'

'That's right,' says Mum. 'Every girl should look nice on her birthday.'

Nice. Yes, that's my limit. Not like Helen, stunning and mysterious, with her huge sad eyes and her high cheekbones, a mournful copper-haired princess in need of rescuing. I'm too solid, too grounded in ordinariness.

Instantly I hate myself for thinking like this. I don't want to harbour ungenerous thoughts on my birthday. I love my sister, even if she is a pain. Only, just for once, I'd like today to be a tiny bit more about me. Is that so wrong?

I don't know why but suddenly I'm compelled to swivel round and check out what the rest of the pub is doing. And it's as I'd have predicted. The waiter, the little girl and her dad, the old men by the beer pumps, the scruffy ramblers who've just walked in, the bar lady herself: not one of them is looking at me. They are all looking at my beautiful sister.

CHAPTER 1

When we got home that night I heard Mum say to Hel, 'You were great. You did really well.' I was on the landing, putting my new top in the washing basket, and I thought about the end of the meal, where the rest of us had tucked into pudding while my sister sat and watched as usual. I don't know who finds these situations harder, her or us.

Laundry sorted, I took myself into my bedroom to check my phone and to go through my presents and cards again, the way you do on your birthday. There'd been nothing yet from Owen, although I wasn't that surprised as I knew he was busy travelling home from Glastonbury, plus his mind's generally on higher concerns than boyfriend stuff. I'd get something off him eventually. Aside from that I'd had a good haul: a green silk scarf, new jewelled sandals, a subscription to *Private Eye*, a copy of Evelyn Waugh's *Scoop* in a retro slipcase, posh cleansing milk, a giant block of Galaxy from the girls at zumba, a box set of *Being Human*, vouchers, money, a stack of cheeky Facebook messages from far-flung college mates. There was also a text from Ned asking how Hel had managed at the meal.

And a happy birthday to you, Jen!! I typed back. He rang straightaway.

'Obviously that,' he said. 'I wrote it in my card, if you remember.'

'I know. I was just messing. And thanks for the book. It looks funny.' He'd bought me a collection of newspaper misprints and humorous headlines.

'My pleasure. You OK?'

'Why?'

'You sound teed off.'

'No, I'm fine. Tired. The new job's still quite stressy. But the meal went OK. Helen settled, in the end.'

It was true she had stayed in her seat, eaten her fishcake and green salad, chatted a little. Anyone glancing over probably wouldn't have noticed she was on edge.

'That's good,' said Ned. 'Sorry I couldn't have been there. I did try to skive off work but they weren't having it.'

'We missed you.'

'Get away.'

'We did. You're our family's steadying influence. You're our metronome of sanity.'

'Bloody hell, Jen. If that's the case then we're all in trouble.'

I could hear the smile in his voice. At the same time I caught sight of my reflection in the dressing table mirror, standing there in my bra and skirt, and imagined Ned being able to see me like that. My cheeks grew hot. Behind me on the wall was the countryside mural Dad painted when I was about six, featuring misshapen squirrels and an owl and a rabbit with one mad eye. There were my shelves above the bed, laden with a jumble of books and ornaments and half-used hair products, and on either side two tall cupboards, both of which were stuffed to the point where you had to jam the doors closed really quickly or everything fell out. I'd ended up tying a belt round the handles for security. My fake-fur rug was rucked up against the skirting; a tower of CD cases had collapsed against the wardrobe. Every one of my drawers had a scrap of material poking out. I had not inherited my mother's cleaning gene.

'Jen? You still there?'

'Yeah, yeah. Temporarily distracted by the state of my room.'

'Gaining the upper hand, is it?'

'It has gone a bit mental lately. I might actually have to tidy up at some point.'

'The day pigs go whizzing past the upstairs window.'

'No. One day soon I'll sort it. Chuck out the rubbish, streamline what's left. Invest in some new storage solutions. Remove all traces of my adolescence and bring the place up to date so that it fits in with my exciting new career.'

'As long as you don't take down your Crazy Frog stickers. I bought you those.'

'Yep, I remember.' A row of them along the bottom of my book case. Ned had presented me with them as a good luck charm for starting secondary school. 'Sorry, though, the amphibians might have to be sacrificed. This room is not an appropriate environment for a thrusting young journo.'

'I love it when you pretend to be grown up. It's cute.'

'Bog off, Neddy. You should probably call my sister now, she'll be expecting you.'

'Yup, I'm on the case. Just wanted to speak with you first. In case, you know . . .'

'I know.'

'But she's OK? Really?'

'She is. We were fine.'

'Good. Right. See you, then.'

'See you.'

And ten seconds later, on the other side of the door, came the theme to *White Horses*, which is Helen's ring tone. It made me jump because I'd never even heard her come up the stairs. When she wants to, my sister can move round this house like a ghost.

The Chester Messenger is situated on the top floor, and my desk is by the window, so I can look out over the Rows and watch the shoppers and tourists and men dressed as Roman centurions leading columns of school kids down Watergate Street. Here, I'm a good distance away from Rosa, Editor and boss, but I'm near Gerry, our other sub, so he can give me a hand if I get stuck. He's in his fifties, has been on the paper for thirteen years, and he's supposed to be training me in practical journalism, although mainly what he says is stuff like, 'Go get us a Crunchie from the machine, will you, Jen? Milk and two sugars for me if you're heading for the kettle.' His theory is that the human mind's only capable of concentrating in short bursts, so it's quite legitimate to continually interrupt my working day with random demands. Maybe he's right. I'm fresh out of uni, what would I know?

This morning I was working on a piece for our lifestyle section, Chester Cream. My brief was 'The Worst Date Ever', and I'd been tasked with extracting sound bites from emails and tweets and interviews we'd garnered, and then pasting them together to form a coherent article. Utter fluff it might have been, but I'll be honest, I was quite enjoying myself. It's always entertaining to read about other people's cock-ups. *He belched in my face. He brought his mum along. Previously unmentioned WIFE came home and I had to climb over a gate to escape.* I was thinking how I might group the confessions. The funny ones and the pervy ones, the disgusting ones and the sad, the ones that just sounded like a plain unvarnished nightmare. Possibly I could rank them, produce a top twenty. That would be quite snappy. It could go on our website as a taster. Then again, some of them were hard to compare. The man who set his own beard on fire because his date wasn't paying him enough attention, or the waiter who embarked on a spectacular nosebleed in the middle of serving the soup – which rated as worse?

I did wonder whether I should chip in anonymously with my own experience, whether Owen might see it and recognise himself. But no, that wouldn't happen because he never went near *The Messenger.* He said it was middle-class toss; he said that if people stopped bothering for five minutes about the right shoes to wear or what tat Hollywood film was showing at Cineworld, they might notice their country was going down the pan and rise up in revolution. So I probably could get away with writing about how, in our last term at uni and after months of mooching round after him and attending his political debates, handing out flyers for him and stacking chairs, I burst into his room one night and declared my love. Only what I hadn't realised was that he'd been on Skype, and a load of his mates were listening in to every word I said. The shame when I'd twigged had been hideous. There'd been a nice outcome, though, when he'd switched off the laptop and listened, and said he did like me and admired my energy but he wasn't interested in a girlfriend, he didn't have time for one. And I'd been so loved-up I'd just ignored this and kissed him and he kissed me back and shortly afterwards it turned out he was quite interested after all. Happy days.

A warning cough nearby. I looked up from my desk to see Gerry's eyes on the main door.

'Our glorious leader's arrived. Chop chop.'

That would be Rosa, returned from lunch. The rest of us have to grab a sandwich, but my boss dines out nearly every day. Networking, she calls it. She came round the corner of the water cooler, headed in our direction. Not an attractive woman in the conventional sense – her chin was too strong for that and she was what Dad liked to call 'broad in the beam' – but she did know how to carry herself. Most likely been to finishing school to learn how to walk with a stack of books on her head. Good breeding, confidence, I don't know what you'd call it, but she had it. A healthy, forty-something county girl. I'd slipped into the habit of calling her Tweed-knickers when she was out of earshot.

'Busy, are we?' she trilled across to Gerry and me.

I nodded guiltily, even though I had nothing to be guilty about.

Gerry said, 'You had a phone message from the new events manager at the racecourse. I've put the number on your desk.' He does that, throws the conversation back at her, refuses to be fazed. I tend to blush and lower my eyes, even when I've been slaving away on an article for hours.

'Good.' She started to walk away, then paused and retraced her steps. 'Jennifer?'

'Yes?'

'How far are you on with the piece on infidelity?'

Infidelity? She'd lost me. 'Do you mean the worst-ever-dates thing?'

She sighed. 'No. If I'd meant worst-ever-dates I'd have *said* worst-ever-dates. I mean the piece on infidelity. The tell-tale signs of cheating. That book we were sent. We talked about it yesterday.'

I glanced over at Gerry but he had his eyes fixed on his PC screen.

'Oh, right. That. I didn't realise you needed it immediately. Did you want me to start it now, Rosa?'

'I believe that's what I asked for.'

Had she? 'I thought you needed this date piece finishing.'

'I do. I need them both, by the end of the day. Or is that going to cause you some kind of problem? Did they not cover multiple deadlines on your university course?'

You didn't say you needed the other article for today, I wanted to snap back. *It's not me who's causing the problem here. Last week we didn't need the Life Class piece till Friday, so why the rush? If you're going to change the timetabling, you need to flag it up. I'm not a damn mind-reader.*

'Well?'

What I'd assumed was a rhetorical jibe clearly required a response. 'Yeah, I'll get onto it. Do you want me to finish the dating stories first?'

Rosa just rolled her eyes as if the question was more than her patience could bear, then turned on her heel and left.

I waited till she was gone. 'Hell. What do you think she meant by "the end of the day", Gerry? Four p.m? Five? In her email folder first thing tomorrow so it's there when she comes in?'

He removed the end of his pen from between his teeth. 'Who can tell?'

'How am I going to get through both pieces in time?'

'You'll just have to squeeze them out. Like toothpaste.'

'I just don't get why she has to be so stroppy with me, though. Why did she even hire me if she thinks I'm so useless?'

But I knew the answer to that. Partly it was because Rosa had been impressed with me on paper, with my degree and with my tutors' references, and she'd offered me the placement before she'd had chance to realise she didn't like me in the flesh. Mainly, though, I was kept on because I was an unpaid intern, doing the job for free so as to get my foot on the ladder. And I considered myself lucky. Of the group I'd graduated with, over half were still unemployed, or in jobs which had nothing to do with the degree. It had taken me nine anxious months to land this position here.

'You're the office junior,' said Gerry. 'It's part of your remit: "Take crap from boss". We've all been there at some point and we've all survived.'

I shot him a grateful glance.

'Oh, and by the way,' he went on, 'I hate to remind you, but you know you're out this afternoon talking to those American quilters?'

'Bloody hell, I'm not, am I?'

'That's what's down in The Diary, Jen.'

'No. No! I'll phone up and cancel.'

'You can't. The photographer's booked.'

'Fuck.'

Urgently I began to root around my desk. Within half a

minute I'd found the paperback guide to detecting infidelity that Rosa had been on about: two hundred and seventy-five pages, no pictures except for the stiletto heel squashing a hot dog sausage on the cover. I flicked through, feeling glum. No way would I have time to complete the dating piece, read this book and condense it into an article by 2 p.m. Unless I just rehashed the accompanying press release, skimmed a few chapter headings, the intro and conclusion and then winged it.

I heard Rosa's shoes tap-tapping over to Alan on the sports desk. She likes Alan. He flirts with her and he never seems to have deadline crises.

'Right,' I said to Gerry. 'I'm putting on my earphones and I'm going for it. Don't let anyone disturb me unless the building's on fire.'

He gave me a little salute.

And with that I was off.

<u>Is he Playing Away? The Seven Deadly Signs</u>
No one likes a paranoid partner. Yes, we've all been struck by the odd twinge of jealousy, a flash of insecurity as your other half shares a joke with an attractive colleague, or eyes a younger woman in the street. That's normal and it soon passes.

But what if those prickles of concern have recently grown into genuine nagging doubts? What if that sense of suspicion's beginning to invade every corner of your life? A new book by Professor Lally Pike, Nail That Cheat!, explains how the answer might not lie with you, but in what your husband or boyfriend gets up to when you're not around. Check our list of possible danger signs to tell whether your fears might be justified.

<u>Looks</u>: *Has your man been trying out a new image? Taking the*

trouble to style his hair where before he just ran a comb through and was done? Perhaps he's been showering more frequently, or buying himself lots of new clothes. Ask yourself – who's he making this effort for? Whose sartorial advice might he be taking?

Secrecy: The classic ploy of a cheating man is to take his mobile into another room to answer it. But watch out too for him closing his email down quickly when you walk in, or the installing of secret passwords which he never bothered with before. What's he trying to hide? If they're totally innocent, why can't these messages be shared with you?

Moods: If he's been grumpier than usual, there might be a sinister reason. Modern life can certainly be stressful with its different demands, but if he's been niggling over details and picking pointless fights then it could be a guilty conscience rising to the surface. Or perhaps he WANTS to put himself in the doghouse, then he can justify looking elsewhere.

Timetables: Has he changed the hours he's been working? Perhaps his boss keeps asking him to work late or springing surprise meetings which mustn't be missed. There could even be nights away at conferences or training courses. Sure, there are some professions which eat into your free time, but if you're noticing a radical departure from normal office patterns then it could be a signal to start investigating.

Names: Has one particular name started cropping up just a little too much in general chit chat? Does a certain person seem to find her way into a lot of his anecdotes? It could be because she's absorbing your partner's mind. These mentions don't even have to be complimentary – they could be neutral or even hostile. A man sometimes hides his interest underneath a barrage of critical comments, the same way the little boy in the playground will yank the plaits of the girl she secretly fancies.

Famine: How are things in the bedroom? You could find your sex life's stalling because his energies are being diverted. Look out for signs such as his being permanently tired, or achy/sick/stressed. Perhaps he no longer comes to bed at the same time as you to avoid any advances, or won't undress with you in the room for fear of revealing love bites or scratches.

Feast: Alternatively, your man might be keener than ever on sex, either as a result of overstimulation or the need to compensate for his cheating. Watch out if he suddenly has a variety of new techniques at his disposal – who's taught him those?

By the time I'd dealt with the quilters and then signed off the cheating article, it was getting on for half six. Gerry had packed up and gone; Rosa was still in her office, or at least her fan was whirring. God knows how late she intended staying. I emailed the pieces across to her and picked up my bag.

I was still fuming, and the content of the article had unsettled me. Gerry laughed at me for it but sometimes I worried about writing copy that could upset people. Who knew what effect my glib, thrown-together checklist might have on individual readers? Spouses collared and challenged, rightly or wrongly, distress caused whichever way the truth fell. Evenings filled with accusations. And all in the name of filling column inches.

Well, thank God I trusted Owen. He wasn't going to be cheating. He barely had enough attention to cover one girl-friend, let alone a bit on the side.

I rechecked my watch now, considered my options. Although it wasn't one of the nights we usually met up, I wondered if he might be free for a quick cuppa and to listen to a moan about horrible bosses. I could pop down there now. Just say hello. I didn't fancy going straight home.

Owen was currently based on the top floor of a tall, thin townhouse overlooking the river. Being an unwaged political activist, he'd never have been able to afford a place like that himself, but back in the day his dad had married money, divorced, and walked away with a very good settlement. Mr Cooke now owned no fewer than four properties in Chester, and allowed his son to live in one rent-free. Which made Owen a lucky dog. I'd have given anything to move out of our three-bed semi, with its pokey bathroom and too-thin walls. Mustn't be ungrateful, though; my parents were already subbing me through my internship, Dad grafting long hours to keep his haulage firm going, and Mum with her part-time receptionist's post. And as I was often reminded, at least I had a roof over my head, not like those poor souls standing outside Thorntons in all weathers flogging *The Big Issue*. In any case, it would have been wrong to envy Owen's wealth since he was using his secure financial position to campaign for a fairer society. His flat aside, he really did care nothing for material possessions. If you gave him an expensive gift he'd most likely pass it on to someone in need (I'd learnt that the hard way). More than once I'd witnessed him stop in the street to remove items of his own clothing – warm jacket, good trainers – and hand them to a beggar.

This July evening it was a quiet, pleasant walk down to the Dee. The shoppers had dispersed but it was too early for the drinkers to be out. As I passed the artisan bakery, speckled pigeons loitered hopefully. The shadows were lengthening, the red sandstone Walls rosy in the sunlight. Bunting fluttered from the tops of the Rows. The atmosphere was festive, English, summertime. How much did Owen notice of the city, its history and beauty? Or did you stop appreciating such details when you lived in the middle of them? I sometimes had this fantasy of him and me sitting on his window-seat in our pyjamas at midnight, drinking hot chocolate while the lights sparkled on the weir below. Except I wasn't allowed to stay over, because one of his quirks was he could never get off to sleep in a shared bed.

A few hundred yards from the house I stopped to phone him, to save myself the disappointment of ringing the doorbell and getting no reply.

'Jen?' He sounded surprised. 'All right?'

'Not really. I wanted to see you. Are you in?'

'No, like I said, I'm busy this evening.'

'Are you?'

'I've got that lecture I told you about.'

'Oh. Yeah.' It was true. I'd forgotten. 'When do you need to leave?'

'I've left already. I'm cycling into Blacon as we speak. Gotta be there for seven-fifteen.'

'Remind me what it is tonight?'

'Social Welfare: Where Next? It's Irma Boyd speaking, she's terrific. You should come.'

'Nah, you're OK. I need to get home and have something to eat.'

'There's a lecture about corporate crime and the multi-nationals coming up soon.'

'Is there?'

'And another about the economic implications of biofuels.'

I know I should take a keener interest in the politics of inequality – Owen has the entire weight of moral right on his side – but I can't always summon up the energy. Some days I can barely cope with the injustices and loose ends of my own small life, never mind trying to take in the global scale of wrongdoing.

'What time will you be finished?'

'Not till late. Look, Jen, I've really gotta go. Sorry. I'll call you tomorrow, talk about the weekend. Yeah?'

'Yeah.'

That would have to do. He rang off and I stood for a while, feeling flat, while the traffic lights went through their sequence two, three times. I thought, should I ring him back and ask where exactly in Blacon the meeting was? Drag myself over there and sit beneath flickering strip lights while some strange woman railed about privilege and corruption? Might it be worth it to see my boyfriend? The answer was no, not this evening. It was a hug I'd been after, not a lecture. I could walk down to the river, though, past his house. Buy a snack from the late-night newsagent. Eat it looking out over the water.

I nipped over the crossroads and made my way in the direction of the Old Dee Bridge. There was Owen's house, with its Georgian frontage and fan-shaped glass over the wide front door. There was the cobbled courtyard, steps, the iron railing, hanging baskets: a genteel space in the heart of the city. I cast a longing look now at the top storey. At the same moment, my mobile began to buzz. I scrabbled for it hopefully.

'Owen?'

'It's Mum.'

'Oops. I meant to ring and let you know I'd be late. Sorry. Were you worried where I was? It's just, I've had the worst day, that bloody woman sprung a load of extra work on me and she knew I had an assignment, but luckily the American quilters I had to interview were really quick or I'd never have managed it—'

'Jenny, we need you here.'

'Yeah, I'm on my way. But I'm going to grab a muffin first because I'm starving, then I'll be—'

'No, straight home, love. I need you to help me with Helen.'

Her voice sounded strained, teetering on that knife-edge between apology and command. *Honestly, sweetheart, only if it's no trouble, but if you don't do what I'm asking right this minute I'll never speak to you again.* I'm too familiar with that tone. And I remember some of the Helen situations we've had before: Mum discovering a strip of laxatives hidden inside a book, the Bank Holiday weekend when the bathroom scales stopped working, the time I accidentally broke Hel's special plate. In a normal family none of these would have been an issue.

'Right, fine. I will just buy a snack from the newsagent though because—'

'Jenny, please. We need you now.'

That high-pitched note of panic, like the singing of a wine glass about to shatter. There's no arguing when she's that near the edge. Hel says boo and we all jump.

When I got home the curtains were drawn, even though it was light outside. This was our drama and no one else was allowed to watch. Hel was squeezed deep into a corner of the sofa, as if she wanted to disappear down the crack between the cushions. Dad was nowhere to be seen. I guessed he'd had his say then taken himself off somewhere, out of the way. Mum stood in front of the TV, her arms folded.

'What do you think?' she said before I'd even sat down.

'About what? You have to give us a clue.'

'Helen. She claims to have a job. A job!'

I glanced across at my sister, who shrugged.

But indignation was already rising from my mother like steam. 'A job, and we knew nothing about it. Nothing. It's all been arranged behind our backs. Not a word. All done in secret. That's what bothers me here. And do you know who gave her a reference? Mr Wolski. Tadek Wolski! So she's gone ahead and confided in her ex-teacher, yet she didn't think to breathe a word to us. That's nice, isn't it?'

I settled myself on the arm of the chair and looked at Hel. She had on her mask-face – no expression other than one of complete detachment. I can't tell whether she uses it because she knows it winds Mum up, or if that's genuinely how she feels. Above and beyond us all.

'What sort of job is it?' I ventured.

'What sort of job? I'll tell you. Something that I'd never have let her anywhere near if she'd taken the trouble to consult us first.'

My mind boggled. Whatever could my sister have in mind? Mercenary? Prostitute? One of those guys who cleans the windows at the very top of skyscrapers? 'Elephant sperm collector,' I imagined Ned saying, and that very nearly started me giggling, which would have probably meant my mother driving me out of the family forever.

'Cut the dramatics, Mum. It's a kennel maid,' said Helen to me. 'I want to work at an animal rescue centre.'

'What, with cats and dogs?'

'No, with performing fleas.'

'OK. Keep your knickers on.'

'Please don't use language like that, Jenny,' said Mum.

'She started it.'

I thought, if only Owen hadn't been going out I could've been round at his now, sipping cold cider and listening to music. Away from this.

Mum tried again. 'Helen, tell your sister what they want you to do at this centre.'

'Clean up, feed the animals. Look after them. Try to rehome the ones who—'

'Which would be fine,' broke in Mum, 'except this kennels or rescue place or whatever they call it, can you imagine what a distressing place it must be? When the animals are brought in hurt and abused, and then they don't get better, and then they . . . they don't get better. How's that going to make you feel?'

'Upset, for a few days. Then I'll move on. Focus on the ones who are healthy, the ones we've helped.'

'But think what state you got yourself in when Toffee died!'

Toffee, king of the cavies. I must have been about nine when he went to guinea pig heaven. A large brown and white boar who ran away whenever I tried to stroke him, but who'd wheek at Helen as soon as she appeared and stand up on his hind feet to be fed. He'd been a good pet on the whole, but he let us down majorly by having a heart attack right at the start of Helen's worst period, when letters of concern were coming from school and Mum was starting to make appointments with health professionals. The death of Toffee had triggered Old Testament-scale mourning. Helen had cried for days.

Now Mum came over and sat on the chair arm next to me. 'Jenny, you can see why I'm worried, can't you? Back me up here.'

'When Toffee died I wasn't myself,' argued Helen. 'I was a teenager, it was a different time. I'm recovered.'

And I thought, *Are you, though? Are you recovered? How far along the spectrum do you have to be to say you're cured?* Even that morning I'd seen her putting low-fat spread on a Ryvita. Scrape it on, scrape it off, reapply, remove a bit more, adjust, refine, scrutinise. No actual eating allowed till the application looked to be exactly the right thickness. Just watching her made me exhausted.

'But is it worth the risk?' Mum went on. 'Believe me, I'm not just blocking you for the sake of it—'

'You're not blocking me at all, Mum. This whole thing is ridiculous. Physically I'm fine. Dr Gerard said that last month; you were there, you heard him. My BMI's healthy, my bone density's passable. You said yourself it was good news. And I need to get into the world and exercise my practical mind. I've done enough academic studying. I've more A levels than I know what to do with. But mainly, I can't stay holed up in here with you forever.'

'We're not expecting you to. Of course you have to make your way in life. We want to support you in that, you know we do. But can you not pick something more suitable? Something less . . . disturbing? Your dad'll help you look for a job, he knows people.'

On the wall behind Mum's head hung her wedding photo. There she'd been, a glowing twenty-something bride, with no idea what deep lines were going to score themselves around her mouth and chin over the next three decades. Everything about today's contours said disappointment, weariness, frustration. She might keep herself smart, have her hair dyed professionally, but the years had done for her skin. It was as if she was collapsing in on herself.

Helen sat up straight, her eyes blazing.

'Oh, for God's sake. Can't you see how mean you're being? I went out and got this position on my own. I checked through the small ads, I applied, I had an interview, I won it fair and square. My first ever job. Paid employment. It was my idea, my effort. I had no help from anyone.'

'Apart from that Mr Wolski.'

'I thought you'd be proud!'

'Well, we are—'

'Looks like it.'

Mum turned to me. 'I give up. This is what we've had all evening. She's deliberately missing the point. Talk some sense into her, Jen. She might listen to you.'

That nearly made me laugh out loud. 'Yeah, right.'

'Well she doesn't listen to *me*.'

My sister sighed and slumped against the cushions.

I said, 'You really want my view on this?'

'*Yes*,' said Mum.

'OK then. For what it's worth, I actually think the kennels placement is a good idea.' Her eyes widened at the betrayal, but I carried on regardless. 'Hel's right, she's got to find something to do at some point or other, and better if she starts with a job she's keen on rather than one that's been thrust on her. What she's chosen here isn't anything high-powered, there's no huge expectations or responsibility – I'm guessing it's going to be mainly filling dog bowls and poop scoops, yeah? – and despite your concerns, Mum, I reckon it'll be quite an upbeat place. She'll be working alongside people who help animals get better, and they're bound to be a supportive bunch. And there'll be success stories every day, pets being rehomed, getting healthy again. It could actually be quite therapeutic for her.'

'Therapeutic. Nice one, sis.' Helen nodded her approval.

I swivelled so I was addressing her directly. 'Anyway, it's about time you started contributing to the household.'

'You mean, like you do?'

Sod off, I vibed at her. *I'm trying to help.*

Meanwhile Mum was glaring at me like I was the biggest disappointment ever. 'That's put me in my place, then.'

'You asked for my opinion. What about Dad, does he think Hel should work at the kennels?'

'Him!'

Helen slid herself to the edge of the sofa and stretched. Then she stood up, her gypsy skirt trailing off the cushion behind her and flopping down around her ankles. She'd cinched in her waist with a leather belt that I knew she'd had to punch extra holes in to make fit. She's still pretty thin in my book, whatever the doctors' charts say.

'Look, is there anything to eat?' I asked. 'Because I'm so hungry I'm starting to feel sick.'

With a swish of Indian cotton my sister made her way out into the hall and up the stairs.

'I've left you a plate of shepherd's pie,' said Mum absently, passing her palm over her brow as if she had another of her headaches. Of course I can see why she worries. We all live in fear of it starting up again. Sometimes the anorexia's felt like a fifth member of our family: Hel's shadowy companion, hanging round the dinner table, casting a chill of bad memories over us all.

I made to get up, but she reached out and held my arm for a moment.

'You know, Jenny, I only ever try and do my best for her. It's not easy.'

Maybe I should have stayed to reassure her, listen to her woes. But I was tired and famished and missing Owen. Fed up, too: I bet Mum didn't spend a tenth of the time angsting over my problems. I'm tough as old boots, I am.

'So cut her some slack,' I said.

I brushed her away and walked into the kitchen, not looking back.

Ten to midnight and I was propped up in bed, playing with the origami animals Owen had sent me. The parcel had been sitting on top of our fridge for days, apparently, not that anyone had thought to mention it. Inside was my birthday card – hand-drawn, a complicated swirl of leaves and feathers – and this paper menagerie he'd created. There were two kangaroos, a swan, a walrus, a seahorse, a fish, something that might have been a cat, a panda, a bat, a rhino and a mouse. Each one had been carefully threaded with cotton so I could hang it from my lampshade or curtain rail. For now I'd lined them up along my duvet so I could take a photo with my phone, except the penguin kept falling over. Its beak was too heavy for its centre of gravity. If I leant it against the walrus, that held it up, but then it looked drunk. 'And nobody likes a drunk penguin,' I imagined Ned saying.

I was delighted and relieved. I knew Owen wouldn't have forgotten. Even last year, before we were going out, he'd taken the trouble to make me a photo frame out of driftwood. Then, that Christmas he'd painted me a watercolour of the weir. In between times I'd had a bookmark decorated with pressed bracken, a pendant made from a Scrabble tile, and a whistle he'd carved himself out of a willow stick. All right, it was no use taking him to a shop window and pointing hopefully at a pair of violet stilettos ('You don't need any more shoes, Jen. You're just giving in to the pressures of consumerism.'), but these little personal gifts he made me – presents that don't hurt the planet, he'd called them – were worth much more.

I was still negotiating with the penguin when I heard a soft knock at my door. I stiffened in case it was Mum, come to have another go at me for not taking her side in the kennels argument. At the same time a small part of me hoped it might be so I could say something soothing and end the day on a better note. But when I called 'Come in', it turned out to be Helen, dressed in her long white robe and carrying a mug in each hand.

'I saw your light on,' she said.

We know Helen keeps late hours. It's a hangover from the illness, when she used the nights to exercise and write weird poetry.

'Yeah, well. I've a lot on my mind.' I gestured at the mugs. 'What's this in aid of?'

'I made you hot chocolate.'

'Why?'

'Do you want it or not?'

I did. I threw down the phone and reached out gratefully. Hel settled herself on the end of my bed, pretending not to notice the state of my carpet or the piles of clothes draped over my chair and stool. My mess annoys her, the same way her obsessive neatness gets to me. We don't go in each other's bedrooms much.

'They're cute,' she said, nodding at the origami figures. 'I like the little moustache.'

'It's a bat.'

'So it is. Did you make them?'

'No. Owen. For my birthday.'

'Right.' The faintest note of disapproval. Not everyone gets Owen or his approach to low-cost gifting. She herself had bought me a smart office set in a mix of primary colours – lime green stapler, tangerine hole punch, raspberry pen pot, etc – to brighten up my desk at *The Messenger*. 'Make you look more organised,' she'd said.

I swept the origami onto the bedside table, out of the way.

She said, 'Anyway, I just wanted you to know, you were brilliant this evening. You didn't have to stick up for me.'

'Mum was wrong. That's all there was to it.'

'I'm glad you can see it. Even Dad wasn't completely sold on the idea because he thinks I can "do better". A nice clerical post, he sees for me. But those points you made were good ones about the kennels being low-pressure and therapeutic. I'd been explaining how I wanted to use my qualifications somewhere, and that I loved animals, only I couldn't get Mum to listen. It was hopeless.'

'She knows now. We told her. And in any case, you're right, she can't physically stop you. What's she going to do, lie down in front of your car each workday morning?'

Hel's lips twitched at the image. Then she looked anxious again.

'I've upset her though, Jen. I feel bad about that.'

'Oh, I wouldn't fret. She's always upset over something.' I blew on the surface of my drink. 'Isn't that how families work? Various members sitting on their hands trying not to strangle each other?'

'Maybe. We're too alike, me and Mum, that's the trouble. We ought to be more laid back, the way you and Dad are. Is your chocolate OK?'

'Yummy. How's yours?'

A slight head shake. 'I've got green tea.'

Obviously.

'This is nice, anyway,' I said.

'Yeah.'

Two sisters sharing a midnight cuppa and a friendly chat. There hadn't been enough of that.

'The other thing was,' she said, 'while I'm here, I wondered if you could do me a favour.'

'Two in one day? Steady on.'

'No, it's important, and I don't know who else to ask. Incredibly important. I'm being serious. I've been wanting to talk to you about it for ages.'

'Yeah?'

The trouble with my sister is she can be quite manipulative. Whether this is a behaviour she took on when she was ill, or whether she was just born that way, I've no idea. I can't remember what she was like before. I do know that when she asks you for a favour, you need to be on your guard. *Don't say anything to Mum about that food in the bin, will you? If you don't let on that I scoffed your Easter egg, I'll buy you one twice as big. Tell Dad I had a migraine and couldn't face going.* Covering for Helen's got me into trouble in the past.

I said, 'Can't you ask Ned, whatever it is?'

'Not Ned.'

'Why? What are you up to, Hel?'

'I want you to check something online for me.'

'You've got a computer.'

'I can't. It has to be you.'

'What, then?'

'It's . . . I want you to find Joe Pascoe for me.'

I put my cup down. 'Joe Pascoe?'

'Mm.'

'Joe you were at *school* with?'

She nodded and lowered her face so I couldn't see her expression.

'Joe who broke your heart?'

'Yes.'

'Why are you asking me?' She didn't reply. '*You* do it, Hel. Go on Twitter or Facebook or Instagram, he's bound to be somewhere.'

'I daren't. I might be . . . I only want to know what happened to him, from a distance. Then I can put him out of my mind for good.'

A lock of hair hung over her cheekbone, and some long-buried instinct made me want to push it out of the way and smooth it down for her. I didn't, though. I kept my fingers firmly round the mug and stared till she raised her head.

'Right, Helen. Let me get this straight. Behind Ned's back you want me to check up on a boy you were at school with, what, fifteen years ago – a boy who dumped you and who you haven't been in touch with since – and report to you and that'll be it, end of story?'

'Yes.'

'It won't be the end of the story. Will it?'

'It will!'

'But why, Helen? Why are you even considering this?'

'What I said. I'm trying to move on, with the job and stuff. I want this year to be the year things change. So I need to draw a line under certain things. Put them to rest. I've been hanging on to the past for too long. I know it's not normal. But it's only because there's not enough in my life.'

'And Ned?'

'I know. I love him, but there's this kind of – ' she waved her free arm, searching to explain – 'this *noise* at the back of my brain and I need to silence it. That's all, I promise.'

Joe Pascoe. The boy who'd smashed open my sister's heart, who'd made her cry even more than she had over the damn guinea pig. Started nasty rumours about her, Mum had told me, which exacerbated the bullying that was already pretty established. Finished with her for some girl called Saskia in the year above, and between the two of them they pulled her apart. Hel had lasted just one more term before she dropped out of school entirely. Perhaps that's why she couldn't let it go now, because she felt ashamed of leaving the way she did, with so much unfinished. When I'd left school it had been with a raucous end-of-year party and a snog under the chemistry block porch with Chris Green. Signed shirts and super-soakers and a banner hanging off the roof and someone passing round a helium balloon to make us talk like mice. My sister had had none of that.

'I still don't think it's fair on Ned.'

'No, Jen, don't you see? It's *because* of Ned I need to settle the past. Because at the moment things aren't right between us, and I think the way to sort them is to nail that bad history. Yeah? One look, one update, that's all I need and my head'll clear forever.'

Those large, appealing eyes, that brave but delicate little

pointed chin. She's so bloody persuasive. That's always been part of the trouble.

And I pictured Ned, his pleasant face, his cheerful smile, the casual, happy lope of his walk that you could recognise from a hundred yards away. Always bringing with him news and entertaining stories, helping out around the house, generally lifting everyone's spirits. He was practically a member of the family. He was like the funny older brother I'd never had.

Except you don't fancy your brother.

I said, 'For God's sake, Hel. I don't like it.'

'Please. Please.'

'Oh, just . . . leave it with me. I'm not promising anything.'

She moved her hand across the duvet so her fingertips were close to mine, but not quite touching.

'I knew I could depend on you,' she said.

CHAPTER 2

The office was sweltering. Rosa was near the sports desk, flirting loudly with Alan and a man from some local supermarket PR department, and next to me Gerry was bantering down the phone with one of the photographers. I squinted at my PC screen.

What's Your Craziest Holiday Experience?

My main task of the morning was to sort through readers' tweets and emails and arrange the most amusing ones into a light summer page-filler. Should've been a half-hour job, but actually it was impossible to organise this dross into any kind of meaningful shape. Every offering was moronic, pointless and self-congratulatory. _I stole a child's inflatable dolphin and her dad chased me down the beach! I buried my mate's phone in the sand and then couldn't find it again!_ Pillock. _I trod on a sea urchin._ How did that even qualify as crazy? Stupid, yes. Clumsy. Unlucky (especially for the sea urchin).

I plucked at my shirt, fanned myself with a sheet of paper.

My mate and I were so drunk we fell asleep on our balcony in the sunshine and got roasted alive. I could use that one but Rosa might want the drunk part editing out. *I yelled SHARK and got everyone to leave the water screaming. I nearly got arrested for defacing a political poster in Chile. I ate a wasp.* No, there was nothing I was going to be able to do with this garbage other than type it up as it was. There was no kind of pattern or order I could impose to shape the piece. In any case, the photo desk would break up the text randomly with stock cartoons and photos. *My girlfriend and I went skinny dipping in the moonlight and ran into a late night beach party – yikes!*

I pulled out my mobile and texted Ned: 'What is maddest thing you've ever done on holiday?' No mileage in texting Owen because I already knew it was that time he locked himself inside a grain silo to protest about world food distribution. Six hours in a police cell he got out of that escapade. The high point of his career so far.

I turned my attention back to the article. What else did we have here? *I dived off a cliff and broke my nose.* Blimey, that gem had been sent in by Mum's hairdresser; I recognised the name. That's the thing about working for a regional paper. You're effectively positioning yourself at a busy crossroads, and if you stand there long enough, all local life trots by.

My shirt was sticking to my skin now and I worried about dark patches appearing under the arms. Once I'd nailed this article I was going to take a trip to the ladies' and jam as much of myself under the cold tap as I could manage.

I dared a mate to drop a crab down his trunks and it nipped his bollock! No, no, that one would definitely have to be edited if it was going to grace the pages of Chester Cream. In fact, I'd probably ditch the entire quote so as to avoid provoking any copycat cruelty to crabs.

I was just putting the piece to bed when my phone beeped with a new message. Ned: 'I don't do crazy. I'm too boring.' As I was reading, another message from him came through. 'Nearly brought home stray cat from Spain but hotel owner took it in instead.'

Yes, that sounded like Ned. If anyone would try and save a starving Spanish mog, it would be him. Our family had known his family forever, and he always was the kind of guy who'd open a window to shoo out a moth, or carefully carry a spider to the doorstep. He was just one of life's thoughtful people. He'd bring in the shopping for Mum, and hold spanners and torches and tape measures for my dad when required. When I was still at primary school and Helen was at her worst, he'd often volunteer to collect me at home-time so Mum wouldn't have to leave my sister unattended. Of course none of these acts of kindness was on Owen's fiery scale of world-saving, but I like to think little gestures add up in some kind of cosmic ledger. I had a sudden memory of him at the school gates, wading in to stop some big lads throwing a younger boy's shoe into a tree.

Without warning, my thoughts slid to Joe Pascoe, and my sister's tremulous request of six nights ago. 'Don't you trust me, Jen?' she'd said, her pretty eyes wide and pleading. 'Look, think about it. If I was after playing dirty, I'd have just looked him up for myself and gone from there. But *you* doing it takes out any element of temptation. That's the point. Your involvement keeps it above board.'

So far I'd taken no action because I wasn't convinced Ned would see it like that. Yet that half-threat hung over me: if I didn't assist Hel, she might take matters into her own hands.

In the background I could hear Rosa exclaiming over

something on the supermarket man's iPhone. Gerry, chat finished, was whistling under his breath as he typed. I tuned them both out and brought up Facebook on my PC. Then I typed in Joe's name. It felt safer to do it here. And a quick peep couldn't do any harm, could it? That didn't commit me to anything.

Mum's always banging on about the dangers of social networking and how people make themselves ridiculously vulnerable by laying out their entire personal details online. She says sites like Facebook and Twitter are a stalker's paradise, and who knows what brand of madmen and crims are sifting through your intimate histories and making notes about your routines, harvesting your passwords, mapping your movements. She says no one understands the concept of privacy any more. We under-thirties are beyond naive and deserve what's coming to us.

For the most part, oldie-talk like this makes me want to stick my fingers in my ears and go la-la-la, but today I wondered if she might not have a point. Five clicks was all it took me to locate the right Joe, the Joe who said he'd been to St Thom's, Cheshire, class of 2002. He was married, it turned out. Not to Saskia – that must have fallen apart – but to someone called Ellie. He lived in Chrishall, a village on the outskirts of Chester, and he designed websites for a living. PortL, his company was called. Disappointingly his photo album only had two pictures in it, one of a sunset and one of a huge fish hanging from a hook. However, a quick scan of Ellie's page revealed a stack of images showcasing life in the Pascoe household.

Ellie-the-wife was blonde, with expensive-casual clothes and a bright white smile. Her two girls were miniatures of their mum. I didn't even have to guess the kids' ages (six and nine) because Ellie had obligingly posted snaps of their last birthday cakes, candles and all. The family garden was large, with swings for the girls and a long, smooth lawn. They had a pond and a pergola. They held barbecues. The girls liked fancy dress. Sometimes they all played boules. It was like looking at pages from a Boden catalogue. Ellie was in a reading group and did Pilates and liked a film called *Molten Days* and had 443 friends.

Joe himself seemed to be ageing well. His hair was cropped quite severely but it suited him. His chin he kept stubbly, though I could see he'd experimented with a proper beard at one point. I squinted at the screen, trying to picture the arrogant teen who'd trampled my sister's heart. He just smiled back at me, a man easy with himself and proud of his achievements. The lovely Ellie was a Global Communications and Engagement Manager with NatWest.

Even as I scanned the info I was wondering whether I should tell Helen about any of this, and if so, how much, and what kind of spin to put on it. Would it be a relief for her to think of him settled and out of reach, or would the idea of his being married be upsetting? What exactly should I say about his wife? Should I mention the children? Would it help if I could detect some tiny element of dissatisfaction in his life choices, or would that be courting danger? Most importantly, should I reveal that he was still living just down the road from us, a mere twenty-minute drive from our house – that so near was he, the gods of mischief might sometime have them bump into each other inside Chester M&S? Helen had sworn to me this business was about closure and recovery, but my sister lied easily. She told you what you wanted to hear.

I tried to picture her reaction to the various scenarios. My main fear, as ever, was that she'd be knocked off-centre again, and all that would entail. Mum's towering fury if she suspected I was involved. God, it didn't bear thinking about. A memory flashed up of Helen sitting at the kitchen table and crying over a plate of spag bol, still in her school shirt, and Dad shouting that they were 'crocodile tears'. I'd never heard the phrase before and had to go away and look it up. Then I'd been both impressed and outraged by the idea someone could fake a crying fit, and also confused because she'd looked in genuine distress to me.

I clicked to study Joe's timeline. 'How did you manage to hurt my sister so badly?' I mouthed at the screen.

'Jennifer! If you could tear yourself away from your dating websites and get on with some actual work, we'd be so grateful.' Rosa's voice sliced across the office, making me jump. At once everyone stopped to look at me: Alan and Tam on sports, the supermarket man, the woman reloading the water cooler. Only Gerry didn't turn round, but I saw his shoulders tense.

'It's not a dating site,' I said, as levelly as I could. But it came out as a whining protest, and my cheeks grew hot as I vanished the page.

'Well, who is he, then, this man you've been gazing at for the last ten minutes?'

'It's research, Rosa.'

'Research? What for?'

'The holiday piece.' I thought fast. 'I remembered there was this boy I was at St Thom's with who had a suncream fight in a hotel foyer. It went up the walls and over the furniture, everywhere. I was just trying to find the details.'

'And how much detail do you need, for goodness' sake? One line per incident, that's all you're required to write. No one's asked you to compose a dissertation.'

The whole of this speech was shouted the length of the room for maximum humiliation. I heard her snort, then she leant in towards Mr Supermarket and said, mock-conspiratorial, 'You see, this is the problem when we take them straight from college. They're just not grown up enough to follow instructions.'

The meanness of it made my eyes sting, and for a nasty moment the document in front of me grew swimmy. I thought, *Come on, Jen, get a grip. It's only old Tweed-knickers. Don't let her see she's hit the mark.* So I lowered my head, blinked a few times, breathed deeply and did what Ned always advises with tricky customers, which is to picture them in some embarrassing situation. I went for a selection of old favourites: Rosa fitted with that scold's bridle they have on display in the Grosvenor Museum; Rosa tied to a ducking stool and dropped into a pond; Rosa in the stocks, covered in raw egg. Meanwhile, back in the real world I saw her pick up her handbag and usher the supermarket man to the door, no doubt off for another working lunch. The click click of heels down the uneven wooden stairs. This is an old building. One of these days she might have a nasty fall.

The fan churned and whirred and still the air was as hot as ever.

Gerry stretched, rolled his eyes in my direction. 'Oi, Jenny-fer,' he said. 'Where are you up to with your work?'

I nodded at my PC. 'More or less finished this piece. I have to be out at two, visiting a nursery.'

'So you've a bit of a window, then?'

'Why? What are you after?'

'I only wondered if you could nip outside for half an hour and gather me some vox pops for a piece I'm doing on pensions.'

'Pensions?'

'Yeah. Just take a clipboard and ask a few people in the street whether they've got one set up, what they think of the state pension, how they feel about the retirement age. That kind of blah. You'll get more responses than me. You've a more approach-able face.'

I grinned. 'You mean I should get out of the office before I chuck my monitor across the room in a fit of pique?'

'The thought never entered my head. Now go on, buzz off, enjoy some fresh air. I'll deal with Madam if she comes back before you, but we both know we won't see her till gone four.'

I hit the street gratefully. Outside it was just as warm, but a different kind of heat, dry and pleasant on the skin, not fuggy with confined bodies and bad feeling. The plan was to grab a can of something cold, then step out among the masses with my clip-board and gather a few useful quotes. Before I'd reached the precinct, however, my phone bleeped with a text message. I opened it up and read that the nursery visit would have to be rescheduled due to a stomach bug sweeping through staff and kids. Call me heartless, but I actually let out a little whoop. I forwarded the text to the photographer, then stood for a minute under the Rows, watching shoppers mill and street vendors blow glittering streams of soap bubbles onto the pavement. In front of WHSmith's a preacher was calling out that each new day was a gift from God, and that His eye was always on us. Pigeons strutted and pecked. A delicious sense of freedom flooded through me.

Obviously I knew what I ought to do was collect Gerry's sound bites for him, return to my desk and try to get ahead with some work. That would be the sensible option. That would show Tweed-knickers I wasn't such a waster. But the cancellation felt like a sign. It meant I could nip down and see Owen, hole up there for half an hour. My heart lifted at the thought. As for the vox pops, I'd get a few on the way.

I wasn't even sure he'd be around because some lunchtimes he visits the food bank and helps sort tins. But no, my luck was in because he answered his buzzer immediately. When he opened the door I was so pleased to see him that I flung my arms round him there and then, in the middle of the communal hall. He hugged me back, then unhooked me, laughing.

'Jen, hello! What's this in aid of? Why aren't you at work? Hang on, don't tell me you've walked out? No, DO tell me you've walked out.'

'Nothing so dramatic. Just fed up and skiving off.'

'Really? Shame.'

He looked so sexy in his loose white shirt and faded jeans, his dark hair mussed and floppy. Hel calls him the Young Bohemian and says he ought to be hanging out in a Paris garret with a bunch of revolutionaries. I've not passed this observation on in case it gives him ideas.

'The sooner you do pack that place in, the better,' he said as we started up the stairs. 'Chester bloody Messenger. Consumer-engineering masquerading as news, that's what it is.'

'I write fillers for the lifestyle section. I report on library events and nursery open-days. Don't make me personally responsible for the evils of capitalism.'

'You run adverts for hundred-quid anti-wrinkle creams when there are people in this city who don't have a roof over their head.'

'You know, I actually came here to get away from the ear-bashing.'

He paused on the stairs and turned, apologetic. 'Shit. Sorry. I get carried away.'

'You do.'

'It is really nice to see you.'

His expression softened. If I'd been able to reach I'd have kissed him again, but his position on the higher step put him beyond me. I closed my eyes as his finger moved down to touch my cheek, trace my jaw line then stroke across my lips. This was what I'd come for. This was what I needed.

'Wish you wouldn't wear this stuff on your face, though, Jen. You don't need chemicals on your skin. No one does. You're fine without make up.'

I opened my mouth to reply, but at that moment from the top landing a girl shouted, 'Hey, Owen, have you got any double A batteries?'

He began to hurry up the stairs again.

'Owen? Owen?' Her accent was twangy – Aussie or New Zealand. Through my boyfriend's flat various strangers come and go with their flyers and posters, news sheets and placards. Sometimes it's like Piccadilly Circus in there. I'd not met any Antipodeans, though.

As we walked through the door she was standing in the lounge, struggling to pull a jumper out of a rucksack: a girl of about my age with tanned arms showing under her T-shirt, and strong legs in shorts and sneakers. She had a muscular frame like a runner, and short, bleached hair.

'This is Chelle,' said Owen cheerfully, as if I was supposed to know who that was.

'*Shell?*'

'That's right,' she said, shaking the jumper free. 'As in Mi-chelle. I'm camping out here for a while.'

'Here?'

'Yup. This is me.' She indicated a rolled up sleeping bag pushed against the table leg.

I said, 'I'm Owen's girlfriend.'

'Yeah, I know, good to meet you. Jen, isn't it?'

'Jin' was how she pronounced it. 'Jin, usn't ut.' The name sounded ugly like that, sort of tight and churlish. She carried on wrestling with the contents of the rucksack. The drawstring looked to be stuck and whatever she was after was near the bottom; she plunged her wrist inside and felt around blindly, like a vet extracting a calf.

I said, 'OK, well, nice to meet you too.'

Owen sank down on the sofa, stretching his long legs out in front of him. 'So she's just gonna doss down here for a couple of weeks while she does some research.'

'Oh. Right.' I wondered what my face was registering. *Did you know she was coming, Owen? Who exactly is she? How long will she be around?* 'Research?'

'Thought I'd see if I could fill in a few blanks on the family tree while I was over in the UK.'

'You have relatives round here, then?' I asked, wondering why she wasn't staying with them.

'Nobody alive. A couple of ancestors, maybe. Mainly I'm here to do some comparative work, study a few businesses and government systems in the UK and assess the way they impact on various social groups. Plus I'm thinking, I'd really like to get to V as well. That would be pretty awesome.'

'The festival? That isn't for another two months.'

'Yeah, well, I'll probably have moved on before then. I've lots to do, places I want to see. Tons to pack in. I'm on a mission.'

She grinned, and Owen grinned back. I looked from one to the other.

'And how did you two meet?'

'Chelle and I got chatting online, in this Worldfair forum. I was asking about working conditions in Vietnam, and she'd visited there the summer before. I wanted to know if she'd seen any sweatshops. We started a discussion on the wage chain, and it kind of went from there. One time I said to her, you know, if your travels ever bring you in this direction, give us a shout. And then it turns out—'

'When? When did you say that?'

'January, February.'

'You never mentioned it.'

'I often chat online, to all sorts of people, Jen. About stuff you're not interested in.'

I knew the stuff he meant: corporate dominance, macroeconomics, the politics of exploitation.

Chelle was unrolling some kind of batik sheet or throw, a brown affair with a fern pattern. She paused and blinked at me. 'Is it a problem, me stopping here?'

'No. God, no. Of course not. Make yourself at home. My boyfriend's very easy-going.'

He smiled his approval at that so I knew it was the right thing to say, but really my heart had sunk. I wanted to rewind the last hour and start again from a better place. Owen, lodger-less, opening the door and greeting me with open delight, asking how my day had been, sympathising, offering at the very least a snog and a shoulder massage. Some South American folk music. A toasted pitta. Space to relax. I loved being in his bedroom, with its strange pin-ups of pre-war Dresden, the Prime Minister morphing into an alien, a glass head full of pills. Some of those posters I'd sourced myself, from obscure shops down the backstreets of Manchester. It felt as if everything in there, from the tatty kelim bedcover to the dangling cobwebs, was at least part-mine.

Even if I was never allowed to stay over. Unlike some. Who was this woman anyway? How sane? How honest? Might she not clear off with all his possessions at some point?

'It's funny, though,' he was saying, 'the way sometimes you meet a person online and you just click with them. I don't know what it is. A coming together of minds, I guess.'

I watched her drape her ferny throw across the sofa. 'So you don't know anyone else in the area, Chelle?'

'There are some guys down in, where is it, Tilford? In Shropshire?'

'Telford.'

'That's right. But I don't really know them that well and they're away travelling. Oh, hey, Owen, did you manage to get me a key cut?'

'I did. It's in the kitchen.'

'Awesome.'

There was a pained silence. I didn't have a key.

As Chelle went off to hunt, he reached across for my hand and drew me nearer. 'This is great, isn't it? It's going to be so cool to be able to compare notes with someone from the other side of the world. The global village in action. We're going to have to make the most of Chelle while she's here. There are so many questions I want to ask. Tonight she can come down the Oak and I'll introduce her to the crowd. You up for that, Jen?'

'Well—'

'What?'

'Nothing. It's my zumba class this evening.'

Owen looked disappointed. 'I thought it would be nice, all of us together.'

'I suppose I can miss it, for once. What time?'

'Eightish, here. Or if you're late, we'll see you in the Oak.'

He pulled me down gently so I was sitting next to him.

'Love that blouse on you, Jen. It makes me think of blood or rubies. Makes your hair look darker.'

'You were the one who told me I looked good in red.'

'I was right, then.'

This was more like it. 'Shut up and kiss me,' I said. And he did. In the second before our lips met I smelt something sweet and malty, a lunchtime beer, overlaid with his rosemary-scented vegan deodorant. I knew he'd have spent his morning writing to Amnesty or emailing an MP or leafleting passers-by about exploitation and greed, and I wanted to say, *I understand you're fighting the good fight and I love you for it, but, just sometimes, why can't you be less interested in the world and more interested in me? Why can't you be ordinary-selfish like the rest of us?*

Because I am who I am, Jen, I imagined him replying. *You knew that when you got involved.*

'Nearly forgot. I picked up this. I thought you'd like it,' he said, drawing away from me and reaching inside his jeans pocket.

When he opened his hand he was holding a pebble, pale cloud-pink and smooth with delicate cerise veins across the surface. I could see why it had caught his eye.

'Pretty. Where did you get it?'

'Down by the river. I thought it looked a bit like a heart.'

He dropped it into my palm and closed my fingers round it.

I laid my head against his chest and exhaled, letting out the complications of the morning. Rosa's nastiness I vanished away easily enough, but imprints of Joe and Ellie's profile photos still hung about in my mind. I wished I could talk to Owen about the Pascoe business. In the past he'd been sympathetic about Helen and her problems and demands; in fact he had a whole heap of opinions regarding the media's portrayal of women's bodies and the unrealistic claims made on young people to conform. *Listen*, I could say, *Hel's asked me to do a thing and it doesn't feel right. Yet I'm flattered she came to me for help and I want to trust her. Will I do more harm than good? Do you think she's being honest? Am I being unfair to Ned? Is it possible to update on an ex and then walk away scot-free?*

But even as I ran through the questions I knew I wouldn't be voicing them. Not to Owen, not to anyone. I was too unsure of what I was doing, too anxious over the morality of it. Simply being here, though, being held close and letting my thoughts run freely was as good as a confession. Better, because there was no risk attached, no chance of judgement or a lecture. I clutched my pebble and breathed into his shirt. I felt him stir against me.

There was a commotion as Chelle marched back into the room and, without warning, pulled the table out from the wall, scraping it judderingly across the carpet. 'That's better.' *That's bitter.* 'Uh, hullo? Guys?'

With extreme reluctance I raised my head and pulled away from my boyfriend.

'What?'

She was standing above us, a power lead in her hands. 'Sockets?'

'Pardon?'

'Yeah, sorry to interrupt there,' she said, not-sorry-at-all. 'But any ideas where I can stick my charger?'

When I got home, Hel was watching TV and eating an ice pop. I noticed she'd put some lipstick on, which meant Ned must be coming round. She was wearing her favourite dress, too, a vintage Laura Ashley with long sleeves. Even in the warmest weather my sister still tends to feel the cold.

'What time are you out tonight?' she said.

'More or less as soon as I've eaten.'

'I thought your dance class wasn't till later?'

'I'm not going to zumba. I'm off back into Chester.'

'Ah. Don't you mind that it's nearly always you who trails in to see him and never the other way round?'

I flopped down next to her. She'd never said it outright, but I knew Hel was pretty lukewarm about Owen. The trouble was, she didn't see him often enough to know what he was really like.

'It's difficult for him because he only has the bike. He can't be cycling twenty miles each way, in the dark, down those fast, twisty A roads whenever he wants an evening drink with me.'

'Well, I don't see why he can't get a car. A cheap little run-around. Surely his dad'd buy him one like a shot?'

'He'd *love* a car. But they're crap for the environment. Even the greenest models.'

'So instead he lets you pollute the air with your carbon emissions.'

'No, because he goes on a website and pays for me to off-set them.'

I let my head fall backwards, too tired to argue any more.

Perhaps she picked up on how I was feeling because she said,

'It was only that Ned wanted to catch you before you went. He has this app on his phone, to do with generating spoof tabloid news reports. He said you'd appreciate it. But he can show you another time. Owen taking you anywhere nice?'

'We're just meeting friends at the pub.' I wondered what she'd think if I told her about the Chelle set-up. 'How was the kennels?'

'Poo city. As usual.'

'That's what you signed up for.'

'I know, I'm not complaining. I scoop and hose, that's basically my day. The dogs are nice. That's what makes it worthwhile. There's this Staffie with one eye, only came in two days ago and he's dead cute. He wags his tail so hard when you talk to him he nearly falls over. They've called him Isaac.'

'Was he ill-treated? Is that how he lost his eye?'

'No, I think it was a disease. But his owners couldn't look after him, he was too boisterous, so they brought him to us. He's a total sweetie. All he needs is a loving home.' She tilted her face appealingly.

'I hope you're not getting ideas. Mum won't entertain the idea of a dog, you know that. Too messy, too hairy. She moans enough about keeping the house clean as it is.'

'Yeah. I did wonder about taking Ned to see him . . .'

'Don't. That wouldn't be fair. Anyway, his landlord won't let him keep pets.'

'No.' I could see the cogs going round. She was trying to work out how she could get her own way.

Mum was clattering about in the kitchen. The front driveway was empty, which meant Dad must be working late. All I could think was that I needed to get under the shower, if I could just summon up the energy.

'And you, how was your day, Jen?' asked Hel, unexpectedly.

'Mine?' I rolled my eyes. 'Put it this way, I'd rather have been scraping up dog mess.'

'That bad?'

'Uh-huh. One day soon you're going to read a newspaper headline about an editor being bludgeoned to death at her desk. Gerry'll slope in one morning and find Rosa sprawled over her keyboard, mouse in hand.'

'And your prints will be on the murder weapon?'

'You guessed it. Why are some people so vile?'

'Good question. Something broken inside. Something that leaks poison into their souls. Mum gets some absolute gits coming into hotel reception. Did you hear about the guy who got fed up of waiting because she was on the phone to another customer? Unzipped his wash bag and wrote "SERVICE" in toothpaste on the counter.'

'Bloody hell. No, she didn't tell me that one. What did she do?'

'Wiped it up and dealt with his enquiry. That's the job, she has to stay polite.' Helen looked thoughtful. 'You know, there's this old guy at the kennels who's been there about twenty years, clearly hates my guts. It got to me at first, but I've worked out that an aggressively pleasant approach winds him up way better than snapping or complaining would. It's become quite funny, watching him struggle to manoeuvre. He's got nothing to batter against, you know? You could try that technique with Rosa.'

'You mean a charm offensive? Hmm. It might kill me in the process, that's the only problem.'

Helen tipped up the ice pop and drained the melted liquid into her mouth. Even an action like that seemed graceful when executed by her. One time I'd been leaning on the saloon bar in The Foxes, trying to order a drink, when a middle-aged man had sidled in next to me and begun a conversation. At first I'd assumed he was chatting me up, but then it transpired he used to work with Dad and was simply being friendly. Except, when I'd got my beer and the barman was handing over my change, he went, 'Say hello to Don and your mum from me, won't you? And that beautiful sister of yours.' The phrase had burned itself across my brain there and then. Your Beautiful Sister. Because what did people say to her in similar circumstances? Give my regards to the Plain One?

I heaved myself up off the sofa. Helen motioned me to wait.

'Don't let Rosa spoil it for you, Jen. Really. You've waited long enough for that job, studied and passed your exams and sent off a stack of applications. You mustn't let some sour old baggage get in the way of your career.'

'No.'

'You deserve to get what you want.'

'Thanks.'

'Well, you do.'

I was touched by her concern.

'While you're here, can I quickly ask,' she went on. 'It's been a week now. I was wondering, have you had chance to search for Joe online?'

I noticed she'd lowered her voice. From the kitchen came a thud, like someone slamming a drawer in anger.

'Um, yes. I've had a quick look. I want to go back and . . . make notes. What I mean is, summarise everything I can find, cover it all, so you don't have to go searching yourself. Then it's done, finished, and you can put it to bed.'

'I see. Like a dossier?'

'No! Not like a dossier. That sounds way too creepy.' But she was right; some kind of information file was almost what I'd had in mind. On my way home from Owen's that afternoon I'd glanced at my watch and noted it was primary school coming-out-time. I'd toyed with the idea of nipping over to the school named on his daughters' sweatshirts, and hanging around to see if I could catch a glimpse of Joe in real life. And then it had occurred to me that if I was thinking those weird stalker-thoughts, what might happen to Hel's brain if she slipped into the same groove? It was vital I kept her away from Facebook.

'I'm on the case. Don't keep asking. I'll tell you when.'

'OK,' she said meekly.

'Trust me, yeah?'

'I will.'

I remembered the half-hour drive back up to Chester that awaited me, a date with Chelle at the other end. 'And just – oh, just enjoy your evening with Ned.'

She didn't reply.

Owen likes the Oak because it's tucked away off the tourist route, outside the Walls. I like it because it's old and gloomy-cosy with thick black beams and leaded windows. In the beer garden there's a broken piece of Roman masonry, and by the bar there's a glass case containing a mummified cat, which the owners found in the chimney breast, together with a Tudor belt buckle and some lead shot. I sometimes think this city has more history than it can cope with.

When I walked into the pub they were settled round one of the big tables in full discussion mode. Chelle was there, tucked in against Owen, and Vikki and Keisha who run the Revolution bookshop out Handbridge way, and Owen's mate Saleem who works in an Indian takeaway and once drove us to Wrexham in his delivery van so we could drop off some toys at a women's refuge. A man I'd met in the bookshop once but whose name I'd forgotten, skinny guy in an oversized mohair jumper, was talking about multiple organ damage in lab rats and the breakdown of weed killers.

Keisha smiled when she saw me, and budged up to let me slide in next to my boyfriend. In truth I'd have preferred it if I could have wedged myself between him and Chelle, but it was good enough. Owen nodded a brief hello. His eyes were alight and I could see he was immersed in the debate.

'So although they knew that there was gene flow between GM and non-GM plants,' hairy-jumper was saying, 'they went ahead and deregulated anyway. And what we've ended up with is the evolution of glyphosate-resistant weeds. And we know what the biotech industry's response will be.'

'Stronger chemicals,' said Owen. 'More poison into the food chain, more genetic manipulation.'

'And a boom in super-weeds. Madness. It's so fucking short-sighted. Why can't the US government see that short-term financial gain is leading us into a long-term food crisis?'

'Because the food giants are the ones doing the political bankrolling. They're all in each other's fucking pockets. Meanwhile the rest of us are hurtling towards Armageddon—'

'You look nice,' said Keisha at my elbow.

I turned towards her, grateful someone had noticed I'd made an effort.

'Oh, cheers. So do you. I like your new hairstyle.' Since I'd last seen her she'd gone from sculpted ebony waves to a natural short fuzz.

'Yeah, I'm transitioning. I've had enough of chemical straighteners and weaves. The problem with Afro hair is it fights you every step of the way. Takes up too much of your time. Kinky's the way forward, I've decided.'

'Good, isn't it?' said Vikki, leaning forward. 'I told her ages ago to just let it grow, let it do its thing. You know, I'm "transitioning" too: from Nordic blonde to grey.'

'There's no grey, Viks. It's in your mind.'

'There is too. I pulled out a pure white strand this morning. I'm growing old before your eyes.'

'You did *not*. You *are* not.' Keisha batted her flirtatiously.

Now Saleem was speaking, his eyes wide, his face full of righteous indignation. 'And what about the StarLink gene? That was actually being eaten in taco shells before it was even licensed. No amount of farmer compensation is gonna put that genie back in the bottle, is it?'

Whatever Saleem's talking about he's always one hundred per cent passionate, but you do have to watch him because he's also full of bollocks, like the way he pretends he grew up in the mountains of Kashmir even though he actually hails from Bolton.

I said to Keisha, 'How's the book trade doing?'

She shrugged. 'Huh. Not brilliant. Obviously it would be better if the shop was nearer the city centre, but, you know, the rates—'

'Tell her about the café,' broke in Vikki.

'Oh, yeah. The café. What it is, we had this idea of starting a little coffee bar at the far end of the shop. Nothing elaborate, only hot drinks and cakes, then customers could wander round and buy a book and sit and read. They'd stay longer. Spend more.

And Vikki reckons we could expand the notice board, use up a whole wall, and have small-press newspapers laid out, and loads more leaflets and posters, so we become a directory of events. Then maybe people would start to come to Revolution as a meeting place in its own right, and have discussions and plan campaigns and demos. Like the old coffee houses in the past.'

'Is there enough room for a café?' I asked, trying to picture a separate eating area within the layout of the tiny shop.

'Yeah, if we take some stock off the shelves and put it upstairs, and bash that cupboard out. Vikki's looked into the health and safety side, what certificates we'd need to be able to serve unheated food. It's doable. More than doable. We're aiming to have it up and running by September.'

'Sounds as if you've got it all worked out.'

Across the room, a girl with long red tresses like my sister's was snogging a man with a shaved head, eating each other's faces as if there was no one else in the entire pub. I thought, how great to be on a night out with the one you loved, just the two of you. To have that level of attention. At the edge of my consciousness I heard Chelle's voice twanging through the debate:

'See, in New Zealand, supermarkets have to label GM products by law, but if you're in a restaurant then it's up to you to ask. They don't print that info on the menu. And I don't think that's morally right, putting the responsibility onto the consumer.'

When I turned back to look, Owen was nodding vigorously. 'No. No, it isn't. But that's how business works. Shift the blame away, keep the guys at the centre clear.'

'Because the power's in the hands of a few, and they cover for each other.'

'Yes! That's exactly it. That's what I'm saying.'

I didn't like the way his eyes were fixed on her fair, round face. I linked my arm through his to remind him I was there.

'Have any of you guys over here been involved in GM crop-pulling?' Chelle asked.

Owen waved a hand towards Saleem. 'He's done a bit. He took out half a test field outside Oxford. Got arrested, fined.'

'Awesome.'

Saleem looked shyly pleased.

'Can I ask, Chelle,' Owen went on, 'how robust is your legal system when it comes to fighting these companies? Do you trust the government to make a stand?'

Vikki at my elbow: 'Jen, will you come to the café?'

'Huh?'

'For our opening, will you come along and do a piece on us?'

'What, *The Messenger*? If you want. Yeah, that should be OK, 'cause Rosa had a supermarket guy in today plugging his charity event, and next week I'm writing up an article about a local nursery. So it's basically the same. Give the office a ring, but let them have plenty of notice because the photographers are pretty busy at the moment.'

'Cool. We badly need the publicity.'

She sat back and I was able to listen again to Chelle.

'The way effective campaign groups work these days is to behave like knot grass, you know? With roots running under the surface and spreading out.' She gestured with her hands. 'Business corporations are based on a pyramid shape, with a leader at the top and then levels two, three, four, whatever, below. But that's not as effective as having a lateral structure. Lateral structures are harder for the authorities to tackle directly and they're harder to stamp out. So you get these small groups using social networking to investigate, expose, broadcast their findings around the globe. Then it doesn't matter how hard the big organisations try, they can't stamp us out. There are too many of us, and we have too many platforms. The internet's become the ultimate democratic tool.'

I said, 'We know that already. It's hardly news.'

'Yeah,' said Owen,' but it's reassuring to hear it pulled together like that from someone who lives on another continent. Sometimes you sit at your computer and you feel like you're on your own and it's easy to lose heart. I'll remember knot grass, though. Great image.'

'So long as it's GM-free knot grass.'

Nobody laughed at my joke. I saw hairy-jumper give me a dismissive glance as if to say, *Who's she again?* I stared him out with my best girlfriend scowl.

'Redeetech,' continued Owen, 'that's who I'd like to get some dirt on. They're right at the heart of the GM conspiracy. I don't suppose you have anything on them, do you, Chelle?'

She grinned in answer, and began to pull her rucksack up from under the table. The rest of the group were transfixed, like people watching a magic show and wondering what was in the top hat. In the end it proved to be nothing more than a smart phone, which she switched on and then tapped and scrolled, pursing her lips enigmatically.

I said, 'Hey, while I remember, have you heard about that new comedy club that's opened up in Nantwich? We had a press release from them this morning, and the line-up looks good. Political satire, all sorts. I wondered about us piling over there sometime. It could be—'

'Got it,' announced Chelle, cutting me off. She leaned in,

angling the phone for my boyfriend's benefit. 'I'd say this is what you've been looking for, Owen. Believe me, you're going to find this pretty awesome.'

Then he was lost again in the murky world of transgenics, and they were craning their necks to see, and I might as well not have been there.

It wasn't until we were on our way to the flat that he spoke to me properly. Though night had fallen, the air was still mild and the streets busy. You could hear snatches of music from pubs and clubs, catch the occasional whiff of fast food. Crowds of normal people enjoying themselves normally. As we passed under the Eastgate clock, I managed to get Owen to hang back a little.

'Hello.'

'Hello.'

'Don't seem to have had much of a chance to chat to you this evening.'

'No, well, it's tricky in a group like that. Everyone was fired up tonight. It was fantastic, wasn't it? I knew it would be. Listening to Chelle, to everything she's got to share. To get that international perspective.'

'Can I ask you something, Owen?'

'Go on.'

'Did you know she was coming to stay?'

'Huh? Oh, not really. We'd vaguely talked about it and then things went quiet. I didn't think she'd turn up. She said she might fly to Bali instead.'

'I just wish you'd mentioned it. Given me some warning.'

He cocked his head. 'You don't mind, do you?'

'No.' I felt myself blushing at the challenge. How could I say yes without making myself sound petty and possessive? So plainly innocent were Owen's motives that it felt shabby to come over all territorial.

'I mean, you didn't mind when Saleem's mate camped out with us last year.'

'No.'

'And she'll be gone in a few weeks. I genuinely think we've a lot to learn from her.'

'OK.'

'The New Zealand government, their environmental laws, their press. There's so much I want to hear about. She's been a terrifically active campaigner.'

'Has she?'

'Oh, the most amazing stunts. I'll get her to tell you about them.'

We walked on a little further. I said, 'When she's gone—'

'What?'

'I'd like us to have more time on our own. You and me.'

Silence.

'Because we used to, didn't we? We used to have meals out all the time, and walks. When we were at uni. We'd go to clubs and parties, and museums, and street fairs. We were always doing something together, do you remember?'

I took his hand and felt his smooth palm against mine.

'Jen, we were students. That was the life then. There were so many more hours in the day. What you have to understand is, I'm really busy now. You can see that. I've always been busy, right from when you first knew me. It's not like I've changed. You've been with me long enough to know that's how I roll. There's a lot I care about and want to pursue.'

'Yeah, you have the world to save, I get that. Can't you take a few more evenings off, though? Pass the flame to Saleem or Keisha for an hour or two?'

He made some non-committal noise in his throat. We were drawing level with The Cross, the monument at the top of the precinct where he'd once stopped to help a homeless man who'd fallen down the steps. We'd righted him and checked there were no bones broken, and then Owen had given him all the money he had in his wallet.

I said, 'Can I at least stay over tonight?'

'Why tonight?'

'Thought it might be nice.' *Because I'm your girlfriend and you should want me to.* 'Chelle's staying over.'

'She hasn't anywhere else to go.'

'I'd like to spend the night with you, Owen. I know it was too much of a squeeze in those old student beds, but you have a double mattress now. How about we give it a try?'

After a pause of maybe ten seconds, he finally went, 'OK.'

My heart jumped, a huge great thud of relief and amazement. I tried not to break my step, but inside I was dancing. I couldn't believe how easily he'd given in. After months of claiming he could never sleep properly if he shared a bed, here he was saying it was fine. We were fine. I wondered whether, in some bizarre way, the presence of Chelle might prove a blessing after all.

I gripped his hand more tightly, heard the sing-song slide of her voice putting the whole of politics to rights. Somewhere under the dark eaves above us birds roosted. Flowers spilling from hanging baskets trembled in the warm air currents.

Then he said, 'Have you brought anything with you?'

'Like what?'

'Change of clothes? Toothbrush?'

'No.'

He looked down at my maroon cami, my frayed jeans. 'How are you going to walk into that posh office of yours tomorrow?'

'Hmm. Hadn't thought about that. I guess I could . . .' I scrambled for a solution. Perhaps if I set the alarm for 6 a.m. and drove back to Mum and Dad's, changed there, got into town for 8.30. But even to my ears that sounded ludicrous and desperate. 'No, I suppose you're right. Next time I could bring a bag, though, yes?'

Before Owen could answer, Saleem was half-turning, calling over his shoulder, 'Come hear this. Listen to what Chelle's found out about GM mosquitoes.'

And with that my boyfriend dropped my hand and hurried to catch up.

It must have been about midnight when I reached home. I'd wanted to hang around the flat to say goodnight to Owen on my own – or as on our own as we could manage with Chelle camped out in the next room – but no one else was for budging. They all wanted to carry on the chat till the small hours. So in the end I'd given up.

I was too frazzled to go straight to bed, though. We'd passed such an important milestone this evening: that theoretical invitation to sleep over had felt critical. Sometime soon – next week even – I'd be staying at my boyfriend's properly, putting my soap bag on his windowsill and my clothes over his chair. A short step from there to asking for a drawer or the bottom of a cupboard. Then, if I was effectively half-moved-in, he was bound to find more space in his life for me and we could rebalance ourselves.

He'd be more available and I'd be less clingy. It would be like it was when we first started going out.

I hung up my bag and loitered downstairs for a while. Mum stopped waiting up for me about a year ago, and although her nervy clucking and offers of late Ovaltine used to annoy the hell out of me, I kind of missed it.

I tiptoed up the stairs and went into my room. Played back the day, wished Rosa a bad night, tormented myself with a few images of Chelle and Owen bumping into each other as the dawn rose. Took off my make up, pulled on my pyjamas. Then I thought, I wonder if Hel's still awake? Not that I necessarily wanted to share what had happened this evening. Though I could ask her what she'd think if Ned moved a lodger in. I might just have ten minutes with her.

I opened my door as stealthily as I could, reached round and tapped on hers. I waited. 12.30 wasn't late for my sister; it was unlikely she was asleep. I tapped again, a little louder in case she hadn't heard. Nothing.

I whispered, 'Hel?' But she wasn't for answering. Tonight she'd decided she was off-limits.

I gave up, stepped across the landing and switched off the light. Along the crack at the bottom edge of Helen's door I could make out the faintest blue glow, as if from a laptop screen.

CHAPTER 3

<u>Under the Gavel – our regular round-up of what's hot in the antique and auction world</u>

<u>This month: vintage dolls' house furniture</u>

How many of us will have played with a dolls' house at some time during our childhood? Whether it was a Lundby or a Tri-ang, or something plywood that a family member knocked together for you, the likelihood is you'll have spent hours engrossed in furnishing and arranging the rooms.

But did you know that some vintage miniature furniture is now highly collectible and fetching good prices in the sale rooms? David Roper, of Holyman Auctioneers, gives some top tips on identifying the real treasures.

'Jen.' Gerry spoke just behind my chair, making me jump. 'Are you busy?'

I clicked save, then swivelled to face him. 'Not critically, no. Just crafting a gripping piece about toy furniture.'

'Do you want to see something funny?'

'If it's that YouTube video of a snake eating another snake, then no. Don't ever show me anything like that again.'

'It's not YouTube.'

'What, then?'

'This.' He reached forward and shrank my file away. Then he brought up Google and typed in a name. A black page with flowing white font filled the screen.

'*Top Flight Dating . . . because sometimes,*' announced the strap line, '*life doesn't send you what you deserve.*'

'Eh?'

'Alan spotted it this morning on Rosa's machine and he made a note of the name. It's a singles' site. But only for your posh, upwardly mobile types. The rest of us can sod off.' He began to read aloud in a fake-sincere newscaster voice: '"Our mission is to provide a superior romantic networking site, exclusive to professionals. Are you smart, attractive, discerning? Hold down a high-powered senior position? Been working hard, and now you're looking to play hard?"'

'Eew, stop that, Gerry. You sound like Joanna Lumley on steroids.'

'"Top Flight Dating offers an efficient, friendly service for the busy executive. We can help you meet like-minded people from your area." In other words, we sift out the scum for you. No free-loaders here, no one who licks tomato sauce off their knife or skulks round Primark of a Saturday. Brilliant, isn't it?'

'Disturbing, more like. You're not saying Rosa's a member? She might just have been doing some research.'

'Alan says he tried to view the page she had open, and it's a restricted area. You can only get in when you're registered.' He stepped away smugly.

'Blimey. That's bizarre. I didn't know she was interested in the squelchy stuff.'

'Apparently.'

'So beneath that tweedy power suit lurks a trembling girlish heart, ripe for romance.'

'Seems that way. I'm wondering how we can break in, see her profile.'

'Yeah.' I felt torn. It was fun to mock Rosa behind her back, especially considering how she'd had the cheek to accuse *me* of surfing date sites at work. But at the same time it felt bad to go rooting through her personal stuff. Even trolls are entitled to a love life.

Gerry said, 'We've tried "password" and "rosa-heffer" and "messenger" and "cream". Alan suggested "cheshire-oaks" because she spends half her life shopping there. Or "grosvenor" because we know she rates their restaurant. I thought you might have some more creative ideas.'

'Hmm. How about "evil-lizard-hearted-boss"?'

'See, I knew I could rely on you to think outside the box.'

'Always.'

My phone bleeped with a text, and Gerry scratched his chin thoughtfully. 'You could register on there yourself. Then it'd be access all areas.'

'I have a boyfriend,' I said primly, opening up my mobile.

'It'd only be for a laugh.'

'A laugh costing ninety quid a month. Or didn't you notice their tariff page? Executive rates, those'll be. To keep the commoners out.' The message turned out to be from Ned, asking if he could meet me for lunch. *OK*, I texted back.

Gerry began to walk away, shaking his head. 'All I can say is, if I was paying the best part of a hundred smackers a go, I'd be expecting a damn sight hotter date than our Rosa.'

'That's because you're a pleb,' I called after him.

If it wasn't for Gerry, I'd pack the job in tomorrow.

When I got to the café, Ned was waiting for me. He was wearing mucky combats and a T-shirt and he looked whacked.

'Busy day, then?' I asked, pulling in my chair opposite him. Ned is odd-job man/caretaker at Farhouses, a gracious, castellated nursing home off the A41. It's one of the Bedevere group of care homes, so top-end clientele and facilities. Ned tends the gardens, fixes pipes and transformers and loose carpets, deals with vermin, and has been known to step in as a bouncer if emergency dictates. I also know he's helping one of the care assistants to pass her EFL exam, and that he sometimes plays the piano for the residents if he's free and they ask nicely.

'We've been shifting furniture out of the dining room,' he said. 'So they can start the renovations.'

'To the ceiling?'

'Ceiling first. Then the walls, the floor, everything else that's been water-damaged. It's a bloody mess. That's the trouble with old sandstone buildings. Randolph's pulling his hair out at the cost. And squirrels have broken into the attic and eaten some of the wiring. I daren't tell him about that yet.'

Ned had taken me up onto the roof of Farhouses once, completely against the rules, and shown me the view from the turrets: flat green Cheshire plain spreading out lushly on all four sides. I'd seen the squirrels from there, leaping between the trees and scratting about on the lawns. He's supposed to live-trap and then shoot them, however I know that he drives them in secret up to Delamere Forest and releases them there. This is completely illegal because they're classified as a pest species, but he'd break any number of laws rather than upset my animal-loving sister.

I said, 'Anyway, it's nice to see you. To what do I owe this honour?'

'Do I need a reason to take a pal out to lunch?'

He was smiling, his body language open, and a casual observer would have thought he was at ease. Yet I could see the slightly too-wide grin, the tension in his shoulders. Our Ned had something on his mind.

I knew if I asked straight out he wouldn't tell me, so I decided to kick off the conversation with a worry of my own. Once we'd placed our orders, I had another moan about Chelle.

'Two weeks she was supposed to be staying, at the outside. It's already nearly four and she's showing no signs of shifting.'

'Ah.'

'And don't get me wrong, it's not that I think she's a proper threat – well – no, I don't. I trust Owen in that way. But the situation's still disturbing. Just, her *being* there. Parading round in her little vest tops and shorts, drinking with him into the night. Plus she has a front door key. How can that be right when I don't?'

Ned was sniggering.

'What?' I asked him. 'It's not funny.'

'It sort of is, though. You can't take her seriously. I mean, what kind of parents call their kid "Shell", for God's sake? Or is it one of these eco-tags she's adopted for herself – "Dances-with-whelks" sort of thing? Hey, over breakfast does Owen go, "Do you fancy an egg, Shell?" Does he go, "Have you seen my razor, Shell?" "Look at my muscle, Shell."' Ned made me laugh in spite of myself. 'And when you first walked out of the bedroom in your jim-jams, was Shell shocked?'

'Enough already!'

'Honestly, you don't need to stress about her,' he said, taking two bottles of lager off the waitress and pouring them into glasses. 'She's just an annoying limpet. One good shove and you'll dislodge her from her rock. Things are going OK with you and Owen otherwise, aren't they? You've managed to win half a mattress. Which is progress.'

'For one night a week.'

'Yeah, well. Don't knock it. Some of us don't even get that.'

It was true enough. Mum and Dad would have been cool with Ned staying over – they've known him for years, his mum's a friend of the family, they think he's all-round wonderful. They'd have been fine, too, with Hel spending nights at his flat: she is thirty. The problem lies with Hel and her insanely territorial attitude to both her personal space and her routines. She loves Ned, but she always has to draw this line between herself and other people. Everything has to be done on her terms. That means no nights away from her own bed, and no one using or moving her personal possessions. She once told me that even the thought of being away from her stuff makes her panicky, and also she hates the idea of being watched while she's asleep. So you see, Owen's not the only one who has issues with sharing a duvet.

I said, 'It's just my sister's way.'

'You think I don't know that?'

69

Our toasties arrived and I tucked in. Ned smiled approvingly. 'You look as if you were ready for that.'

I nodded, my mouth too full to answer. The cheese was stringy and salty on my tongue, the bread fresh and crunchy. Later I was planning to have a slice of apple pie with cream. I love eating. I celebrate the social and individual joy it brings. I could never turn food into an enemy, the way my sister has.

'Is yours OK?' I asked after a few minutes. Ned had taken a few half-hearted bites, then put his toastie down on the plate. He glanced up at me, back to the table, at me again. I thought, Here it comes, whatever's been bothering him.

The question, when it landed, took me by surprise. 'Jen, I have to ask you. Do you think Helen's getting ill again?'

'Christ, I hope not. What makes you ask?'

'She's been kind of secretive, lately. More than she normally is. Like, if I walk into her room when she's not expecting me she's really twitchy and tries to cover up her laptop. Last week she had a sheaf of printouts she shoved under the bed and then claimed was a list of RSPCA addresses. It might have been, except why did she hide them?'

My heart began to thud uncomfortably. 'Did you check when she wasn't around?'

'No! I'd never go poking into her things. Not least because if she saw me, she'd go berserk. But I wouldn't anyway. That's not my style.'

'Hiding papers isn't a sign of an eating disorder.'

'Not on its own, no.'

'What else?'

'Ah – she's – she doesn't – she won't, you know. We're not as close as we were. Physically.'

God. He was trying to say they'd stopped having sex. 'Are you quite sure you want to share this with me, Ned?'

'Sorry. Only, I thought it might be because she'd lost weight and didn't want me to see her body.'

'I don't think she's lost weight.'

'Is she eating?'

'Far as I can tell.'

We both knew Helen was a past master at appearing to consume normal meals. Her food-avoidance strategies were many and devious. They'd fooled us all at some point or other. Another problem is that, although she's officially recovered, anorexic-thinking for Hel's become a permanent mindset that she has to manage daily, whatever weight she is. She still puts huge amounts of effort into setting and maintaining the various mealtime rules that make her feel safe; she still weighs herself every morning and at the same time, and woe betide anyone who's in the bathroom when she needs to get in.

Ned took a long breath. 'It's probably nothing, then. I shouldn't have worried you. For God's sake, don't mention it to your mum.'

'No fear.'

We laughed uncomfortably. The thought of my mother's reaction if she believed we were entering another phase was unbearable.

'Back when she was at school,' said Ned, 'can you remember how it started?'

'No. We never talked about it. So I didn't catch on for ages. I mean, I knew something was wrong because there were a lot of arguments and people hushing when I came in, and talking behind closed doors. But I didn't take that much notice. You don't at that age. I was, what, seven, eight? I was more interested in what was on TV or who got bollocked at school that day. I do remember early on, though, when Mum actually smacked me and I think it was because of Helen, because I'd seen her refusing food so I tried it on as well, just for attention if I'm being honest, and she went ballistic with me. Slapped my face, screamed in my ear. Told me I'd sit at the table the whole night if I didn't clear my plate. I'd never been smacked before, I was in total shock. Then Dad came in and *he* started shouting at *her*. Horrible. I couldn't work out why everyone was getting so hyper over half a plate of stew. But I suppose Mum was venting the stuff she never dared say to Helen. And then there was another evening when my dad caught Hel scraping her dinner into the bin, and he ended up shaking her by the shoulders.'

'Jesus. I didn't know about that. I don't know most of it. Not the beginning and the middle. I came in towards the end, when she was getting better.'

'Oh, it's shrouded in mystery and you still haven't to ask. Once upon a time you might have got some sense out of Dad, except he doesn't want to go there because for a while he was the villain of the piece. He always had a whole lot less patience with the anorexia, used to reckon we should just be holding her down and force-feeding her. Like that would sort it! But he was desperate and frightened. And because Mum always takes the opposite side to whatever Dad thinks, she used to be super-protective of Hel, all softly-softly-let-her-be, and then beat herself up in case she was aiding and abetting the illness. So they were always falling out. There was some sort of crisis or row every day. I'd say I was about ten before I had an idea what was going on, and only then because I'd heard one of my friend's mums talking about it in the playground. No one thought to tell me outright.'

'Maybe they didn't know how. It's not something that's very easy to explain.'

'Maybe. You came on the scene about then, so I bet you know as much as I do. She really won't talk to you about it?'

'Nope.'

I looked across, and the fair skin of Ned's brow was crinkled. I wanted to reach over and smooth it for him, straighten his blond hair where it stuck up on the crown. Over the café's radio, Simply Red was playing *Holding Back the Years*; it made me think of an evening long ago when I'd been at the kitchen table revising for my GCSEs and Ned had wandered in to make a coffee. The song had been playing then, and Ned had swayed about in front of me cartoonishly, then grasped his earlobes and pulled them out from the sides of his skull as far as they'd reach. 'Holding back the ears,' he'd sung at me. Daft, but I was so wound up with exam nerves it had seemed hilarious. Even sitting in the school hall next day with my Eng Lit paper in front of me, I'd kept recalling the incident and giggling. I think now that was the point when my crush on Ned began. *This song*, I wanted to say to him. *Do you remember an evening when you mimed Mick Hucknall into a pan scrub for me?*

I reached out and took his hand. 'Let's not go backwards. It's not helpful. For what it's worth, I don't think Helen's ill again. I think she's a moody madam – I'm allowed to say that, I'm her sister, and anyway I've said as much to her face – plus we both know she's weird and obsessive. That's just her. But I honestly don't think she's sliding into anorexia again. I truly don't. I'll keep a close eye on her, if that'll make you feel any happier.'

'Would you, Jen?' He squeezed my fingers. 'It'd be a load off my mind. And obviously don't let on to her I'm worried. That wouldn't help.'

'No.'

Like some delicate piece of antique machinery, my sister, all finely-balanced cogs and springs wound up to the nth tension and tiny ticking parts. One of those brightly coloured miniature mechanical singing birds. Sometimes you're worried to even breathe near her.

After a moment, Ned drew his hand away. I'd like to have said he looked happier, but he didn't.

I nodded at his toastie. 'Aren't you going to finish that? Because I'll have it if you don't want it.'

He blinked, smiled, then pushed the plate towards me. The radio had changed to the Kooks, 'She Moves in her Own Way'.

'It'll be OK, Ned. She'll pass through whatever's bugging her, she always does.'

'Yeah, I'm sure you're right.'

But his eyes were clouded, as if he was focussing on some sort of interior film clip being played out.

'The trouble is, Jen, I've been dating your sister for ten years, and yet sometimes I feel I don't know the first thing about her.'

I took my time walking back to the office, mooching down narrow Tudor alleyways clogged by foreign students with their humongous rucksacks, by businessmen and -women shouting into mobiles, by shoppers laden with smart carrier bags. I pictured Ned walking in the opposite direction, headed for his car and an afternoon of furniture removal.

What it could be with Hel, I might have said to him, *is that she's been obsessing about a boy she went to school with. Has she ever mentioned him? Left her for a girl called Saskia? A boy who she apparently dated for a mere six weeks, and who, after they broke up, spread it around that she was a 'nut-case nympho'.*

Helen had been grudging in the detail she'd give me; I'd had to push for anything at all. But I'd said to her, 'If you're going to implicate me, the least you can do is be honest.' Then, of course, when I heard how he'd behaved, I'd laid into her.

'He said what? The dickhead! For God's sake! How can you still be in love with a man like that?'

She went, 'I don't love him, Jen, I hate him.'

'So why are we doing this?'

And she'd just looked sad and confused, as if she couldn't fathom the answer either.

Instead she'd switched to telling me a story about him: how he'd once followed an elderly teacher down the corridor, mimicking the man's slightly limping gait. The teacher, suspecting something, had whirled round, and on impulse Joe had thrown himself to the floor and pretended to be having some kind of a fit. He'd bitten his cheek as he fell, either accidentally or on purpose, so he was able to spit real blood onto the lino. The teacher had been so convinced by the performance that he'd bundled his own jacket under Joe's head and knelt by him while they waited for the dedicated-first-aider to come. At the end of the day he'd even popped into the sick room to see how the lad was doing.

'It was funny,' Hel said, 'even though it was cruel. The whole corridor was laughing over it.' When she saw my face she said, 'Everyone thought like me, the whole class. It wasn't just because I had a crush on him. Joe was *so* popular. He had this confidence, it drew people, boys and girls. He was magnetic.'

Again I'd scoffed. But a tiny part of me tingled with a kind of guilty recognition. How many times had I checked his Facebook pages over the last fortnight? Carefully noting the updates – Joe had bought a Snow Patrol album, been jogging along the canal, had joined Sports Locker's loyalty card scheme. What was I looking for? What did I think I'd find? One week ago, when my job had taken me out towards Chrishall for the afternoon, I'd found myself parking my car outside his daughters' primary school while he and his wife picked up the kids. I'd even tried to take a photo (why? For Helen?), but he'd moved at the last second and I'd only snapped her, in her purple striped tee and cropped leather jacket. I'd watched as the family climbed into their shiny 4x4, the older girl struggling with a guitar case. Joe was wearing an open-necked plaid shirt and cut-off jeans with trainers. After they drove away I deleted the picture.

And I'd felt, sitting in the driver's seat with the sun blazing through the windscreen, as if Hel had infected me with her own mad brain-itch. Because whatever Joe had, he had something. I didn't like him – I loathed him – yet I too was falling under this compulsion to know what he was up to, to get inside his life and see how fate was really treating him. And when I thought of how often this man was invading my head, I'd told myself there and then to get a grip and I'd gone that same night to Helen's room and laid out everything I'd discovered. I made sure to use the blandest, most direct language to explain about his status, job and family. I tried to avoid specific detail and words which were in any way loaded – I said he had two young children but I didn't say they were angelic, like pretty dolls, the image of their mother. I made no comment about Joe's good looks having lasted. Nor did I name the branch of the bank where his wife worked, or his web design company. I just set the facts out for her as neutrally as I could manage. Helen had been good. She hadn't interrupted to ask for information which would have caused extra pain. She made me pause only once, when I was telling her how he played football for a local amateur team. 'At school they thought he might make a professional,' she said. 'He went for trials.'

When I'd finished, I asked if she was OK. She thought about it for maybe half a minute – it felt like half an hour – and then declared she was. I said, 'Is that it, then? Is it over? No more digging?'

'I promise,' she said.

Now it seemed, from what Ned had confided, that despite her vow she hadn't been able to resist a peep herself. I suppose it was inevitable. I just hoped that was as far as it went. A few photos printed out and sighed over, a few days of unsettled, non-specific heartache. Perhaps if I'd stayed to talk it through further with her, ask how she was feeling about the news, I might have stalled her. But she'd closed down on me. Nothing more to be said, dear sister. Thank you for your detective work, and good night. I'd left her sitting under her duvet, pulling her fingers through her long red hair and staring abstractedly at a poster of The Lady of Shalott.

All Gerry had a chance to do was flash his eyebrows at me in warning before Rosa came storming up to my desk, a scrap of paper clutched to her chest. She's no sylph, but my God she can move fast when she wants to.

'It looks as if I need to spell something out to you,' she said, slapping the paper down on my mouse mat so that I flinched.

Fuck-fuck-fuck, I was thinking. What had I done? What had she found? Had I somehow missed a deadline or appointment? Had I said something inappropriate during an interview? Or was it – oh, dear God, no – was it that she'd found out I'd been browsing her dating website and poking about her personal business? She must have been checking my internet history while I was out and seen the URLs. In which case I was toast. I was out, and goodbye internship and decent references and any chance of getting another reputable job in the field of journalism for which I'd spent three years studying. I sat there wide-eyed and horrified as she towered over me, her beaded necklace swinging past my nose. And I wondered, during that second before she spoke again, whether I'd be heroic enough to take the blame for the whole thing, or if I'd try and save my skin by blaming Alan too. *He spotted the site to begin with, Rosa. He was the one snooping about your office. He's senior sports editor, I'm just a trainee. Take it up with him.*

But before I could marshal my thoughts, she was off again, stabbing at the paper with a manicured nail. 'This note I found on my desk twenty minutes ago. What do you think it says, Jennifer?'

Not being a mind-reader, I couldn't possibly say. 'I don't know, Rosa.'

'Don't you?'

Well obviously fucking not. 'No.'

'Did you or did you not tell the Revolution bookshop we would be sending out a press team to cover the opening of their café? Well, did you?'

My mind struggled to make a narrative out of the words. Hazily it formed: last month, me and Keisha and Vikki sitting round a pub table while Owen and Chelle preached about GM crops. Keisha telling me about how they were going to rearrange their ground floor to make room for tables, me casually promising to send a photographer round if they just rang in and gave their details to the desk.

'Yes, I did. What's the problem?'

She stood up to her full height, sighing exaggeratedly. 'Because if they want an advert, they can damn well pay for one, like everyone else. Who are you to give away free advertising space on our pages? What made you think you had the authority?'

'But we often send out reporters to cover that kind of event. That nursery allotment last week. And the charity fun day outside Sainsbury's, we did a full-page spread on that. I thought it was about supporting local businesses.'

'My God, Jennifer, are you really so dim?'

'Evidently yes.'

I couldn't believe I'd said the words aloud, but I was glad I had. I was sick of being spoken to as if I had no right to answer back. Rosa's nostrils flared, and she leaned in again.

'Let me explain in nice, simple language, then. If *The Chester Messenger* decides to report on the shifting of a few tables at the rear of a cupboard-sized hippy store, then what do you think will happen next? I'll tell you. We'll have every shop in the district on the phone telling us to come out and see they've painted a wall, or hung up a new painting. Expecting a column and a photo on the strength of it. So then the people who actually pay for genuine advertising space – who keep the damn ship afloat, in other words – will withdraw their custom because why should they put their hands in their pockets when we're dishing it out for free? Yes? Can you grasp that? Do you need me to go over it again?'

My face bloomed with heat. *But then why is the supermarket different?* I wanted to ask. *Or the nursery? Doesn't the same rule apply to them?*

She must have read my mind. 'The nursery and all the major supermarkets round here are regular advertisers with us. They generate thousands. Without them, our newspaper would go bust. We have a relationship, links, history. They are reputable and established companies. Names that local people know and trust. Whereas your tin-pot Revolution bookshop are a bunch of freaks peddling joyless dogma. We don't want the association. Unless, of course, they can stump up the fee for a conventional advertisement.'

She knew perfectly well they couldn't. A single full spread cost five hundred quid, and even a quarter-page was beyond the means of Keisha and Vik's budget. The shop made a pittance, there just wasn't anything left over for advertising. Sometimes they got lucky: I do know that once – and I didn't ask the details – some flyers magically reproduced themselves on the photocopier of a nearby private school, and on another occasion Vikki spotted the owner of the regional free paper in a bar with a woman who wasn't his wife, and thereafter got six weeks' space in his business section. But mostly they had to do without, and the shop was on the edge of the city centre and its customer base 'niche'. The margins were so slender they were nearly invisible. That's why the promise of even a tiny bit of press coverage had meant so much.

I hung my head. There was no response I could make to Rosa, because if I started to argue I knew I'd never be able to stop until every shade of abuse had spilled out of my mouth and I had no internship any more.

Luckily for me, she seemed about finished. Across the office Alan was calling her name and holding up his phone, miming a kind of flapping action which clearly meant something important because she only bothered shooting me one last withering look before hurrying across to take the mobile and coo into it, smiley smiley.

After a minute, I restarted my PC and tried to bring the day's schedule back into focus. Rosa's words were still loud in my head, and little hot flares of temper and humiliation kept leaping up under my breastbone. I imagined waiting till the end of the day, then challenging her, without the pressure of an audience. *I know what your problem is*, I would say. *It's because the bookshop people are different, isn't it? Different from the so-called smart set you hang out with. It's because the crowd at Revolution have creative hair and FairTrade clothes and because Keisha and Vikki are lesbians. So they don't quite measure up to your ultra-bland standards. Too common and outrageous to waste newsprint on.* And I pictured Owen saying, *I told you when you started working for that paper they were a bunch of capitalist gits.* And I thought of having to take myself round to the shop to explain that, despite what I'd promised, we wouldn't be turning up with a notepad and camera after all. Damn Rosa. Damn her to hell and right round again. In my whole life I'd never met anyone as objectionable. As I sat now at my desk, hatred for her was pumping round my veins and filling up the chambers of my heart.

Just as I was about to expire through my own poison, Gerry cruised past on his way back from the water cooler. Without pausing, he bent his head in my direction and muttered, 'You know what the problem is there, don't you? Nasty case of thrush.'

I let out a yelp of angry laughter. At once Rosa's head whipped round, but I stared her out and she returned to her call.

These tiny rebellions are what keep you going.

After work I wanted to go straight to Owen's, but I felt I had no choice other than to make my way over to the bookshop and explain myself. I'd done nothing but stew all afternoon, trying to work out whether there was any way I could slip a mention of Revolution into print *somewhere*, just to spite Rosa. But I knew it was impossible. In practical terms she had editorial control, and had to approve the entire submitted text before it went to central press. So she'd weed out any reference she didn't like, and roast me into the bargain.

By the time I reached the shop I was flustered with guilt and resentment. Keisha's grin as she let me over the threshold only made me feel worse.

'Spot any changes?' she said, nodding towards the far end of the room.

'Bloody hell. I'll say.'

Since I'd last visited, the place had been transformed. The customer space used to be labyrinthine with ranks of free-standing black wood shelves, the walls covered in a jumble of cheaply produced flyers, the ceiling clad in orange pine. They'd taken down a partition and removed a massive cupboard, repainted the ceiling so it was cream, and pushed the shelving to the edges of the room. More books were displayed on tables and on white wire racks. In the rear half, which I could see still wasn't finished, one stretch had been left bare and primed; I guessed that was for notices. Keisha followed my gaze.

'Vik's got a friend who's an artist and he's going to paint us a tree on that section. Then we can stick posters and cards on the branches and trunk. Give it more of a visual impact than an ordinary notice board.'

'Cool. Where have you put all your books?'

'They're still here. Just better displayed. I know, it's amazing, isn't it?'

I took a breath. 'And your café's going at the back?'

'That's right. Saleem's sourced us six old school desks that were being thrown out. Covered in graffiti and ink stains, very cool. Plus one of those long wooden counter tops from a science lab. The cakes can sit on that. And then in the evenings, we can push the tables aside and make a performance space. People can come and do readings and make speeches and have discussions.'

She looked so happy. I felt like the biggest heel in the world for what I was about to say.

Keisha frowned. 'Don't you like it, Jen?'

'Yes, I do. I really do. It's tons better. Who's going to be making your cakes?'

'Viks. She's not done a lot of baking before, but she has been reading up.'

As if on cue, the shop door jangled open and there was Vikki, carrying a basket of poorly looking fruit.

'From the market,' she said. 'They were more or less giving it away, just 'cause it's got a few bruises and lumps. But we like imperfect round here. Hey, Jen, what do you think of our makeover? Good, isn't it? We're on track with budget and schedule, too, it's coming together. I can't wait to see the photos in your paper.'

I said, 'You'd better sit down for a minute. I've something to tell you.'

They're so sweet, those two. They sat and listened politely, Keisha pressing her lips together in a rueful way, and Vikki pulling a sympathetic face when I described Rosa's outburst.

'I'm sorry,' I said.

Vikki sighed and poked at her fruit. 'It's not your fault. It's the system: you have to be inside it for it to work. But, bugger. It is a set-back. I suppose we could always arrange for a nice dramatic news story to happen, get coverage that way. I could chain myself to something. The drainpipe outside.'

'It would have to be a popular landmark to get maximum attention. The Eastgate Clock.'

'The Town Crier.'

'You mean the pub?'

'No, I mean that geezer who walks around the precinct in highwayman gear. I could stalk him, wrestle him to the ground, then shackle both of us to The Cross. That'd have him ringing his bell.'

'Honestly, Vikki, between now and opening day you could rescue a dozen orphans from a burning building and Rosa would boycott the story on principle.' I plucked a withered grape out of the basket and held it aloft. 'See that? That's the size of my boss's humanity. That's exactly how large it is.'

Keisha nodded. 'We're done, then. Who'd like a brew? Shall I get the kettle on?'

'I can hand out leaflets for you, though, if you want.'

'We might take you up on that, Jen.'

They made me a peppermint tea, and I took my mug and sat in the window, watching passers-by and nursing my shame. There I let my thoughts wander back over the day, beyond my boss's rant to my various other failings, and finally to the conversation with Ned and what he'd said about Chelle. An annoying limpet, he'd dismissed her as. Nothing to fret about, 'easily dislodged'. Was he right? Part of the trouble was, she never left Owen and me alone. Even if we closed the bedroom door she'd be bumping about outside, playing the radio and singing along in a penetrating nasal voice. And it felt as if no conversation could run for more than two minutes without her butting in, diverting the subject onto yet another anecdote about her activist experiences. The time she'd hijacked a crop sprayer, the time she'd sent a singing nun-o-gram to the environment minister, the charity gigs and student protests and shop sit-ins she'd organised. Owen lapped it up, treated her like a guru. 'You know, Jen,' he said to me one night as we lay in bed together, 'I sometimes listen to Chelle's ideas and think she's been *sent* to us.' *Ooh, like an angel*, I nearly said, but I managed to bite back the sarcasm. His admiration was naked and intense. If he'd told me she could speak to dolphins I wouldn't have been surprised. *Don't you find it irritating the way she finds everything 'awesome'?* I wanted to say to him. *Have you seen how she's left wet towels on the floor? Did you realise I had to go out and buy more coffee because she finished off the jar without telling anyone?* And more than that, I wanted to ask, *Do you like her better than me? Do you find her attractive? Are you ever a little bit tempted?* But I knew how intolerant that would sound, and if there's one thing Owen can't abide, it's intolerance.

Keisha came over to flip the sign on the door. ''Cause we don't want to be besieged by crowds of customers all night,' she said drily.

I heard myself say, 'What do you think of Chelle?'

She blinked. 'Hmm, Chelle. She's very interesting. She's led an interesting life, hasn't she? Packed a lot in.'

'But do you like *her*, as a person?'

'I don't know her.'

'From what you've seen?'

'Well—'

'We think she's a free-loader and an attention-seeker,' called Vikki from across the shop. 'Does that make you feel better, Jen?'

I blushed. 'Oh, God. Am I that transparent?'

'It's all right, your secret's safe with us.'

Out of the corner of my eye I saw Keisha shuffling with embarrassment. She obviously didn't think such bluntness was appropriate or wise.

I said, 'I didn't mind her visiting for a bit. She's Owen's mate and it's his flat at the end of the day; he's had other people stay over when they've needed somewhere to crash for a day or two. Only, Chelle's not showing any sign of moving on. If I had a specific date when she was leaving, it wouldn't be so bad. When I ask her she just shrugs. And I don't feel I can put up much of a protest in case I come over as jealous or petty. You know what Owen's like. He's allergic to pettiness.'

Vikki laughed. 'Owen needs to wake up. Chelle's a sponger – she's got him paying for everything: food, travel, drinks, the lot. He bought her a new rucksack last week because her old one had split. A pretty good one, too. Top of the range.'

'Did he?' That was news to me.

The women exchanged glances.

Keisha rubbed at the face of her wrist watch. 'He said to me it's because she couldn't manage without one, and she hasn't any other resources right now. You know what Owen's like when he thinks someone's genuinely in need. He can't help himself.'

'But Chelle can. If you're not happy, Jen, you should speak up,' said Vikki.

'Don't push her,' replied Keisha. 'It's not really our business, is it?'

'Yeah, because I don't like to stand by . . .'

I barely heard them. New rucksack? New bloody rucksack? I couldn't believe it. My heart was swelling at the unfairness. I tried to think what had Owen given me lately. A second-hand poetry collection. And I'd been really touched because he'd gone back to the bookshop specially after I said I wished I'd bought it. 'What's this for?' I'd asked when he handed it over. 'No reason,' he'd said. The floppy, yellowed paperback had cost him £3.50, and at the time I didn't even think the price mattered. Did it matter? Was I being an ingrate or a mug? The value of a gift was the intention behind it, surely?

Whatever the arguments, Chelle was clearly taking the piss. She'd stepped over a line.

So far I'd made myself hold back on the criticism because it's hard to point out someone isn't very nice without sounding not very nice yourself. I knew how it would come across. I had rehearsed a few openers, but each time I'd ended up sounding, at best, ungenerous and, at worst, a bitch, and I could picture all too clearly Owen's appalled face. *Just tell the woman to buzz off*, I could hear Ned saying. *It's straightforward enough*. To which I'd reply, *To you, from where you're standing, maybe*. Easiest thing in the world to solve someone else's problem. 'Just insist your husband gives you more respect.' 'Just take your boss aside and demand a pay rise.' We all know the theory, but how many of us live by the manual? These set-ups always seem so clear if you're on the outside. It's different altogether when you're in the middle of them. What could I say to Owen that would make him see it my way?

'She'll be here in a few minutes, anyway,' said Vikki, breaking into my thoughts.

'How come?'

Vikki frowned. 'We're all off to the Oak for a strategy meeting about this new website he's putting together. Didn't Owen say? I thought that's why you were here, to meet him.'

'Huh? No. I was just going to go round to the flat as usual—' I made myself stop, but the damage was done. I'd already made myself look a fool in front of her. I couldn't bluster and pretend, *Oh, yeah, I remember. He rang me this morning.* It was too obvious that my boyfriend had planned an excursion without bothering to tell me.

And there you had it. One final V-flick from the World's Worst Day.

'Well, you're here now, so that's OK,' said Keisha unconvincingly.

As it happened, we didn't have to wait long for them to turn up. Within five minutes Owen and Chelle stumbled through the door laughing, his face shining and hers registering a self-satisfied smirk.

'Oh, that's brilliant,' he was saying. 'Wait till I tell the others. That's classic. Classic.'

'Something's funny?' said Vikki.

'It is, it is.' Owen wiped his eye with his cuff. 'Chelle, tell them what you told me on the way here.'

Chelle perched herself on the corner of the nearest table.

'Well,' she began, 'this was a couple of years ago, in Wellington. A group of us were at this store, this supermarket, and we were doing a demo dressed as cows—'

'You were protesting against GM milk,' Owen chipped in.

'Yeah, that's right. And we were wearing these cow heads with horns, yeah, and zip-up cow-print onesies with kind of leather hooves over the hands – they were pretty awesome. Everyone was stopping to look at our signs and take our leaflets, we were getting loads of attention. And then I looked along the row and I counted one cow too many. There were supposed to be six of us, but I counted seven. So I said to my mate Mitchy, Who's the guy on the end there? And he said he thought it was a friend of Bev's – she was our secretary then. And I said, Who is he, though? And Mitch said he thought his name was Ryan, but Glen said he'd heard he was called Frankie or something. So I kept a watch on Mr Extra, and when he thought we weren't looking I could see he had his phone out and he was taking photos of us and texting. Then he dropped his phone – he was having to struggle because of the hooves, yeah? – and I went over to help him and heard him speak. And I knew his voice. I knew who it was. It was this guy out of Sector Twenty-Twenty, which is this right-wing group we've had some problems with – I'd seen him a few weeks before ranting away on YouTube and I recognised him. Basically he'd been spying, trying to get some dirt so he could discredit us. I whipped off his cow head and I shouted to the others what was going on, he made a run for it and we started this chase round the car park, still in our costumes. It was epic. There were shoppers standing there, gripping their carts, with their mouths open. Fantastic publicity for the cause. It made the regional TV news.'

Owen was shaking his head in admiration. 'Fantastic, isn't it? Why haven't we ever done anything like that?'

'Run round a supermarket dressed as cows?' said Vikki. 'I could give you a few reasons.'

'Ah, come on, Viks, where's your sense of adventure?' I said, from the window-seat behind him.

My boyfriend did a double-take. 'Hey! Jen! I didn't see you.' To my delight he came straight over and hugged me hard. He seemed genuinely pleased I was there, or maybe that was just an overflow of bonhomie. 'I was gonna text you about where to meet.'

'She popped in to ... admire the shop,' said Keisha diplomatically.

'Excellent! Then we can all walk up together, soon as Saleem and Noolan get here. We've been bouncing round some ideas for a new website, one that draws together fringe news and events. I mean, I know there's Limitation.org, but a lot of that's animal rights. I wanted to put together something purely on environmental issues.'

I said, 'I do a fair bit on the newspaper's website. I might have some tips.'

'Yeah?'

'Like I was telling you earlier,' broke in Chelle, 'there's this neat web-design package I used when I was in New Zealand. I'm pretty handy with that. What I did was use it to create a database of interest groups, and then once that was up and running we were able to sort them into categories and sub-categories . . .'

She stood by the door, sturdy legs planted apart, hands on hips as she laid out in detail for us her experience in IT. No surprises for guessing she happened to be an expert in the field. That the pages she designed got more hits, that her colleagues at the time had been amazed by her creative ability. They'd urged her to take a screenshot and have it printed onto T-shirts, so she'd bowed to popular demand and run up a dozen, and even sent one to the Prime Minister. The Prime

Minister of New Zealand actually owned one of her T-shirts. Think about that.

I found myself trying to picture this rucksack, wondering why I hadn't clocked the upgrade. Thought of what I might say to Owen on the subject. What he'd say to me. *The stitching had bust, she couldn't carry her belongings any more, it wasn't like a luxury item. She needed help, Jen, and I was in a position to give it. That's all.* Then I was dropping back into a memory of Manchester, a day he'd got chatting to this homeless guy in Piccadilly and it transpired they knew each other, had been at the same school only a few years apart, and Owen brought him home and phoned round till he managed to get him into a hostel, and for months after that we'd see the man about and he'd give the OK sign. It made me proud, because as Owen said, you should never judge anyone purely on their circumstances. Any one of us might be sleeping on a bench if the fates conspired. Life was luck, and those of us who were on the up had a duty to help those who were on the way down. To him, it was that simple and pure. I loved him for his optimism, his energy, the way he made you feel you could change the world. I remembered how we'd toast bread together on his gas fire, watch comedy DVDs with the duvet pulled over the sofa because the student flat was so damn cold. One morning we'd found a starling lying on the grass under his window – he reckoned it must have banged into the glass – and we brought it inside till it recovered and then we opened the door and let it fly away.

Meanwhile, back in the present, Chelle was still droning on. I reached over for my boyfriend's hand and squeezed it, and encouragingly, he squeezed back. And with that single gesture, my spirits lifted and the situation seemed to clear itself in my mind. Viks was right. Of course she was. Dumb patience was getting me nowhere. I needed to trust my boyfriend's feelings for me, have confidence in my status. Confrontation might not be the way, and open challenge would probably just be counter-productive. But I *could* deal with this woman. I was more than a match for her. I could see her off without needing to involve Owen.

'. . . And although design's important, content's the critical thing because it's no good if there's no substance underneath your flashing logos . . .'

I stared at her as she talked. Her sun-bleached hair was already darkening and her tan fading. Brand new bloody rucksack. Well, no more. It was time to match her at her own game.

'. . . So that's the way I'd structure it,' she was saying. 'If you're after a serious, professional website. As opposed to something that looks like a candy-coated lifestyle magazine.'

She shot a sly look at me, and I answered with a broad, warm smile which confused her no end.

Candy-coated, am I, madam, I vibed back. *We'll see. Just you watch.*

It's fair to say, that evening in the pub, I was on fire. Instead of mainly sitting and listening, I jumped right into the discussion. I suggested the name Just-Iz, which everyone liked, and some possible logos and some home page features. Thinking of the various press models I'd worked with, I was able to put forward four or five sponsors Owen might try contacting. I offered ideas for getting media attention, and reminded them of the best ways to approach journalists. As the August sky finally darkened through the window, I saw Saleem staring up at me from his notebook, and Keisha grinning and Chelle scowling, and my boyfriend for once hanging on my every word. Chelle butted in repeatedly, and I'd just let her finish and then start up again, sometimes rolling the conversation along as if she'd never spoken. Once or twice I told her, 'Well done,' which I could see pissed her off mightily. All the while I held Owen's hand, or pressed his knee with mine, or leant against his shoulder. Once, when he returned from the bar with a drink for me, I took his face in my hands and kissed him full on the mouth.

And when the bell rang for last orders I simply went, 'So I'm coming back to yours for the night, yeah?' and he didn't throw up any obstructions. Maybe he knew about the spare set of clothes I'd cached under the wardrobe.

I texted Mum to let her know my plans, then walked out of the pub with my arm round my boyfriend's waist. Behind us Chelle was boasting to Saleem about a flash-protest she'd organised outside Britomart, and how it had been awesome because they'd all suddenly lain down as if they'd been shot, and shoppers had to step over them and some people were calling the police and holding tissues over their mouths in case it was a gas attack, and you could still find the footage on a site called Freestreamers. But I tuned her out.

As we strolled up the main precinct I raised my eyes and spotted a plane flying directly above us, winking across the blackness to land who knew where. A tube full of passengers leaving England's shores, some perhaps forever. Easy as that.

It may not have been a shooting star, but it was worth a wish anyway.

CHAPTER 4

'The best thing about Saturdays,' said Ned, easing off the handbrake as the traffic lights changed, 'is when you wake up and you think it's a Monday or something and then you remember it isn't.'

Helen shifted in the passenger seat and half turned to me. 'Yeah, and then you pull the duvet up and roll over again. Bliss.'

I said, 'Sometimes, on a winter's morning, I poke my arm out and let it get cold solely for the pleasure of bringing it back into the warm again.'

'You crazy, thrill-seeking fool.'

On either side of me Chelle and Owen sat silent, unable to contribute to this working week discussion.

It was meant to be just my sister and her boyfriend's trip out, but the night before Ned had asked me along too.

'Why?' I'd said.

'Hel wants you.'

'Why?'

'Because we think you'll enjoy it. You like *Downton Abbey*, don't you? Well, that's Bersham Hall, basically. You get to wear a mob cap and make butter pats. If you want.'

'And if I don't?'

'You can park yourself in the tea room and scoff cake all afternoon. I've heard their lemon drizzle's won awards.'

So I'd sort of agreed, and then I'd asked Owen and Owen had asked Chelle.

Now here we were, she and I, hip to hip in the back of Ned's Fiat. I heard her intake of breath as she prepared for another one of her anecdotes.

'The best thing about Saturdays in Auckland,' she began, 'was rowing across from the CBD after a night out. The CBD's the central business district, where all the clubs are – well, that's the Viaduct – and if you missed the last ferry you'd have to borrow someone's boat and then row it back in the morning. And sometimes as you crossed you'd see killer whales poking their noses up out of the water, and little blue penguins right there in the harbour. They swim on the surface on their sides and they flap their flipper like they're waving to you, it's so cool. And there are colonies of ducks, and I've seen floating mangroves. It's awesome to be paddling across there in the moonlight. Totally awesome.'

There was a silence while we digested this. 'Wow,' said Owen.

'I saw a pigeon poop on the postman's head yesterday,' I said. 'That was fairly awesome.'

'I once saw a pigeon fly into a man's face,' said Ned.

'Bet that was intense.'

'It was for the pigeon.'

'Have you ever seen baby pigeons?' asked Helen. 'They're so ugly they're cute.'

Chelle cut in. 'We have pigeons in New Zealand too. Plus we have these birds called keas, I don't know if you've heard of them. They're a bit like a parrot, and they're super-intelligent but they're on the endangered list. Farmers used to kill them because they attacked sheep. They'd sit on the sheep's back and peck through the wool to eat the fat. Well, so the farmers claimed. But keas'll have a go at anything. They've got these mega-sharp beaks and they'll strip out a car faster than any mechanic, snap off your aerial and steal your wiper blades. They'll tear the lead flashing off your roof. And conservationists are saying that their diet's poisoning them. And they're still being shot by some hunters. It's tragic.'

'Who'd be a kea,' said Ned. I thought there was the very faint edge of a snigger in his voice.

A sign on the verge announced we were crossing the border. 'Welcome to Wales,' I read aloud.

'Sheesh, that reminds me.' Chelle leant forward so she could address Owen directly. 'Did I ever tell you about that time we tethered an inflatable bleeding whale over the Prime Minister's house?'

'Is it much further?' I heard Helen ask.

'Twenty minutes,' said Ned. 'If you can hang on.'

The driveway leading up to the house was about two miles long. Ancient trees lined the road, parkland stretched beyond. Every few hundred yards squirrels dashed out in front of the car, which meant Ned slamming on his brakes.

'They've bloody followed me from work, they have,' he said, scowling as one hopped lazily from verge to verge. 'Like bad spirits. Look, that one can't even be bothered to shift out of the way. It'll be a flat squirrel in a minute.'

'Don't be mean!' said Helen.

'In New Zealand we get possums squatting on the tarmac. They're a lot chunkier than these guys.'

'Course they are,' said Ned.

But we all went quiet when the hall came into view. It was exactly like an old watercolour. The long, broad building, backdropped today by a china-blue sky, was red brick and symmetrical with matching chimneys and ranks of tall, arched windows. Along the roof edge was a balustrade, while over the door there was a central pediment, and at ground level a gracious flight of white stone steps flared to the gravel frontage. Everything about the aspect was designed to say, *This is an age of elegance and harmony, balance and reason. We are classical, we are regulated.* Blink, and Mr Darcy would draw up in his barouche landau.

After we'd parked and paid for our tickets we were shepherded towards the house and in through a side door. 'Servants' entrance,' muttered Owen. He was right as it turned out, because we found ourselves inside a vaulted kitchen with a vast iron range and lots of scrubbed wooden counter tops. The walls and ceiling were hung with cooking implements; a spit with a pretend roast revolved over a flickering electric fire. Someone had draped stuffed rabbits and pheasants across one end for added authenticity, which made Helen shudder.

'If you feel that way about animals you should think about going veggie,' said Chelle.

'My sister's diet's fine as it is,' I said threateningly. God knows, we didn't want any more food groups being cut out.

Meanwhile, Owen had wandered to the far end of the room and was assessing four shelves' worth of jelly moulds.

'How the hell could one family *need* so much, Jen?' he asked as I came up behind him.

'It's not about need, though, is it? It's about showing off. "Look at me, I've put twenty different puddings on the table. See the girth of my blancmange."'

'Yes. And how many poor people were supporting this ridiculous lifestyle?'

'I think that's what we're going to find out on the tour.'

He sighed deeply. 'The problem with society is that some sectors of it think they deserve more just because of who they are. It's expectation that drives inequality. Expectation and apathy. That's all it comes down to in the end.'

'Up the revolution,' chirped Ned, passing us by as he headed for the next room.

Owen shot him a look.

I said, 'You were getting a touch loud, that's all.'

We moved out into a stone-flagged corridor lined with very old photographs.

'Here are the outdoor staff as they were in August 1912,' read Helen from a caption below the largest group photo, 'including the gamekeeper, the head gardener and his team, the grounds keeper, the gate keeper, the head coachman and working coachman, the stable master, the groom and stable boy. Detailed records were kept of each man, and his photograph taken biennially. The owners of Bersham Hall were unusual in that they took an interest in the lives and fortunes of their servants as individuals in their own right, instead of simply as employees of the estate.'

'Big of them,' said Owen.

Pale, stern faces from the past stared back at us coolly. It was hard to tell whether they laboured under a sense of oppression or not.

We trooped on past the butler's pantry and the housekeeper's study. The windows were ill-fitting and draughty, and there was nothing to cover the bare floorboards save a rag rug.

'Must have been cold,' said Hel, nodding at the tiny grate. Ned reached out and put his arm round her shoulder, and I thought I saw her flinch. He didn't seem to notice, though. After a moment she relaxed and let him draw her close. Perhaps it was just that the touch had been unexpected.

We visited the servants' dining room and the gun room and the laundry, and then a guide pointed us up the stairs towards the posh part of the house. We quickly realised we were entering another world. Under our feet, as we climbed the ornately carved stairs, was patterned carpet. At the windows hung thick curtains and the walls were richly papered. This was the territory of comfort and indulgence, silk and satin, tassels and quilting. I could feel Owen seethe. When we came out into the main hall, he stood in the centre of the marble floor and scoffed at the ranks of portraits and antique weaponry on display.

'It's pretty obscene, isn't it? You have to admit. I mean, you could house a whole family just in this one room.'

The space was larger than his whole student flat had been. In the far corner, a guide in conversation with another visitor was pointing out something on the ceiling, and we all raised our heads to look. What we saw was an impressive filigree of white plasterwork piped across a Wedgwood blue background, a border of fleurs-de-lys and a series of criss-cross panels drawing the eye in towards the centre. There sat a rich and glowing fresco depicting (as far as I could tell) an old man dressed in a sheet and standing in a river. I sidled nearer to the guide so I could eavesdrop; found out that the old guy was supposed to represent St Christopher bearing the infant Christ across the foaming waters, and that the Earl who'd commissioned the painting in the late 1700s had ordered the saint's face to resemble his own. Arrogance on an epic scale.

'You can see it in their eyes,' said Owen, glaring at a portrait of a man in a fur-trimmed cape. 'There's no self-doubt there, no spark of humility. These people think they're born to order the rest of us around.'

'I suppose at least they commissioned some grand art. Without that wealth, we wouldn't have architecture like this, would we?'

'So?'

My gaze swept round the delicate panelling, the Chinese-lacquered furniture, the silk drapery. 'It's our cultural history. And it's good that artists got the chance to practise their skills and produce beautiful objects, and that those objects were then cared for and preserved so that we can all enjoy them today.'

'Worth centuries of human suffering and exploitation, Jen?'

'When you put it like that—'

Helen came gliding up behind us. 'Owen, my love, why did you come today if you're just going to be angry about everything?'

He had the grace to look sheepish. 'It's just, it's hard for me to see a place like this without thinking of its political and social impact on the ordinary working man. I came here because I wanted to learn more about the history of oppression, take the opportunity to gather some facts.'

'So actually, despite the grumbling, you're sort of enjoying yourself?'

'Well, it's been interesting.'

'OK, then. "Thank you, Jen, for inviting me on this trip".'

'Yeah. Thanks.'

'Good.' Helen pressed her lips together, then turned and skated her way across the shiny floor tiles to where the arrow signs pointed.

The next room we visited was lemon yellow. It was full of musical instruments – clavichords and fiddles and flutey things – and round the edges were positioned hard, upright chairs that no one was allowed to sit on. This part of the house, the guide told us, had been severely damaged by subsidence in the 1970s and painstakingly restored. The onyx mantelpiece had cracked, and new stone had to be sourced from abroad at terrific expense. Top craftsmen had worked round the clock to minimise the damage. The wallpaper above the dado was hand-blocked and cost thousands to replicate. In fact, upkeep of a building on this scale was unimaginable, a constant nightmare for the owners who nevertheless struggled on, staunch in their duty to preserve the country's heritage for future generations. If, in the light of that, we felt we wanted to make a further contribution to maintenance on top of the entrance fee we'd already paid, there was a donations box by the exit.

I dragged Owen out before he had a chance to respond.

Bersham Hall's bedrooms, when we got to the upper storey, were plush but uncomfortable-looking, with their commodes, their stunted four-posters, a jug-and-basin set up for washing. One of the beds had apparently belonged to an earl who'd never married but had kept his sweetheart waiting till she was too old to find anyone else. Which sounded plain mean, but recent evidence had come to light suggesting he'd caught syphilis as a young army captain, and had felt compelled ever after to remain a bachelor. She'd died a spinster, while he'd expired abroad and alone in a hotel. All that wealth, all that rank, and he'd had neither friend nor lover at his bedside when he passed.

The children's nursery I liked much better. Near the front, within mane-stroking distance, there was a rocking horse with a stack of painted wooden blocks by its feet. Under the window was a row of large, fancy dolls and an impressive toy fort. There were skittles and hoops, moth-eaten teddies, a pair of bladed ice skates. One of the earls had commissioned for his son a pedal-car replica of his own Bentley, shiny green and leather-upholstered and complete with flying B hood ornament. Even Owen was drawn, I could tell. But the little lad didn't have long to play here, the guide explained, because boys were sent away to boarding school at seven. Girls didn't merit a proper education, full stop. They were landed with a governess who'd deliver only the basics, just enough to keep them occupied till they grew up and got themselves safely married.

The same guide told us the story of one countess who'd died trying over and over to produce a male heir, and another with mental health problems who they'd treated by locking her up for six years till one day she broke open a window and jumped to her death. I wanted to whisper to Owen that actually life in the eighteenth and nineteenth centuries must have been tough whatever social class you were.

When the indoor tour was over we were released out into the gardens. It was a warm day and the grasshoppers were chirping.

'That noise reminds me of the cicadas we get in New Zealand,' said Chelle. 'Except they're a lot louder. Does anyone mind if I take my shoes off? I like to walk around in bare feet when I can.'

Beer feet, it came out as. Ned snorted.

'Beer feet? Is that what you get when you've drunk too much? I think I've had beer feet myself some nights.'

I couldn't resist a grin. The number of times I'd wanted to take the piss out of her pronunciation and never dared.

'Right,' announced Hel. 'Time for the best bit; I wanted to save it till last. Over the other side of the gardens here they have this rare breeds enclosure, pigs and cows and sheep and chickens, but also giant Belgian rabbits that you can pet. Big as cats, we're talking. Bigger. Imagine that, Jen.'

'Rabbits?'

'Uh-huh.'

'Ah. I see. And this is, in fact, the real reason we've come?'

'No. Not just that. There's the whole heritage thing, and the architecture and the landscape which we've been enjoying—'

'Thirty miles we've driven, essentially so you can molest some bunnies? What are you like?'

'Come on, everyone loves a rabbit.'

'In New Zealand they're actually a major pest—' Chelle began.

I choked her off. 'OK, sis. If that's what your heart truly desires, we can give you half an hour to prod your outsize rodents. Show us where they are. Lead on.'

We made our way through close-clipped hedges and along neat paths, past mellow brick walls and espalier fruit trees. As we passed under one ornate metal arch, Owen paused and nipped off a rose with his fingernails. I wondered if he was doing it for spite, a miniature act of rebellion, but then he stepped over to me and pushed the stalk behind my ear, gently.

'That velvet-red so suits you,' he said.

His way of saying sorry. I touched the edges of the petals with my fingertips.

'Hey, yeah, good idea. Let's all grab a flower,' said Chelle. 'Share out the wealth among the peasants. It's not like there aren't enough to go round.'

I watched as she stepped in front of him, cocking her head in expectation that he'd do the same for her. But he didn't seem to get what she meant and instead walked on past her, and she was reduced to picking her own rose, thrusting it into her own short hair.

At last we came out into a cobbled, farm-style courtyard with a stone trough at its centre. A chalkboard sign told us that the rabbits were housed in a barn next to the present earl's vintage car collection, and you had to wait to be let in, a group at a time.

Helen at once hurried across and put her face to the barn window. 'Oh, wow, look at them. You won't believe it. These animals are *huge*.'

I came and peered in beside her. Under the orange strip lights the rabbits were monstrous, muscled and powerful. They looked like pulsating boulders scattered across the straw. I could see their eyes glinting, the strong claws poking out from their massive feet. A young girl crouched next to one, touching its flank nervously. She didn't much look as if she wanted to be there.

'Good God, Hel. I've never seen anything like it. Do you think they're safe?'

'Of course they're safe. They're rabbits.'

'That one looks a bit evil.'

She glanced at me as if I was mad.

'You OK if I go and ogle those rich-man cars?' said Owen from behind me.

'Me too,' said Chelle immediately, as I'd known she would.

I shrugged because I didn't have a choice.

So my boyfriend and his hanger-on took themselves off to the building next door while Ned, Hel and I stood at the entrance to bunny world with a bunch of chattering Brownies. Then, when it was our turn, we had to wash our hands in sterile gel and hear a lecture on health and safety, which was mainly about not sticking your fingers between their mighty incisors and also watching out for their powerful hind legs.

At the last minute I bottled it.

'Actually, you two go ahead. I'll admire from out here,' I told them.

I'm not sure Hel even heard me. All she was interested in was getting to her mutant coneys. She pushed forward, elbowing Brownies out of the way.

I was left on my own, leaning against a warm wall in the September sunshine. Over to my left was the vintage car collection; I knew if I wanted I could wander across and annoy Chelle some more. But it was quite nice to be alone for a few minutes, imagining what it would be like to be the owner of an estate with twenty bedrooms and a lozenge-shaped carp pool. There's something deeply restful about being surrounded by beautiful objects. Halfway through the tour I'd noticed, for instance, that if the ceiling moulding included a lion, then that same motif was taken up again in the design of the carpet; that a curve or flourish here matched a curve or flourish there. Every pattern had its echo, and the attention to detail was stunning. What must it be like to live amongst such calm, classical forms every day? And I pictured myself transplanted here, sumptuous dinners served up in front of me and afternoon teas on the terrace, slinky evening gowns and distinguished men in dinner jackets. There would be grand staircases to descend. Heads would turn. String quartets would strike up. As lady of the manor, you'd be above the stress and fret of having to make your own way in the ordinary working world. No more run-ins with a sarky boss. No more office politics. All that weary business swept aside for a life of privilege, grace and order. Then I remembered Owen and I thought, *How appalled would he be if he could read my mind right now?*

The barn door swung open and Ned appeared. 'You OK, Jen?'

I jerked out of my daydream. 'Oh. Yeah. Fine.'

'Not so struck on the rabbits?'

'Not wildly. I take it Hel's having a ball.'

'See for yourself.'

We stood side by side to squint through the glass. Helen was on the far side of the room, kneeling among the hay bales next to a meaty black specimen and stroking it along the length of its ears. There was a brown rabbit by her feet and another at her elbow. Her expression was one of rapture.

'Has she even noticed you've left?' I asked.

'Nope. I am surplus to requirements.'

'She does love her mammals. It's such a shame Mum won't let her have something. Even a hamster would do it.'

'Why doesn't she? Is it the hygiene aspect?'

'That and the scope for bereavement. But yes, mainly it's the mess. You know how wound up my mother gets if anyone undoes her housework. The idea of anyone trailing bags of sawdust or poo-strewn cages through the house would probably bring on some kind of attack. You're not allowed pets in your place, are you?'

'No. Otherwise I would. I know how happy it would make her.'

'I suppose you could always move. I mean, get a place together. You've been dating long enough. Then Hel could pack it to the gunnels with as many critters as she wanted.'

Ned sighed. 'I have broached the subject – several times – but she always warns me off.'

'She likes the current set-up too much.'

'Yes, basically. It makes her feel secure. She has her room at yours, and she has me. There's that space between she needs to preserve. Living *with me*, or any step beyond that – we're kind of stuck.'

'I'm sorry.'

'Yeah, well. I do know not to take it personally. It's her way of coping.'

On the other side of the window, my sister bent to whisper into her rabbit's ear.

I tried to lighten the mood. 'If you will choose such a high-maintenance partner.'

'Hah! Forgive me, Jen, you're one to talk.'

To our left, Owen and Chelle came strolling out of the vintage car building, deep in conversation. He was waving his hands around to emphasise whatever vital point he was making.

I said, 'Then again, you have to look below the surface stuff, don't you? Look at what matters in a person.'

'You do.'

Still several yards away from us, my boyfriend came to a halt, pointing first at the main house then back at the building where the cars lived. His brow was furrowed with disapproval.

'And not let yourself get hung up on the little irritations. I mean, I appreciate Owen can be a bit . . . intense. But his vision and energy, they're extraordinary. He makes me see the world through different eyes. It's like taking off sunglasses and appreciating the colours properly; everything's more vivid. Plus he's taught me that you don't need *things* to make your life happy or meaningful. You don't have to spend your time acquiring possessions. Like, last Christmas he took me to the cathedral precinct and whipped out this tatty old hymn book and we stood and sang carols and collected money for Shelter. And it was bitterly cold but I hardly noticed because people were coming up and smiling and handing over their cash. Loads of it. Notes and stuff. And then this homeless guy joined in, he was drunk but it didn't matter, and some clubbers walking past stopped and did a stint, then a couple of choristers came out of the cathedral and sang with us, and it was magical. The best Christmas memory ever.'

'Better even than when we went out at midnight and put a bra on your next door neighbour's snowman?'

'Better even than that.' Again I touched the cool flower petals resting against my hair. I thought of a music festival the previous summer where he'd plaited me a crown of ivy to wear; potatoes baked in the embers of his garden bonfire; the blood-thrilling beat of drummers during an anti-racism demo. 'Seriously, when it's working, it's great. And it is coming right again. I am making progress. I get to see more of him these days, and just, I feel like his girlfriend, properly. All I need to do is oust the limpet and we'll be there.'

Chelle was still shoeless, and I could see the cobblestones were causing her problems.

'Good for you, Jen. Although I'd say the sooner she shifts herself, the better. You weren't exaggerating: she is truly annoying. Awesomely.'

Another minute and they were level with us.

'How were the cars?' asked Ned.

'Pretty nice,' Owen replied. 'They've got an E type in there, 1971. And a Jensen Interceptor and a Lotus Elan convertible.'

'What colour's the Lotus?'

'British racing green.'

'Nice. Any Triumphs?'

'I think a TR4 and a TR6.'

'I like open-top cars.'

'Yeah.'

'If I had the money I'd have a blue TR6. Or maybe a maroon Stag.'

'Stags are smart. Classic lines.'

'A maroon Stag with beige leather seats and a walnut dash. That's what I fancy—'

'It's still about the iconography of privilege.' Chelle sliced across the conversation.

A light in Owen's eyes died. 'Oh, yeah.'

'Because status symbols on that scale have no moral justification in today's society. It doesn't matter how shiny their bumpers are or what top speed they can do. It's still basically money tied up in selfish, showy objects. Money that could be out in the system, doing people some good.'

'You're right.' He nodded soberly. 'I mean, transport should just be about getting from A to B. There's no need for a car to cost two hundred grand, is there?'

'I'd best cancel that Lamborghini, then,' said Ned.

Chelle bent to brush grit off the sole of her foot. I noticed how she put her palm against Owen's bicep to steady herself. 'Anyway, I reckon we should go over to the gift shop now.'

'The gift shop?' I said to her. 'I don't think you'll like it there.

There might be model icons-of-privilege on sale. Tea towels with symbols of oppression printed on them.'

'I want to ask,' she said, 'how many of their products are FairTrade. And get them to stock more.'

Ned and I exchanged glances.

'Looks like that's where we're headed, then. I'll go drag your sister away from her new friends,' he said. 'In the meantime, ladies, you might want to hide your stolen roses.'

When we got home that evening it seemed my mother was engaged in a major clear-out. The front of the bureau had been opened and emptied, as had all three drawers. Mum herself was stretched out on the sofa with her feet up and her hand over her eyes.

'I've decided I'm sick of hanging onto clutter,' she announced as Hel and I stood in the doorway, taking in the scene. 'I'm sick of it taking up space in my house. Rubbish. I don't need it. It has to go.'

The bureau's contents she'd grouped into piles, on the dining table, on the chairs, at various points across the carpet. There was an open bin bag against the wall.

My sister just shrugged, but I was instantly on high alert.

'Hey, you're not throwing out my fox ears!' From the pile at my feet I snatched up a plastic hair band with two brown felt triangles glued to the top. This had been part of my costume during Year 2 Nativity, that famous Bible scene where Jesus gets a visit from a posse of woodland creatures. Klara Peplinksi's squirrel tail had become detached halfway through and, in a moment of inspiration, she'd laid it over the baby's neck for a scarf.

Mum uncovered her eyes. 'Anything you want keeping, put on the chair by the window. If you haven't saved the things you want by the time the bin men come tomorrow, they're going.'

'And that's certainly not rubbish,' I said, picking out a tatty programme from my school leavers' ball. 'It's a souvenir, it's part of my personal timeline.'

'You look worn out,' said Helen to Mum. 'Shall I make you a cup of tea?'

'Thanks, love, yes. I've had such a day at work.'

'And this is my college rag mag. I helped edit this,' I said, pushing through the piles. 'God, we had a laugh doing it. And look, here's a Red Nose that Ned bought me. And my koala purse I had in the juniors. Oh, yay, and my Gareth Gates fan club pack. There are stickers and, aw, see, there's a little badge with his face on. Bless him. You're not getting rid of this lot, no way.'

My mother made no reply so I carried on rooting, moving between the different heaps. There was a huge bag of loose batteries, one of emergency candles, some shoe cleaning equipment. Here was my old calculator with my name and form scratched on the back panel. Inside a hockey sock, along with my gum shield, were stuffed a load of pom pom animals I'd made in Year 6 Craft Club. Lindsay Pagett and I had sold some of them door to door to raise money for new playground equipment.

And what was that exercise book, half hidden under an ancient TV warranty? A St Thom's planner! Yes, I'd recognise that orange cover anywhere. I pulled it out, expecting to see my name on the front, only to find it was one of Helen's. That was a surprise as she normally kept her academic stuff in her wardrobe, boxed and catalogued.

I ought to have put it aside or handed it straight to her, but I couldn't resist a quick flick through while she was out of the room. It felt like a chance to glimpse a side of her I barely knew.

She'd been a fan of multiple pen colours, and columns, and double underlining. Bullet points and highlighting she liked as well. Every page was covered with general Year 10 classwork, her neat, slanted handwriting setting out timetables and homework instructions methodically. Since this was a book which never got handed in for marking, she'd also allowed herself some doodling down the margins: figure-of-eight patterns, hot air balloons, turrets and castles with birds flying over them. Sometimes she drew glossy red lips, smiling. On one page was a list of term test results: 87%, 79%, 91%, 84%, and next to each figure she'd drawn a little flower. It was nice to peek into this world of Helen-past, to compare her notes with my own untidy Year 10 scrawl. What a clever girl she'd been. How the teachers must have loved her. Then I flipped the page and blinked in shock. After all the pristine entries, suddenly I was looking at a burst of violent scribbles, the maths equations beneath almost obscured with thick and angry red marker. I could tell at once it hadn't been done by her. Hel's corrections were always precise and measured.

With a sinking heart, I carried on through the planner. There was more red marker, some scrawled obscenities, a smear which might have been mud. Several of the later pages had been torn right out. Witnessing the damage with my own eyes made me feel terrible, as if it somehow made me complicit in the bullying that had gone on. Poor Hel. Day after day, walking into that bear-pit, wondering what was waiting for her.

As I went to put the book down, it flopped open at the back

page. And here was a work of wonder. Margin to margin was a mass of manic biro, scored so deep and intense into the paper there was hardly any white left to show through. *JOE* my sister had written at the centre, in 3D capitals with cross-hatched sides. His name she'd surrounded by clusters of stars and beaming suns, and further out she'd drawn rockets, ringed planets, moons and comets. Two stick figures floated against the black background, holding hands; one of them had long hair. The whole design was bordered by a pattern of tiny, interlinked hearts. Hours, the design must have taken her. There was so much love coming off this page, so much hope. The level of need was painful.

'Here you are,' she said, coming in from the kitchen and putting a steaming mug down next to Mum.

As if it was on fire, I dropped the book in a bin bag, out of sight. Perhaps my parents had hung onto it as evidence against the school. That seemed most likely. I couldn't imagine Hel wanting to preserve such a humiliating memento. But whatever the reason it had been stashed away in our bureau, it was time to get rid. The idea of her spotting it now made my insides turn over.

'Let's see what we've got, then,' she said, wandering over to the table. With her slim fingers she sorted through crocheted mats, nail varnish remover pads, hair bobbles, jam jar labels. She paused for a moment at a booklet on guinea pig care, then slid it away. There was a *Radio Times* cover showcasing something called *Vets in Practice*, a tatty certificate announcing Helen Crossley had won second prize in a junior science competition, a bundle of greetings cards from various home tutors wishing her good luck with exams, and an uncashed book token from her old teacher Mr Wolski. Then there were her Children & Adolescent Mental Health Services notes.

'Oh, those,' said Hel when she spotted the folder.

'What is it?' asked Mum, raising her head.

'Nothing. Only my medical file.'

'I meant to put that away.'

Helen picked it up but didn't open the flap. 'Shall we just whizz it?'

'No!' This time my mother sat up properly. 'We need to keep those letters and charts.'

'Why?'

I thought it was mean of Hel to ask that. We both knew what was going through Mum's head: *In case you get really ill again and need to go back to the Mental Health Services and we can hand the records over without any delay. Because getting into the system can be such a battle and if it ever happens again I want us to be prepared. I want to tackle the situation as early as possible, before it gets too strong for you to deal with.*

But there was the difficulty. To keep hold of Hel's anorexia history was almost like inviting that possibility, signalling to her daughter that we expected the full-blown disease to return. I remembered the one occasion Mum'd opened up to me very slightly about it, during the course of a long night when I was kept awake by raging toothache. I'd been home from uni, and she'd sat up with me and tried to distract me by chatting. She'd said, 'If I could take the pain off you and have it myself, I would, you know. There's nothing worse as a mother than seeing your child suffer.' I'd been impressed because she seemed to mean it. Then she went on, 'Except when they're making themselves ill, there's *truly* nothing worse than that. When Helen starved herself it was the cruellest thing she could have done. I thought my heart was going to break.'

Now Hel was holding the notes over the bin bag provocatively. 'Well, I say sling it.'

Mum was dithering, her hands coming to her mouth and away again. 'Yes, OK, if that's what you want, obviously. Only, we could just – perhaps we should—'

Helen replaced the folder on the table. 'All right, don't stress. It makes no difference either way. The health centre has copies. So I don't see the point of hanging on to it.'

'Well, if you feel that way—'

'I do. Shall I?'

After a moment Mum nodded and the folder went into the bin bag.

Meanwhile I'd recovered enough to unearth a plastic carrier of Dad's belongings: cassette tapes, a video he'd shot to promote his company, some headed notepaper, company pens and a baseball cap I'd bought him with the legend *Keep on Truckin'* embroidered on the front. The joke being that Dad would never have worn a baseball cap, even if it had been raining fire from the heavens. There was also a bunch of newspaper and trade magazine clippings about the development of his haulage firm over the years, and a letter dated 2002 saying he'd been nominated for a Midlands regeneration business award. It was some achievement, considering he'd built the company up from nothing. He'd worked hard. He'd done well.

'You can stick that lot in with the rubbish,' said Mum, nodding at the carrier I was holding.

'Hang on. I take it you're going to check with Dad first that he doesn't want it any more?'

She just lay back with her head against the cushion. I placed the bundle under the table, out of sight.

'Right, well,' I said, 'if this is what we're doing, I think my best option is to grab a bin bag of my own and use it to take some of my things upstairs. Where they're safe. Have we any spare?'

'In the drawer by the sink.' She began to struggle up once again.

'No,' said Hel. 'Jen'll get it. You stay there.'

I trailed through to the kitchen, noting the brilliant sheen on the chrome and the glossy work surfaces. The sink gleamed like a TV advert. Even the bowl of apples on the windowsill had a polished look about them.

There were in fact no spare black bags in the drawer, only the torn wrapper off a roll plus some flimsy little pedal bin liners. They wouldn't do at all for what I had in mind. My plan was to harvest at least half those batteries, for a start, so I could keep my own private cache. I'd also spotted a universal battery charger and an unopened box of biros.

'There's none left,' I called to Mum.

'Yes there are. Try the pan cupboard.'

I did as I was told, but the only stores I found in there were fresh dishcloths and scouring pads. Then I had a thought: Dad kept a load of green garden refuse sacks in the garage. I could pinch one of those (and get considerably more in it).

I grabbed the keys, then slipped through the back door and down the side of the house. The outside light was on and I could make out a bat flittering around our roofline, a little black scrap against a navy sky. It made me smile to watch. Another night I would point that out to Hel.

Fumbling, I turned the key in the lock, stepped inside and

reached for the light switch. But a split second before, I was aware that the room wasn't completely dark, that a glow was coming from the far corner near the metal shelving. A soft glow, and smoke.

Under my fingertips the light snapped on.

'Hello?' came my dad's voice, slightly wary.

'Dad?'

'Oh. Jen.' He sounded relieved.

'Dad! What's that smoke? Are you on fire?'

'Not so's I've noticed. Come round, see for yourself.'

I quickly skirted the bonnet of his Juke and squeezed myself between the metal shelves and the lawnmower. From there I could see against the rear wall a sort of niche made from cardboard boxes, and my dad sitting in the middle of it on a leather footstool, coat on and holding a cigar. A portable radio was positioned at his elbow. The music coming out of the speakers was jaunty, hippy-style.

'What *are* you doing?' I asked.

'What does it look like?' He swept his arm around. 'Enjoying a smoke, listening to Mungo Jerry. Reading my Wilbur Smith till it got too dark to see.' A fat paperback lay face down at his feet.

'But out here?'

'It's not cold. Anyway, I've got my sheepskin.' He tugged at his coat collar. 'I would say sit yourself down but there isn't room.'

I took a step forward, bewildered.

'Does Mum know you're in here?'

'She might do.'

Mum indoors, reclining on the sofa, surrounded by her labours. I was baffled. 'Did you have a row or something?'

'No. But she was busy, I was in the way. It seemed easiest to come in here. I sometimes do. You know, when things are—'

'You're saying she drove you out of the house?'

'No, no, it wasn't like that. I fancied a smoke. Some time on my own.'

'But this is ridiculous!'

Dad took a drag on his cigar, blew out in a long stream. 'What was it you wanted in here, love?'

For a moment I struggled to remember. 'Um. Garden sacks.'

'Behind you. Above the tool box.'

I turned and there they were, nestled between a tin of assorted nails and a bottle of engine oil. As I drew out the roll, I said, 'You do know she's throwing your stuff away. Your tapes and clippings that you collected.'

'Ah, well, let her. None of it matters any more. Not really.'

'What? How can you say that?'

He looked me straight in the eye. 'Because it doesn't. It doesn't, love. Don't go back in and make a fuss. Leave it. For my sake.'

The footstool strained under his weight. I thought how old he seemed, how defeated and apologetic. I wanted to go up to him and shake his shoulders, say, *Get in there and claim your place by the hearth. It's your house. It's your right.*

'Honestly, Jen, don't worry about it. I'm fine here for the minute, with my cigar and Mungo J. Just chilling out for ten minutes. We all need a space of our own now and again. Think of it as my gentleman's club.'

So he came out here other evenings too. Sometimes when I thought he was working late, he was shut up in here with his books and his tobacco. I laughed awkwardly. 'Very exclusive.'

'Oh yes. Membership of one.'

'Can I bring you anything?'

'I'm grand, thanks.'

Grand. Huh. Whatever else he was, it wasn't that. There was the reek of diesel in my nostrils. The floor felt gritty under my soles. My dad, semi-detached from his own family.

I stood for another few seconds and then, not knowing what else to say, I left him to it.

Late that night Hel came to my room with hot chocolate again. This time she'd also added a plate of thickly buttered crumpets, which she knows I love. Although she denies herself continually, she does get a kick out of treating others. A mass of contradictions, my sister.

'Thanks for coming along today,' she said as she settled herself on the end of the bed.

'No problem. Why *did* you ask me, though?'

She shrugged. 'I think we should start hanging out more. It's always been tricky with the age gap, and then you were away at college. I'm not sure I've ever got to know you properly. As an adult, I mean. More than just my sister . . . You enjoyed yourself, though?'

'I did. Some of the art and the architecture we saw today was stunning. Uplifting, actually. Although you were probably too busy fiddling with your rabbits to notice.'

'Yeah, the rabbits. Weren't they something?'

'They were. I won't say what. By the way, I'm sorry about Chelle tagging along. She just invited herself.'

'I got that. Urgh. What an annoying little tick she is. That business with the pampas grass!'

Helen had been sitting on the wall by the gift shop talking to Owen about women's body image in music videos. The next moment, Chelle had run at them with a length of pampas grass she'd pulled up and started whacking them over the shoulders with it. 'Toy toys,' she was yelling. We thought she'd gone mad, but apparently the toy toy (toe toe) is some kind of New Zealand plant that kids use for play-fighting. It was pretty embarrassing to watch. Owen took the thrashing in good spirit but Helen was livid because it meant her hair got covered in clingy feathery seeds which wouldn't be brushed away.

'Did you get it out?'

'Only with conditioner and an old nit comb. Stupid cow. Oh, and those endless bloody stories: "I blocked an Auckland jeweller's doorway with horse manure because they were selling coral." Who does she think she is? St Joan? God knows how you've kept your patience with her all these weeks.'

'Well, I haven't much choice. Owen thinks the sun shines out of her. She's a model activist and virtue personified as far as he's concerned. And he'd be *so* disappointed in me if I criticised her outright.'

'I suppose he hates me, then.'

On the journey home Chelle had been waxing lyrical again about the wonders of her home country – how much greener it was than the UK, how much outdoors there was to enjoy, how much better the weather was – when my sister turned round in her seat and asked, 'Why don't you go back there, then?'

Cue a shocked silence. Owen's eyes appalled, Chelle's furious. Ned focussing hard on the road ahead, me silently cheering.

'I will, that's my plan,' she'd said icily. 'But while Owen needs me for his campaigning work I want to stay and help.'

I said, 'By the way, what happened in the end with the V festival and the mates you were supposed to be meeting there?'

She put on a pious face. 'Couldn't afford a ticket. Owen offered but I wouldn't let him. I already told him I'm not taking his money.'

Oh, fuck right off, I'd nearly said.

'Well, you'll have to go home pretty soon if you haven't got a visa,' observed Helen.

'Who says I haven't got a visa?'

'Well, have you?'

'No. But I can soon stick in an application.'

'I can help you with that,' Owen had offered.

At the end of my bed Helen shifted and sighed. 'Look, sis, it's not my place to give advice.'

'But . . .'

'I'd say you need to watch her, that's all.'

'She won't be around forever.'

'Until she goes, then.'

I shook my head emphatically. 'Owen's on the level. He'd never be unfaithful, it would go against his moral code.'

'Wouldn't he?'

'No!'

'OK. You know him, I don't.'

She watched me eat my crumpet, butter dripping down my fingers. Butter's something my sister would never eat, even now she's supposed to be recovered.

I licked the side of my palm clean. 'It's fine for you,' I said. 'You've got the perfect boyfriend. Ned's entire focus is on you. He barely even notices other women. You have *nothing* to worry about in that department.'

'No, I haven't, have I?'

And she shot me a look that was almost frightened. In the next instant, right before my eyes, Hel closed down again. Her mouth became a tight line and her expression detached. She leaned away from me blankly. I remembered that moment earlier in the day, the way she shrank into herself when Ned touched her.

'Helen?'

'Have you finished?'

'What?'

'Your crumpet. Give me your plate, Jen. Don't just leave it on the side there for Mum to deal with. I'll wash it up.'

'Hel, listen—'

'And your mug.'

'OK, but, you know, if you want to talk any time. About Ned or anything. If there's ever a problem, you can always come and chat. You're right, we should hang out more often—'

She stood up, a piece of crockery in each hand.

'Helen, wait a minute.'

'Shh.' She tipped her head to one side, as if she was listening out for some far-off sound.

'What?'

'Nothing. I'll see you tomorrow,' she said.

CHAPTER 5

<u>*Stop with the Stalking! How to Break your Addiction to your Ex.*</u>

We're well used to the TV thrillers that portray stalkers as creepy, controlling men who hang around in bushes and leave sinister answerphone messages. But nowadays an increasing number of women find themselves drawn into spying on a previous boyfriend, checking out his Facebook status compulsively, bombarding him with texts or tweets or calls. Both a blessing and a curse, social networking has provided ways that we never dreamed of to track someone's movements, and some of us are finding that hard to handle. Because now the temptation is always there, just a click away.

So what happens if you find you can't control your impulses any longer? What if the person doing the stalking is YOU?

I read over my copy guiltily, images of Joe Pascoe rising up between me and my monitor. I'd been about to call it a day there, I really had. I'd given Hel the information she needed.

She'd asked no more. The case should have been closed. But then I'd found myself on the outskirts of Chrishall again one afternoon, having interviewed a campaign group about speed bumps, and I thought, since I'm here anyway, I'll just nip down the high street and have a peep at his house.

Obviously I'd tracked down his address long before; had a look on Street View and Zoopla so that I knew his Victorian-fronted farmhouse was worth £750K and that there were two four-star restaurants nearby and the local crime rate was seventeen per cent lower than the national average. But as I was practically driving past I thought I'd like to see it in the flesh, just as a way of signing off the project.

I parked up by the corner shop, treated myself to a Cornetto, and then I strolled back along the road casually, like a tourist enjoying the autumn sunshine. The house itself, with its mellow aged brick frontage and graceful bay, faced a village green bordered on the opposite side by a row of candy-coloured mews cottages. This was the view onto which Joe and his wife looked out daily. Along the side of the house was a drive paved with herringbone brick on which sat a sports-styled Audi in silver. A high yew hedge screened the drive from next door, and the front garden bloomed with blue hydrangeas and some tall pink plants whose name I didn't know. Honeysuckle wound its way around the front porch. And I thought, You do not deserve all this, man-who-broke-my-sister's-heart.

Time ticked by. The sun was warm on my skin and I found myself slipping into a fantasy about how things might have been for Hel if we'd been closer in age and I'd been there at school when she got into difficulties. Would I have been able to help? Would I have stood up to the bullies, to Joe? There'd been a girl in my year – Lindsay Flood – who none of us had much liked because even at fifteen she seemed middle-aged and boring, and on non-uniform days she wore horrible mumsy dresses and her haircut was rubbish. Once or twice I'd asked her to join us on the lunchtime bakery run, but she'd said no and after that I never bothered again. Now I wished I'd tried harder. How had it made her feel, watching us shrieking in the cloak-room and larking about? The teenage years are harsh, but you don't see it till later.

I was still standing on the opposite side of the road, spindling my ice cream wrapper, when without warning the side door opened and a woman stepped out. I could see at once this wasn't Mrs Pascoe. Some friend of theirs visiting, it must be. This woman was dark-haired and curvier, and I'd have said five or ten years older. She wore a Sophia Loren-style belted mac and sunglasses, very glamorous and assured. Very much their style of acquaintance. For a second or two I was thinking, *I wonder what I'll look like when I'm thirty-five or forty? It might not be so bad being old if you can keep up the grooming.* And then I spotted Joe.

He was standing just inside the threshold and my first thought was, *Why on earth are his legs bare?* Because his hairy, finely-moulded shins were on view underneath his dressing gown. *Dressing gown?* Next thing, he was bending forward to give her a kiss, and it wasn't a friendly peck on the cheek like these Cheshire types give after a dinner party, mwah-mwah. This was a proper full-on snog. His jaws were working and her neck was stretched to reach him. After a while he tried to draw her inside but she broke free, glancing around. I stayed where I was but turned my head as if I was engaged in studying the view across the green.

Next thing, I could hear her footsteps coming down the path towards me, and a small cyclone of panic started up in my chest. Oh my God. What if she clocked I'd been gawping and strode over and challenged me? What would I do? Whatever would I say? I wouldn't give my name. I'd pretend I was someone else. Give a false name. Christ, if she found out I was a journo, and got onto Rosa with an accusation of spying . . . But then again, all I'd been doing was standing on a public highway. A cat can look at a queen. She didn't know about my Joe-dossier, she couldn't prove any dodgy motive—

When at last I risked a glance up, she'd gone right past me and was on her way towards the corner of the street. I watched as she took some keys out of her pocket and pointed them at a black BMW, which winked as it unlocked. In she climbed, briskly rearranging the sun visor, her headscarf, something on the passenger seat. Less than a minute later she'd driven away. Back at the house the side door was now shut, the windows empty of movement.

So there we had it. Whilst Ellie was safely occupied at the bank, Joe the home-worker was free to get up to whatever he fancied. He could see this woman every weekday, if he wanted. Or different lovers, in rotation. It was the perfect set-up for an adulterer.

The experience had left me rattled. My first impulse had been to take the story straight to my sister and give her a blow by blow account of the incident, spell it out to her that Joe Pascoe was *still* a love rat all these years later and that, however hurt she'd been at fifteen, she'd had a lucky escape. After the news had sunk in we could pin a photo of him to a dartboard, kick some cushions around, make sympathetic noises about his poor wife.

By the time I got home that evening, however, I'd decided to hang on and keep the information to myself. I wasn't sure why. I suppose I was worried by what Ned had told me, because Hel did seem fragile at the moment and I didn't want to risk destabilising her. Only last night she'd claimed to have a sore throat and had left her lamb chop and her mashed potatoes, which Mum had made specially, a separate, butter-free portion. Then later that night I'd heard Mum and Dad arguing. I'd caught Hel on the landing and I'd said, 'Have you really got a sore throat?' And she'd said, 'Look, it's going round the kennels. Am I not allowed to catch germs like anyone else?'

Behind my swivel chair I could hear Rosa's tinkling laugh as she flirted on the phone to some businessman or other. I tried again to focus on my stalking article. What the hell right had I to be dispensing advice here when I was still checking Joe's Facebook page every day? But however hypocritical I was feeling, the piece would have to be written within the next hour because right now I was in so much trouble with Rosa it was like a black cloud hovering permanently above my head. Not just Rosa either: with the whole of the office.

What had happened was that The Diary had gone missing – The Diary being our most precious piece of hardware, over and above even the ranks of PCs or the phones. Without that simple A4 book, no one knows who's doing what or when, and interviewees are left stranded and photographers wander adrift and the whole of the structure of the day falls apart. We'd turned the place upside down, and I'd been as peed off as anyone because I urgently needed a scribbled mobile phone number so I could confirm the details of a Halloween event coming to Northgate Arena. Then Alan had walked past my desk and accidentally knocked my bag to the floor, and what should slide out but The Diary, sandwiched between some loose papers and a brochure for Carden Park leisure hotel. The upshot was, no one was speaking to me. I'd racked my brains over how it might have got there, because I honestly had no recollection of having handled it that day. It did cross my mind that Rosa herself might have planted it; it felt like the sort of warped thing she'd do.

I cast a sneaky look at Gerry, but he had his head down, working. He'd been late for an appointment with an MP so he'd every right to be as annoyed with me as anyone else.

'Jennifer! I hope you're making progress?' barked Rosa from across the room.

'Uh-huh.'

'Because I want that piece by midday. Forty minutes, you've got.'

'Mm.'

She could probably see how little I'd done. I wondered whether it was possible to spontaneously combust with anger. The writing gears in my brain had seized up the moment she'd spoken. I would never get this article finished. I would flunk the deadline and Rosa would tear me up and this time I might lose control and hit her and end up in a police cell as well as jobless. Not that this even counted as a job, seeing as I didn't get paid. So much flak for nothing.

A movement at Gerry's desk. I looked over and, his gaze still fixed on his screen, he was tilting a piece of paper carefully, so that I could see it but Rosa couldn't. I squinted to make out the detail. It was a printout of a bird with a brown back and a spotty chest. 'THRUSH' said the caption underneath. Then he gave me a lightning-quick wink.

'GOD save us from incompetence,' I heard Rosa mutter, followed a moment later by the clunk-shut of her office door.

One bright spot in the day was that I'd be spending my lunch hour at Owen's. Chelle was still hanging around, but I was a lot less troubled by her than I had been. Over the past few weeks I'd scored several small victories: I'd got her to contribute to the household bills by making her do a midweek shop for milk, bread and other basics we'd run out of; I'd removed my toiletries from the bathroom and stored them in Owen's wardrobe, which meant she had to go out and buy her own instead of filching mine; I'd even dared challenge her over one of her protest-memoirs, because I'd read the very same story on an internet forum and I knew it had actually happened to some Canadians in the 1990s. In front of Owen she'd denied all knowledge of this other group, which was stupid as what she should have said was, Yes, I know, we copied them. Instead she claimed it was the sort of stunt that could have occurred to anyone, great minds think alike, etc. But I'd said, 'What? *Two* sets of illegal trawlers boarded by activists dressed as mermaids? Really?' And she'd shut right up.

I'd also taken to asking her lots of questions about New Zealand, in the hope that might prompt a bout of homesickness. What was her house like? Was it large or small? Rural or urban? Did she miss her parents? Her mates? The culture? What were the shops like? How did their education system work? Did she have any friends who were Maoris? Was the climate very hot? Very rainy? What did they do for Christmas? Was there more or less traffic on the roads than in the UK? What was their biggest-selling newspaper? Could you buy a Mars Bar over there? Where was the best holiday resort? Had she ever seen an echidna? A volcano? A real live kiwi? On and on I went with my stream of bland, annoying enquiries, knowing I was driving her up the pole and that there was nothing she could do about it.

And Owen-wise, I was making real progress. I now sometimes stayed over twice a week, and I was planning meals and doing some of the cooking. I was using his washing machine. I'd brought along a hairdryer, shoe cleaning kit, a dressing gown and some better towels. The one thing I hadn't had much time for was the website development I'd promised him the month before, but there were so many other to-dos on my list and Chelle was putting a few hours in here and there and, unlike the newspaper, it wasn't as if we were working to a deadline. In any case, Owen himself seemed to have gone off the boil with the project after chatting online to a man who was raising money to send bicycles to African midwives. Now he was all fired up with that campaign, and badgering the customers at the bookshop café with sponsor forms and petitions.

So, the stalking article put to bed, it was with a fairly buoyant heart I trotted down the hill in the direction of my boyfriend's flat. I'd picked up a bit of gossip about a dodgy councillor which I knew he'd be pleased with, and then I thought I might rustle us up some French toast, because I'd made some last week and he'd said how much he'd enjoyed it. Heck, I might even go mad and make a slice for Chelle.

I did my special doorbell ring, then let myself into the hall with the key he'd finally given me. Music floated down the stairs, some jaunty Antipodean band that I was sick of hearing, but I wasn't going to let that bother me. This building was my refuge from office-hell and I was going to be nothing but smiles and lightness and sizzling, vanilla-scented bread.

When I reached the landing I saw the door of the flat was ajar. I pushed it open, and at the exact same second the music stopped. Owen was sitting in the middle of the sofa with his head in his hands, the flat around him strewn with papers and magazines and odd pieces of household equipment. I paused on the threshold, trying to work out what was going on. Briefly I wondered if he'd been burgled, because there was something disconnected about the layout of the scene, the placing of the furniture odd – as if there were gaps, maybe, though I couldn't at first identify what had been removed. The table seemed bigger and the room lighter. There were dust-shapes marking some of the surfaces. An electrical socket extension cord trailed untidily from behind the chair.

'Everything all right?' I said. 'What's happening? Owen?'

He made me wait a few beats, then he raised his eyes to mine. 'Well, Jen, you got your way.'

'Got my way with what?'

A clatter from the direction of the bathroom made me jump.

'Owen?' called Chelle, her voice echoing slightly. 'Is it OK with you if I take this half-tube of toothpaste?'

A moment later she walked in carrying her rucksack by its straps and plonked it on the floor in front of her. 'Oh,' she said when she saw me.

Now I understood that the table looked bigger because the balled-up sleeping bag underneath it had disappeared. The extension lead trailed out because Chelle's phone charger was no longer in situ. The sofa was lighter because her fern-pattern throw was gone.

'I've left you those leaflets about recycled bike parts,' she went on. 'And the addresses you wanted. If you need to contact me, use my Hotmail account, yeah? I can still work remotely on the website. Just let me know what needs doing.'

There was an awkward silence. No one looked at anyone else.

'Anyway, that's me packed. Looks like I'd better be off.'

'Please don't,' said Owen, getting to his feet.

'Ah, I've got places I need to be. My work here is done.'

'But you've weeks before your visa expires. You don't have to move on yet.'

'I think I do.' Chelle jerked her head in my direction.

This whole situation felt horrible, almost as if I'd been caught out in some act of vandalism or poison-letter-writing. *What? WHAT?* I felt like shouting. *So she's off? Well. Why the long faces? She's had a bloody good run. She never was a permanent fixture. Isn't it time for her to move on, spread her enlightenment elsewhere?*

She came and stood right in front of him, hands on hips. 'So thanks for having me, Owen. I think we've made real strides together. You're an awesome person, you know. It's been a total blast. And Jen,' she half turned and gave me a sarcastic salute, 'well done you. Mission accomplished.'

Too stunned to react, I watched as she and my boyfriend came together in an embrace, then held onto each other as if they might never let go. *Get off him!* I wanted to cry out. *He's mine! Have you no shame? Just go!* Owen's eyes were closed; I couldn't see her face because she had her back to me.

They swayed, broke apart.

'That's me done,' said Chelle, bending to pick up her rucksack.

Owen was shaking his head.

She said, 'Keep in touch, yeah?' But she was addressing him, not me.

In three or four strides she'd crossed the room and was gone. We heard the door bang shut behind her.

'Oh, Jen,' he said bleakly.

My heart was thundering in my chest, my mouth dry with fury and dread. She'd made me out to be a villain, had she? The jealous girlfriend who'd driven her out? God knows what tales she'd spun. I knew I had to keep calm and not overreact or I'd risk playing into her hands. But how to redeem this moment? How to hold my nerve?

'Well, that was a surprise,' I ventured.

Owen sank down onto the sofa again. He looked sick.

I said, 'I shouldn't worry, she'll most likely reappear in ten minutes.'

No response.

'I mean, it's a shame she couldn't have stayed. I know you'll miss her. She's been useful with her ideas and that. But at least you've got your floor back. You can pull the chair forward now and we can use the table properly again. You can spread your papers out. See what you're doing. So that'll be better. And anyway, she's still here in a virtual sense. You can always email and Skype her, can't you? Take your laptop to the pub and it'll be as if she's sitting round the table with us. These days no one's truly absent. They're only ever on the end of an internet connection. She's not gone at all if you think about it in those terms.'

Still he said nothing. There was a massive weight of words in him, though, ready to burst like a dam. I felt it. I knew I had to ask.

'What was it made her decide to leave today?'

At last he met my gaze. 'For God's sake. Stop it. Stop

pretending, will you? Chelle and I talked through the night. She'd just had enough of you making her feel not-wanted.'

'What? What's she been saying? I bet she's been making stuff up. She's always doing that!'

'I said, stop it, Jen.'

'But she has. I've caught her out on all sorts.'

'You've made it your mission to undermine her, I do know that. You and your friends.'

'No! No, I was just trying to—'

'Enough. I don't want to hear it. You've let me down. Honestly, I'm not even sure I know you any more.'

He slumped against the cushions, staring at me, and to my horror I saw his eyes were full of tears.

After I'd left Owen's flat I wandered up to The Cross, unsure what to do with myself. I knew I was in no state to return to the office, so I sat on the monument steps and texted Gerry that I'd been taken ill and needed to go home. A transparent lie, but it was the only excuse I could come up with on the spur of the moment. Then I let my head tip against the stone column and lost myself in the flat and clouded sky, my mind boiling with words said and unsaid. How had I come to mess up so badly? After all the careful gains I'd made, how had it come crashing down around me? Why had I not defended myself better? Made him see the Chelle that I could see? Why had I answered him back and put myself so squarely in the wrong?

She was my guest, he'd said. *You had no right to decide when she went.*

A woman with an afro walked past The Cross, and that made me think of Keisha and then of Vikki. I imagined taking

myself round to the bookshop now, and their surprise and
concern as I told them what had happened. They'd be kind.
They'd feed me one of their dense and lumpy cakes. But I knew
even as I played with the idea that it wasn't a serious option
because, no matter what they thought of Chelle, they were
Owen's mates first and foremost.

The air began to spot with rain. I felt it on my cheeks and lips
first, as cold, spiteful prickings. Fine, I thought. Let it pour. Let
it drown me where I sit. I'm not shifting. However, as the drops
grew larger and gathered momentum, it eventually occurred to
me that if someone from the newspaper happened to walk past
I'd be in even worse trouble than I already was.

I stood up, scanned the precinct, then made a dash for the
nearest side street. Thunder rumbled in the distance and shop
awnings flapped in the stiffening breeze. People were beginning
to walk with their heads lowered and their collars up. I gathered
speed, found myself following a series of old and narrow lanes in
the general direction of the city car park. It seemed my feet were
taking me home, even if I didn't especially want to be there.
Where else was there to go?

*I'm not telling you what she said, no. It doesn't matter anyway. I
know you were trying to push her out, I heard some of it with my
own ears.*

On and on Owen's voice echoed round my head. The windscreen wipers swished crossly against the rain as I drove down
the A41, wondering who'd be in when I got there. Helen was
working odd hours at the kennels and I wasn't on top of her
timetable. It was Mum's half day so she might be about, but
then again she could have nipped out to see Ned's mum or to

check on old Mrs Harris across the road, or to the shops. Dad had said this morning that he wouldn't be home till late (cue more cupboard door slamming from my mother). So I didn't know what I'd find when I opened the front door. Part of me craved company and comfort, but part of me needed to be miserable alone.

You've let me down, Jen.

Far off, the sky over the southern horizon seemed brighter, as if I might at some point drive out of the rain. For now, though, I was right in the middle of the squall. Branches overhead waved in the wind and yellow leaves spattered against the car. On my right I saw a sign for Hampton Primary School and the attached GCSE unit where Hel had gone for a while after she'd dropped out of St Thom's. I'd only visited the place once, an afternoon when I was recovering from chicken pox and Mum couldn't get a babysitter for me. We'd driven out to pick up my sister and I'd hung around in the main hallway while Mum had words with the unit tutor next door. I remembered cut-out daffodils and decorated eggs, so it must have been around Easter. Birds with fat triangle beaks, a pink-faced Jesus popping up from behind a boulder. I remember thinking, with the superiority of a top junior, how some of the written work on display was rubbish: 'My dad youses a hamma', with a scratchy stick figure of a weapon-wielding maniac drawn underneath.

I switched my headlights on against the gloom. Sticks and small branches were flying out into the road, and lane-wide puddles forming in the dips. I was constantly braking to drive through sheets of treacherous water. Along the edge of the field, telegraph wires swung between their poles, and I turned up my wipers a notch to try and clear the screen. Here came The

Dragon Inn, previously Rajah's Curry House, previously The Gables, where we sometimes used to go for sixth-form birthdays. In that car park Nutter Cook had wrenched the wiper blades off a Micra, thinking it belonged to Hannah Brierly, only to discover the car was actually owned by some random blameless punter. By that half-barrel planter I'd kissed lanky John Lucas, and Nia Hughes had pranced along the adjoining wall singing that her milkshake brought all the boys to the yard.

As I drove into the outskirts of town the rain was starting to slacken off. At the first roundabout onto the bypass was a signpost for the industrial estate, and that made me think of the times when I was a kid and Dad had taken me to his office and bought me a bacon sandwich from the van parked on the corner, or we'd nipped down to the Midway Café for a Trucker's Brunch. On a couple of occasions he'd let me climb inside a lorry cab and investigate the drop-down bed and the mini TV and fridge, everything you could want for a perfect life. That had blown my mind at eight. I'd questioned why anyone bothered with houses. Just buy yourself a kitted-out HGV and trundle off round the country. I remembered the office building itself, but the way it had been in the early Noughties, just a spartan prefab affair with stacks of papers everywhere and boring charts on the boards. The drivers would stand outside the door and smoke and swear and I'd have to pretend not to hear. Sometimes Dad would go out and say, 'Keep it down, lads, we've got a visitor.' Then they'd give me the trucker salute, which was a pretend blast on an air horn. I recalled two secretaries, one blonde and smiley who kept sweets in her drawer, and another, more matronly woman with a Welsh accent. I liked them both; they made a fuss of me. Looking back I suppose Dad took me to the haulage yard to give Mum a break, but it had felt like a special treat, something just for me and not for Helen. I didn't recall him ever taking Helen there. And hadn't there once been a Christmas tree up, and I'd been given a plastic sparkly tiara which he let me wear on the way home?

Even though it was years since I'd last visited, I had an impulse to go there this minute, call in on the pretext of admiring the new buildings and just to say hello. Not to tell him anything personal. To see a friendly face, that was all. But then again, if I did appear at his office on spec, how would it be? I could picture his flustered surprise, his concern in case I was there to deliver bad news. He'd be wrong-footed, maybe impatient that I'd come during a busy period, maybe even embarrassed, and I wouldn't know what excuse to give for dropping by. I was too big now to stand in the swivel chair, jerking it from side to side, scrounging Fruit Pastilles and making chains out of paper clips. What had happened to that sparkly tiara in the end? Why didn't we take better care of the things we prized?

Mum was home when I let myself in. I could see she'd just returned from shopping because there was a receipt on the table and the fruit bowl was full again.

I stood in the doorway for a minute and watched as she went round tidying stuff away – Dad's glasses thrown in a drawer, his headphones unplugged and tucked down the side of the book case, his magazines and slippers pushed out of sight under the chair. Eliminating him from the scene, basically. One day he'd wake up from a nap to find himself shut in the cupboard.

'What are you doing back at this time?' she said, glancing up.

I shrugged.

'What does that mean, Jen?'

'Feel sick,' I said, because it was easiest.

'You do look a bit pale. What's brought that on?'

'Dunno.'

She stopped what she was doing and narrowed her eyes at me. 'Have you got a headache?'

'Yeah.'

'Then take some Panadol and go lie down.' She went back to her tidying. 'Probably too much staring at a computer screen. I've told you, you need to watch your posture.'

'Yes, thanks for that.'

I hate it when she tries to turn a problem round so it's somehow your own fault. I wondered what she'd say if I launched into the truth about my day. Would she even have time to listen?

'Oh, and Jen, while I've got you on your own—'

'What?'

'Helen.'

'What now?'

My mother paused in her activities again. 'She told me this morning before she left for work that she wants to go to zumba with you.'

'She's not said anything to me.'

'Well, she does.'

'Oh. OK.'

'And?'

'And what?'

'Are you going to *let* her?'

The question took me by surprise, so much so that even in my deep-dark misery I almost laughed. 'I can't say no, can I?'

Mum's mouth went tight. Her face became a cartoon-face with a thought bubble over her head: *Yes, and if this is the beginning of an intense exercise regime that starts to make her poorly? If she moves from one hour's zumba a week to three and then seven and then ten, fourteen? If we find she's doing it on her own in her room at night? Dancing till she's exhausted, and then she can't function in the day and gets confused and confrontational and the disease manages to get a grip again? You've no idea. I've been there. I remember. We had to take that treadmill away in the end.*

I said, 'Look, a session of dance might do her good, have you thought of that? Get her out of the house, meet some new people. Release some endorphins. Improve her bone density.'

'Make her all conscious of her body again,' finished Mum.

'And what do you expect me to do? Stop going to classes myself? If Hel's made her mind up, you know what she's like. If she doesn't come with me, she'll just find a class of her own.'

'You always go against me.'

'No, I don't.'

'I'll be checking with the doctor.'

'You do that.'

For a moment we stood facing each other, crackles of frustration sparking across the distance between us. Then Mum seemed to sag, defeated. Her hand came up and gripped the edge of the sofa.

'I worry.'

Yeah, you worry about her, I longed to say. Not about me. Try asking what sort of day I've had. Ask me where my life's going. Go on. I'm your daughter too. But no. You think the whole world revolves around the twisting rope that is your relationship with Hel.

'It doesn't do you any good, you know. All your fretting only winds her up.'

'I know.' Her head drooped.

I said, 'Look, if she does decide to come to zumba with me, I promise I'll keep a close eye on her. I'll make sure she paces herself and drinks enough. And I'll let the teacher know her background. OK? Can't say fairer than that.'

My mother's brow remained pinched with anxiety. She obviously wasn't going to be talked round.

'Oh, you know what? I haven't time for this,' I said. Suddenly I was on the verge of tears. I needed to escape.

'Are you really not well?' I heard Mum say as I turned and ran for the stairs.

The whole drive home I'd longed for the sanctuary of my room, but now I was here it seemed like the crappest place on earth. I threw myself on the bed and stuck my earphones in, hoping to blot out the last two hours but unable to stop events replaying on their horrible loop. I don't know how long I lay there, tormenting my own brain. At first I kept my phone next to me on the pillow, just in case Owen texted me. Then, after a while, I switched the mobile off and threw it onto the floor with the rest of my rubbish. Because what message could he ever send that would undo the words he'd said?

'But Owen,' I'd pleaded. 'I don't understand. Why are you so upset? I mean, I know you enjoyed having her around to give opinions and stuff, but to be *this* distraught. It's beyond reasonable. Not if she's just a mate. What else is going on?'

'You don't get it, do you?'

'No, I don't. Unless . . . no.'

He'd run his fingers through his hair distractedly.

'Last night Chelle and I sat up and talked till late. We talked about the future, about what she wanted. I told her to apply for a visa so she could stay here, 'cause she'd fitted in so well. I said she could look at getting a job nearby, finding a place of her own, putting down a few roots. I'd have helped her with it all. And do you know what she said? She said she wouldn't because it would make you angry and she didn't have the energy to fight you any longer.'

'That's ridiculous. It's a front. She was always going to take off sooner or later, she was only ever visiting. We all knew that—'

'Plus she told me about how uncomfortable you've been making her feel.'

'Aw, come on.'

Owen's jaw went tight, as if he was biting back words.

I said, 'You mean because a few times I ribbed her slightly about the stories she told? I'm not being blamed for that. Some of those things she claimed, I just didn't believe them. Did you? I mean, insisting she came up with the idea for Captain Pollinator when we know it was that Swedish cartoonist.'

'She knows him. They email.'

'She *says* she does. Has she ever shown you any of the actual messages?'

'See, this is what she found difficult, Jen. You were so hostile. So negative with her. You told her to go home, for fuck's sake.'

'That was my sister, not me! I never said anything like that. OK, I maybe took the piss a little, when she was showing off. It wasn't nasty, though. Only like joking between mates. Like we do with Saleem when he waxes lyrical about his days in Kashmir. He takes it, he laughs.'

'This was different, and you know it. There was an edge to how you were with Chelle. You hurt her feelings. She tried to be your friend.'

I'd meant to play it cool, I really had, but my alarm was spiralling.

'Hang on. I'm not being painted as the baddie here. I've been patience on a bloody monument, I have. How many other girl-friends would have put up with an alien woman parking herself in their boyfriend's flat and refusing to shift for months? Tagging along everywhere we went. Helping herself to anything left lying around. It was a ludicrous situation, only you couldn't see it. You do realise she was completely taking advantage? She was scrounging off you.'

'I share what I have, you know that. She never asked me for anything.'

'Not much. Only a brand new rucksack, for starters.'

'Not that again.' He sounded utterly dismissive.

'Yes, that. I never pressed you for how much it cost, but I know they don't come cheap. Not being funny, but when was the last time you treated me?'

'I give you presents all the time.'

And I blushed, because that was true.

'I'll say what I said before, Jen. Chelle was a stranger in a foreign land. She depended on the kindness of those around her. I saw she needed a new rucksack – she didn't ask, I offered – so I got her one. A good brand, as it happens, because cheap is false economy and I didn't want her stuck with another split one six months down the line.'

'And what if *I*'d needed a new rucksack? What then?'

'But you didn't. You don't need anything.'

'Don't I? Don't I really? A bit of respect and understanding would be a start! To be treated like your actual girlfriend instead of some minority interest. To *matter*.'

His eyes widened, as if he was seeing me properly.

Looking back I think that was the moment I knew I'd lost him.

I sat up on my bed, nauseous at the memory . All around me was my own childish clutter. I wanted to sweep it away and burn it. The scuffed Crocs, the balled-up tights, the jam jar of dusty felt flowers I made when I was about ten, the wind-up comedy false teeth Ned had given me last Christmas, the fairy lights, the bin stuffed with fashion mags, the bubble mix, my Lobster of Loveliness mug, the multipack of sherbet dib-dabs, the beagle-ears hat, the tumble of badly managed make up: it was the stage set of a failed life. Open on the carpet was a magazine I'd saved because I thought Owen might like the tribal-print bean bag I'd spotted on the centre pages. I bent and picked up the mag, then tore it apart down the spine, flinging both halves at the door where they struck my dressing gown and landed with a soft, unsatisfying thump.

I was so angry I hardly knew what to do. I wanted to seize my bottle of Argan oil and smash it against the stupid wallpaper, draw slashes of red lipstick across the stupid mirror. I'd rip down the stupid curtains and take scissors to the stupid rug. I'd hire a sodding skip and junk the lot and then climb in on top and wait for the disposal men to come and cart me off too.

As I scanned about for something I could reasonably damage, my eye lighted on the corner of a shoebox poking out from under my bed, a stupid shoebox decorated with stupid ladybird stick-ers. I wrenched it free and kicked it across the room so hard it collided with the leg of the dressing table and ricocheted towards me. Then I got down on my knees and clawed off the lid. This was the box I'd started when Owen and I first got together, a collection of mementoes charting our time together. There were flyers from student events, a photocopy of the letter about Starbucks he'd had published in the *Guardian*, a drawing he'd done me to illustrate the Vicious Circle of Consumerism. It was in here I'd stored his birthday origami and the card he'd drawn himself. Towards the bottom of the box was a slim pile of photos I'd printed out, from the early days, the top one showing me and Owen sitting on the stairs at some uni house party with our arms round each other. I lifted it up for closer examination, even though the act of doing so was like plunging a knife under my own ribs. That was the night he'd told me about his mum having left while he was still a kid, and how his dad gave him loads of cash yet was always too busy, and about some of the ways the world needed changing. There'd been crazy dancing going on around us and some sort of fight happening in the back garden, but we felt cocooned and separate and above the clamour. 'I never imagined I could feel so close to anyone,' he'd said. 'I've never felt like this before. Is it love?' And he'd stroked my hair in a wondering, reverent way.

I remembered another night when we'd gone to float tea lights down the Manchester Ship Canal in support of Amnesty, and afterwards he'd taken me back to his room and just held me for ages. And the day he drove me to Chew Reservoir and we lay on the grass and he told me I made him complete.

I stood up and dropped the print on the bed. Then I tipped everything on top of it. As well as papers, other rubbish cascaded out: pin badges, bottle caps, a plastic pen-topper shaped like a victory fist. Every one of them had had a special significance when I'd been part of a couple. Now it was just junk. Even the heart pebble he'd given me the day Chelle arrived.

I scooped up the first few flyers and began to tear them up systematically, letting the pieces fall into the shoebox. The sheets ripped in half, quarters, eighths, sixteenths, and then into tiny unreadable fragments. And throughout, my head rang with voices as if I was listening to a radio play I couldn't turn off.

'It's obvious you like Chelle better than me.'

'That's the language of the playground.'

'I think you're in love with her.'

Owen let out a deep and weary sigh. 'Jen.'

'My God, you *are*.' In that moment I was convinced I could see it all. 'Yes! That's what this is about, isn't it? Isn't it? Bloody hell. How stupid have I been? You've fallen for her – while I stood back and gave you the space to do it. Christ knows, she's been trying hard enough. Everybody was warning me but I said no, Owen wouldn't behave like that. Owen's moral code wouldn't allow it. He's got principles. God, I'm such a fool.'

'No.'

'Oh, I think so.'

I was giddy with indignation and fury. I'd had to reach out and touch the wall to steady myself.

'Well, you're wrong,' said Owen emphatically. 'I do like her. A lot. Not that way. But listen to me – no, don't start – because the thing about Chelle is, she *knew* me. You've never understood me, never been on my wavelength. You've never truly sympathised with my concerns. Chelle did.'

'Wait a minute,' I spluttered. 'I've "never sympathised with your concerns"? Bloody hell, it's *all* revolved around what you want. I've spent *hours* doing the things that matter to you.'

'Precisely. That matter to me, not to you. It's been a chore as far as you're concerned. A sacrifice. And then you've always made it plain you expect to be paid back somehow, toothbrush rights and that possessive stuff, then you've sulked when I wouldn't deliver. Even though you knew that wasn't the way I tick. That's not the kind of girlfriend I want, Jen. Territorial, jealous. I need someone who understands what truly matters. The bigger picture, the injustice of the world.'

'*We* matter!'

Another sad shake of the head.

I said, 'Stop making me out to be a selfish person. I donate to charity. I help if someone's in trouble. I give money to that guy who sits by The Cross.'

'It has to be wider than that. If right's going to triumph, you have to give it all your energy. You have to want to move mountains, not little stones.' There was this evangelical light in his eyes and I remember wondering whether he'd gone slightly mad. Perhaps Chelle had leached his sanity too.

'Owen, I'm going to ask you something and I don't want you to lie.'

He looked at me full on and my heart contracted with fear. 'You'd better be sure you can cope with the answer, then.'

'Did you have sex with her? Just say it, get it over with.'

'No, Jen,' he'd said straightaway. 'I would never cheat on you. And I don't know how you can even ask me that.'

'So what's happening here? Spell it out for me.'

He'd buried his face in his hands, a pose of anguish.

'I don't want to say it. I don't want to hurt you.'

'You *are* in love with her.'

'No!'

'What, then?'

'All right. This is it: having Chelle here hasn't made me fall in love with her. It's made me fall out of love with you.'

There'd been a moment of complete stillness, a hurricane's eye, before the reality of what he'd said sank in.

Now I'd reduced every sheet of paper in the ladybird box down to tiny scraps that couldn't be ripped any smaller. I carried it over to my bedroom window. The damp autumn air had swelled the wood so at first the catch wouldn't budge. I put the box down and began thumping hard at the frame till eventually it shifted. A final furious push and the glass swung open, wrenching the hinges. I bent to lift the box, settled it on the ledge, then angled it so that flakes were shunted out into the air. At first they came away in small, hesitant drifts, individual scraps spinning on the breeze and flittering towards next door's front lawn. But as I nudged more violently, whole clumps slithered over the cardboard lip to shower down thickly and vertically like a very localised snowstorm. I can't explain why it gave me a weird satisfaction to litter my own garden like that. I only know it did.

I carried on tapping and shaking, leaning right over the sill so I could see the shreds of my relationship scatter. There it went, those months I'd believed I was happy, reduced to remnants, destroyed. Pulped.

And it was at that point, through the swirling confetti of despair, that I saw Ned standing on the drive below, his anxious face upturned towards me.

Two minutes later there was a knock at my bedroom door. It opened a crack and Ned peered round. 'Can I come in? Your mother's – hmm – quite interested to know what's going on.'

'Yeah, I bet she is.'

He stepped forward, onto the remains of the broken magazine. I saw he was wearing the tartan shirt Hel had bought him last Christmas, and his thick boots and jeans. His fringe was ruffled from where he'd jammed it under his cap while he worked. 'So. Ah. You OK, Jen?'

'No.'

'What's the story?'

I sat down on the bed and started to cry in earnest. At once he came forward and plonked himself next to me. 'Jen? Jen. Oh no. Shit. What can I do? Have you got a tissue?'

He began patting his pockets and bringing out all kinds of useless articles: a conker, a small spanner, a wrapped barley sugar, a fifty pence piece. Meanwhile I let myself weep, not the kind of elegant crystal tears my sister sheds, the ones that slide silently over her porcelain skin, but soggy trails that made my cheeks go blotchy and my nose run. My mouth was twisted down and I was making whimpering noises like a dog. I knew my make up would have smeared, but I just couldn't stop.

After a minute or so I managed to gather my wits enough to bring my hands up and shield my messy face from Ned. He responded by lifting my hair out of the way and tucking it behind my ear.

'Don't,' I said.

'I've found you a hanky. It's almost clean.'

I reached out and took it blindly.

'Can you tell me what's upset you, Jen? Is it Tweed-knickers again?'

'No.'

'Chelle? Owen?'

I let out a moan.

'*Shit*,' I heard Ned say under his breath. 'What's he done now?'

'Finished with me.'

And off I went again, into a fit of fresh sobs.

'What? Oh, Jen.' He twisted round and gathered me into his arms. I pushed my face against his shirt and lost myself there while he rocked and shushed and patted me and murmured that it would be OK. No it won't, I thought. It'll never be OK again. I let him say it though, because what was the alternative? *That's it, love. You've blown it. Your life's knackered.* Ned smelt of wood shavings and disinfectant and Swarfega, and his body was warm against mine. I wanted never to move from this position.

After a bit I heard him go, 'Would it help if I told you he was a tool?'

'He's *not*.'

'He must be to have upset you like this.'

'Well, he's not.'

'Is this anything to do with the Limpet?'

I loosened my grip and moved away from him. 'Sort of.'

'I knew it.'

'Not the way you're thinking.'

'How, then?'

Through the open window came a whining drone that I guessed was probably the mini hoover at work: Mum clearing up my paper storm before the neighbours complained. Even from here I thought I could detect a martyred tone to the motor. God knows what she'd have to say when Ned left and I was forced to go downstairs for tea. I'd have no defence. It was a stupid gesture from the outset. I could just have thrown the stuff in the bin and been rid.

'It was like this,' I said. Then in a small voice I told him what had happened.

I tried hard not to begin crying again, and I more or less succeeded. Ned sat and listened without interruption. Occasionally he sucked in his breath, or frowned, but mostly his expression stayed the same: concerned, disturbed, sorry. When I was finished, I asked him what he thought.

'I refer to my previous judgement.'

I flushed miserably. 'Don't say that. I know you and Hel've never much rated him, but he's my first serious boyfriend. I know it wasn't perfect – what is? – but it was getting better. It would have worked out eventually. I loved him. I thought he loved me. I was kind of *banking* on him.'

'What you said needed saying, though. He needed to be told. You know he did.'

'And look where it's got me.'

'You're too good for him, Jen, that's the critical issue. Sorry, I know you think he's some kind of saint, and probably I should keep my mouth shut—'

'No, you've got it back-to-front. *He's* the good one. It's because he's so good that he couldn't see through Chelle.'

'But he didn't deserve you. He never let you be yourself.'

'He was trying to get me to be a *better version* of myself. The thing is, he's so generous—'

'Bollocks. Sorry, I've had enough of this. It's all right him giving away a pair of expensive trainers to a tramp in the street when he knows his dad's just going to buy him some more the next day. The reason he's so generous, the reason he never bothers about money, is because he always has it. Not like the rest of us, having to count every penny.'

'But he genuinely isn't interested in material possessions. It's not a pose. And he does make sacrifices. He'd love a car but he won't have one, on principle. He just wants to help the world.'

Ned shrugged. 'Why doesn't he work for a proper licensed charity, then, instead of faffing about inventing daft campaigns?'

'Because, because . . . he doesn't want to be restricted by corporate hierarchy. He wants the freedom to put his creative energy into lots of different areas.'

'Doesn't want to be restricted by having to get up in the morning like the rest of us.'

'You barely know him!'

'OK.' Ned held up his hands, palms out. 'You're right. If he wants to live like that, I suppose it's his choice. Whatever else is going on here, though, I'm not having you beating yourself up about any "moral inferiority". That's crap. Just because he makes himself out to be the saviour of society doesn't mean you have to believe the hype.'

'I can't hate him. Not yet.'

'No.'

'He said I lacked zeal.'

'Well, he knows where he can stick his zeal, doesn't he? Come here.' I let him draw me into a close hug again. 'The bottom line is, Jen, the way he's been treating you is just wrong. He's had you running about after him like a servant. As far as I can see, he's never appreciated you. And yet look at you. You're great. You're pretty and funny and smart. You're kind, you're sane. You've got a decent set of pins on you. Most guys would fall over their bar stools to get a date with you.'

'They wouldn't.'

'Trust me, they would. Don't do yourself down.'

I let myself rest against him once more. Thoughts spun in my mind's eye like the barrel of a fruit machine: Chelle's sneer, Owen's brimming eyes, the slam of Rosa's door, everyone in the office looking as The Diary fell out of my bag. Useless, I was, on every front.

'And weren't they queuing up to date you at uni?' Ned went on. 'I remember Hel said you had three boyfriends in your very first term?'

'They were dorks.'

'Ouch. Cruelty, thy name is Woman. OK, look, I know it feels shit at the moment, but that won't last forever. It won't. You're going to have a pretty dark few weeks, and then things'll begin to lift and you can get out there and enjoy yourself again. Doing what you want to do, and no one to drag you along to Save the Woodlouse demonstrations or Smash the Rich leaflet drops. No more sitting in draughty village halls being lectured on your failings. That's got to be a silver lining, yeah? Instead you can get on with ordinary fun stuff like, I dunno, going to the cinema and shopping and watching live comedy. I've been meaning to check out the Civic's Laughter Nights for ages and never got round to it. How about we start a monthly comedy club, the three of us, and take it in turns to pick a show. I really fancy that. What do you say?'

I didn't answer at first because I was thinking how bloody lucky Helen was to have a boyfriend like him, and whether she fully appreciated him. Thinking about whether the ghost of Joe Pascoe had been truly erased. Joe and his smug philandering; Owen and his platonic crush on Chelle. It came down to the same hurt in the end.

'What do you say, Jen?'

I realised Ned was staring at me, waiting for some kind of

response. 'Mm. Perhaps, when I'm feeling more in the mood. Right at this minute I don't feel as if I'd have a lot of tolerance for comedy.'

'No, obviously. When you're ready.'

'Yeah.'

'Deal.' He lifted my chin with his fingers. 'This business with Owen – I won't be so crass as to say it's for the best, but in the end you'll be grand, you know. You will.'

His other arm was still round my shoulders, and he felt so nice I heard myself blurt out, 'God, I wish you had a brother.'

'Hah! When I was born my mum took one look at my ugly face and went, "That's it, no more."'

You were never ugly, I thought.

And through the window came the sound of an engine idling, cutting out, a car door slamming, a stamp of boots on the step, the rattle of the porch being opened. My sister was home, to claim her property.

She came to me after dark, bearing a Walnut Whip.

'What's that in aid of?' I asked, sitting up in bed.

'I thought it might help.'

I shook my head. 'Can't face eating. Even if Mum is going to go mental with me.' On the bedside table sat my plate of sausage and mash. I hadn't been able to manage a bite earlier so she'd made me take it up to bed.

'She won't go mental with you. She's sorry. She wishes she'd known what was the matter.'

'Well, I'm not going to risk it. Has Ned gone?'

'Yup. And Mum's watching people on TV murder each other and Dad's lost inside his earphones. It's a riot.'

'What time is it?'

'Half eight.'

'Feels way later than that.'

Helen perched on the end of the duvet. 'Seriously, can I do anything?'

'No. Yes, finish what's on that plate for me.'

I'd meant it as a joke, but to my astonishment she got up and went over to my abandoned meal. She frowned, picked up a fork and speared one of the sausages. Then she held it to her lips. For one crazy moment I thought she was actually going to take a chunk out of it, but after a cheeky mime she instead walked over to the window, unhooked the sausage and flung it out far into the night.

'Don't! For God's sake, Hel! I'm in enough trouble for littering as it is. If Mum steps through the front door tomorrow and squashes a sausage, I'm dead.'

She looked at me as if I were simple. 'Oh, sweetheart. Haven't you heard of my good friends Mr Fox and Mrs Cat? Nature's little hoovers, as I like to call them. Hugely useful. Happy to dispose of any amount of evidence as long as it's edible. In fact, let's give them a double treat tonight. Chuck us the other sausage and they can have that as well.'

I did as I was told, imagining what my mother would say if she could see us. Me still blotched and washed-out in my fuzzy dressing gown, Helen at the window like Rapunzel, her white shirt loose around her cuffs and her cheeks slightly flushed. My beautiful, complicated, grown-up sister, one day sneaking into my infant bedroom to tell me Santa was on his way because she'd heard hooves on the roof, another day thoughtlessly filling the front pocket of my school bag with her unwanted porridge.

'Ned's been telling me about his comedy night idea,' she went on. 'I think it's great. I'm up for it. And you know, we could have some girly time together, you and me. Now you'll be around more. Like, didn't you always want to try out gel nails? And you never would because Owen hates that sort of thing. Well, sod him, you don't have to bother any more. You can do what you want. We could go to a salon together and I could have a facial or something. Go mad and get a fake tan, false eyelashes, the works. What do you reckon?' She made a pouting face.

'Maybe.'

'I just thought it could be fun. And I'll take you shopping if you like. Treat you. We could hop on a train to Manchester and have a trawl round there. We've never really done that kind of stuff, have we?'

'No.'

She was trying so hard.

I said, 'I know you think Owen was a dick, and that I'm better off without him, and that I'll get over it. But whether that's true or not, right at this minute I miss him. It hurts. It bloody hurts.'

She turned to face me, her huge eyes full of tenderness.

'You don't need to justify yourself to me, sis. I know exactly what it's like when someone breaks your heart.'

CHAPTER 6

<u>*Join the Litter-Picking Gang!*</u>

Anyone keen to make Leewood Green a nicer place to hang out can meet this Saturday and take part in a family litter-picking day. Members of the public are invited to come along and complete an hour's tidy-up of the footpath, wood and river banks, followed by a warming cuppa in the village hall.

'It's an opportunity for local people to get involved with improving their community and to meet with friends and neighbours at the same time,' says 17-year-old Daisy Williamson, who came up with the idea of the litter-pick. 'We'll have live music and tea and cake, and we're confident everyone will have a fun morning. Just come along and get stuck in!'

Daisy came up with the idea when she was walking her dog Scoffie along the public footpath and noticed the messy state of the grass and hedges. 'Now the hedgerows are bare you can really see what a mess they are. I just thought, instead of moaning about it, why not get busy?'

Plastic refuse sacks, easy-grip litter-pickers and gloves will be available on the day. Meet at 10 a.m. on the Rovers car park.

What else was there to do but throw myself into work? Already this morning, as well as blasting through my first article, I'd cleared the office sink, washed everyone's dirty mugs and wiped the drainer. I'd tidied the mini fridge and chucked away a black banana, a half glass of something horrid and cloudy and some curled-up cheese slices. I'd disinfected the salad tray, taking care not to contaminate Rosa's carrot batons, and then scrubbed all the tannin off the teaspoons. I'd watered the plants and sorted the post. I'd been through the competitions cupboard and binned an unclaimed basket of dried flowers and a box of out-of-date local restaurant vouchers. I'd bought, out of my own pocket, a large wall planner as a back-up in case the damn Diary ever went missing again, and I'd jotted down some notes for a new feature on the website.

'What the bloody hell's up with you?' said Gerry as I plonked an unasked-for Crunchie on his desk.

'I'll have it for myself unless you're properly grateful.'

'Oh no you won't. Hey, how about making us a coffee, since you're up?'

'Made you one. It's by your elbow.'

He gave me a considered look. 'Seriously, what is the matter?'

'Nothing. I'm trying to be more professional.'

'Hmm. Right-ho.'

I watched him unwrap the Crunchie and snap the end off. Flakes of honeycomb exploded across his keyboard, and I knew that if Rosa had caught me doing that I'd have had such a telling off.

'Also, I've got this idea,' I said. Gerry carried on chewing. 'What it was, you know how we do the Bonniest Baby comp in the summer, and it boosts circulation because families buy extra copies to get hold of the voting coupons? And Rosa was saying she wished we could run it all year round?' Gerry nodded and took another bite. 'Plus, you know how popular TV talent shows are right now?'

'Uh-huh.'

'Well, I was wondering if we could combine the two. If we could organise a website-based comp where people could send in clips of their kids demonstrating some sort of skill – doesn't have to be showbiz, singing or dancing. It could be football control, or gymnastics. Anything that can be filmed.'

'Times tables? Scrabble?'

'If they wanted to send it in. No one would vote for it, though, so it would just filter out. The good stuff, the entertaining and interesting clips, would rise to the top naturally.'

'Unless there was some corruption involved. Pushy parents block voting.'

'Which would also be good. Circulation-wise, at least.'

Gerry scrunched up the chocolate wrapper and leaned back in his chair. 'Pff. I'll be honest, Jen, it sounds bloody hideous. Badly filmed brats performing their party pieces. "Look at me, aren't I clever?" Hell-on-a-stick, I'd call it.'

'Child-hater.'

'Yep, that's me. The fewer kids I have to come into contact with, the happier I am.'

'I expect the feeling's mutual. But you wouldn't have to go anywhere near this comp. I'd organise and judge it.'

'God, you are ambitious all of a sudden, aren't you?'

Rosa's office door opened and she paused on the threshold for a moment, studying the screen of her mobile.

'I'm just trying to climb out of the hole I seem to have dug for myself lately,' I said.

He grinned. 'You'd better go for it, then. Off you trot, share your creative genius.'

'Do you think she'll like it?'

'There's only one way to find out.'

Rosa had been undergoing a transformation of her own these last few weeks. She'd lost weight, had her hair restyled, and she'd taken to wearing bright silk scarves. She'd also invested in a new and vivid lipstick, which left stains on cups and imprints on the cheeks of visitors. I thought this was a mistake; her face was alarming enough without any of its features highlighted. But Rosa herself seemed chuffed with her new look. There was a spring in her step, a sheen to her cheek. 'Word is, she's bagged herself a man,' Alan at the sports desk had confirmed one lunchtime when our boss was out schmoozing some director or other. 'She met him on that dating website. I don't know any details, only that he drives a Merc and lives in Alderley Edge.' Which sounded about right. We'd all stood round the water cooler, wondering whatever kind of guy could be moved to look on Rosa and go misty-eyed. I said, 'Personally I don't care who she dates as long as it keeps her pleasant.' She'd definitely been less snippy, a fraction more forgiving.

I glanced at Gerry for reassurance but he had his head down, working. I took a deep breath, then stood up and went across to her.

'Rosa? Are you busy?'

She let out an incredulous huff. *How can you even ask? I run this office. Of course I'm busy. And so should you be, worm.*

I stood my ground. 'I've come up with an idea you might like. One that might really boost *The Messenger*'s circulation.'

Typically she made me wait another few seconds while she jabbed at her phone; just making the point that I was well down her list of priorities. Most likely she was only surfing the John Lewis website after some even scarier lip colour. 'Well, go on,' she snapped.

So I quickly outlined a format for my talent show, stressing the likelihood of parents multibuying voting coupons, plus the publicity that the comp would generate in its own right. I explained how we could get schools to spread the word as well as the usual social media, and stressed the fact that I'd do most of the admin myself. I said we could maybe market the idea to the whole *Messenger* syndicate, and in years to come, when momentum had built up, even hold cross-region contests. The more I spoke, the more feasible it sounded, until by the end I was feeling quite confident. All the while Rosa listened, lips tight and unreadable.

Finally she said, 'Judges.'

I said, 'It'll be chosen by the readers. That's nice and democratic.'

'No.' She shook her head firmly. 'Readers can vote for a shortlist. The finalists will need to be chosen by a celebrity.'

'Who?'

'We'll have to see who's available.'

My heart was speeding up. Was Rosa actually approving an idea of mine? Acknowledging for once that I'd done good? Put the flags out.

'When should we run it, do you think?' I asked cautiously.

She frowned. 'Not this year. January, perhaps. Some pre- and post-Christmas plugging, a January the First launch, and then the finals over the Feb half term, when the kids should be available to come and perform. Yes, that ought to work. I'll check on venues – the manager of Marshall's owes me a favour – and see whether Gyles is free . . .'

I wondered if Gerry was listening and what he'd say to me afterwards. High-five. Go Jen. This felt like my first proper step up the ladder, my first real stake in the newspaper. My own comp ready to go syndicate-wide.

'. . . Oh, and while you're here, Jennifer, I've been meaning to say, do you think you could do something with your hair?'

'Sorry?'

'I was just pointing out that your fringe needs a cut. And your jacket, there's fluff or something on the shoulders. You're out this afternoon, aren't you?'

'Yes.' I was down to interview a pair of posh dieticians, a local husband and wife team who'd cadged a slot on morning TV.

'Student life is one thing, but now you're an employee you represent this office when you go out to meet the public. You are, for that period of contact, the face of *The Messenger*. And for that reason I'd like to see you making a little more effort with your grooming. If it's not too much trouble.'

'Oh.' It was all I could do not to gape at her rudeness. Always, always she had to squash me in public. I couldn't be allowed one uninterrupted moment of triumph.

'So go write me up a schedule for this thing – timings, blurb, promotional channels, prize packages – and have it on my desk by twelve. I'll take it from there.'

Abruptly she pushed past me and went to bother Alan at the sports desk.

I sloped back to my PC and sat gazing at the screen for a moment.

'Those tweed knickers can chafe something terrible,' said Gerry from beyond my field of vision. 'Though I've heard live yoghurt can be very soothing.'

'Thank you but shush,' I told him. 'Some of us have work to do.'

In an effort to give myself a boost I thought I'd spend my lunch hour somewhere different, so I took myself to the Empire Hotel. It's seriously posh in there. The staff wear brocade waistcoats and the coffee comes in tall glasses, while gilt mirrors reflect and double the whole gracious space. There are even potted palms. The fittings are polished brass or wood or leather, and the tables against the walls are partly screened off from each other for extra privacy. The atmosphere's how I imagine a London club to be, calm and unhurried, no piped music. It was also the one place in Chester I knew I could go and be sure of not meeting Owen. He'd never set foot in such an arena of privilege, would have scourged himself for even considering it. Owen, whose face I searched for every day in the city centre crowds.

It was still quite early for lunch and there was barely anyone else in yet. I settled myself at a table in the window, placed my order with the waiter and sat back to read a couple of texts that had come in. One was from Keisha asking how I was, and the other was a video clip from Ned of an angry lemming squeaking at an Alsatian dog. *That supposed to be me?* I texted back. Keisha's message I left so I could have a think about how to reply. I thought it was unlikely we'd stay in touch long term, me and the bookshop girls. That made me sad, sadness on top of sadness. You don't just break up with one person. You lose way more than that.

Before I could get too wobbly, though, my drink arrived in a cup that was literally the size of a half melon. The hot chocolate here's the same price as a sandwich in some other places, but you get at least a pint and it comes with whipped cream and cinnamon and marshmallows so it'll do you as a light meal. I picked up my teaspoon and poked the surface experimentally. The steam rising to meet my nose smelt delicious. *See? You'd never have dared come here if you were still dating him*, went Ned's voice in my head. I scooped off a marshmallow and ate it.

Then I turned my attention to my phone again. First I updated my Facebook page with a snapshot of the cup in front of me: 'Should I drink this or go for a swim in it? ☺' Then, in spite of myself, I found I was somehow on Revolution's page and clicking my way onto the photos they'd posted of the café opening: pictures of the girls in matching bowler hats and Saleem dressed up like a Bollywood star and a packed shop of people enjoying themselves. Within this album I knew there was also a close-up of me and Owen sharing a slice of cake. After the break-up I'd been sensible, unfriended him so I could no longer get onto his profile page and brood over his updates. But now, like a masochist, I scrolled down to see his photo once more.

It was gone. Saleem was still there, standing on one of the tables and striking a pose, and you could make out the back of Owen's head in one of the crowd scenes, together with the sleeve of my coat. But our couple-portrait had been deleted. Emotion flushed through me then: temporary relief, the pain of the break-up revised, gratitude at Vikki or Keisha for taking the picture down. It was Vikki who, a fortnight ago, had collected my belongings from my ex's flat so I could pick them up from the bookshop. It was Keisha who, when I went round there, pushed into my hands a book about surviving relationships and told me to call round any time. I appreciated that she'd said it. It was a kind gesture.

I closed the screen and dropped the phone in my bag. Finally I put my elbow on the table, rested my chin in my palm and just observed the crowds as they milled up and down the precinct.

There are various tribes I like to pick out. A lot of the pedestrians in Chester are day-trippers, there to wander vaguely, dipping in and out of shops and generally soaking up the heritage. They stop without warning to hold aloft guidebooks, to point, to take photographs of interesting Tudor frontages. Then you get the business types, suited and upright and striding with purpose to their Very Important Meetings. They have to dodge and weave a bit to keep the pace up because there are always so many slow people in the way. Occasionally they get it wrong. Once I saw a guy in pinstripe go full length over a tartan shopping trolley.

The ones I find most fascinating are the ultra-smart females who dangle prestige carrier bags over their wrists, fresh out of Brown's or Tessuti. These are the women Rosa likes to imagine are our readership: Cheshire Wives, Cheshire Daughters. Their outfits are always immaculate, lots of neutral tones and patent leather, plenty of telling designer detail. It's impossible to guess the ages of these women because the young ones look old for their years, while the older ones are hanging onto youth like grim death. Probably if you examined their teeth, like horses, you'd be able to tell.

A man in a charity tabard was chatting up a lumpy matron; I

watched her glow, touch her own cheek, reach for her bag and credit card details. A harassed mother trudged past trailing a sobbing boy. None of them glanced into the restaurant at me. None of them was Owen.

I'd been idly following the progress of a teenager on crutches when my consciousness snagged on – what? – on a familiar face. No, not the face. It was the top peeping out of the half-zipped coat that was familiar, purple-striped, a distinctive blue pendant resting on top. I knew that outfit, I'd seen it countless times on Facebook. I recognised the woman loitering in the doorway of Americana. As I stared, she put her mobile to her ear and simultaneously checked her watch as if she was waiting for someone.

Obviously I ought to have stayed where I was. Ellie Pascoe was nothing to do with me. We'd closed the book on that business. But without stopping to analyse my actions, I found myself snatching up the bill, fumbling for my purse, slapping cash on the table. I couldn't have told you what I was doing. Some hot compulsion, no logic behind it; I just felt I needed to see her close up while I had this chance. Perhaps at the back of my mind there was a half-formed fantasy where I'd rush over, take her to one side and tell her straight out what her husband was up to. Set her right. Disabuse her of the idea he was decent and faithful. Tell her in such a skilful, discreet, compassionate way (as we stood in the foyer of a busy city clothes store) that she'd be nothing but grateful for my intervention. Mostly I think I just wanted to see her move about her ordinary life in her bubble of blissful ignorance. Passing me where I stood, unaware that a tap on her shoulder, a whisper in her ear, would bring ruination.

By the time I got outside, she'd disappeared. Had she gone

into the shop or walked on? There was no sign of her in either direction. I scooted across the road, cutting up suits and tourists alike, and half-ran through the entrance of Americana. I made directly for the women's section and looked about. No. Not here. Nothing. And why wasn't she working in the bank today? Was she pulling a sickie? I carried on through, moving from department to department. No joy in shoes or men's either – but wait, was that her in children's? Was it her blonde head showing above the racks of party dresses? She twisted to the light, holding up a hanger, and yes, it was. I flicked my gaze away, pretended to examine a selection of toddler coats. When I checked again she'd wandered on and was browsing T-shirts.

Casually I let myself edge closer, noting with each sneaky glance how different she appeared from when I'd last seen her, that time on the school run. Today she wore no make up and her hair hung limp and unstyled. She kept on touching her wrist to see her watch, and scanning about her as if she was expecting someone. Very keyed up, she seemed. I thought for one mad moment, *What if the person she's expecting is a man? What if she's here to meet a lover?* She *and* Joe sneaking about, doing the dirty. God, that would be ironic. But no. You glammed up for an assignation, didn't you? Ellie was drab and washed-out, a long way from the bright-eyed, dewy-skinned wife smiling from her Facebook page. Perhaps she did know about Joe after all. She certainly looked glum enough. I wondered what her status said right now. *Shattered. Betrayed. Divorce pending.* Or would her last post be yet more photos of gingham bunting, pastel cup cakes, rose petals, suede wedge shoes? She draped a T-shirt over her arm and parted another set of hangers to peer at sizes. As soon as I left her, I'd check her profile.

Up came the wrist watch again. She sighed and replaced the T-shirt, then began to make her way back towards the shop entrance. I stayed where I was. To follow her any further would just be too stalkery. Instead I focussed on her shoulders and sent a huge wave of sympathy in her direction, a great, strong mental hug from one wronged woman to another. *Go, Ellie, and good luck to you, whatever happens with your marriage, because you're going to need it.* I'd have loved, loved to drop Joe in the shit by revealing his infidelity, but I'd never want to inflict hurt on her. Dear God, she had enough to contend with. I watched her slight figure weave her way amongst the stands and mannequins till she was out of sight.

My muscles sagged. I took in a deep breath, and then another. How long before I needed to return to the office? Twenty minutes. I still had time to wind down, clear my head. Perhaps I could restore my spirits with a quick peep at the jeans and jackets here, and then before I left, grab myself a flapjack from the café on the top floor. My energy was running low. I ought to have something solid in my stomach.

I returned to womenswear and flicked half-heartedly through a few items, unhooked them, held them up against myself. It was hard to concentrate at first. I kept remembering Ellie's pale face, her clouded eyes. You could see an unhappiness there, I wasn't imagining it. But whether it was caused by Joe or something else, who knew. Could be work issues, ill parents, the kids in trouble. Perhaps it was something entirely trivial. Her bramble jelly hadn't set or she'd mislaid her Toast catalogue. Perhaps she was simply depressed for no reason. An attack of the ordinary blues like we all get.

A cherry-coloured blazer distracted me temporarily, and I

slipped it off its hanger and tried it on. Mmm. Yes. Wow, that was nice. The effect was really flattering, the nipped-in waist giving me extra shape and the narrow lapels slimming my shoulders. The colour too was gorgeous. Perhaps I could ask for it for Christmas. I took out my mobile to photograph the tag. And that done, while I had my phone in my hand I thought, Why not just bring up the Pascoes' profiles one last time and see what's happening there?

I went first, as I always did, to Joe's, but there was no change and nothing significant. No posts for three weeks in fact, and the last one only a video link to a football compilation.

Ellie's, though, was a different story. Now when I tried to get onto her Facebook page, I couldn't. She'd changed her privacy settings, locked me out. Only her Friends could see her page, and I couldn't help noticing there were a lot fewer of them. The numbers had been slashed to less than a dozen, and most of those family members, going by the surnames. It had been a drastic cull. I didn't like the look of that.

I shut the phone off, suddenly weary of social networks and the murky virtual windows by which we all spied on each other. It was sick, this obsession with the Pascoes, sick as my sister's. I'd had enough of it. I would nip up to the café, buy my flapjack and restore my blood sugar, ready for a hard afternoon's work. I needed to plug myself back into normality.

But I should have known fate wasn't done with me yet.

At the top of the stairs I paused to get my bearings because they'd changed the café round since I was last in. It was soft furnishings where the tables had been, and the eating area had been moved to the opposite side. I began walking towards the sign, still (in spite of myself) pondering Ellie's Facebook page and how I might get past the block, when there she was again, sitting with a grey-haired woman near the food counter. They must have slipped past me while I was preoccupied. Ellie's face was bowed and her companion was leaning forward urgently.

I didn't know what to do. For a while I stood by a shelf of cushions, watching them. The grey-haired woman might be her mum, I supposed, although she didn't look anything like Ellie. She was built on a large scale, broad and florid, with a frizzy mop of curls. Her calves under the table were encased in thick sheepskin boots. She took Ellie's fingers in hers and it was like a slab of meat closing round them.

Whoever she was, she certainly had a lot to say.

The position of their table meant I could legitimately have gone right up to them, stood close by as I ordered my cake. That way I wouldn't have been able to help overhearing their conversation. With a spot of strategic lingering, I could probably have found out who this woman was and what was the topic that absorbed them. Then I saw that Ellie was crying. My own heart was gripped by a spasm of both pity and self-pity, a connection so intense for that moment that I was amazed she didn't sense it and turn to look at me. Grey-hair frowned and soothed and patted about for a hanky. She ended up offering a serviette which Ellie took, but after half a minute screwed into a ball and threw on the table. *What?* Grey-hair seemed to be asking. *What can I do?*

With a decisive action Ellie got to her feet, waving the other woman away. She pushed her chair under the table and set off in my direction, then veered off to the left. I realised she was seeking refuge in the ladies' loo.

I wanted to do some good. That was my excuse. I wanted to

be able to help, if only in some tiny way. As Grey-hair rooted in her handbag, I darted out of my aisle and followed Ellie into the toilets.

The place was empty when I got inside, one cubicle door shut. I thought it was important I was up-front about my presence so that she didn't believe she was alone and do anything embarrassing. I started by running a tap and splashing my hands in the sink. Next I used the dryer, and when that had finished I set off a tap again. *Someone is here*, I vibed at her. *Someone who wishes you well.* I thought at random of my poor sister: how many hours of her teenage life were probably spent hiding away in school loos, mopping her tears. If only she'd had a kind word or two to buoy her up.

With a click the cubicle finally opened. I was facing the mirror, reapplying my lip balm, but I could see Ellie had made an attempt to dab her face dry and repair her equilibrium. She was still very flushed, though. Our eyes met via our reflections. Then she stepped up to the sink and began to wash her hands. *I'm sorry*, I said in my head. *I noticed you were upset. Are you OK? Can I help?*

She caught my gaze again and I gave what I hoped was an encouraging smile. Immediately fresh tears welled and ran down her cheeks and I felt awful. But it was the prompt she'd needed.

'God,' she said, her voice high and girlish. 'What a mess. Bloody men.'

'Yes,' I said. 'Bloody men. They're not worth it, are they?'

Then, before I could add any more, she'd wiped her hands, dried her face with the towel, and left to face the world. Those were the only words we exchanged. They were the only words she needed to say.

*

As I traipsed back to the office I passed a young homeless man sitting in a doorway with his coat spread on the pavement, begging. The world was grim, there was so much badness sloshing about. I paused, opened my purse and handed him a twenty-pound note, my lunch money for the week. His face showed such surprise.

"Kin 'ell. Cheers, beautiful,' he said in a Manchester accent.

'I'm not beautiful. But thanks.'

'You are, you know.'

I shook my head.

He shrugged. I walked on.

Although I was out of the office that afternoon, I needed to pop in and confirm the destination address, pick up my notebook and Dictaphone.

As soon as I stepped through the door I could tell something was amiss. Gerry was hunched right over his keyboard in the manner of a schoolboy who doesn't want anyone copying his test. Over by the water cooler two photographers huddled, looking as if they'd rather be anywhere else. Meanwhile Rosa circled the room with a face on her like a sulky baboon.

I tried to telegraph a query to Gerry with my eyebrows, but he wasn't taking me on.

'It was *there*,' snapped Rosa, pointing at the fridge. 'It was in there, on the top shelf. *Somebody* has taken it.'

'Taken what?' I asked before I could stop myself.

'My lunch!'

'Oh.' The swell of dread subsided. Unless Rosa's lunch had been a rotten banana or some leathery cheese, I was definitely in the clear. Whatever nasties I'd chucked in the waste bin that morning, I knew I definitely hadn't touched her carrot sticks.

I grimaced to demonstrate innocent sympathy, then lifted my jacket off the back of the chair and reached into my bag to double check the appointment details.

'*Someone* must know where it went,' Rosa continued. 'It hasn't just disappeared on its own. It hasn't grown legs and walked off.'

The couple I was scheduled to interview lived out in Tarporley. I seemed to remember reading they had a clinic on the high street. In fact I thought I could picture it, a row of bronze-tipped railings running along the outside.

Alan walked in carrying a multipack of Coke. He too picked up on the atmosphere. 'What's the matter? Something amiss?'

'Yes. My glass of Lemon Accelerator has been removed from the place I left it.'

'Lemon what?'

My boss's lip twitched with irritation. 'It's a special formula, lemon juice and metabolism-boosting supplements. You mix it up and then it has to sit and chill overnight. It's very expensive. They use it at the Chanterelle Spa. I'd put it in the fridge, and now it's gone.'

'Ah, right. Like lemon juice, is it? A cup of lemon juice? And it's disappeared, you say?'

Lemon juice. Oh fuck. Fuck fuck fuck. I speeded up my movements, struggled to get my coat on, failed to insert my arm into the sleeve and gave up. So that glass of horrid cloudy stuff I'd slung down the plughole at 8.50 a.m. had in reality been my boss's wallet-busting diet gunk. I bundled up the coat and let it drop onto the chair. The bag strap had caught, but I tugged and it came free. I overbalanced slightly and knocked into the desk, making the pen pot fall over. Everyone looked in my direction.

Leave it, leave it, I told myself. All I had to do was keep my mouth shut and exit the building. I was past Gerry's desk, I was by the water cooler, I was almost within reach of the door.

'You know, I'm pretty sure Jen mentioned she'd had a clear out of the kitchen area just this morning,' I heard Alan say behind me.

I really needed my dance class that night. I needed to be flinging myself about to Latin music for an hour in the company of non-judgemental women.

I'd half expected Hel to cry off the zumba. I knew she was nervous about going because she kept asking me about it – was the teacher nice, was everyone very fit, was it quite competitive? Though her figure looks graceful, her coordination's poor. It took her five goes to pass her driving test. So she was worried about making the wrong dance moves and everyone seeing. I told her it didn't matter, and that even the instructor sometimes forgot the steps. I said, 'What do you think'll happen if you do go wrong? The zumba police will turn up and cart you off? No one watches anyone else anyway; we're each in our own world of salsa rhythm, jigging about.' But Hel has to get things right and be perfect, and struggles when she falls short of that.

She was also bothered about what to wear. She still doesn't like exposing much flesh if she can get away with it. I said she could arrive in a baggy jumper if she wanted, but it would have to come off at some point unless she wanted to collapse with heat exhaustion, and wouldn't that be embarrassing. In the end she settled for cargo trousers and a vest, with one of Ned's short-sleeved tees on top of that and a long cardi over the lot. Her hair she insisted on wearing loose, even though I said it would get in the way (she did agree to a sweatband round her forehead). As we went out of the front door, Dad called to us to have a good time and Mum threw him a look so sour it ought to have shrivelled him where he sat, except he never takes any notice of her.

But I wasn't going to let her sulking ruin my evening. I love zumba, had always been fed up when Owen made me miss a class. It wasn't only the buzz I got from dancing, it was the whole package I enjoyed – the cheery lights shining from the village hall as my car drew up, the greetings and banter as I walked through the double doors, the funky music playing in the background. My feet would be tapping before we'd even started. And it was such a friendly mix – young teens to pensioners, women from all walks of life. We had farmers and nurses, chemists and teachers, a dog-walker, a pilot, a landscape gardener. One of our student members had been an extra in a zombie film.

'Are you positive no one'll laugh at me?' Hel asked, shivering as I led her through the foyer.

'I promise. They're not like that.'

She managed a tiny smile and we slipped inside.

It was noisy with laughter and chat. Sally, the instructor, was already up on the podium because I'd deliberately timed our entry so we'd go more or less straight into the dancing and Hel wouldn't have chance to stress. I knew introducing her to people and fielding their polite questions would be an ordeal. I made my way to my regular spot at the front, and my sister came and stood bravely beside me.

But before we kicked off, it seemed that this week Sally had an announcement. She adjusted her head mike, then cleared her throat.

'Hello again, and a special hello to our newbie,' she said, with a little wink at Hel, who blushed and lowered her eyes. 'Now, I know you're keen to get going. Champing at the bit, aren't you? That's my girls. But first, I have a special message from Lydia regarding her sponsored cycle trip.'

All heads turned to Lydia, who was standing in her usual place near the corner.

'Yeah, hi folks. What it is, as most of you know, my son and I did this charity bike ride from Land's End to John O' Groats and I just wanted to update you on the final totals and to say thanks again for your sponsorship and support, which was fantastic. In the end we've raised three thousand eight hundred pounds and it's going to Cyclists Fighting Cancer.'

There she paused while we took in the figure and applauded.

'Seventy-five hours in the saddle, wasn't it?' said Sally. 'You were walking funny for ages after.'

Lydia nodded. 'Ten days' solid riding.'

More applause, a few jokey comments. 'Jesus,' Hel said under her breath to me. 'How many miles is that?'

'Dunno. Eight hundred, nine hundred?'

'Wow.'

'She did tell me. I'll show you her charity page when we get home; it'll be on there.'

Sally gave Lydia a final thumbs-up and reached for the dial on her iPod dock. Then the music swelled into a thudding bass line that vibrated right through you. 'OK, just follow me,' I mouthed, and we were off.

For me, the attraction of zumba is that you can completely lose yourself. I've been coming to this class for so long that the sequences are programmed into me. The tunes are catchy and bursting with energy, the lyrics often in a language I don't understand but which sounds yearning and poetic. For three or four minutes at a time I switch off my brain and become simply an extension of the music, an abstract thing wired up to the pitch and beat, so that I'm throwing out my limbs without thinking and springing into the air and gulping in great joyful breaths. When I'm stamping my feet, I'm stamping away the frustrations of the day. When I shake my head, I'm emptying it of cares. Tension drains away until the only thing that's left of me is the dance. I love it. Of course this session was different in that I did have to keep half an eye on Helen, but the warm-up was slow-paced and easy to follow and she seemed to be having no problems. I thought, *if she gets through this class OK, she'll like it. She'll come away exhilarated, the way I do, and it'll do her so much good.* Her colour was up already. She looked excited.

Four songs later and we were both pretty flushed. We paused between tracks for a drink and I said to her, 'At least take your cardi off.'

I'd expected her to say no, but she did as she was told, and in dragging at the sleeve she pulled the oversized T-shirt almost off her arm. For a moment she hesitated, holding the material away from her burning skin. Sweat was beading her brow above the headband and her eyes were feverishly bright. *Don't tell me she's actually going to strip down to her vest?* But then the next song started and she let the T-shirt fall and hurried back to her place.

She kept up well on the whole. Slim as a wand my sister may be, but she's not especially fit. I could tell she was struggling towards the end of the hour. The rest of us know how to pace ourselves and if we're getting puffed we take it down a notch, cutting out the odd leap or kick or arm-pump. Helen was having none of that; she was going to do it right or not at all. When we got to 'Danza Kuduro' there are these multiple twirls which I could see were making her giddy. I said, 'Go sit down for a minute. No one'll mind.' She just shook her head and carried on.

It wasn't till the stretches at the end that she let herself flop.

'You OK?' I asked as she leaned against the wall, breathing hard.

'Uh huh.'

'How're you doing?' asked Sally, hopping down from the podium while we had a minute's break. 'Have you been drinking enough?'

'Uh huh.'

'And you've enjoyed it?'

'Yeah, I have, actually.'

'Good. Are you ready for your cool-down exercises?'

Helen frowned at me. I could tell she thought she'd had enough.

I said, 'We have to do those or we'll ache all over tomorrow. Won't we, Sal?'

'We certainly will. Listen to your sister.' She gave Helen another wink and returned to the dais.

The quiet music came on. Gradually the women put down their water bottles and face towels and wandered onto the floor again, ready to stretch. Next to me, Helen at last tore off her T-shirt and threw it against the skirting board.

I'd said to her before class that no one would be watching her, and I thought I'd been telling the truth. But I'd forgotten what a compelling figure my sister is. Now she was stripped down to her vest, her narrow waist, flat stomach and porcelain-smooth arms were on full view. That striking curtain of orange hair draped like wavy silk down her back. She just draws the eye, she can't help it. She always has done.

'So we begin,' said Sally, 'with feet hip-distance apart. Then take a brave step forward, and *lean* into the lunge. And hold. Check your bent knee, it should be over your ankle. Feel the calf muscles speaking to you. What are they saying? Are they saying hello yet? OK, arms out at the sides, and bring them slowly round in front of you as if you were embracing a giant beach ball . . . That's right. Mesh the fingers and try to pull them apart. Keep your shoulders down. Chest open. Chin lifted so you're looking straight ahead. Breathe.'

I got into position and glanced across at Helen. She was like an ivory carving, her skin so pale you could see the veins at the inside of her elbow, the shadows of bone definition at the base of her neck. There was something so fragile about her. I thought of Ned and his recent worries. *Had* she got any thinner? Not that I could see, not obviously. Perhaps her cheekbones were that little bit sharper. There were bluish tinges under her eyes, but there often are because she stays up late. And that made me remember other times I'd secretly studied my sister in the past. Once when Mum had talked her into taking me swimming – God knows what threats or bribery she'd employed to wangle that – and Hel had sat on the poolside wearing a sarong over her one-piece and I'd been fascinated by the extreme sharpness of her elbows and the fact her tummy was actually concave. Her arms had been mottled purple and yellowy, the way your skin goes if you play out in the snow in just short sleeves. And she had been cold that day, even though the pool was heated and steamy. I recalled another afternoon when I'd come home from primary school and she'd been laid out on the sofa with cushions piled underneath her. She said she couldn't get comfortable, that however she lay, the seat was digging in. I said it was like the fairy story about the princess who was so refined she could feel a single dried pea through twenty mattresses. That had made her smile.

I thought of a day I'd brought home a friend from primary school. I think I was in the top class then, and this girl had wanted to go in Helen's room and poke around, and in fact she had done and I'd had to drag her out. She'd got hold of one of Helen's belts and tried it on (it was way too small) and then asked whether my sister was going to die. When Mum heard about that exchange she banned the girl from our house and gave me an earful for having invited her.

Because there's always been this secrecy around Helen – her body, her room, everything. Considering we've grown up together, I feel I hardly know her. So much of the person she is has been shrouded in mystery. Then again, I suppose it's to be expected. Even if she hadn't been anorexic, she's seven years older than me. That's a gulf which is hard to cross.

Yet here we were, dancing together. Who'd have thought it? When the class was over and we were filing out, she grasped my arm.

'You were right, sis. I admit it. That was amazing.'

'You enjoyed it?'

'God, yeah. I'm knackered, though. Phew! How do you remember the different routines? I'll never learn them.'

'You will. It's muscle-memory, half of it. Your body recalling the moves without you even having to think.'

'If you say so.' We walked out onto the car park and she pointed to the pub across the road. 'So what's The Duke like?'

'No idea. When the zumba girls go out, it's normally to the Queen's Head. Why do you ask? Don't tell me you're in need of a drink.'

'I just don't want to go home yet. Do you?'

'To the land of the Arctic stares? Fair point. Come on, then. Let's put our heads round the door.'

The Duke turned out to have one of those old-men's saloons, horrible carpet and splitting seat covers. It was empty of customers, too, which is never a good sign. There was, however, a good log fire going.

'Sure you want to stay?' I asked.

'You want to go home and sit in front of the TV with our parents?'

Hel pulled off her headband and settled herself by the hearth while I got us two Diet Cokes, plus a bag of peanuts for myself. I'd have quite liked a shot of something but I was driving.

'So you'll be zumba-ing next week?' I said, sliding in next to her.

'If you'll have me. It's a pity I was so rubbish.'

'You were not.'

'Oh, I was, Jen. Like that move where we had to lean over and shimmy our boobs – I've no boobs to shimmy, have I? And no bum to wiggle. I must have looked ridiculous. You know me, I can't really do "sexy".'

I understood what she meant. Hel's beautiful, but it's aesthetic, abstract admiration rather than the blatantly carnal she tends to arouse. She'll never have a luscious body, plump and ripe, curvaceous. Her beauty's always going to be the sort that puts you in mind of wood nymphs or Rivendell. Out of the blue I recalled what Ned had confided back in the summer, that they weren't sleeping together any more. Dear God, horrible image. Why had he ever told me that?

'Don't stress,' I said quickly. 'We're all sizes and shapes in there. You just have to go with the music. Have fun.'

'I did! And the weird thing is, I'm exhausted, but at the same time I feel so fired-up I could leap tall buildings at a single bound. Do you know what I mean?'

'I do.'

She grinned at me and I grinned back. Well done, Jen; well done, little sis.

We sipped our drinks and watched the fire flickering in the grate.

'How are things with you, anyway?'

'You mean Owen-wise?'

'If you like.'

'You don't want to know.'

'I wouldn't have asked if I didn't.'

I let out a long sigh. 'What you'd expect. I miss him, Hel. I miss him every day and every night. Some evenings I don't know what to do with myself. I come out of the office and I have to fight the urge to turn and walk across the square and down towards his flat. Or to the shop to see the girls, or to the Oak. Those places that were ours. And then when I get home I'm in a mood, and Mum's asking all these questions, but never the ones that might make me feel she actually cares about me as a person.'

'She does care. She just doesn't know what to say to you. She's trying.'

'Oh yeah, very trying. But the worst aspect of this whole break-up thing is that I keep going over and over in my mind how I ought to have played it with Chelle. This idea that he blames me, that he's got me down as – I don't know – a *bully* – that hurts. That's hard to bear.'

'Owen's a tosser.'

'No. He's just naive. He misread a situation. I just wish I could have another chance to explain myself properly. It still goes round and round my head, what I should have said, what I wish I hadn't. It's killing me, Hel.'

She nodded. 'Maybe you need to contact him again, then.'

'I do think about it. But I haven't the nerve. If we met up and he repeated that stuff about how I never understood him and how I was too pushy . . . I can't risk putting myself through that. Not right now.'

'It would be a resolution. Which is better than the state you're in.'

'I don't know. I change my mind twenty times an hour. Ned thinks I'm better off single.'

'Huh. Does he? Who died and made him king? Look, Jen, if you want to contact Owen, you go ahead. Or not. Your choice. Only it seems a shame if you think you could still talk him round, not to at least have a try.'

'Life's tricky, isn't it?'

'It bloody well is.' She flicked her hair back carelessly, and across the room the barman cast a longing glance.

I said, 'You two are OK? You and Ned?'

'Great,' she said, and I thought I'd never heard a syllable invested with such bleakness.

The pub door opened and an old man tottered in. He had with him a dog on a lead, a faded collie with a drooping head. I smiled a greeting but he ignored us.

'My God, they make a pair,' I whispered to Hel. 'You have to ask yourself, who's going to keel over first?'

She nudged me with her foot. 'Don't be mean. That's exactly the type of animal we help out, the ones who get left behind when their owners die.'

She began to talk about the kennels then, and about the cases that were currently on her mind. I wanted to know about the man who'd been a pain to her when she first started.

'Oh, he's still a pain. Every day he finds something to carp about. Last week he threatened to file a written report about my not locking the meds cabinet, but actually I hadn't been anywhere near it and then the centre director admitted it was her fault. He was furious.'

'What have you done to annoy him so much?'

'Nothing that I know of. It could be Lucinda-Syndrome.'

I nodded. Lucinda had been a tutor hired about ten years ago, when Hel was ploughing through her science GCSEs. She'd taken an instant dislike to my sister, sniping and inventing complaints against her, and after a while we'd worked out it was basically to do with the way Hel looked. That does happen sometimes. Mostly beauty like hers provokes a warm reception in people, but there are always one or two who react to it by getting defensive and hostile. Lucinda herself had a hairy mole and a monobrow, but as we said at the time, that wasn't Helen's fault.

'Perhaps that's why Rosa doesn't like me,' I said drily.

'She *could* be jealous of you. It's not such an outrageous idea.'

'Ha.'

'No. You're young, you're at the start of everything. It's all before you. God, Jen, I wish I was still twenty-three.'

'Because thirty's *so* old.'

'It is when you've done nothing with your life.'

'Get off. Tell me more about the doggies.'

So she described a foxhound rescued from a hunt that they'd successfully rehomed as a pet, despite various people telling them it couldn't be done. There was a Jack Russell-cross with a withered hind leg whose owners had got bored with him, but who'd found favour with a boisterous vicarage family. The blind Staffie, Isaac, was still around; he'd become the centre's mascot and everyone on the staff made a fuss of him. Every week brought new refugees and new matches, and a few losses. Some days she cried but I hadn't to tell Mum that. Mostly it was good. 'I want to make a difference, Jen. Like that woman tonight with her charity bike ride. Imagine achieving something like that. I can't stop thinking about it.'

'If you announce you're biking to John O' Groats, Mum'll have a heart attack on the spot.'

'I was only thinking aloud.'

'Well, no thinking aloud in front of her. Not unless you want another earful.' I took a sip of my Coke. 'You know she's going to be furious when you get back and say you've enjoyed yourself.'

'So she is.'

I thought of my mother's anxious, resentful face as it had been over the dining table that evening.

'Actually, I don't know how you stand it, the constant scrutiny. She's getting worse. You can't even cross your legs without her being on high alert, can you?'

'Ah, she's OK.'

'She needs to stop being so controlling.'

'It's only because she worries about me.'

Suddenly I was annoyed.

'Tell me something, Hel. Why do you always defend her? I know she irritates you to death. She does nothing but monitor your movements and try to stop you doing stuff. She's like a bloody prison warder. Plus she's so damn miserable. She never has a good word to say about Dad and she's just not interested in me. I could shack up tomorrow with an axe-murdering junkie and she wouldn't bother. It's totally unbalanced, like you get twice the attention and I get none. Not that I'm complaining; I couldn't stand it the other way. I don't know why Dad puts up with it, though. The way she is with him, it's awful. If I were him I'd tell her where to go.'

I felt a lot better for having got this off my chest. I was fed up, and it was nice to have the opportunity to offload to someone who understood. This evening with my sister had been good. I felt we'd made a new connection. I wondered if she thought the same, wondered if we would sit and chat like this next week, and the week after that.

'I mean, why did Mum go on and *have* a second child if she wasn't that fussed? Do you think I was a "mistake"? And why did she get married to a man she obviously can't stand? It's wearing on the rest of us. Do you reckon she was she always this sour? Was she a sour kid, was she *born* sour?'

Helen frowned. Her fingers laced and unlaced in her lap.

'You shouldn't go on about her. She's your mum. I know she's hard work sometimes, but she's had a difficult life.'

'Has she? How?'

'It's not that easy to explain, Jen. There are things—'

'Things?'

'Family things. You didn't pick them up because you were too young.'

'Pick what up?'

A pause.

'OK, listen,' she said. 'I'm going to tell you something, and you're not going to overreact to it. You're an adult and you ought to know how your own family works.'

'You're scaring me.'

'No, I just think you need to know the truth.'

'Come on, out with it now you've started.'

'Jen, the reason Mum's so angry is that Dad had an affair.'

There was a moment where the words sat intact, like droplets of water on material before they're absorbed. Dad. An *affair*? My dad? Old, fat Dad? My lovely dad? No. *No*. 'Fuck off, Hel.'

'I'm sorry. It's true.'

'It can't be! No way. *No way*. It must be some story Mum cooked up to make you feel sorry for her. The plot of some bloody TV soap she's been watching and fancies trying on for size. She's mistaken, she's confused. The whole thing's sick. It's *sick*. Shut up!'

Helen sat impassively till I'd finished. Then she said, 'Mum didn't tell me.'

'So how do you know?'

'I found out myself.'

'You're trying to tell me you saw them together?'

'I came across this pair of earrings in his car. I took them to Mum because I thought they were hers. They weren't. They were Jeanette's. You remember, his work secretary?'

My head was ringing. 'Not that blonde?'

Helen shook her head. 'You're thinking of Steph. Jeanette had brown hair. Quite plump and mousy.'

'When? When was this supposed to have happened?'

'I was still at high school. You'd have been in first year juniors, so about six, seven.'

'But earrings don't mean anything! Dad might have simply given this woman a lift somewhere.'

'No, he admitted it there and then. You know Dad, he's not the world's most artful liar, is he? Mum challenged him and he just confessed. Swore it was over and would never happen again. I heard it all; I had my door open, listening.'

That description of Dad made my eyes prick with tears. Hel was right, he'd be rubbish at deceit. He wasn't built that way. The very last person in the world I'd have thought would cheat on us. My dad.

She said, 'And don't you remember the rows, Jen? God, I mean, they tried to hide it from us, but there were so many arguments that bubbled up over nothing. You must remember that business on holiday where Mum completely lost it, dragged us out of the café and announced she was taking us home?'

Yes, I did recall that. Sitting in the Cornish sunshine on a plastic chair, Mum snatching at her handbag and standing so abruptly that the table nearly overturned. *I've had enough*, she'd said. Enough of what? I didn't know at the time. I thought it must be me or Helen, or the heat. The shot of pure fear as she took my arm and started to lead us away down the road. Were we going home? I didn't want to go home. It was our holiday. Then Dad was running after us. And unbidden came another memory overlaying the scene – this morning in the Empire Hotel, and Ellie eating her heart out over Joe—

'Are you OK, Jen?'

'No, I'm bloody not. How could I be? Why would Dad cheat on Mum? He's *nice*. I thought he was nice.'

'I think it was my fault.'

'Aw, come on. You?'

Helen drooped, and her voice sounded small. 'I think things were so bad at home. I mean, things with me. The bullying and school phobia, and Mum going on at him to solve it when it couldn't be solved, and me getting ill. I think – you know what Dad's like – Jeanette was probably a sympathetic ear. Obviously more than that in the end. I don't know. I've tried to make sense of it, and that's the best I can come up with.'

Part of me was still completely stunned. Everything I thought I knew about our parents was upside-down. The good guy was not the good guy; the mean-spirited turned out to be the betrayed. Over the years, all those moments of allegiance and outrage and triumph and pity that had been misjudged. My family memories were founded on a lie. Why hadn't Helen told me? Why *had* she told me? And here, now, in this fag-end of a pub which even the locals shunned.

'I can't get my head round it.'

'It's OK.' Hesitantly she put out her hand and placed it over mine.

'No it isn't.'

'No. It isn't.'

I said, 'But if she was that upset, why didn't she kick him out?'

'Because she needed him around. She couldn't cope on her own. Everything was such a mess. Which of course was my fault too.'

'So she let him stay and just got angrier and angrier.' My God. It explained so much. The constant sniping, the way he blocked her out. And she'd been living with that. How *had* she lived with that? My dad, in the wrong for so many years. 'I don't know either of them any more. Fuck, it's as if my real parents are gone and there are these two imposters in their place and I'll never get them back again. It's horrible. I still can't process what you've told me . . .'

Hel shuffled closer on the seat and attempted to embrace me. After a second's embarrassment I let her, though it was hard to relax against her unfamiliar contours. Nothing, nothing what it had been half an hour ago. If only I could unwind my life and return to where I had been before.

'I'm really sorry, Jen. Maybe I should have told you sooner, only I wanted to protect you. That's why I kept quiet. You seemed too young to be burdened with it. But then lately – for a while, actually – it's felt almost as if you were older than me. More mature. Like you've caught me up and passed me by.'

'Don't say that.'

'Anyway, you had a right to know why Mum's the way she is. When she's cross, it's not with you, or me, even if it feels that way. Do you see?'

'I'm not sure.'

'So you'll be nicer with Mum, yeah?'

'I am nice with her.'

'And Dad . . .'

'I can't think about that.'

'He's spent a lot of time paying for one slip.'

'Don't.'

'I'm just saying, no one's a villain. Some things happened.'

Some things. I pulled away from her and took hold of my glass. 'And I thought this was going to be a relaxing drink together.'

'Well, I mean, it's been good to talk. We don't do it very often. Even if what's been said is a bit painful.'

I felt a flush of heat rising up my chest and realised it was fury. With Dad for turning his back on the family to pursue his own lust, with Mum for putting up with it, with Helen for uncovering the affair, with all of them for being in on it and excluding me. Wires of tension criss-crossing around me, sly and meaningful looks exchanged, with me in the middle of this cat's cradle of secrets. I was tired of people closing doors against me and mouthing over my head. Helen's illness, Dad's affair. God knows what else had gone on that I hadn't discovered. I'd had enough of being the baby of the family. I'd had enough of the family. I wanted to step over the lot of them and stride off into my own life. Wherever that was.

'And I know you're upset now, but that'll lessen, Jen. I sobbed my heart out when I first realised. You get used to it, though.'

'Do you?'

The barman reappeared and began polishing glasses. The log fire spat and crackled, the old sheepdog scratched its ear. How long we sat in silence like that I don't know. I was aware of my own thumb stroking up and down the side of my Coke with ever increasing speed. Before my eyes rose that picture of Ellie bent over the sink, her face pink and tender with crying. I'd not been intending to tell my sister about what I'd witnessed seven hours ago in the Ladies' at Americana because I wasn't sure what effect the news might have. It could be reassuring for her, make her finally understand what a lucky escape she'd had when she and Joe broke up, and therefore banish some of those tormenting memories. On the other hand, depending on how she felt towards Ellie, it could dredge up sympathies that would draw her again into her own darkest place. It might even, worst-case scenario, lead her to believe Joe was on the market again and in need of consolation. Potentially dangerous. So at the very least I'd wanted to mull over the possibilities.

But I was overtaken with the surge of power that comes from holding charged information. This was my turn to break a revelation over someone's head.

Beside me Helen sat twisting strands of bright copper hair around her index finger. 'I'm really sorry, Jen.'

I took a deep breath.

'You know, it's odd you should mention people having affairs,' I heard myself say, my voice trembling slightly, 'because you'll never guess who I saw in Chester today.'

CHAPTER 7

WOMAN'S WORLD

The Festive Five – our Top Tips on How to Avoid a Stressful Christmas!

You know what it's like: so much build-up, so much expectation, so much darned hard work. No wonder many of us have come to dread the demands of the yuletide season. Tensions run high as family members are cooped up together in overheated rooms for hours on end. There aren't enough kitchen helpers, or there are too many, and meanwhile the rubbish bags are piling up and the TV remote's gone missing and no one thought to check the household battery stocks before the shops closed. You're convinced that under every other roof in the land, Christmas is going like a dream. The reality is, though, very few households are advert-perfect, and almost everyone's bound to run into conflict at some point over the holiday. Here are our simple suggestions for relieving the pressure and making sure we all have the relaxing break we need and deserve.

I read back my copy and it sounded like the most pat advice ever. Because God knows how my own Christmas was going to be this year, playing happy families with parents-who-no-longer-felt-like-my-parents. For so many years I'd believed that, for all our spats and grumbles, everything was basically fine with the Crossleys, when in fact it was nothing like. World War Three had played out behind my back. The idea was unbelievably hurtful. I felt like the biggest fool in the world.

It had been a long process of reorientation. Lately there'd been nights when I'd sat next to my mother on the sofa, pretending to watch TV but in reality scrutinising every line and contour of her face and wondering how on earth she'd held herself together during the discovery of Dad's infidelity. My whole life she'd just been 'Mum'; I don't think I'd ever *seen* her as a person, as a woman. Lately I realised there was so much more to her, a darker, stronger, fiercer core which must have carried her through the worst. No wonder there were days when she was raw and snappy. Helen helped me see this as she let me talk it over endlessly in the small-hours privacy of my bedroom. I wanted to tell Mum that now I understood better, I was sorry I hadn't been more patient with her. But how would she react if I came out with such a speech? Could either of us bear that sudden burst of intimacy? The raking up of the painful past? I doubted it. So I just carried on watching, and badgering Hel, and thinking.

At the same time I found myself assessing my father's body language – the furtive glance up from his newspaper whenever someone walked into the room, or that slight shrinking of the shoulders he always did when the telephone rang, as if he was expecting bad news. I'd never noticed before but it seemed to me he still moved like a guilty man. Or was I imagining it? Was

I overdramatising? I couldn't tell. I loved him, I hated him. I had no idea who he was. It was a relief when he took himself out to his den in the garage.

Then there was the more basic (but increasingly urgent) matter of what to buy these people for Christmas. Because how do you shop for the truly damaged family? I'd flicked through catalogues and browsed online as usual, trawled the Rows of Chester, but every idea I had seemed loaded with subtext. Aftershave for my father? *Yes, but who are you attempting to smell nice for?* Speciality chocolates? *Grow fatter, Dad, then there's less chance you'll cheat again.* Posh hand cream for Mum? *You're dry and wrinkly, no wonder he strayed.* A pretty scarf? *Hide that withered neck away, old woman.* As for Helen, who knew what she wanted at the moment? My revelation about Ellie she'd absorbed in a cool silence, which could have been relief, triumph, anger, pain. However she felt, she wasn't for sharing. Perhaps I should just buy us all a bumper box of Kalms and have done.

'Hey, Gerry,' I said, looking away from the screen.

There was no reply. When I glanced over he was swivelled round in his seat, looking at Rosa's empty office.

'What's going on?' I asked. 'Don't tell me she's on the warpath again? Do I need to brace myself?'

'Nah, you're fine. Do you want a laugh, though?'

'Depends.'

'OK.' He lowered his voice. 'Soon as the boss walks in, take yourself over to the wall planner and pretend to be making notes. But keep an eye on her window. Alan tipped me off. Apparently you should see something funny.'

'What sort of funny?'

'He didn't say. Some prank he's set up.'

'Where is he, anyway?'

'Out interviewing the contractors for the new sports stadium. He should be back any minute.'

I saved the Festive Tips document, vanished it and got down to my next project, which was a feature about local restaurant events over the festive period. Gerry had done the spadework on this one but then Rosa had passed it on to me to finish. Scanning down his notes I was surprised to see that one of the chefs interviewed was my old food tech teacher, Mr Dickson. Wee Rory, we'd called him. Had hours of fun imitating his Glaswegian accent. But it looked as if he'd known what he was talking about when he chivvied us to roll our pastry thinner. Now he was *Asperge d'Or* Chef of the Year. Well, good for him. A brave step to pack in a secure job and start up on his own. And I thought of how, as well as cookery, he'd also taken us for PSHCE in Year 8, when some of us hadn't been as mature as we should have been and weren't ready to discuss citizenship and social responsibility. I remembered Stuart Lyons, who'd started a craze for stapling stuff to your tie and who'd attached himself to his text book cover in the middle of a debate about substance abuse. I suppose we must have been a pain to teach, but you don't think about that when you're drunk on your own wit. Stuart's daftness sparked off another recollection, this time of a male PE instructor who we called Wiggo because the popular myth was that he wore a rug – 'Nobody's hair's that crap in real life,' people used to argue – but we never found out the truth. Which in turn reminded me of my sister's favourite, Mr Wolski, because he had his hair spiked like some of the sixth formers and wore almost-trendy shirts. My favourite teacher had been Mrs Patterson because she taught English, which I loved, and she was the person who told me I could make a career in writing if I worked hard and stayed focussed. Sometimes her name popped up in *The Messenger* because although she was retired, she was very active in the Quakers.

And I remembered Nia Hughes and her Year 9 'Term of Dares', where every day a group of us had to do something mad and usually boy-related. Note-planting was high on the agenda, and the sending out of inflammatory texts or gossip. Because those were the days when, if someone fancied you, they'd drop a message to you via their mate and you'd just say yes or no and then it was sorted. The news would get around, you might be an item for a while, and then later, you wouldn't. After the break-up, a couple of days of smarting or embarrassment and you'd be on track again, ready for the next event. You were high, you were low, but it was never deadly serious either way, and in between there was so much larking about you couldn't stay miserable for long. How I missed the simplicity of that time, the giddiness and fun. It was a shame for people who'd been bullied at school or who couldn't keep up with the work or make friends, but for me, right now, I'd have gone back in a heartbeat.

'Hey up. Bandits at six o' clock,' said Gerry, bringing me back to the present with a jolt.

Thankfully you could always hear Rosa before she appeared because she wore these clicky heels and they made a racket on the wooden stairs. One second later the office door burst open and in she swept, her fur-collared coat flapping. There was still no sign of Alan.

Gerry nodded significantly towards the wall planner, and after a moment I picked up my pen and went to stand near it. He was right. From this position you could see right into her annexe and make out clearly what was on her desk. Today, planted among the piles of papers and gadgetry, was a shiny red parcel, about the size of a slim book and done up with gold ribbon. 'To Rosa', said the label in thick black pen, 'Merry Christmas'. Nothing else. What was Alan up to? Was it from Alan? Or was this gift courtesy of Mr Top Flight Dating? According to our man on the sports desk, that romance was still going strong. New Boyfriend had taken her to a hunt ball and they'd had their picture snapped for a county mag. She'd shown Alan some photos from her own camera, and he reported that she'd been a vision in fuchsia silk. 'I expect there was tweed underneath,' had been Gerry's comment.

Rosa hung up her coat and drew off her black leather gloves, scanning the room as she did so. Her eyes gleamed when she saw what was waiting for her by her monitor. Immediately she strode over and snatched up the parcel, weighed it in her hand, then shook it. I put my pen to one of the planner's squares and pretended to make notes there.

At first her touch was delicate – a tweak of a ribbon, a dainty lifting of the red foil edges. Then she abandoned any restraint and in one greedy movement tore off the wrapping whole. Two items fell out, the first a long, flat packet that looked as if it might be sexy stockings. She reached for her reading glasses and held the packet up to the light to peer at the description. But I could make out the picture on the back and they weren't sexy stockings at all, they were those dodgy crotchless 'hygiene' tights you wear to keep your nether bits cool. Puzzled, she put them down and switched her attention to the other part of the present. This was a rigid box, narrow and about the length of a pencil. Because it had been wrapped separately, Rosa had to use her fingernails to pick away the piece of Sellotape at the end before she could get into it. And then it came loose and she was able to draw out the box, leaving the paper like an empty shell. Her brows came down as she took in what she'd uncovered. It was a box of Boots' own-brand thrush cream that lay across her palm.

The next second she looked up and her eyes caught mine. I saw hurt in there as well as humiliation and anger; it felt like a pin stabbed in my chest. I turned away fast but it was too late. She'd seen me watching. She understood beyond doubt that I'd stationed myself there to be a witness. And I heard her thoughts as plainly as if she'd bawled them across the office: *YOU set this up? This is your idea of a joke? How dare you! You're NOTHING, NO ONE. I'm your BOSS. You're going to be sorry for this, Jennifer Crossley.*

The envelope was waiting on my desk when I returned from lunch. Not that I'd had much of an appetite after Rosa's evil stare had burnt its mark on my brain.

'This'll be her firing me,' I said to Gerry, holding up the envelope. 'My marching orders.'

He had the grace to look ashamed. 'Look, I'm sorry, Jen. I thought he'd set up a harmless prank. I'd no idea of the detail. I assumed it would be a fake spider or something.'

'Why did you even tell Alan about the thrush joke?'

'Dunno. We were chatting, it was just something I said. I didn't know he was going to act on it. You were unlucky the way it worked out.'

I slapped the letter down on the table.

'Unlucky? You're kidding. I was set up there.'

'You reckon?'

'Totally. He can be a nasty piece of work, can Alan. Always trying to score points off someone. Do you not remember last week him asking Tam why she'd put in a claim for mileage when she was getting a lift in every day off her boyfriend? He dropped her right in it.'

'I know he can be sly.'

'I've been wondering for a while now if it wasn't him who planted The Diary in my bag. I bet it was. The way he happened to "discover" it.'

'Have you crossed him lately?'

'Oh, I don't think it's personal. I think he just loves to get other people into trouble because it makes him look better. He knew what conclusion Rosa would jump to when she spotted me gawping through her window. Anyway,' I went on, picking up the letter again, 'if this *is* my notice to quit, there's not a lot I can do about it.'

'If it is, she posted it yesterday.'

Gerry pointed at the envelope and it was indeed franked and dated. That calmed me slightly. Rosa wouldn't have drawn a smiley biro face in the top corner either.

I flipped it over, slid my finger under the paper flap and prised it open. A Christmas card – of course it was. Not your conventional sort, but a sheet of folded paper with a photoshopped image of Ebenezer Scrooge protesting against cuts to the welfare budget. 'To Jen, have a groovy Christmas', Keisha had written, and underneath, '(We didn't know your home address!) Pop into the shop soon – we miss you. XXX'.

At the bottom of the page Vikki had added her signature plus the message, 'PS Owen says hello'. At once my anxiety levels shot up again.

'Listen,' continued Gerry, 'I tell you what. This is partly my fault, so I'll go to Rosa and say it was me.'

'What?'

'I'm not having you take the rap. It's not on. I'll go and see her.'

'But then it's not fair on you either.'

He let out a short laugh. 'I don't care. I'm coasting towards retirement, me. Don't give a stuff what she thinks of me either way. But you, you're just starting out, you might need a reference soon.'

Owen says hello. I struggled to focus. 'You mean tell her it was Alan who planted the parcel?'

'Nah. She wouldn't believe that. She thinks the sun shines out of him. She's had a soft spot for him since the day he came for his interview. I'll just say it was me, a moment of madness. I'll say it's my new blood pressure tablets affecting my brain.'

'She'll be furious with you.'

'Yeah, well. The world'll keep on turning.' He ran his finger round the inside his collar as if it was too tight for him.

I put the card down. 'I don't know what to say.'

'Don't say anything. Leave it to me. Gerry'll sort it out.'

And with that he straightened his tie, patted down his shirt and began to make his way towards Rosa's room. I knew I should probably follow him, but my legs felt weak and my heart was racing and I couldn't imagine how my presence would help his story. All I would do was make things worse. Meanwhile, the torn envelope lay across my keyboard. *Pop into the shop soon – we miss you. XXX* Who exactly was missing me? Whose were those kisses at the end? Did Owen volunteer that hello himself? Did he specifically ask Vikki to write in the card? What did 'hello' mean anyway?

The door to Rosa's room shut with a clunk. On the stairs I could hear Alan's voice growing louder as he shouted cheerfully into his mobile.

If anywhere does Christmas with aplomb, it's Chester. When I left work at nearly six it was dark and the fairy lights strung along the Rows were twinkling. We'd had a covering of snow and it was still coming down, those very small flakes that you can barely feel on your skin but which stick to your clothes and hair. Shop windows glowed warmly. I could smell cinnamon from the French bakery, and scented soap as I walked past Crabtree & Evelyn. When I raised my head, the snow was swirling round the street lamps in a way that made me think of Narnia. I knew I should get home before the roads got bad, knew my mum would be getting the tea ready, knew there was no way I ought to be bending my steps towards the Revolution bookshop. *For goodness' sake*, went my commonsense, *one second-hand casual greeting is what you've had off Owen. It's nothing on which to build any hope. He hasn't even sent you a card himself.* But I somehow couldn't help being caught up by the sparkly magic of the night. I mean, I could go along and just see how things were. Just see the girls. Catch up on news, let them know I missed them too. Buy a book or two and casually return his hello. How could that hurt? How could it be wrong to meet old friends, to wish someone well on this Advent eve?

As I hurried along, slaloming between late-night shoppers, I saw couples everywhere, holding hands and arm in arm, embracing in a café porch. I caught a glimpse of a youth shyly collaring a female assistant in a perfume shop, and an older man studying a jeweller's display of heart-shaped pendants. The world seemed full of lovers looking to please.

There were no lights on in Owen's flat as I passed.

By the time I'd crossed the river and climbed the hill towards the shop I was feeling faint with nerves. Oh for God's sake, get a grip, I told myself. All I was going to do was put my head round the door, say Merry Christmas, and – if I got the chance – ask Vikki whether the note on the card had actually been prompted by Owen or was simply her being kind. That was it. Nothing to get in a state about. I could hear music drifting down the street, some slow, old-fashioned American jazz.

I drew near and crossed to the opposite side of the road, wanting to approach from an oblique angle rather than stroll straight in. The shop entrance was ajar, in spite of the weather, and a sandwich board parked on the pavement outside announced 'Late Opening'. The jazz was coming from a speaker on the front table. I could see several customers, or at least several bodies moving among the books, plus the café area was almost what you'd call busy, with every one of the four tables occupied. In the window was an artificial Christmas tree laden with the oddest selection of ornaments. I counted a baby's bootee, a doll's head, a CD with a ribbon looped through it, a cocktail umbrella, a plastic dinosaur, a mini box of cereal. Paper snowflakes had been stuck along the bottom edge of the glass.

And there was Keisha, a tinsel crown resting on her afro and a tray of biscuits balanced on her upturned palm. She offered the biscuits to a guy in a long coat and he took a great handful and dropped them in his pocket. Luckily she seemed to find this funny. I craned to see if Vikki was about. She wasn't behind the counter serving drinks. That was Saleem, in a striped apron. She wasn't one of the people sitting down having a drink. Perhaps she'd popped out for a while, to top up supplies or drum up more custom. Then I spotted her. She was at the top of a stepladder, half-hidden by a beam, attempting to hang a paper chain.

I sucked in a breath. OK, what I'd do was scuttle over, make a smiling, happy-Xmas entrance, grab some cheap paperback and do an 'Oh-by-the-way' as I was paying. That would sort it. That would be enough. I checked for traffic through the drifting flakes.

That's when I saw Owen. I'd missed him because he'd been at the foot of the stepladder, holding it steady. Now he gave his hand to Vikki as she clambered down. 'Bloody uneven floors,' I imagined her saying. My heart did a great thump as he emerged into the light and I saw him properly. He'd had his hair cut shorter since I'd last seen him, so it no longer hung down over his eyes. It made him look older and harder, less of a dreamer. And he looked sad. No, he really did. For minutes I watched, and he'd smile quickly at some joke or comment, then the smile would die and it was like a light going out. There, a flash, a fading, his mouth a set, grim line again.

Oh, Owen. Part of me longed to run over to him and fling my arms around his neck. Simultaneously, a surge of anger flooded my chest as I remembered the things he'd said about me, about himself, about Chelle. It made me want to march in and slap him for being so consummately played. Yet another part of me was just desperate to be inside the bookshop group, eating cookies under a poster of a butterfly with the CND logo across its wings. Safe inside a world I knew, before everything changed. I stood on the cold pavement dithering, playing out the various scenarios in my mind. *Jen!* he'd exclaim. *Thank Christ you're here, I've missed you. I wanted you back but haven't been able to pluck up the courage to say.* Or, *God, Jen. I wasn't expecting you. Whatever do you want?* Or, *Shit, look who it is, that's the cue for me to leave.* No. He wouldn't be cruel. He might turn me down, but he wouldn't be malicious about it. There was that sad mouth again. I ached to touch his lips with my fingertips.

A bus trundled past, blocking him out of my sight for a few seconds. If only I could make my legs work.

Then I heard my phone beep. I pulled it out, fingers fumbling, and checked the screen to find a text from Mum asking what time I'd be home. Typical, that, breaking into my drama with her irritating concerns. I typed that I was already on my way and sent the message off. Mothers make liars of us all.

Behind the shop glass, Owen was spreading out some leaflets on the table and Vikki was bending over to read them. Keisha was nibbling one of her own biscuits, while the man in the long coat was pointing at something in a book he'd picked off the shelf. Saleem leaned on the counter, his apron rucked up. The jazz played on.

I thought, *Right I'll do it. I'm ready. I will do this thing, and then if it all comes to nought, I'll turn around and leave forever.* And at least I'd be sure. That'd be an end to it.

I took one step forward and my phone started to ring.

'What?' I barked into the mouthpiece. 'Who is this?'

A brief pause, and Ned's voice. 'Jen? Hi. It's me.'

'Oh, hi. What's up?'

'Nothing. Nothing at all.'

'What's up, Ned?'

Another bus passed by in the opposite direction. On the back seat a teenage girl stared out, bleached pale by the interior lights. She looked completely fed up. I wondered whether she was going home to an annoying family.

'I was just wondering when you'd be home.'

'Why?'

'Nothing really.'

'Just say it.'

'Your sister's in a spot of bother.'

Bloody hell. 'Bother? What do you mean? What sort of bother?'

'Nothing to worry about. Bit complicated to go into here. Are you on your way?'

The shop door opened fully and the man in the long coat swept out. I noticed both of his pockets seemed to be bulged out of shape, and also that he had what could have been the end of a baguette protruding from one cuff.

'I wasn't, no. I'm actually in the middle of something important, if you must know.'

'Right, OK.' He sounded nonplussed. I don't often snap at him. 'That's fine. No problem. Really. Sorry to bother you, forget I rang. We'll see you when we see you.'

'For God's sake, Ned. You can't just drop something like that and then back track. What's going on with Hel? Tell me.'

But the phone was dead. He'd rung off. Across the road Keisha came and stood in the shop entrance, looking up and down the street for more customers. I waited for her to spot me, braced myself for it, but instead she simply went inside again. It was almost as if I'd become invisible.

Even as I pulled into the drive I could tell something was going on. The porch and hall lights were blazing and the garage front was wide open. Mum's festive door wreath had been knocked off centre.

I climbed out of the car as Dad was emerging from under the

steel shutter. He was puffing and panting and attempting to manhandle a two-metre-wide roll of green plastic sheet into the house. I heard my mother shout for him, a high, panicky bark.

'What's happening?' I said, locking the car.

He shook his head as if the situation was beyond explanation.

I followed him in, hung up my bag and coat next to the Christmas tree and went through to the living room. Dad carried on into the kitchen but I stayed to see what was the matter with Helen. She was sitting on the sofa with Ned, her face taut and pale. Between them, laid across the cushion and squirming, was a blanket-wrapped bundle.

'Now, Hel, see who's here,' said Ned.

My first thought was, *Holy fuck, she's stolen someone's baby.*

'I won't tell you again, get some newspaper under it,' shouted Mum from the stairs. The thing in the blanket whimpered. Above us all a silver foil Christmas star rotated serenely from the ceiling.

'What have you got in there?' I asked.

'It's a puppy.' Ned reached over and gave my sister's hand a squeeze. 'Someone brought it into the shelter today and because it's so little it's going to need round-the-clock feeding. Hel volunteered. You're going to be its foster-mum, aren't you, Hel?'

'There were six of them,' she said.

'That's right. They were found under a bridge in a sack and the others didn't make it, but this one, this chap here, he's putting up a fight. We're going to save him, aren't we?'

'He's got a heat pad to keep him warm.'

'Yeah, and we've found a puppy-sized box. And you've brought home some special milk and a feeding bottle. He's well set up. He's landed on his paws, this one.'

Mum came marching in. 'Has your dad laid that tarpaulin yet?' She didn't wait for an answer, just went on through. From the kitchen we could hear rustling and swearing, then scolding.

- It's not wide enough.

- How wide does it have to be?

-The whole floor.

-Why?

- Because this is where we eat! This is where I'll be cooking the Christmas dinner in a couple of weeks' time!

- That dog won't stray from its box tonight. Have you not seen the size of it? Like a flaming guinea pig. It's going nowhere.

- Says you. I'm the one who'll be clearing up after it.

'No, Mum,' Helen called. 'I'll be the one clearing up. I'll do everything. It's only for a night. Or two.' She lowered her voice for the last bit.

The dog whined again and then made a sort of choking noise. Immediately my sister bent over it, using her index finger to move the blanket away from the muzzle. I could make out a very pink and naked-looking nose, eyes closed into slits. What fur there was looked to be white. 'You're OK, sweetheart,' she told it.

'Hold that edge and I'll pull it across,' went Mum's voice. You could tell she was furious. Her lovely house, decked out for the holidays with the holly tablecloth already laid, the red velvet napkin holders and Spode plates on standby, the frosted twigs pinned over the mantelpiece. In the corner burned her mulled-wine-scented candle. Somewhere under the crackling of plastic and my dad's grunts, a TV show of carols was playing. All is calm, all is bright.

'So what breed is he?' I asked.

'We can't tell yet. It'll be a mix; no one dumps pedigrees. There may be some terrier in the face, my boss thinks. You know, I keep thinking about his mum. She'll be beside herself.'

'Don't,' said Ned. 'Focus on this little guy. He's the one who needs your attention.'

'But what kind of bastard leaves baby animals to die?'

Mum appeared in the doorway. 'Wouldn't the dog be better off in the garage? Because it's quieter in there and there wouldn't be so much disturbance for it. We wouldn't be stepping round it every five minutes. And if there are any accidents—'

'Don't be daft, it's about minus twenty in there,' called Dad.

A darkness crossed her face that was horrible to see. *You're all against me*, she was thinking. *Again*.

I said, 'It's only for a few hours and we'll clean up if there's any problems. You honestly won't know he's here. Everything'll be dealt with and tidied away at the end. And you can see how much it means to Helen to see him recover. After the rotten start he's had, we want to do our best by him, don't we?'

On cue the puppy squeaked again, a heart-rending sound. We felt it.

'For God's sake,' said Mum, but she had no argument to counter with. Instead she jerked her thumb over her shoulder. 'You're not to use any of my kitchen equipment, is that understood? Any tea towels you use go straight into the machine on a boil-wash. And use the antibacterial handwash. I don't want us coming down with salmonella or e-coli.'

'Or worms,' said Ned under his breath. Mum didn't hear but Hel and I did. It was hard not to giggle.

Mum disappeared again and I went over to the sofa to get a better look. The puppy's muzzle was all I could make out, along with an upturned mouth, like a sleepy smile. I knew the dog wasn't really smiling. Nevertheless it seemed a sort of hopeful sign.

'How often will it need feeding?'

'Every couple of hours,' said Hel.

'And you're going to get up right the way through the night?'

'I am.'

'Good luck with that.'

She smiled, reached over for the pup and lifted him onto her lap. It was cute to see her cradle the tiny body against herself. The action, however, revealed a small stain on the cushion below.

'Uh-oh,' whispered Ned.

'No! Is it wee?' I asked in appalled fascination. These were my mother's replacement cushion covers, the ones she'd bought last summer after Dad had left a topless Sharpie pen resting on the chair arm and it had rolled off onto the seat.

Helen shook her head. 'It'll be drool, or something that was on the blanket. It'll sponge off. Probably.'

'What? *What*'ll sponge off?' Mum again.

Expertly Ned slid across so his bum was hiding the mark. 'Grass stains on my knees, Mrs Crossley. They're a swine. It's an occupational hazard when you're edging the lawns. Hel was saying, though, a dab of Ariel and they'll come up grand.' As she peered round the door frame at him, his eyebrows were so comically pitched I couldn't help let out a little squeal of laughter.

'Jen,' said Helen, in warning. But then she too began to laugh.

Ned responded by making his eyes wider and more innocent, and that was funny too. And my mother, staring at us like a grumpy bird of prey, trying to work out what crime we'd committed, and Dad stumbling through behind her, tripping on his own tarpaulin and swearing, became in that instant the funniest sequence I'd ever seen.

'Ssh,' said Helen, her shoulders heaving with mirth. 'You'll scare the pup.'

'Yeah, shush, you two,' said Ned.

'Sshhh!'

We all just carried on.

Mum watched us disapprovingly. 'I'd love to know what the joke is. I don't suppose anyone's going to tell me?'

Dad, squeezing past, put his hand on her shoulder. 'Oh, ignore them, Maureen. Come up to the box room and help me find that extension lead. The sooner this doggy hospital's set up, the sooner we can shut the door on it and relax.'

She paused to wipe her hands on a tea towel, then followed him. When they got to the foot of the stairs he stepped aside to let her go first, and she gave a little half-nod of acknowledgement. It was one of their rare moments of unity.

I woke at 3 a.m.; maybe I'd heard Hel's alarm clock going off through the wall. Sometimes when you surface in the small hours it's a matter of rolling over and sinking back into oblivion, but not on this occasion. I lay in the dark with my eyes wide open, feeling wired. There would be no snuggling down under the duvet and trying to chase sleep now. Sometimes you know it's pointless. So I got up and threw on my dressing gown, shoved my feet into my slippers and made my way downstairs as softly as I could.

My sister was in the kitchen, as I knew she'd be. Only the hob light was on, casting a gentle glow over the puppy's box.

'Is it OK if I come in?'

She looked up from the sink where she was filling a bowl from the hot tap. 'Yeah, fine. Don't make too much noise, though.'

Carefully I brought in a dining chair, placing it near enough to view the dog but not so near I might scare it. I took care not to rumple up the plastic sheeting, too. Meanwhile, Hel had filled a bottle with special milk and was warming it in the bowl. She was still wearing her jeans and sweatshirt.

'Trickier than it looks, this,' she said. 'I've already had to throw one teat away. I made the holes too wide and the milk was coming out faster than it should, and if that happens then the puppy can end up inhaling it and that can give them pneumonia. Oh, I'd best just check his temp while we're waiting.'

She rummaged about in the bag she'd brought with her from the shelter and pulled out a thermometer and a jar of Vaseline. With deft movements she popped a sterile plastic tip over the sensor and then dabbed the end with petroleum jelly.

'Is that going where I think it is?'

'Uh huh.'

I couldn't really see much as she bent over the box, so instead I found myself gazing round the kitchen, at the pinboard of bills and coupons and recipes and flyers; at the decorative wall plate of Lake Windermere; at the base unit where Hel kept her own food supplies, which none of us was supposed to touch. Not that I'd be tempted to run amok with her Rich Tea Fingers or her dry Ryvita. At one time she'd got into using Post-It notes and there'd been coloured tabs and labels all over the cupboard door, the microwave, the fridge; some system to do with what she was and wasn't allowed to eat.

With a reassuring murmur at the puppy, she stood up and

took the thermometer over to the light where she could read it. 'OK, that's fine.' She flicked the used plastic tip-cover into the bin and placed the thermometer back in the bag. Next she went over to the bowl of water and picked out the feeding bottle, pressing it to the inside of her arm to test the warmth. 'Another minute, I reckon.'

'I never asked you if he had a name.'

'The dog? Pepper. That was my idea.' She looked pleased with her choice.

'Yeah? Why?'

'Dunno. I looked at him and he just seemed like a Pepper. Ned thinks we should call him Runty.'

'Harsh.'

'I know. Pepper's no runt or he wouldn't have got this far.'

'He's going to be staying with us over Christmas, isn't he?'

Hel busied herself with the bottle again. 'We'll have to see how he goes. Unless we can find him a surrogate mum he'll have to be hand-fed for weeks.'

'By you?'

'The guys at the centre'll share him round. But I've said I'll have him again when it's my turn.'

'You know Mum's going to go nuts.'

'That's a cross I'll have to bear.'

She tested the milk one last time, then went to sit on the floor by the box. The pup was snuggled into a corner and she had to fish around to root him out. That done, she laid him on his stomach along her skinny thigh and began to try and match up the rubber teat with his mouth. There was a struggle at first, but then he latched on and began sucking. Now I got the chance to examine him properly. It was strange. He reminded me almost of a slug, with his pointed bottom and short tail, or maybe a scaled-down baby seal. He was mainly pinky-white, a few darker patches on his flanks and haunches. Hel was keeping a close watch on his rounded stomach, and on the level in the bottle.

After a minute or so she stopped. 'Better not let him have too much at once. Little and often, that's the way.'

The puppy was still rooting about hopefully. Hel slid her palm under his body, lifted him up and placed him against her shoulder so she could pat his back, the way you might a baby.

'What are you doing?'

'Burping him.'

Objective achieved, she placed him on a towel and, using cotton wool dipped in water from the bowl, she started to wipe round his willy. 'You have to do this to mimic the action of the mother licking him,' she explained. 'Otherwise he can't pee.'

Newborn pups weren't capable of widdling unaided? I couldn't help but marvel at the competent way my sister was handling him. She was like a vet or a nurse, measured and deliberate in every action. Eventually some wee did come out and a bit of poo as well. Hel tidied up his rear end, checked the heat pad in his box by pressing it with her knuckles, and popped him down in his bed. She pulled the blanket so it was against his body. 'They are utterly useless at this age. They can't even shiver. Normally they'd leach their mother's body heat, only poor old Pepper doesn't have that option.'

A final fuss round the box and then she was up and at the sink, scrubbing her hands and the bottle and making up sterilising solution in a plastic jug.

'Have you been doing this routine all night?'

'Yup.'

'Bloody hell. It's like being a new mum.'

'I suppose it is.'

'Can you ever see yourself—' I'd begun before I'd thought the sentence through.

'See myself what?'

Too late now. 'Kids. Having babies. With Ned, I mean.'

She shook her head vigorously. 'No way. Not ever. Not with Ned or anyone else.'

'You seem very sure.'

'I am.'

'Fair enough.'

'I'm not going to try and justify it. I don't want children, end of.'

'OK.'

And what about Ned? I thought. *Does he know this? Does he feel the same?*

She shook the rinsed-out bottle and then submerged it carefully in the steriliser.

I said, 'It's gone half-three, you know. You must be knackered.'

'I was. I've kind of got my second wind. How about you?'

'Wide awake.'

'Well.' She shot me a conspiratorial look. 'How about I make us some nice hot toast?'

As soon as she said it, I wanted nothing so badly. 'I'll do it.'

'No, you stay there, Jen. I'm already up.' Plus she'd rather prepare her own food. I knew the drill.

Helen took the unsliced loaf out of the bread bin and proceeded to cut three slices, two the depth of doorstops and one thin as a wafer. She set them under the grill and assembled butter, Marmite and some fancy strawberry conserve Mum had got in for Christmas. She checked the bread, flipped it, brought out plates and knives. The scent was making my mouth water. When the toast was cooked she brought it out and scraped her single slice with a tiny smear of Marmite, then began to slather my two with butter and jam. I laughed as a vast blob of strawberry gunk fell off the knife and landed on the floor.

'What you want to do, sis, is pile more jam on because there's only about half a pot on there.'

She smiled and pushed the plate at me. I rose and followed her out of the kitchen, and we settled together on the sofa next door.

'It's running down my sleeve,' I said, trying to intercept the trickle of melted butter as it slid along the side of my palm.

'That's why I have Marmite. An altogether better-behaved spread.'

'I'll say.'

We studied each other as we ate: Hel's small teeth nibbling primly at her brittle slice; me biting great chunks of still-doughy bread and chewing them eagerly, jam clinging to my lips. 'You're enjoying that,' she said.

'My compliments to the chef.' There was something moist on my chin. I wiped it away with my dressing gown sleeve.

'Good.'

And it struck me once again how weird she was, the way she loved to feed other people and yet continually denied herself. I said, 'I could never do what you did, Hel. Cutting everything right back. I love my food too much.'

She nodded. 'Yeah, I love food too. Some days it's all I can think about. I could sit down and eat and eat and eat and eat.'

I paused, mid-bite. This revelation stunned me. If I'd ever stopped to think about it, I suppose I'd always assumed the basis of my sister's illness was that she'd effectively killed her appetite, that it had become easy for her to deny herself food because she simply didn't feel the same urges as the rest of us. But here she was saying no, she was as hungry as me. Hungrier, probably. It was outrageous.

'Then why don't you?' I heard myself blurt. 'Why don't you just let go and eat what you want?'

'It's hard to explain.'

'Try. Please, Hel. I want to understand. Why would it be so terrible if you did get fat? Why would it matter? Plenty of people are fat and happy, fat and healthy, fat and successful. If you put on a few pounds, it wouldn't be the end of the world, would it?'

Her brow crinkled. 'It would. For me. Because . . . the way I am with food, the rules I have in place, it's sort of . . . at the centre of me. It's like a reference point that helps me negotiate the world. It's what makes me feel I'm me.' She saw me looking doubtful. 'It's like a charm almost, a talisman, warding off the chaos. A guarantee. Like that programme we watched about OCD where a man thought his family would die unless he did certain actions in multiples of four. And he was washing plates over and over, and locking and relocking the door. Oh, and like the way Mum has to have everything neat and tidy or she gets in a fluster, and I know you and Dad laugh at her for it, but I actually get where she's coming from. It genuinely matters to her. It's her security. So if the numbers on the bathroom scales stay steady, to me that's order. It's my reassurance.' She paused and raised her beautiful eyes to mine. 'Does that make any sense to you, Jen?'

'Perhaps. Some of it. But you're recovered.'

'I am. Only, when you've been used to thinking a certain way for years – especially the years when you're growing up and your personality's forming – it's a mind-set you get into and I can't imagine ever getting completely out of. Even though I've got things contained.'

'It's not right, though, is it, even now?'

She laughed. 'My head, you mean?'

'I just meant—'

'No, it's OK. It's difficult to find the right words to talk about anorexia. I *am* recovered, Jen. I think of myself as recovered. But we all need our talismans. Do you remember when you were learning to drive? You wouldn't go out for a lesson unless you had Dad's St Christopher with you. You said it made you feel in control. You knew it was only superstition, but still you wouldn't be parted from it. In fact, you freaked that time you thought you'd lost it. You turned the house upside-down.'

'Yeah, I suppose.'

'That's a little bit how I am today. But then multiply that need for one small, specific area of control by about a thousand, and that's what it's like when you have full-blown anorexia. Till it becomes the single most important thing in your life and what holds everything else together. And even though a tiny, shrinking part of you knows it's not a right or normal way of thinking, there's this other voice, the anorexia, going, "OK, then, but what have you got left if you reject me, hey? Nothing. You're nothing." That's what was playing on a loop in my head when I was at my worst.'

'Even though we loved you and wanted you to get well?'

'It was even stronger than that, Jen. When it speaks, it's deafening.'

I paused, wondering whether to push further, decided to try. I don't know what it was – the late hour, the earlier shared laughter – but I felt very close to her just then. 'Can I ask you something else? You don't have to answer.'

'Go ahead.'

'Well . . . I've always wondered, how do you *not*-eat? I mean, when you're desperately hungry and you need to fill your stomach, how do you stop yourself from clawing open the biscuit tin or grabbing a chunk of cheese out of the fridge? Because when I need refuelling, the idea of food completely fills my head till I satisfy the craving. That's the body's normal impulse, isn't it? It must be nearly impossible to fight it.'

Hel looked shifty. 'There are tricks. Techniques. You learn to fool your body.'

'How?'

'Well – having loads of water, tea, diet fizzy drinks to fill you up. If you're feeling like you need to eat but instead you have a glass of water, the urge quite often passes. And ice cubes and ice lollies are good because they take a while to finish, and they keep your mouth busy. Oh, and I got through a lots of mugs of Oxo. A lot of sugar-free jelly. A lot of sugar-free boiled sweets.'

'I remember your jelly phase. All those pots in the fridge.'

'Yeah. And as well as tricking yourself, you have to trick other people. So I'd say I was taking my plate through to wash up when really I was scraping half my dinner into the kitchen bin. I got away with that for ages. Before they started watching me. There are loads of ways you can hide food, dispose of it discreetly. Then what happens is, you find the less you eat, the less you want. Your stomach shrinks. You get accustomed to living on very little. In fact it's quite a nice, light, buzzy sensation – you feel clean and energised. Being hungry actually gives you this amazing feeling of achievement, of being "on top of yourself" – I know, it sounds weird, but that's how it is – and that offsets the physical discomfort of an empty belly. Hunger becomes something you have to beat. And meanwhile the other threads of your life seem to—' She broke off. 'No. I'm not telling you any more.'

'Why?'

'Because.'

'I won't say anything to Mum, I promise.'

'It's not that. It's the look on your face.'

'What look?'

'Fascinated. As if you want to give it a try.'

I laughed. 'No way. Truly, Hel! God, I've never even been on a diet. Not a proper one. I last about three hours and then I think, "Sod it" and scoff a Twix.'

'Good. You don't need to diet. You've got a lovely figure. You know, Ned's always checking out your cleavage.'

'He is not.'

'I don't blame him. It's not like there's much going on in my chest department, is there?' She patted her breastbone ruefully.

I put down my plate.

'How did it start? Were you trying to lose a couple of pounds so you could get Joe back? Because I know when Owen dumped me, I had days hating the way I looked, wondering how I could reinvent myself so he'd regret what he'd done. So I can see how that might have triggered something in you. Trying to look like that Saskia girl. Or was it the bullies? Did they try and say you were fat?'

Over the quiet of the room I could hear the house night-creaking, the gurgle of the radiators. I imagined Mum and Dad upstairs, their breathing deep and even, oblivious. All in the kitchen seemed peaceful. Pepper must be out for the count. The night was ours. I waited for my sister to unpack her madness.

'Again, it's hard to explain,' she said at last. 'I honestly don't remember why I decided I had to lose weight. Maybe I didn't know what else to do with myself. Maybe half a stone came off naturally because I was upset, and then that sort of became important. Like a little tiny island of positiveness in the middle of a great sea of shit. And so you get this boost, which you need, and so you try a bit harder and lose some more. It's easy at first. The weight drops off. People pay you compliments. Next thing you've developed a habit, you've got yourself into patterns of eating and meal-avoidance which are regulating your day. That's when the trouble starts because your family notice and ask questions and put pressure on you to break those patterns. Obviously you're not going to, because that would be undoing the one area of your life where you're succeeding, the one that feels as if it makes any sense. Plus it seems outrageous – how dare anyone dictate to you how much you should weigh? So you react by becoming secretive and lying. It becomes you against the rest of the world, and the harder they push, the stronger you resist. You know, like the lock gates at The Poacher, where the more weight of water's behind them, the tighter they shut. So for me that was when the eating disorder bedded in. God, there was this one evening Mum followed me upstairs with a plate of steak pie and she said she was going to stand over me till I ate it. The level of emotion I felt then was unbelievable. I actually hated her. I wanted to stab her with my fork and run out of the house. '

'Hang on. You're saying that if we'd simply left you to starve yourself, you'd have been OK?'

'No.'

'What, then?'

'I don't know. I can't . . .' She held out her palms in a gesture of bafflement. 'I'm telling you how it took hold, that's all.'

'Have you ever explained any of this to Mum?'

'How could I? We're not allowed to talk about it, are we? In any case, for ages I couldn't have articulated what was going on. I didn't understand and I didn't have the words. I was just a seething ball of self-loathing and paranoia. It's only in the last few years I've begun to see how anorexia works. And even then, only how it worked for me, and only some of it. So much of the disease contradicts itself. You have to be twisted in your head to see any logic there.'

'OK.' With every question I was edging further and further out onto an ice-covered lake. Each step forward was a risk, a potential plunge into disaster. Mum had drilled me over the years and I knew there were things I hadn't ever to ask – what her weight was now or what it had been, for example. I must never say she looked well, in case she heard it as 'fat', and I must never say to her face she looked thin in case she took it as praise. But there was so much I longed to know. 'And did you – did you ever make yourself sick, Hel?'

She shook her head. 'Thought about it, couldn't bring myself to do it. I tried laxatives a couple of times and they were a disaster. They gave me the most awful cramps and then, eugh. It was pretty rank. You don't want to hear the details.'

I wanted to ask her why she'd sometimes stolen chocolate from me, but I didn't want it to come out like an accusation. 'I've read somewhere that however thin you get, you look in the mirror and see a fat person staring back?'

'For some, I think. Not with me. I understood that I was thin. I was just never thin *enough*. I knew I was making myself ugly, I knew what a state I'd got my body into, but looking dog-rough actually becomes an excuse to despise yourself even more. The whole thing about anorexia is it's carefully tuned, designed to fuel itself. And by then it had become about much more than the way I looked, anyway. It was about denying myself and excluding myself. I decided I didn't *deserve* nice food and treats. I wasn't worthy.'

'Why, though? Was it because of the bullies? Or was it seeing Saskia and Joe together? Did that make you feel second best?'

Hel seemed surprised. 'Joe never went out with Saskia.'

'Oh! Didn't he?'

'No.'

'Really?'

'Really.'

'Where have I got that from, then?'

'I have no idea, Jen.'

I tried to think back to the snatches of Hel's history I'd managed to glean from Mum. The trouble was, all I'd ever got were dark hints and disconnected warnings. 'Saskia was involved, though? She was around at the time you got ill?'

Helen's expression became guarded. 'I thought then she was the best friend I had. The only friend.'

'So what happened?'

'She moved away.'

'I see. That was upsetting as well, then?'

'I don't want to talk about it.'

'OK.'

For a minute or so I wondered whether I'd blown the mood,

whether the shutters would come down. But no, her body language relaxed again and she laid her head against the sofa, wriggling to get more comfortable. Then she closed her eyes.

I said, 'Why *did* you ask me to check up on Joe? I mean, if it was such a miserable time for you, I can't see why you'd want the reminder. Wouldn't you just try to forget him, block him out?'

'What I wanted to know was how life had treated him,' she said, still with her eyelids shut. 'I wanted to know if he'd got what he deserved.'

'But fate doesn't work like that. Otherwise Rosa would wake up covered in boils.'

'I know. Events are mostly random, we're all careering around like atoms in a cloud. I get that. Except, the trouble with the anorexia mind-set is, you turn everything in on yourself. Therefore if I fail, it's always my fault. Always. Whereas if you make a mistake at work, say, you might blame Rosa or a computer virus or put it down to plain bad luck. Well, you might say it's your own fault, but the point is it's not an automatic impulse, the way it is with me. And last summer I couldn't stop thinking about what happened with Joe and how utterly shit it had been – yeah, even though it was so long ago. I don't know what stirred it up again so vividly. Perhaps it was making myself think about the future. But I found myself reasoning that if karma *had* caught up with him, then in a way that let me off the hook. It would mean I wasn't as crap as I thought I was. The voice of the anorexia had been wrong. The blame lay on him and he'd been punished. Do you see?'

'Karma has caught up with him, Hel. Now Ellie knows he's cheating.'

'Yeah. A mess. What do you think she'll do?'

'I've no idea.'

'Do you think she'll get a divorce?'

'I don't care. And nor should you.'

'I don't.'

She opened her eyes and lifted her head to look at me. 'Let me ask you something, Jen. Since I've bared my soul so much tonight.'

'God, yeah, go on. Anything you like.'

'Have I been a terrible big sister to you?'

The question caught me completely off-guard. 'Eh?'

'Because I know over the years I spoilt a lot of things for you. Meals out and parties. There was that night at The Riverside. Do you remember that?'

Ah, yes, The Riverside restaurant, with its velvet chairs and stunning views of the Dee. The meal had limped to its conclusion and then Dad had wanted Hel to have a dessert, but she wouldn't. He'd gone ahead and ordered her one anyway, and put it down in front of her: a huge plate of chocolate fudge cake with vanilla ice cream melting against the sticky dark icing. I suppose, looking back, the situation couldn't have been any more intimidating. We'd all gone on and eaten our puddings while she sat with her eyes screwed tight shut. She refused to even pick up her spoon. Then the waiter came with the bill and Dad said, 'We're not finished, are we? Are we?' Mum was going, 'Leave it, Don,' but then Dad started ranting about how much the cake had cost, and Helen said she'd told him she didn't want it, and Mum said yes, she had, and Dad picked up the plate and slammed it down on the table top so a load spilled onto the cloth. 'Eat it!' he'd shouted in her face, and everyone around went quiet and watched. And still she wouldn't touch it. In the years since, I've heard some people claim eating disorders are about attention-seeking, but believe me, the last thing my sister wanted then was attention. It was no wonder she still hated meals out with the family. We'd left the restaurant with her and Mum crying. That had been my ninth birthday.

And I remembered another day, Mum taking us on a girls' shopping trip to the Bullring, stocking up on new clothes and school equipment for when I started at St Thom's. But when it came to lunchtime Hel turned her nose up at every café in Birmingham, insisting she wouldn't eat anywhere that didn't serve baked potato with low-fat Philadelphia. That was what she wanted. Mum had been so grateful Helen had named a food she *would* countenance that we'd then trailed round for an hour and a half, till my feet were blistered and I was nearly faint from hunger. An early train home and a cold pasty from New Street Station was what we ended up with, while Hel sat nursing a diet Coke and glowering at passers-by. Not the fun excursion I'd looked forward to.

'Hmm. I won't pretend you haven't been a pain at times. But that's siblings for you. God, there was a boy in my class tried to kill his brother by pushing a wardrobe on top of him. I'd say, compared with that, we've rubbed along OK.'

'Compared with wanting to kill each other?'

'No, honestly.' I nudged her knee with mine. 'Honestly. You were plenty nice to me when I was growing up. What about the surprise fairy lights you clipped to my swing? And the way you helped me build that papier-mâché volcano for geography? Those friendship bracelets you said were a present from the guinea pig? You didn't need to do any of that stuff.'

She nodded faintly, and for a while said nothing. I let the

silence lengthen while we both blundered around in the mists of the past, trying to get our bearings. All the versions of Helen and Mum and Dad and me that had sat here over the years, inside these beige and cream walls.

Then she said, 'Do you want to know a secret? A huge, mad, stupid secret?'

'What?'

'They think it was deliberate.'

'How do you mean? Who?'

'Who do you think? In their heart of hearts, when you strip away the stuff fed to them by counsellors and advice leaflets, my parents believe I just didn't eat in order to spite them. They do, Jen, they truly do.'

'No.'

'Of course they do. They haven't said it in front of me – they trot out the accepted line, "Ooh, it's an illness" – but look at their reactions. Underneath everything, Dad still thinks I was just being stubborn. You remember what he was like, the threats and yelling and the way he'd jab his finger at me. "Stop being selfish, think of your mother." Meanwhile, Mum's convinced it was to do with rebelling and because I hated her, which means the eating disorder was really her fault and she can beat herself up about it forever. And this is where we are now: for all the meetings with doctors and counsellors and CAMHS staff we ever had, at the root of it my parents still won't accept anorexia's a mental illness.'

'Don't be daft. They do, Hel. They must do.'

'Their heads accept it, but when you get down to it they think it was just me, hurting them on purpose.'

I wondered whether she could be right. Far off I could hear

the siren of a police car or an ambulance as it passed a few streets away. The night was a dangerous place.

She went on, 'Don't get me wrong, I'm not thrilled with the label either. But it is what it is. When you're starving, the lack of food affects your brain. Your thought processes and judgements become properly screwed with the nutrient deficiency on top of the mental condition. You just can't think like someone healthy. That's why, from the outside, the illness makes no sense and why it drives everyone around you up the wall. Some people see you as basically rational but making bad decisions, whereas you're not capable of making decisions at all, the anorexia's doing your thinking for you. *I* didn't want to upset Mum and Dad. The part-of-me-that-was-still-me didn't. I hated seeing Mum cry and Dad shout. But the other part was stronger.'

'I believe you. If you'd been yourself, you wouldn't have deliberately hurt the people you loved. I know that.'

She shot me a look of intense gratitude.

'Look, Hel, you need to explain this, get it cleared up. Sit them down and tell them what you've told me. Or 'fess up to Ned and get him to tell them. God, I'll do it if you want, although to be honest, I'd rather not.'

'Nah, you're fine. It wouldn't do any good, whoever did the talking. You know what they're like. If I so much as hint at anything to do with eating disorders, Mum all but sticks her fingers in her ears. Dad walks out of the room. It's the great taboo. They're terrified.'

'Of what, exactly?'

'They'd actually rather believe my motivation for not-eating was wanting to punish them than that I was at the mercy of a mental health condition.'

It took a few moments for me to accommodate what she was saying. But then I could see it, and I knew she was right. How could they have allowed their home to be invaded by some strange entity, a shadowy evil that, in front of their eyes, took over their daughter? They were supposed to be the guardians at the gate. Her protectors. They should have been able to chase the bad ghost away. It must have been easier to decide their daughter just didn't love them enough, however painful that alternative might feel, because that version of events kept Helen as Helen, and not some awful changeling. If the anorexia ever returned, they needed to believe they could reclaim her.

She watched me thinking it through, then pulled her sweat-shirt cuffs over her hands as if she was cold, although it was plenty warm enough in the room. 'Really, Jen. It's best to leave it. Say nothing. Trust me.'

I found myself trying to recall the worst period. Hel had gone into hospital for a month and I hadn't been allowed to visit. That had been horrible. Mum took in board games and jigsaws while I made Get Well cards and copied cartoons I thought she'd like. I wasn't sure exactly what happened during the time she was away, but around that point the anorexia seemed to plateau, and then over the following year she began a slow recovery. Ned started having meals with us, and chatting to Helen afterwards while we were still at the table, making her laugh and distracting her. Sometimes he'd draw her into an argument about a story in the news or about the environment. She always enjoyed that. I suppose she'd been starved of intel-lectual stimulation after dropping out of school. Then it got so Mum would sort of tiptoe out of the dining room and motion me and Dad to exit too, so they could be left alone. And I remembered how one day there were just the three of us watching TV in the lounge – me, Ned and Helen – and I'd looked across and they were holding hands. I can't imagine that was their first date, crashed out on the sofa watching *Richard and Judy* while little sis goggled from the sidelines. There must have been some private moment between them, weeks or months earlier. Bless Ned for all he'd done. Without him our family might have fallen apart.

I said, 'However ill you were, though, you must've hung on to some idea of yourself to be able to find your way back.'

She nodded vigorously. 'Oh, yeah, you don't totally lose your identity. You stay *you*. It's just that a lot of the time, the anorexic voice is louder than your own. Until the day it's not and you can start to recover.'

'Well – the main thing is, you're in a very different place.'

'I am. I truly am. When I was fourteen, fifteen, a lot of stuff happened together at once. Like planets in alignment or something. It felt overwhelming and beyond my control . . . So I'm not saying I couldn't ever get ill again, but that part of my life feels a long way away. I guess I'll never be able to sit down and just eat without thinking. My brain got rewired while I was ill, and that's stuck. But it's not so *urgent* now because I'm on top of more stuff generally. When you're a teen you're surrounded by people pushing you around and making your decisions for you, and the fact you have no say in most of it can be incredibly stressful.'

'And now you have a brilliant boyfriend and a job you enjoy.'

Her face lit up. 'Oh, the job's fantastic, Jen.'

'And you love Ned.'

'Yeah.'

'And Saskia's gone, for better or worse, and the bullies have gone. And you're not hung up in any way over toss-pot Joe Pascoe any more, are you? Are you?'

'Absolutely not.'

'That's definitely all in the past, isn't it?'

'It is.'

Above our heads the Christmas star revolved slowly. Hel's eyes as they looked into mine were clear and serious, her brow smooth and sincere. The face of an angel, my sister has. How could anyone not believe her?

CHAPTER 8

Are you good enough to TAKE THE MIKE? Chester Messenger's looking for talented young performers 5–16 to enter an exciting new talent competition! TAKE THE MIKE is our chance to showcase the region's up-and-coming school-age singers, dancers, comedians, acrobats and any other type of entertainer you can think of. Tired of singing to yourself in the bathroom mirror? Fed up of performing magic tricks to your pets? Feel ready for a personal challenge? Then TAKE THE MIKE could be just the kind of break you're looking for!

Hail battered the diamond-leaded window pane, and at the far end of the office, Rosa's flirty laugh sliced across the general hum. The desk next to me was empty; Gerry was away at his aunty's funeral. On the other side of the room Alan had downloaded a new ring tone which had been going off continually, the blary theme to some 1970s sports programme. This morning had lasted about twelve hours already. Mondays are never great at the best of times, but this one was a topper.

Rosa-wise I was in disgrace again, this time for writing something in The Diary, but not on the planner – my planner, the one I'd instigated – which meant the photographer had ended up double-booked and there'd been no one to cover the dragon-boat racing on the Dee. I felt thick-headed, too, and my throat was scratchy as if I was brewing a cold. And last but not least, a flyer had arrived from Keisha inviting me to a comedy evening at Revolution, where there was an excellent chance I'd run into Owen, and was that why I'd been invited and was I mad to even think about going along? The world was against me, and I'd have sloped off at lunchtime and rung my sister for a therapeutic moan. Except we weren't speaking.

Last Friday I'd driven home early because, for no reason, I'd come over nauseous and thrown up by the water cooler. Rosa had cast one look at me and told me to get out. And take your nasty, common germs with you, she might as well have said. I'd driven myself home, confident at least I'd have the house to myself, because on Fridays everyone in our family's out at work. So when I walked into the hall and heard a man's voice coming from our kitchen, it was a shock, I can tell you. I'd gone cold with fear in case it was criminals come to do the joint over. I called out, 'Hello? Hello?' Then the back door banged and there was another thump, like someone slamming a cupboard or a drawer. Straight after that the radio came on. I thought, what kind of burglar likes to listen to Radio 2 while he goes about his ransacking?

I'd taken a deep breath and grasped my keys so they poked out of my fist, street-weapon style. But when I marched into the kitchen, all ready for a fight, what I found was my sister sitting calmly at the breakfast bar, drinking a cup of tea. 'What are you doing?' I'd said. 'What are *you* doing?' she'd replied. I said, 'I vomited over my boss's shoes. What's your excuse?' 'Headache,' she said, 'there's obviously a bug going round.' Embarrassment was flashing over her head like a neon sign. She didn't know where to put herself.

I said, 'Helen, whose voice did I hear just now?'

She shrugged. 'Jeremy Vine.'

I said, 'It wasn't. It was too deep for that.'

She said, 'He was interviewing some bloke about wheel clamping regulations.'

I said, 'Who went out of the back door?'

And she said, 'No one. I was . . . shooing a cat off Mum's flower bed.'

I pointed to the cup in the sink and said, 'And whose mug is that?'

And she said, 'It's one I made when I first came in – so I could take my tablets. Haven't got round to washing it up yet.'

She tried, but she was struggling. Not only was her colour high, I noticed she was also wearing mascara and lipstick, which she never normally does for work. *Liar* was written all over her.

'Where's your car?'

'I had to park round the corner. There was a delivery van blocking our drive.'

There and then I wanted to run outside and check the street, even if it meant I might catch, oh God, Joe's flash Audi disappearing round the corner. More than that, I wanted to shout at her to stop being so ridiculous and at least credit me with some intelligence, after what I'd done to help her.

And yet at first I couldn't. I couldn't bring myself to challenge her, couldn't make myself ask, Who was it, Hel? Was it Joe? Did you arrange to see him when you thought the rest of us would be out? Did you get in touch with him after I told you about his wife? How many times have you met him? What are you doing? What are you *doing*?

Instead I blurted, 'How's Pepper?'

She blinked, cleared her throat. 'Oh. Great. Yeah. He's in with a litter of labs and getting along well. We might even have found a home for him, although he's too young to go yet. Next month, probably. Mid-Feb. Did you really puke over Rosa's shoes?'

'Nearly. Next time I'll aim better.'

We were both pretty rattled. Immediately after, she'd taken her coffee away to drink upstairs, leaving me in the kitchen alone, but before she went she'd cast me a long, unhappy look.

'I'm sorry, Jen.'

'Is it him?' She knew who I meant.

'No.'

'Come on, I'm your sister. We can talk to each other. I could help.'

'No.' Then: 'It's not like you think. I want to tell you . . . I will do. Soon.'

I thought of the hours she and I had spent these last months building up our friendship. She'd played me for a fool. And I thought of Ned, so trusting, so honest. He had no idea what she was up to. Something in my heart hardened over.

'Yeah? Well, maybe I don't want to hear any more,' I said. She'd winced. I didn't care if I hurt her.

When she'd gone I couldn't resist going over to the sink to touch the mug that sat there. It was still warm, as I knew it would be.

And now the incident sat between us like a grenade and I was finding it hard to focus on anything else. Mum would speak to me and I could see her lips moving, but I had no idea what she was saying. Dad was barely around anyway. Ned I just avoided. I couldn't bear to be in the same room as my sister. Even outside the family – here in this overheated office, with the hail spitting against the glass next to me and Alan's stupid bloody ring tone going off every five minutes – nothing made sense. I'd be reading reports and instructions, and my eyes would slide down the page without any understanding. On the desk in front of me was a list of jobs I needed to get through within the next forty-eight hours:

email new recording studio manager and set up interview

write copy for spring fashion feature

compile top 10 healthy-eating tips for part 3 of New Year New You pull-out

track down who at the council responsible for flood management

There my notes sat. I couldn't lift a finger to deal with any of them. Alan answered his phone by going, 'Y 'ello!' and I wanted to march over and thump him.

Into the corner of my vision swam Rosa, a vision in lime green. She stood in front of me so there was no avoiding her bulk.

'Are you not better yet, Jennifer?' She made it sound as if I were being deliberately obstructive.

'I'm fine.'

'You don't sound fine. You sound like a frog.'

Whereas you look like one, I nearly said. 'I've a sore throat, that's all.'

'Have you been sick again?'

'No.'

She narrowed her eyes. 'You're not pregnant, are you?'

'No!'

My cheeks grew hot with outrage as she carried on peering at me. I knew Alan's ears would be pricked, and Tam had just walked in and was unloading her camera bag.

'If you say so.'

'It's a *bug*, Rosa.'

'Stay away from me, then, and make sure you wash your cup separately. We don't want your infection spreading about. I have a charity gala at Cholmondeley Castle this Saturday.'

Oh, sod off, you social climbing old trout. Go bother someone who's actually interested.

She leant over my desk, frowning at my notes. 'What have you got on this afternoon?'

'Two lifestyle articles. A couple of appointments to set up.'

'So, nothing pressing. Right, then, I think we'll send you out to Bankburn.'

'Why? What's there?' Bankburn was a scrap of a hamlet about halfway between Chester and home, bypassed by a fast stretch of dual carriageway. My understanding was that nothing in the history of all world news had happened there ever.

'Asda-baby.' She was turning away from me as she spoke. 'Saturday afternoon. Mum goes into labour in the deli section, no time for an ambulance, staff step into the breach.'

'God. I hadn't heard about that. Was it OK? What did she have?'

'Girl, I think. The story only came in this morning. We've got photos but we need some quotes from the mother.'

'Can't you just ring her?'

'We've tried but the number's unobtainable. *Someone* must have taken it down incorrectly.'

I racked my brains: no, not my fault, for once. I hadn't been near the phones today. I didn't know anything about this woman and her supermarket delivery. 'You want me to go out and do an interview, then?'

'That's what I said.'

So you'd rather I passed my germs onto a newborn than to you? Nice one, Rosa. 'OK. You'd better give me the address.'

I scribbled down the instructions while Alan's phone blared out its arrogant, jaunty tune once more. It was so asking to be dropped down a toilet.

'Oh,' she finished as I picked my coat off the hook, 'you can email me the piece from home, if you like. Or file it tomorrow. There's no need for you to come back to the office afterwards.'

I slipped out of the door before she could change her mind. I suppose I should have been grateful.

Surprise-baby lived down a farm track rutted and waterlogged and in serious need of resurfacing. The cottage itself was like a lot of them round here: picturesque from a distance but, when you got closer, a mess. This one had a jagged crack down the end brick wall and a wonky roof line that spoke of subsidence. The fence bordering the garden was broken, the lawn all molehills, and a busted pallet lay by the front steps.

Inside wasn't much better. The mother led me into a small lounge heated by a portable electric fire, and invited me to sit. My armchair looked as if it well pre-dated the use of flame-retardant materials, and the fabric was faded down one side where it had been in the sun. Under my feet the cheap corded carpet was lumpy and worn. Air freshener couldn't disguise the smell of damp.

While I watched the baby sleep in its Moses basket on the sofa, mum made herself coffee in a kitchen not much larger than a walk-in cupboard. On the table at my elbow sat an open bread bag and a bottle of Coke: her lunch, maybe. It was a poor place. I was glad Rosa hadn't come out here. She wouldn't have been able to disguise her scorn.

The mother, however, didn't seem anything other than happy and tired. A year younger than me, she was fair skinned with invisible lashes, a generous mouth and wide, plump hips. She sat across from me and spoke with matter-of-fact pride about her baby's swift arrival and the commotion it had caused. The manager hadn't known what to do – he was only a boy, she said – but the elderly woman from the deli counter had blocked off the aisle, rigged up a screen using clothes rails, and then got down on the floor with her to help steer the baby out. Afterwards no one had known whether to cut the cord or not, and there'd almost been an argument. In the end they'd left it for the para-medics, which turned out to be the right thing to do. She'd worried in case they made her pay for loss of earnings or some-thing, but when she got out of hospital there'd been a basket of fruit and toiletries waiting for her from the store and a card signed by everyone. Wasn't that nice? Her husband reckoned there was at least a hundred quid's worth.

I was out of my depth when it came to childbirth stories, but I at least knew the questions I should ask about timings and pain relief and the weight of the newborn, and I remembered to peep (from a germ-safe distance) into the basket and admire. She somehow made me feel immature next to her own capable life, this woman with her mouldy windowsills and tatty furniture. *No, Rosa*, I thought. *I very much wasn't pregnant, and nor was I likely to be at any time in the near future given that I didn't have a boyfriend because he'd dumped me three months ago.* And if I ever did have a baby of my own, would I manage her as calmly as this mother did, scooping her up out of the crib with firm, meaty arms, blouse unbuttoned deftly for breastfeeding?

Just then there was a knock at the front door. I got up to answer, because mum had her hands full, and found on the doorstep an infant girl dressed in school uniform and with a book bag under her arm. She turned to wave to a knackered old Fiesta before coming inside.

'Oh,' I said to the mother. 'Yours?'

She nodded. So there was an older sister. Bloody hell. I'd just assumed Asda-baby was her first. Rookie error! Rosa would have chewed me up for such an omission, and rightly so. But I wasn't myself today.

'And how old are you?' I asked, trying to recover some ground.

'Six,' she said, dropping her bag on the cluttered table and coming to sit on the sofa by her mum.

'You've been at school?'

'Yeah.'

Six. That must mean her mum had her at sixteen, maybe got caught at fifteen. Wow. What petty crap had I been fretting over when I was that age?

'And what did you do in class today?'

A shrug. 'Can I have some milk?'

Her mother sighed.

'I'll get it for her,' I said.

'No,' she said. 'I'll go. The kitchen's a mess.'

As if the rest of the house wasn't. She laid the baby back in its basket where, luckily, it seemed satisfied to be, and heaved herself up. This left me and the girl eyeing each other. She swung her legs, waiting.

I said, 'What do you think of your little sister, then?'

She pulled an exaggeratedly thoughtful face. 'She's going to be my friend. Because I'm older, I'll teach her things and show her what to do. And I need to look after her and make sure she doesn't be silly. And I'll put my toys on a high, high shelf so she can't reach them. I won't let her eat buttons. And if she's naughty I can tell her off. A bit. Not smack her, though. No smacking.'

'Cool. What did you think about her being born in the supermarket?'

'And I get to have a rabbit on my birthday.'

'Yeah? My sister had a guinea pig. It squeaked like a demon.'

She wiped her nose on her sleeve. 'Is your sister a baby?'

'She's older than me. She's my big sister. Like you. She used to teach me things. She taught me how to tie my shoelaces, and how to keep my make up bag tidy. Once she made me some puppets out of wooden spoons. And sometimes she'd mute the sound on the TV and make up silly voices for the actors. She could be very funny sometimes. I used to think she was brilliant.'

But the girl had lost interest in me and was hanging over the basket, watching the baby.

I said, 'Your sister'll grow up thinking *you're* brilliant. If you're nice to her.'

If you don't shut her out for years and then pretend to want to be friends again just so you can get her to do some dirty work for you and then throw her trust back in her face.

In came the mother, mug of milk in hand. 'Couldn't find a clean glass,' she said. 'Can't find anything clean in here right now. Never mind. You'll have to have it in Daddy's mug.'

'Daddy's mug!' said the girl, as if this was some great treat.

When I switched off my Dictaphone and packed away my notebook, they were sitting together again, the girl nestled into her mum's side and the baby quiet at their feet. Behind them I could see tiny cobweb tunnels woven palely into the folds of the curtains; the wallpaper round the light switch was dark and greasy. Which made me think of our house and its unremitting cleanliness, the regimented cushions, the dust-free surfaces, the smearless windows. The scent of fresh pine overlaying the tension and bitterness.

'You will let us know when it's in the paper?' she asked. 'We don't want to miss it, we want everyone to see. To see our baby's lucky start. Haven't we been lucky, eh?'

'I think you have,' I said.

Nowadays, letting myself into the house made me nervous. I kept replaying that previous shock, the man's voice in the kitchen, the slamming back door. This time, however, all that greeted me was quiet. I let out a sigh of relief and chucked my keys onto the hall table with a clatter. That's when I heard Mum calling.

She was using this breathy martyrish tone that, despite my intentions to be more patient, instantly irritated me. In fact I nearly didn't answer. If I could have sneaked past and run up to my room, I would have done. But the lounge door was open and I knew she'd see.

'Jen?'

Or I could turn tail and go into town. Browse the high street, sit in a café for an hour and dose myself with carbs. My sore throat was getting worse and now I had a headache as well.

'Jen!'

'What?' I said, coming into the room just a few paces. I wondered what was eating her on this occasion. A complaint against Hel or Dad, or maybe something I'd done, some domestic crime. Failure to rinse the sink after tooth-brushing? Maybe. I'd been really rushed this morning. I might have left the toilet roll holder empty, too.

'Jen. Help.'

It was her legs I saw first, sticking out from behind the sofa. For a daft couple of seconds I assumed she was down on the floor to clean the castors or polish the metal studs along the bottom edge of the frame. She likes to pay attention to these details no one else notices. It gives her more to moan about.

Then as I came round and saw her properly, the penny dropped. She'd had some sort of fall. She sat half-propped against the cushion edge, her face grey and clammy, her teeth gritted. Her skirt was ridden up on one side, exposing the top of her tights.

'Jesus, Mum. What happened? Did you trip? Have you broken something?'

'No,' she said. 'Hurts. When breathe. Jaw. Arm. Feel sick.'

That's when I guessed she was having a heart attack. I'd seen enough on TV dramas to recognise the signs.

'Oh, God! How long have you been like this?'

'Not. Long. Call Dad.'

'He's at work,' I said stupidly.

She just rolled her eyes, as well she might.

'OK, right,' I said, attempting to pull myself together. 'I'm going to make you comfortable and then call an ambulance.'

Quickly I wrenched off my coat and laid it over her, packed

her round with cushions so she was more supported, then I snatched up our phone and dialled 999. At first I was anxious about saying 'suspected heart attack' within her hearing in case it added to her stress, but then I looked back at her ashy skin and closed eyelids and realised she was beyond caring. Fortunately the guy on the other end of the line was soothing and clear. He assured me they'd have someone there within fifteen minutes. I prayed he was right.

Mum was trying to speak again. 'Don. Don.'

'He's next on my list, Mum. As soon as the paramedics arrive.' I didn't want to tie up the phone in case the ambulance needed to ring us. Was that the right thing to do? Or would refusing make her worse? Chat to her, keep her calm, the man had said – what else, what else? I could try her with a sip of water. No, because of anaesthetics – I could half remember an episode of *Casualty* where they fed a man aspirin to help his heart, so was that an idea? Oh, my mobile! Idiot! I could ring Dad on that and leave the land line clear. And Hel, I needed to call her too . . .

Next thing I was tipping my handbag upside down so the contents scattered across the carpet. Mum's hand came up to claw at her shoulder, as if she was trying to take off something tight.

'I'm calling Dad,' I said. *Do not cry, do not cry*, I told myself. *Do not cry yet*.

It wasn't until the paramedics were lifting her onto a stretcher that I managed to make contact with my dad. He'd been away from his office when I first rang, his personal mobile switched off, and his secretary had to go and fetch him. I managed to get the story out coherently and in a way that I hoped would stop him going straight into panic mode. But I could hear his distress and confusion loud and clear as he took in the news, and that nearly set me off. None of us had seen this coming.

I got him to take in the key points: that he was to meet us at the Countess hospital, that he needed to update Hel on the situation, that I was going with Mum in the ambulance so I wouldn't have my car with me. I said, 'They did an ECG so they know what's going on. She'll be all right now the medics are on top of it,' which was a bald lie because I hadn't a clue how she was doing. Very badly, I suspected. *Her lips are blue, Dad. She couldn't seem to get her breath. I think she'd wet herself. I'm frightened.*

And then I dropped everything to follow the stretcher out of the house, shutting the door behind me on the handbag, duster, coat, cushions strewn across the floor. The debris of a disaster.

They put the sirens on. It was half an hour up to Chester if the roads were clear. Mum lay with an oxygen mask over her mouth and nose, her eyes wide and pleading. They'd sprayed something under her tongue and then she'd been told not to speak. I sat beside her and held her hand. Tried not to look at the IV line feeding in painkillers, tried to stop myself thinking the worst. Made myself imagine – for something to occupy my brain – what the ambulance must look like from the outside, to car drivers and their passengers. They'd be speculating, and crossing themselves physically or mentally, saying, 'Thank God that's not me. I thought I was having a bad day but at least I'm not that poor sod in there.' Or perhaps they'd just gaze after us in a ghoulish way, spectators at a drama without any sense of human connection. There was a boy at school used to shout, 'They're coming to take me away, ha-ha!' whenever he heard a distant siren. And I remembered Mum once saying that too many people were being desensitised by television and computers and that they needed to switch off their screens and get out into the community more, say hello to their neighbours. At the time Helen had been surfing YouTube on her phone and I'd been watching *Britain's Got Talent*, and we'd both just waved her away.

I looked down at her and saw properly and close up the grey roots showing, the papery skin under her eyes. When had she got so old? Because somewhere in my mind I still maintained as my default image the mum I'd had as a little kid, a woman coming up to forty, buzzing with energy, powering through the daily chores. I think she'd been more balanced in her attitude to housework then, fussy but not obsessive. You could put something down without having her bark at you for leaving clutter. Occasionally she'd even sing as she worked, if only underneath the drone of the hoover. And in those days she'd done a lot of baking. I'd come home and there'd be a delicious rack of cooling cakes waiting in the kitchen. My small fingers poking the jam tarts before they were ready, picking chocolate chips off the top of muffins. Those cakes were the end-of-the-day, shoes off, satchel down, children's TV, home, love. But then Hel got sick and there was the business with Dad's secretary, and everything in the house went chill. Not Mum's fault. But I hadn't understood. I'd backed off, lost myself in school life, where everything was a laugh and family was a drag, an embarrassment not to be mentioned. There were no more cakes for a good long while; the tins sat in the drawer under the oven, unused.

I thought, *If Mum gets better and the hospital let her go, I'll bake* her a Victoria sponge and ice it WELCOME HOME. Helen can help me. Dad can clean the house ready. Actually, we'll do anything, anything if she just pulls through.

'OK, love?' The paramedic touched my shoulder.

All I could do was nod because my throat was too choked to speak. The ambulance leaned to one side as we turned onto the expressway. Mum's hand was sweaty in mine.

For half an hour I hung about the hospital corridor on my own, waiting for news.

I asked one of the doctors, 'Was I right, has she had a heart attack?'

He said, 'She's having one now,' and strode off through the double doors.

On one side of the corridor was a display board with notices about the patient care contract, plus some colour photos of clogged arteries. Opposite there was a picture window onto a scrubby garden. I went and stood looking out at the frost-blackened shrubs. The planters held only bare soil. Between two exposed twigs, a stripy spider trembled.

I thought, *I'm not ready for this. This should be happening in the future, far off, years away. Not yet. I want my mum here with me, and not-sick, telling me it's OK. I want someone.* I kept checking my watch and wondering what had happened to my father and sister. They should have been here by now. I couldn't text or call them because, like an idiot, I'd left my mobile behind in the house. Such a stupid, basic mistake. *Hurry up, Dad*, I willed. Every time the hospital doors opened, my heart bumped with fear. I didn't want to be the one the doctors came to with their bad news.

And then, oh, thank you God, Dad appeared at the far end of the corridor as if I'd magicked him by the pure force of need. He walked with the rocking gait of an overweight man, whilst my thin sister stalked along beside him, upright and clenched.

'Where've you *been?*' I said as soon as they got close enough.

'I had to wait for Helen to get home from the kennels.'

'I dropped everything and rushed up here,' she snapped back. 'What's the latest? Why the fuck didn't you answer your phone?' Her turn to accuse.

'Nothing yet. The doctor told me to wait here and they'd tell me.'

'And what have they said so far? What are they doing?'

'She's in surgery. There was a blockage in an artery and they found it using dye or something. They're putting in a stent to keep the artery open. What is a stent? Does anyone know?'

Dad flopped down onto one of the plastic chairs. His face was red and he was out of breath. If anyone had been due for a heart attack, you'd have thought it would be him, not my trim, groomed mother.

Meanwhile Helen remained standing.

I said, 'I left my phone behind. I wasn't thinking straight.'

'Well bloody hell, Jen. Have you any idea what it was like, not being able to get through to you?'

'I had a few other things on my mind.'

Now Dad spoke up. 'I want to talk to someone. Who do I talk to? I want to know exactly what's being done to my wife.'

'I've told you all I know. They said to wait—'

Far off a familiar figure was making his way up the corridor, coat slung over his shoulder. Ned.

'He drove up behind us,' explained Hel. 'So we'd have another car for getting home. Because Dad might need to stay. I didn't want to drive mine because I was too jittery.'

'I'm not going home,' I said. 'I'm staying here till we know she's out of danger.'

But I knew this was a silly statement. None of us knew how long Mum would be in theatre, and I hadn't brought a thing with me – no phone, no purse – only my house keys in my pocket. I wasn't carrying so much as a spare tissue. And I doubted Helen was much better prepared; she was still wearing her bib and name badge from work.

'So how are we doing?' said Ned when he caught up with us.

'Waiting.'

He nodded. 'I was thinking, my uncle Derek had a heart attack ten years ago, do you remember? And he's fine. I mean, I don't know if it was the same sort, if there are different types. Your mum's younger than he was. Which is good. Plus she doesn't eat her own body weight in chips every week. Like he did, I mean. So, you know, that's . . .'

I felt for him, twisting on the spot. Hel was busy plucking at her cuff and Dad was staring at the doors as if he hoped he'd develop x-ray vision.

'I said, 'She's only fifty-eight. Anyway, I thought it was mainly men who had heart attacks.'

Dad said, 'If they don't come out soon and tell us what's happening, I'm going in.'

Through the window a flock of sparrows had landed and were hopping about the dead garden.

'She's been working too hard, that's the problem,' said Hel. 'She got too tired and *no one noticed*.' Daggers at me.

'Aw, come on. You don't have a heart attack just because you're slightly over the top with cleaning.'

'Plus there's the stress of her job. It may only be part-time, but some of the people she has to deal with on reception are foul. No wonder she comes home wound-up. How many times did I tell you to help out more around the house?'

'I did! I did help out! I always stripped my bed every week!'

'Your own. No one else's.'

'You'd never let me into your room to do yours! I vacuum, I wash up.'

'You live in a tip.'

'God, I do just as much housework as you. You're the one who left porridge flakes all over the cooker this morning, which *I* had to clear away.'

'Well if you've wiped that hob it'll be a miracle in itself—'

'Girls.' Dad's voice was cracked and desperate. 'Please. Now's not the time.'

'But Hel's blaming me for Mum being ill and it's not fair.'

'I wasn't *blaming* you. I was saying you need to be more aware.'

'It bloody well sounded like you were blaming me.'

'Don't make this about you, Jen, because it isn't.'

'Tell you what,' broke in Ned, 'I can at least go and get us a drink, yeah? I think we're tired and stressed and probably a bit dehydrated as well. What does everyone want?'

That sobered us, slightly. One by one we gave our orders, and then he started off back down the corridor. You could see the relief in his shoulders that he was getting away.

A moment later I ran to catch him. 'I can help carry the

cups,' I told him. He nodded. There'd been no need to bother with an excuse.

He led me past the vending machine and across the hospital grounds to the main café. Once there he sat me at a table, brought me a latte and, without asking, tipped in something from a hip flask. I raised my eyebrows.

'Brian gave me this,' he said, tapping the little silver bottle.

'Who's Brian?'

'Brian the escape artist. You remember. The old guy at Farhouses who kept making a break for it. Once hitched all the way to Ellesmere Port before we caught up with him. He never went anywhere without his flask, called it his Pep-Up. And when he died, he left it to me. It comes in handy every so often. Go on, have a sip.'

'What did he die of, this Brian?'

'Chasing women.'

'No he didn't.'

'Yes he did. Every day he'd be scuttling round the grounds like Benny Hill.'

'He died of a heart attack, didn't he?'

'No.'

'You're a terrible liar.'

'He was nearly ninety, Jen.'

Ned ran his hands through his fringe distractedly. His eyebrows registered despair. I thought, *No, Jen. However shit my head is, the one thing I mustn't do is take it out on him.*

'We can't stay here too long,' I said.

'I know. But Hel'll text us if anything happens. You just relax for five minutes, yeah?'

I took a deep drink of the zinged-up coffee. The warmth of it soothed my throat.

'It was such a shock. When I found her. I didn't realise. I almost walked past her. God, imagine if I'd done that, just gone straight on upstairs and *left her* . . . And then I saw her legs sticking out. It was, it was just—'

'Horrible for you.'

'At first I couldn't make sense of it. Then I didn't know what to do. Don't ever tell anyone, Ned, but my very first instinct was to scream and run away. Isn't that awful of me? I was almost looking round thinking, Who else can deal with this? Not me, I can't deal with it.'

'But you did. You sound as if you coped brilliantly.'

'I rang 999. The paramedics did the rest.'

'You kept your mum calm. You were great with your dad. He was saying how "in charge" you sounded when you told him, how sensible you were. I think that made a major difference. Because you kept on top of the situation, that made it easier for him to break the news to Helen.'

Helen. 'How's she doing, would you say?'

'Ah, you know your sister. Not much reaction yet. But it'll all be going on inside, you can bet.'

Two middle-aged women queued up at the till, their plates piled high. They were nattering away happily to each other, ready to enjoy a feast. And I wondered who they were visiting here today that they could bear to be in such high spirits, heartless gluttons. Then after a moment I thought, Perhaps they've just had good news. It could be a celebration I was witnessing. People do get well again, have reprieves.

Ned touched his fingers to mine.

I said, 'I feel like I'm standing on a cliff edge and I can't bring myself to look down. This is my mum. My *mum*. I know we haven't always got on, but she's the only mum I have. If suddenly she isn't around—'

'Don't.'

'But what if? What if?' Tears welled up at last. I'd been holding myself together for hours. What if my mum died and left us, what family would there be? The three of us stumbling about, disconnected, not knowing what to say to each other. Perhaps I'd go and sit alone in the garage myself some evenings. The absence of my mother was simply too awful to contemplate. I longed to go back to when I was really young and life was safe and straightforward, and she was right at the heart of things. What we lose as we grow into adulthood is incalculable.

A young woman leaned by the café door, wiping her eyes on her sleeve. As I watched, a guy I guess was her boyfriend or husband came up and put his arm round her. She crumpled into him and he embraced her while she sobbed. That protective gesture made me think of Owen: how once I'd been followed from the car park by a man who grabbed my shoulder and swore at me and threatened me, and how great Owen had been when he heard about it. He'd got me a leaflet on self-defence and a Reclaim the Streets sticker for my bag. For a week he'd walked me to my car to keep me safe. Squeezed me extra tight as we kissed goodbye. And I'd *felt* safe. I thought of summer afternoons sitting on the Walls with him watching the weir, and evenings laughing in the pub with Vikki and Keisha and Saleem. A spike of unbearable longing pierced my breast. I needed to be held like that girl.

'Can I borrow your phone, Ned?'

'Yeah, course. Anything to help.' He pulled out his mobile and slid it over to me. 'Who're you calling?'

I didn't answer because I knew how he'd react.

'Jen?'

'Um . . . no one.' I should have lied. Why the hell didn't I say 'Gerry' or 'Rosa'? That would have been perfectly legit, letting them know I wouldn't be in the office tomorrow. Or even one of the zumba girls. A college mate. Anyone. Only, my mind was scrambled. I turned away to shut him out because I'd mistyped the number and had to begin again.

'Aw, it's not Owen, Jenny? Please say you're not phoning him.'

'Just give me a minute.'

'Jen, please.'

'I want to let him know about Mum, that's all. As a friend. Keep him in the picture.'

'Don't.'

'It's none of your business.' Now I'd pressed End Call instead of Call.

'It *is* my business because I care about you and at this moment you're vulnerable and this is not the right thing to do.'

His voice was getting louder. The happy women glanced up from their plates.

'How do you know it's not the right thing to do? When did you become the expert? I want to speak to him, I'm going to. God!'

'But your timing's all wrong. You're in crisis. You're confused. Look, if later on, after things have settled down, you decide you want to get back in touch with him, and you've given it careful consideration—'

'*Careful consideration?* Who the *fuck* do you think you're talking to, Ned? This isn't the Jeremy bloody Kyle show! I want to phone my ex and that's what I'm going to do.'

'Not on my phone, you're not.'

He made a grab. Startled, I dropped the mobile, which fell with a thud onto the vinyl tiles, bounced once and landed against the central table leg. I was on my feet inside a second. Never in my entire existence had I wanted anything as urgently as to speak to Owen.

'No, you don't,' said Ned, lunging towards the floor.

'For fuck's sake!'

I'd nabbed the phone first, but he had my fist imprisoned in his and was trying to prise my fingers from round the casing. 'Don't be stupid,' I gasped. The scuffle, I was acutely aware, was ludicrous, as if we were kids scrapping in the playground. We were still both kneeling on the floor under the table.

'Give it to me, Jen.'

'No.'

'Jen!'

'I only want—'

I was breathless with adrenalin, and an ace away from breaking into furious, hysterical giggles. At that moment I hated him, would have hit or kicked him if I could.

But he was stronger than me. Slowly he forced my arm up against my chest.

'Drop.'

'Don't speak to me like I'm a bloody dog.'

'I'm serious. I will have this phone. You are not calling Owen.'

'What's it to you anyway?'

His face was centimetres away and out of focus. Then his lips met mine with a dazzling shock.

Once, when I was about ten, I was in a hotel lift on my own which got stuck between floors. I'd waited for a minute or two, pressed a few buttons, pulled faces at myself in the mirrored wall. Then without warning the mechanism gave and the whole lift cage dropped down a couple of feet. My heart had nearly exploded, my blood booming in my ears. When the doors opened I'd staggered out into the carpeted corridor and fainted. That was how I felt right now. Ned's mouth was on mine, working, seeking, kissing me like a lover. Kissing me the way I'd tried not to fantasise about because he wasn't mine and never could be. The pressure on my flesh was the sweetest sensation I'd felt in my whole life. His free hand was reaching round the nape of my neck to draw me closer. Shakily I let the phone fall, but he didn't break contact, just shifted his weight so that the angle was better and he could reach me more firmly. The kissing went on. I didn't pull away. God forgive me, I didn't pull away.

A crack like a gunshot made us spring apart. I fell backwards onto the floor, sprawling, while Ned bashed the top of his skull on the underside of the table. On the floor next to my elbow I saw the broken salt pot; we must have knocked it during the struggle so that it rolled over the edge. White powder glistened on the lino. Wasn't spilled salt terrible bad luck? My muscles felt weak. I hardly knew where I was.

'Are you OK?' I heard a woman ask from behind me. I gave an automatic nod, even though I wasn't sure at all, and sat up gingerly. Opposite me, Ned was dragging himself onto the chair. He looked as disorientated as I felt. With trembling limbs I clambered onto my seat. Eyes burned into my back. Every customer in the place was watching. What must they think? I hung my head, trying to hide behind my hair.

'Oh God,' I heard Ned say. 'Oh God, I'm sorry.'

I swallowed. I knew what I should reply.

'Jen, I'm so sorry. That was unforgivable of me. A moment of madness. Say something.'

I should go, *Don't worry, it was nothing. I knew it was nothing. A clumsy collision. We were both wired and a touch mental, that's all. With the stress. It was like being drunk. We weren't ourselves. Forget it. It's wiped, it never happened.* But that would be a lie. That kiss had unstrung me. Kissing Ned was every bit as blissful and right-feeling as I'd ever imagined. Some kind of touch paper had been lit inside me and now kindled in my chest. I could feel the heat spreading through me. And already the guilt, the awful, sickening guilt. *Oh, Ned, what have you done? What have we done?*

I raised my face to begin framing the lie.

It was then that his phone beeped with a text. Ned spun the screen to face him, pressed a button.

'Hel,' he said simply.

CHAPTER 9

The Cool Girl's Valentine Survival Guide

It's just a date on a calendar, you tell yourself. An event driven by commercialism, hyped up by greetings card companies and restaurateurs and florists. Who cares if you find yourself without a partner on Valentine's Day? Big deal!

Nonetheless, it can be hard to keep cheerful when everything around you seems designed to make you feel a romantic failure. The radio's playing slushy dedications. Friends text and email to show off their Valentine haul. Every shop window you pass is plastered with red and pink hearts. Fine if you're part of it, but if not – bleurgh. Just how DO you keep your sanity and humour under that level of tacky provocation?

Rosa peered over my shoulder.

'Remember, I don't want anything bitter,' she said, flicking a finger at my opening paragraph. 'It's to be an upbeat piece, not an extended bitch about those of us in pairs.'

Seven, eight, nine, ten, I counted silently, shutting the laptop down.

Sun streamed through the tall windows of the Caxton House Hotel, creating pale rectangles across the monogrammed carpet. We were in the conference room, checking out its suitability for the final of Take The Mike. It was a job I felt I could have handled myself, but Rosa insisted on coming along on the basis that We Had To Get It Right (subtext: I don't trust you not to book the event in a broom cupboard).

A porter came and hovered. 'The manager's on his way. Well, another five minutes or so. Sorry for the hold up.'

Rosa huffed, but I knew she was secretly pleased that the hotel proprietor had been delayed because it meant she got to have a good poke around on her own. At one end of the venue was a stage, and in front of that a modest dance area. The rest was audience or dining space. Tables and chairs were stacked against the walls in readiness for the next big do, a wedding or a Rotary dinner perhaps. Ned had told me that the Masons met here.

'We're clearly going to be kept waiting for a while longer, Jennifer. If you want, you can ring your mother.'

The kindness of the gesture took me by surprise, although, to be fair, Rosa had been good about my mum. She'd let me set up remote access on the *Messenger* website so I could work from home, and she'd reallocated various duties to Alan and Gerry without fuss or complaint.

'Oh, could I? Just a quick call to see how she's doing. That would be great.'

'As long as it is quick.'

'Yeah, yeah. She comes out of hospital today—'

My boss raised a hand to tell me to stop. I saw she was checking her own mobile.

I took myself into a corner and tried my sister, who had booked the day off so she could be there when Mum got back. Hel picked up straightaway.

'They home yet?'

'No. Dad said it would be after eleven before she was discharged, and then there are those roadworks at Bankburn, that'll hold them up.'

'Have you vacuumed round?'

'Vacuumed, dusted, mopped the kitchen, wiped the windows. Oh, and descaled the shower head because I know she hates it when that's all chalky.'

'Have you hidden the little stepladder?'

'Mrs Harris has taken it and stored it in her shed for us.'

'Good. We don't want Mum straining after cobwebs or de-fluffing lampshades. She mustn't have any excuse to exert herself.'

My mother was being let out of hospital under strict conditions. She was on a cart-load of drugs, for one. Also, she'd been signed up to a cardiac rehabilitation programme where she'd be taught to reduce her risk of another heart attack. From now on she'd have to get regular flu jabs and watch her diet and take particular note of any pain or breathlessness when exerting herself. She'd be off work for two to three months.

'You've been lucky,' concluded the surgeon who did her angioplasty. 'Because we got to you quickly, there wasn't much damage to the muscle. But your family history puts you in a high-risk group so we need to be on top of that in future.'

The rest of us had just looked at each other. Family history?

Turns out her mum and her aunt had both been victims of heart disease. The aunt had moved to Australia and died before I was born, so her health problems were well off our radar, and Hel and I had always assumed it was old age killed Grandma Lyons. Apparently not. Mum's arteries were furred up with cholesterol, and that meant a new regime of low-fats and statins. 'It's time to let your family take care of you for a change,' the consultant had finished, leaving Hel and I skewered together on our own guilt.

Across the other side of the room, Rosa's phone snapped shut. 'Finished, Jennifer?'

I said to Helen, 'Got to go. I'll ring you later, find out how she's gone on.'

'If you want. But *don't* be late back tonight.'

'Obviously.'

'Because Mum'll want us all together and Ned's coming round and I'm cooking a—'

I pressed End Call quickly.

'He's still not here,' growled Rosa. 'As if we didn't have enough to get through today. I told the manager ten thirty. Ten thirty, I said. And *we* were here on the dot. It's common courtesy to be punctual.'

I said, 'Shall I fire up the laptop again so we can see the latest rankings?'

She shrugged, so I took that as a yes. I brought up the Take The Mike webpage with its rows and rows of video uploads. Competition-wise, the first nine finalist places had been assured via the reader coupon system, but there was another week of voting for the tenth, plus a wildcard to be chosen by us (my idea). We'd ended up with a good spread of talents, and no one pushed to the top who was awful. My favourite was a six-year-old ballet dancer with ebony skin and hair scraped into high, fat bunches like Minnie Mouse ears. But I also liked a skinny teenage boy comedian with a broad Liverpudlian accent, and a floppy-fringed girl who played classical guitar. Gerry's favourite was a high-stepping, baton-twirling majorette, while Alan's money was on a kid of twelve who did tricks with a football.

I scrolled through the most recent uploads.

'What's that there?' asked Rosa, pointing with a plum fingernail. She really does have an unfortunate tone at times.

'It's a lad doing close-up magic.'

'He's in a wheelchair.'

Full marks for observation. 'And?'

'That'll pull in some interest. Does it say anything about his background?'

'Only that he's been interested in magic since he was tiny, and that his favourite performer is Dynamo.'

'Do we know why he's in a chair?'

'I don't think so. It doesn't say.'

Rosa looked thoughtful. 'Hmm. Well, I think we could do something with this. Get more info, for a start. Make him a feature. And isn't there another disabled entrant?'

'On Monday we got sent that clip of the two brothers who perform an extract from a film. One of them has Down's syndrome.'

'Really? Excellent! How did I miss that? Then we should definitely make a feature. It would be better if we had at least one more performer, though. Are you sure there's no one else? Have you been right through them, biogs and all? It doesn't have to be an obvious disability. A prosthetic limb would be great. Even someone with a skin disease, or mild hearing loss, something like that. If they weren't *that* disabled we could always play it up. Then maybe we could have a special section during the performance.'

I gaped at her. Sometimes she was so offensive it left you temporarily speechless.

'Or alternatively, Rosa, they could compete on an equal platform and be placed in the competition on their own merits without anyone patronising them.'

She shook her head in exasperation. 'The trouble with you, Jennifer, is that you don't see the possibilities. People like a sob story.'

'Who says either of these is a sob story? Because these performers are disabled, you mean? No. Not acceptable, Rosa. See our magician: he's there because he's skilled at magic. The wheelchair has nothing to do with anything. The boy with Down's syndrome is in a proper drama group. He performs professionally; his mum says he's auditioned for TV. The point is, he's a good actor.' I saw her brows come together in a frown as she processed what I was saying. '*You* might want to run a Tragic-but-Brave narrative, but it's old-fashioned, it's not relevant here, and it could be construed as really insulting. Hauling these kids out specially and patting them on the head – there, there, well done you – it's naff. Can you not see that?'

Her lips were tight with annoyance. It wasn't like me to stand up to her with such force. I wasn't even sure where that speech had come from. I was glad I'd made it, though.

We were spared any further discussion by the arrival at last of the hotel manager, a buzz-cut, sharp-suited guy who looked not much older than me. He looked familiar too, and when I read his name badge I realised he'd been head boy at St Thom's two years above me. Not that he'd remember a lowly Year 11, as I'd have been. Unless he'd been among the group of prefects who'd reported us for our spontaneous foam party in the sports block toilets. His head girl partner had gone on to find brief and local fame on a reality TV show set in a Chester gym, *The Bod*. I'd done a piece about her last year, just after I started at the paper.

Rosa took charge, as I knew she would. The manager was all apologies for keeping us waiting, all your-humble-servant, which is what she likes, and they immediately got down to layouts and formats and timings and how many perks *The Messenger* could squeeze out of the deal in return for some hotel promotion. I stood by and took notes as I'd been primed, and wondered how Mum was getting on. I remembered how she'd been after her op, how she'd looked up at us woozily and said, 'Sorry,' as if her having a heart attack had been some deliberate inconvenience. A chock inserted in the family mechanism for devilment. Then her eyes had refocused and, hooray, she'd begun telling me off for having a hole in my sweater. Hel and I hadn't stayed long that visit because we were frightened of tiring her; we'd left her with Dad for a spell. As we were leaving the ward I'd glanced back and he'd been stroking her hand, and it was amazing because that was the most intimate gesture I'd seen him make towards her in a long time.

'That won't do,' my boss was saying. Her powerful shoulder muscles moved under her cobalt blouse as she pointed at the stage, swept her arm around the seating area, tapped the brochure. I thought with a pang of envy how easy her life must be, barging through each day untormented by any personal doubt or inadequacy. Life was gilt-edged for Rosa. According to Gerry, her suitor kept a holiday house in France, somewhere on the coast. Well of course he did. Probably had a private jet to take him there. Alan thought the guy might be a solicitor, although last month Rosa had gone to a fundraising dinner at the Nuffield along with a bunch of surgeons . . .

The consultant's face popped into my mind again, his gold-rimmed glasses and beaky nose. 'Will she be OK now?' my sister had asked him as soon as Mum was out of theatre. 'She will if she's sensible,' was the reply. 'She's had a warning and she needs to take notice. You need to take notice.' Cue evil eye at me from Helen. And then there'd been that horrible drive home from the hospital, Hel with Ned (thank Christ), me in Dad's car feeling so churned up and ashamed, I'd had to have the window rolled down in case I threw up. Home to a dark, motherless house that smelt upsettingly of pee, and the sense that nothing in our family would ever be the same again.

'OK, OK, I think we can do that if you can get hold of some better lighting, and if we can look at bringing down the cost of drinks – maybe do some sort of voucher system as part of the ticket price.' Rosa turned her head to me, imperious. 'I hope you're getting this down, Jennifer.'

And I dropped my eyes to my notebook where I hadn't written a thing.

As soon as we returned to the office, she sent me out again, this time for a bottle of champagne. 'For a client,' she said. Behind her back, Gerry mimed a glugging-out-of-the-bottle action. I couldn't have cared less. It was a walk in the cool sunshine to M&S, past the flirty *Big Issue* vendor and the street stall selling scarves, and the Christian evangelist and the scented doorway of Lush cosmetics. I was wondering whether it was too soon to ring home and enquire after Mum, or if I should leave it an hour till she was settled, when someone plucked at my jacket from behind. I spun on my heel to find Vikki, looking apologetic.

'Sorry,' she panted. 'I've been trying to catch you up. You can't half move quick.'

'Ah, well, I'm on a mission. Rosa's sent me to fetch champagne.'

'Yeah? Coincidence. I was just off to buy a bottle myself.'

'Really?'

'Er, no.'

We stood for a moment while she got her breath. She'd braided her hair across her scalp, Heidi-style, and it suited her. Under her jacket she was wearing a red T-shirt with 'Sisters of the Revolution' written across the chest together with the bookshop's website address. She saw me looking. 'Do you like it? We've just had them printed. There's a "Brothers of the Revolution" too. I can get you one if you want.'

'Yeah, go on. Why not? I'll wear it to work.'

'I bet you will.'

We smiled at each other.

'Anyway,' she went on, 'how are you doing? Because I saw some messages on Facebook. About your mum. She's not well? Is it something serious?'

I exhaled noisily. 'God, Vikki. Yeah. Since you ask, it's been pretty awful. My mum's recovering from a heart attack.'

'Oh, my God.'

I shepherded her to one side, out of the main flow of pedestrians, to where we could talk properly. Then I told her how it had been for us, the events of the week, and how we were going to have to change and look after her better. I gave the impression that we were pulling together. I did not say that my sister and I were speaking to each other through gritted teeth and that my head was a seething mess of fear, resentment and desperate, desperate longing. That when I wasn't worrying about Mum having a relapse, I found myself consumed by replays of Ned's kiss, and heated, shameful fantasies of us getting together, overlaid with towering fury that Hel should ever even think about playing away, let alone with a git like Joe Pascoe. Shame too that I'd played a part in rekindling that relationship. This narrative was so loud in my head, there'd been occasions when I thought I'd open my mouth and simply shout out the truth and damn the consequences. But for now it was vital I kept everything to myself. No boats must be rocked while my mother was still so fragile or Lord knows what doom I'd unleash on the family.

Vikki was shaking her head. 'That's terrible. Poor you. I wish you'd let us know.'

'I would have, if Owen and I were still . . . It's tricky, the way things are.'

'You know, he sent me today to look for you.'

'Then why didn't he come himself?'

'He was worried how you'd react.'

Somewhere in the background the Christian evangelist was shouting that each new day was a gift. It is *precious*, he was yelling. It is an *opportunity*. It is *granted to you through God's love*.

Vikki said, 'Look, I don't want to put you on the spot. But could you just call him? Update him. He wants to know you're OK, that's all.'

'*Is* that all, though?'

'You need to speak to him, Jen.'

'And if I don't want to?'

'That's up to you.'

And every day that dawns is a *promise*: that through His grace, *you can be washed clean and start again.* No matter *what* came before. Begin again *spotless.* That is God's offer to *you.*

I said, 'So much is happening. I don't know where I am.'

'We miss you, though. Sometimes I watch the shop door because I'm convinced you're going to come walking in any minute.' She touched my arm sympathetically. 'It's such a shame how things turned out. Bloody Chelle.'

'Yeah, bloody Chelle.'

'You know she told him she was going to help out in an orphanage in Phuket? Turns out she's met this guy and is just hanging around the beach bars with him instead. Scrounging off ex-pats. Owen was very disappointed in her. Gutted, actually. It's made him question a lot of things.'

'Good.'

'Yeah.' Vikki looked rueful. 'Too bloody late now, of course. Anyway, all the best with your mum. Text us and let us know. Text me if you can't face him. Oh, and if you've a spare minute, pop into our new Facebook page, we've revamped it. We do a Book Hero of the Week, and the shop events are listed. You might see something you fancy.'

'I might.'

'See you on there, at least.' Then, with a brief apologetic grin, she was gone, retreating into the crowds of shoppers and quickly lost in the masses.

At the end of the day I came home to a house which was super-heated and reeked of disinfectant; Hel always added too much Dettol when she mopped the kitchen floor. But the main thing was Mum was home. They'd set her up on the sofa, along with all the cushions we possessed, plus a padded stool for her feet and, at her elbow, a shabby tea trolley Dad must have unearthed from the garage. On the trolley were bottles of pills and water, her reading glasses, a paperback, half a sandwich, a pear, a magazine, her mobile phone and the TV remote. Everything she needed to keep her content.

Hel was perched on the low stool, reading a British Heart Foundation leaflet on cardiac rehabilitation. From the clicks and clunks and cursing going on in the kitchen, I guessed that Dad was attempting to put on a clothes wash. I saw that some furniture had been pushed against the wall, out of the way, and a few of our ornaments were missing. Hel had said she might put the fiddlier ones into storage to save on dusting.

I dropped my bag and ran over to my mother.

'Don't leave that there. Mum might trip over it,' said Hel immediately.

I pushed the bag with my foot so it was under a chair. Then I switched my attention to Mum.

Now she was home, amongst these familiar surroundings, you could gauge the effect of her illness better. To my eyes she seemed to have aged even more. Her hair was wild and unset, she wore no make up, and her hand when I took it was dry and unmoisturised. Really I just wanted to gather her against me and hug her tight. Or rather I wanted her to hug me tight and say everything was going to be OK and I was safe.

'Hello, love,' she said.

'So glad you're back!' I leaned in and kissed her brow, feeling a wave of emotion break over me. 'Was it a good journey?'

'Not too bad.'

'"In the first few weeks after you come out of hospital you are likely to have good days and bad days. But as time goes by, you should improve steadily and gradually feel better,"' Helen intoned.

Dad walked in and set down three cups of tea. 'Oh,' he said when he saw me, 'I didn't realise you were here. I'll go stick the kettle on again.'

Hel tutted. 'No, Jen can get her own.'

'I'm fine,' I said.

He sat down heavily and she returned to her booklet. '"For the first two or three days it is best to take it easy . . . each day, try to get up, wash and dress, do some light activities such as making drinks and snacks, go up and down the stairs a few times and do some gentle walking." Are you listening, Mum? Take it easy, the book says. Anything that needs doing, I can do it.'

'Or me,' I said. 'Ask me. Hey, are you warm enough? Shall I get you a shawl from your drawer?'

Mum smiled and shook her head.

'"You can begin doing *light* work in the house as soon as you feel fit and able – for example, washing up and dusting. After a few *weeks* you may feel well enough to do other jobs such as vacuuming." So no going near that Hoover, yeah? In fact, if I find you've even opened the cupboard and looked at it, I'll be cross. We will, won't we, Dad? No joking.'

'I defrosted the freezer for you yesterday,' I said.

'Yeah, and flooded the floor. And all the tea towels needed washing afterwards.'

'I cleared up. The towels are clean and aired.'

'Thank you,' said Mum.

'"When you can start driving again depends on your heart

condition and the sort of treatment you have had. You need to contact the DVLA to make sure it is safe for you to start driving again. Many people who have had a heart attack are not allowed to drive for the first month.'"

'We know that,' said Dad. 'The doctor told her. It's on my list.'

I said, 'Shall I put your Get Well cards up, Mum?'

'Done it,' said Hel.

'Where?'

'In the hall. Didn't you notice when you came in?'

'She can't see them there. They should be in here, on the bureau.'

'I thought they'd keep getting knocked off.'

'But there's a draught in the hallway. Every time anyone opens the door they'll be blown over.'

'Yeah? Do you want to go test it out, Jen?'

I actually would have, but then I glanced at Dad's expression and stayed where I was.

'"If you have had an uncomplicated recovery, you can usually start sexual activity when you feel—". Oh, God, you can read that chapter on your own.' Helen dithered with the pages of the booklet, trying to find a blander section. With her lips pressed together disapprovingly, her expression was for a moment so like Mum's it was uncanny. They don't look much like each other – Hel doesn't favour any of us, though she gets her red hair from Dad's gran, apparently – but in that moment she was her mother's daughter. 'OK, this is a good bit: "What happens on a cardiac rehabilitation programme." Do you want to hear?'

Mum opened her mouth, then shut it again. We waited, poised to hear what it was she desired.

But then Dad leaned forward on his seat. 'You know what, girls? I reckon your mum's ready for a nap. Yes? Do you want to go up and have a proper lie down, love?'

'Well, if no one minds. I didn't sleep well last night. You don't in hospital. All the noises and the lights. And the woman in the bed next to me kept muttering to herself.'

Helen sprang up. 'Good idea. I need to get on and make the meal, anyway.'

'I'll help,' I said.

'You need to come through and see what I've done with the fridge,' she told me over her shoulder. 'I rearranged the cupboards today, sorted out the healthy foods Mum needs. Because we're going to have to change, as a household.'

With care and concentration, Mum got to her feet and reached for Dad's support. We watched as he led her out of the room and to the foot of the stairs, where she began to climb the steps gingerly one by one. I could feel the effort myself, the grip of her knuckles on the banister, the strain of her thigh muscles with each haul upwards; tried hard not to imagine the dark and blood-rich heart muscle pumping away beneath her rib cage. After a few moments I made myself look away, and in doing so noticed one of her Get Well cards had fallen off the telephone table onto the carpet. *Hope you're flying high again soon!* If Hel spotted it, she didn't say.

Hel had indeed reorganized the kitchen. One cupboard was full of pulses and seeds and tinned tomatoes and tuna and sardines and brown rice. Our usual jam had been replaced with a high-fruit version, and the salt with a low-sodium one. Certain bottles of sauce had vanished, and in their place were ranks of herbs and spices. Even some of Mum's baking ingredients were different, so the shelf now boasted a packet of wholegrain flour and, alongside the sugar, something called Splenda. The cooking oil had been pushed to the back and there was a bottle of Flora Cuisine and a can of FryLight sitting in an easy-reach position. We seemed to have a whole supermarket's worth of Shredded Wheat stockpiled. Hel hadn't got rid of my favourites, she explained, just put them in the corner cupboard to make us think first about using them. She reckoned she was going to buy one packet of chocolate digestives a week, and when they were gone, they were gone. 'Because there are only four of us in this house, and I don't touch them, so that ought to be enough.' As soon as she said this I had a craving for an entire plate-full.

Finally she revealed the fridge, packed with salad and fruit juice and lean meat and more low-fat dairy. When I protested about missing my butter, she said, 'We need to support each other. Can't you do this for Mum?' Then, as she closed the fridge door she said, 'Anyway, there are implications for us, too.'

I'd not wanted to think about it, but she was right. If heart disease ran in the family, Hel and I could well be next in line. It was certainly something we needed to factor into our lifestyles. This was a good point to take stock, she said. It would do the lot of us good to eat better, get ourselves checked over at the doctors'. She placed an onion in my hand and I stared at it, stunned by a spike of fear at my own mortality. 'Chop that,' she told me.

Together we began preparing a lasagne, one which used quorn mince instead of beef, and cheese sauce made with reduced fat cheddar, and twice the usual amount of veg. She boiled up tomatoes with garlic and mixed herbs for extra flavour.

'See. No need for salt, then, is there?' And I watched her lecture, like some TV presenter, and I thought, *She's actually enjoying this. She's almost happy because now there's a reason for her rules and we're all in tune at last.* It was hard not to be annoyed by the preachy tone, yet I also had to admit it was a relief that she was ready to take on the responsibility, just sort out the shopping and menus for the rest of us. I could always eat butter at work, if I wanted. Maybe I would and maybe I wouldn't. I'd get my cholesterol measured first.

'Pass me the whisk, will you?' Hel asked, and as I pulled it out of the pot with the daffodils on the side, my memory was jolted and I thought of the bunch of flowers I'd bought for Mum while I was in M&S, and left wilting on the parcel shelf of my car.

'Back in a sec,' I said, and nipped out to get my keys.

It was dark and spitting with rain when I opened the front door. I put my head down and scuttled to the car, unlocked it and reached over the rear seat for the flowers. That's when, out of nowhere, I felt someone grasp my shoulder hard, in a pretty much exact replay of that time I was harassed on Chester Walls car park.

'Get *off* me,' I shouted, stamping my foot down hard and jerking my elbow backwards. I was only acting on instinct.

There was a winded yelp, and then Ned's voice went, 'Fuck's sake!'

I pulled my head out of the car, turned to see, and he was bent over, stumbling across the tarmac, in obvious pain. 'God, are you OK?'

'What do you think?'

He straightened up cautiously, rubbing at his stomach.

I should probably have been apologetic, but I was a bag of

jitters after the shock of being grabbed, never mind the other feelings he aroused in me at the moment. 'What did you think you were doing?'

'Trying to speak to you, Jen.'

'Not now.'

'Yes, now. You've done a great job of avoiding me for two weeks, and I'm not having it any longer. You won't return my texts or emails, you won't speak on the phone. What am I supposed to do?'

'Nothing. Leave it. That's the point. Can't you take a hint?'

'Not in the circumstances, no. We have something we need to talk about.'

'No, we don't. There's nothing to say.'

'But there is.'

I ducked into the car once more and fished out the bouquet. I was drawing a line under this conversation. But as I slammed the rear door shut, he came at me again, took my arm, pushed his face close to mine. 'You have to listen. Please. Two minutes. I won't go away, you know. I'll keep on trying till you let me speak. I'll send a bloody carrier pigeon if I have to.'

'Just leave it.'

'No.'

'Jen, I'm begging you.'

I twisted my neck as far away from him as I could and held the pose. With a sigh he eventually let me go and stepped away, his shoulders drooping. I felt a pang, in spite of myself.

'What can I do here?' he said.

'Nothing. Don't do *anything*. That's the point.'

A cat crossing the lawn made next door's security light click on, and I jumped guiltily. In that moment of distraction, Ned strode forward and took my free hand, leading me down the side of the house to the garage. I let myself follow. I could have fought him, but what was the point? He'd only come back at me another time. Perhaps it was better to get it over with.

In the narrow gap between the walls we were sheltered from the rain but not the wind. A sharp breeze whipped my hair across my mouth and into my eyes. With clumsy, fumbling fingers he brushed it away and held the sides of my face so I was forced to look directly into his eyes.

'You're angry with me, I get that. But tell me what you think happened in the hospital café,' he said.

'I don't want to talk about it.'

'We have to.'

'No, we don't. We need to forget it and move on. "Least said, soonest mended," as my mum says.'

'Give me strength!'

His fierce tone stung me. I gripped the bouquet and tried once more to dodge past him, but he blocked my path.

'OK, listen,' I said. 'Nothing happened in the café. We were wound up and confused. We bumped into each other and there was a friendly moment of reassurance between us. That's it. Finished.'

'"A friendly moment of reassurance"?'

'Yes.'

'You really believe that?'

'Look, Hel'll be coming out any minute to see where I've gone. I'm supposed to be cooking tea with her—'

Ned touched my chin gently. 'I know I should be apologising here, but I can't. I mean, I don't regret what I did. The timing was way off, I'll grant you, I should have waited . . . But you were there right in front of me and I've never wanted anything as much as I wanted to kiss you then.'

'Stop it.'

'You know, don't you? I've wanted to kiss you for ages. You've felt it.'

'No.'

'You kissed me back.'

'I did not.'

'Jen, for God's sake—'

'What good will it do?'

'I'm in love with you. I'll go insane if I don't say it.'

I shrank deeper into the shadows, terrified someone might see or hear. Just my breathing in this narrow brick space sounded incredibly loud. 'Well you mustn't. You're not free to come out with stuff like that. You're attached, if you remember. To my sister. Practically engaged.'

'Not engaged.'

'But . . . *promised*.' I couldn't think how else to express it. Ned had taken Helen on when she was ill, had been her friend and saviour and supporter as well as her lover. It wasn't like an ordinary relationship, you couldn't just walk away from something so intense. Switch horse mid-race. That would destroy her. More, it would destroy our family. 'She needs you.'

'But she doesn't love me any more.'

My throat went tight as I thought: *He knows! Oh, dear sweet Jesus, he knows about Joe!*

Even in the midst of my alarm I wondered how I was going to play the next few minutes. Surprised? Indignant? Or confessional, a sharer in his righteous outrage and betrayal? *Yes, yes, she fooled me too*, I could say. *She drew me in and got me to search for her ex on*

the internet, and I did it because I believed her when she said she only
wanted to put to rest a ghost, and now I hate her for the way she's used
me and for not being the sister I thought she was and for choosing to
pursue a tosser – who's married, with children even – and for cheating
on you, you lovely-lovely-man-who-deserves-so-much-better.

Part of me prayed like mad this moment was it, that despite
the pain and fall-out there'd be, the uncoupling of Hel and Ned
was now going to happen and would be nothing to do with me.
And then he'd be free and mine, and the world would slot rightly
into place around us. My head swam with possibilities.

'Hel does need me. Or she believes she does. But she doesn't
love me.'

'How can you be sure?' I whispered.

'Little things. When you've been with someone that long,
you just know. We're running in parallel, just mates. Not
boyfriend and girlfriend. There's no intimacy. We're like an old
married couple who rub along. It's been that way for at least a
year. Eighteen months, maybe. I've stuck it out – I do care
about her, a lot – I don't want to hurt her or send her off-
balance again, God knows – but there's no real joy in it any
more. We've come apart.'

'Has anything happened?'

He thought for a moment. The hesitation seemed to last an
age. 'She's changed. No single thing I can pin-point. But she's
gradually drawn into herself. No, that's wrong; she's drawn away
from me. Grown, I suppose, with having the job. You must have
seen it too, how she's going off on her own more. Going to a
different dance class to you. I mean, she still wants to see me, but
there's just more in her life. Which should be good. It is good. If
she's happy. Is she happy, Jen?'

It was on the tip of my tongue to tell him the truth about his girlfriend. *I'll tell you what's distracting her, Ned, and it isn't bloody zumba.*

So why couldn't I break the news? Because I wasn't one hundred per cent certain it was Joe she was seeing (although I was, really). Because underneath everything I loved my sister, and still felt nostalgic for the days when we'd been getting on better. Because I felt implicated, and I couldn't bear for Ned to think ill of me, even if he only judged me to have been naive and stupid. But more than any of those, because I couldn't bear to be the one who delivered the blow. Whatever his feelings for my sister, the knowledge that she'd been cheating on him for months would just unman him. The fall-out would be horrible. Our house would be hell. And what if Mum's worst fears were realised and the upset kicked off Helen's illness again? The bad planets aligning over her head once more, the feelings of powerlessness surging up. Joe nowhere to be found, I'd be prepared to bet. And my mother in her own fragile condition, fretting from the sidelines.

Not on my conscience. I simply could not be the one to detonate the bomb.

'I've no idea whether she's happy, Ned. But if you want to end it with her, then you have to find a way to do it. Don't make me your excuse.'

'No. But if I did end it—'

'I'm not answering.'

'If it did finish, would you be—'

'Don't ask me.'

'I think I already know. The way you kissed me back.'

My heart was thudding at his nearness, at the trembling in his voice. I could hear how much this was costing him. I longed to say what he wanted to hear, to throw my arms around him and soothe, to rub my cheek against his, and smell his scent, fold myself against him. The moment was there, opening up and ready for me. But he wasn't mine, he wasn't mine. Move away. Hands by your sides, girl.

'Please, Jen. I'm going mad here.'

His forehead coming down gently to rest against the top of my scalp. The bunch of flowers falling from my grasp.

The next moment we heard the noise of the front door clunking open and TV music drifting out. Before we had chance to rearrange ourselves into a less compromising pose, Dad's bulk appeared round the corner. There he stood for a few moments, squinting into the shadows, trying to make out who it was hiding themselves down his alleyway. Peering, stepping forward uncertainly. 'Jen? Who's that?'

Realisation dawning, and surprise, and then his disappointed, confounded, moon-shaped face hanging in the gloom, just staring at us.

'It's quite like old times,' said Mum, settling herself at the table. Hel had gone to some trouble, laying out the embroidered cloth and arranging my flowers in a vase at the centre. Now she stood at the end with the serving spoon poised over her lasagne.

'OK, pass up your plates.'

The truth was, none us of had any appetite. Mum looked zonked, still blinking from her nap. Dad was tight-lipped and glum, and Ned and I were too guilty to feel hunger. One by one we accepted our food without enthusiasm. Only my sister began to tuck in with relish, while the rest of us forked pasta and quorn mechanically into our mouths, not daring to do otherwise.

'Everything OK?'

'Delicious,' I said.

'It's lovely, darling,' said Mum.

Helen glowed. 'Loads of veg in there. Under ten grams of saturated fat per portion, no added salt, four hundred and seventy calories all in. I've laminated the recipe and I'm going to put it in a ring binder, for easy reference.'

'That's thoughtful of you.'

'When you're feeling better I can show you some more.'

'Great.'

Dad kept throwing me looks, as if he was trying to work something out. I refused to meet his eye, which I suppose only made him more suspicious.

'Is it still squirrel-city at Farhouses, Ned?' asked Hel.

'Yeah. Caught a couple more last week. Bopped them on the head with a length of piping.'

'You did not.'

I said, 'How's Pepper doing? Did he go with that family in the end?'

'Mmm. They were so excited to take him.'

Dad cleared his throat but said nothing.

'We had some more pups in yesterday, been left in someone's front garden. So at least they were found quickly.'

'Will you have to hand-feed those too?' I asked, worried in case we might cop for one.

'No. We've put them with a foster mum. The problem for Pepper was we had no lactating bitches in at the time. But this lot have landed on their feet. All black, they are, and all boys. Four of them.'

It seemed to me that as we sat and ate, the room became

more and more echoey. Our voices sounded small, as if we were in some big, high-ceilinged room, and the cutlery clattered on the china and my drinking glass clinked against my teeth. The silences between each line of conversation were loud as thunder.

'Did I use too much garlic paste? I could use less, and more herbs. No? It's fine, is it? Is the mince cooked through? Can you tell it's not meat? You can get quorn fillets too. Do them like chicken pieces. Marinate them.'

My mind churned with images of the day: the grand, swagged curtains in the Caxton House Hotel; Rosa's talon tapping at my laptop screen; the black-skinned girl in her shell pink tutu, revolving; Vikki standing amongst the crowds, holding her jacket open to show her new T-shirt; Ned looming out of the darkness, touching my face, pleading. Ned. Ned. I'd have given a hundred pounds to be out of this room.

'And there's stewed apricots for pudding,' Helen went on. 'Sweetened with Splenda, and I've made a sort of crumble topping out of low-fat digestives. But you don't have to have that if you don't want. It's in a separate dish so you can spoon it on. Or you can put fat-free vanilla yoghurt on top if you'd rather.'

I glanced across at Mum and she was making pretty slow progress. I reckon she'd eaten maybe a fifth of what Hel had dished out for her, and she was stalling, pushing the food around her plate and chopping the pasta into smaller and smaller pieces.

'The trick to healthy eating is not to have the bad stuff in the house to begin with,' said Hel.

What would Owen be doing? What would he be eating for his tea, and where, and who with?

After a few minutes more, my mother gave up the charade.

'I'm so sorry, love, I can't manage any more.' She laid down her knife and fork carefully.

'What?'

'Do you mind if I don't finish? It was delicious, but I'm just very, very tired.'

Hel struggled to keep her expression calm. *Two hours I've been working on this meal!* said the thought bubble over her head. *Two hours, and look at you all.*

'Oh. OK, Mum,' she said.

'What I might do is pop upstairs and have another nap.'

'Well, I can bring you some up later. I'll save your plate under foil, then reheat it, it'll be fine.'

'No, really, I've had enough.'

'Your mum needs to lie down,' said Dad, pushing his chair away from the table. He'd eaten about half of his lasagne. 'Come on, love. I'll take you.'

Slowly, slowly, as if his wife were made of something fragile, he drew her arm though his and led her towards the hall. There was something pitiful about the small, shuffly steps she was taking.

'I'll save you some pudding, shall I?' called Hel after them.

Mum didn't reply.

On my plate the bright red sauce was congealing round the edges of the pasta. By sheer effort of will I forced myself to swallow another forkful, but it felt like leather in my throat.

CHAPTER 10

<u>*Spring Forward to Easter!*</u>

With the holidays on the horizon, and family gatherings imminent, why not start planning your Easter table? The shops right now are full of those inspirational finishing touches to make your home look – and smell – its best. Lift your décor and impress your guests with these witty and original pieces, all sourced from local craftsmen.

* 1. Lavender and rose door wreath, £25–£39, from Heavenly Gardens at The Tannery, Fourgates Heath, www.heavenlygardens. co.uk*

* 2. Woven bulrush door mat, six designs, £52, and vintage-style boot scraper £95, from That Smart Shop, High Street, Tarporley, www.thatsmartshop.com*

* 3. Laurel and robin's egg mantelpiece swag, £89, from Amelia-Grace, Watergate Street, Chester*

* 4. Cloisonné table centrepiece with scented egg-shaped candles – light individual candles, or combine for a stunning mingled perfume*

*effect. £77, from Joyful Days, Church St, Tarvin, www.joyfuldays.
co.uk*

*5. Hand-painted Italian lanterns for indoor or outdoor use, £40–£60
each; matching marguerite jug and beaker set £45; laser cut crystal rose
bowl £100, from Romanza glassware, Abbey Square, Chester*

I finished the piece, cast a glance at Rosa's closed office door,
and pressed send. 'Christ on a bike, a hundred quid for a boot
scraper?' I could imagine Owen exclaiming. 'Ninety for a string
of flowers?'

Except he hadn't said that, or anything like it. No word of
criticism had passed his lips in the week we'd officially been back
together. Only amazement and delight that, when he'd turned
up nervously to meet me one day after work, I'd gone to his flat
with him and listened to his apology. Listened to him confess
how much he'd missed me. Listened to him beg for a new start.
'I was wrong,' he said. 'Wrong about Chelle. Wrong about you
and me. I've realised it doesn't matter, the differences between
us. I just care about you too much not to have you around. It's
been agony without you. Please forgive me. Please.'

How could I refuse him? Last night he and I had spent the
hours between seven and nine assembling a flat-pack chest of
drawers especially for my stuff. A modest thing, not much higher
than a piano stool, but large enough to take a couple of sets of
folded clothes, and with castors at each corner which meant it
could be slid away under the table. It was Owen himself who'd
suggested and bought it. As he was popping on the last screw
cover and I was picking up the little bits of polystyrene packag-
ing, the doorbell rang and it was Saleem with the shop girls,
bearing a takeaway. Vikki was also carrying two bottles of cheapo
cider, and we got stuck in. The mood was almost like a party.

Owen put on *Question Time* and we took the piss out of George Galloway. 'It's good to see you,' Keisha whispered, and I just thought, *Well, the main thing is, I have a boyfriend again – see, Dad? Ned? I'm safe.*

Meanwhile, on the home front, things were gradually returning to normal. Mum was getting stronger and every day the family seemed to shake down into something more secure and stable. There was one evening we'd sat down and watched a nature documentary together and I'd seen this moth, newly emerged from a chrysalis with its wings pathetic and crumpled. The moth had gathered its reserves and pumped moth blood or whatever into the veins, and gradually they unfurled and swelled till they were standing out like brilliant flags. And I'd looked at Mum and thought, *That's you; you're in the process of uncrumpling yourself.* Every day she walked a little bit taller, grew a little bit more confident. Every day one of us took her out for a stroll that lasted a couple of minutes longer than the previous one. The weather was kind for March and we'd witnessed fresh skies, birds carrying nesting material, blossom starting to flush. Off she'd trot with Dad or Helen or me or Ned, almost like a child being led along to school. It had become a ritual.

She and I had begun to use these little excursions to talk, about all sorts. It must have been the relief of knowing I'd nearly lost her, but I suddenly felt as if all the old tensions between us had dissolved away. Or perhaps it was just that I'd grown up. For the first time I was able to fill her in properly about the Owen and Chelle business, and she listened and was cross on my behalf. 'Don't go back with him if you're not sure,' she told me. 'You deserve someone who takes you as you are.' 'I am sure,' I replied, even though I wasn't.

In turn she'd confided about a boy she dated in the early 1970s, who claimed she'd 'never learn to drive' and anyway, 'women should stay off the roads'. He didn't believe in equal pay, either. 'Why ever did you go out with him?' I asked. She shrugged. 'I was young. In those days opinions like his weren't uncommon. It was perfectly legal then to pay a woman a lower wage for doing the same job. When I worked on reception at Heaton's garage, I did longer hours but I got less at the end of the week than the lad who swept the floors. It wasn't fair but you had to just get on with it.' 'I wouldn't have,' I said, 'I'd have campaigned, I'd have made a fuss.' 'I know you would,' she said.

She talked about how she and Dad first got together, how sorry she'd felt for him because, at twenty, both his parents were already dead and he had to look after an ageing uncle. 'He needed taking care of himself,' she said. She'd decided to marry him in a lay-by on the A49 at Peckforton, where his Morris Marina had broken down. He'd asked her to get a rag out of the glove compartment and a ring box tumbled out onto her lap. At first he was mortified. He'd been planning the proposal for weeks, had a table booked at Lorenzo's. 'He was so crestfallen, bless him,' said Mum.

We reminisced about my childhood and Helen's, and how impressed the teachers at my primary school had been with my reading, and how, in the infants, I'd had to go up to the junior classrooms sometimes to get books which were appropriate for my level. She described how a ten-year-old Helen had cornered an injured fox in the playground (a story I already knew) and had stopped the other children from throwing stones at it. For myself, I recalled the infant Christmas party where Mum had flu so my sister took me along, and we'd been late and had to sneak round the rear of the building where, to my horror, we'd spotted Father Christmas coming out of the men's staff toilets. 'Think about it, though: even Santa has to wee,' she'd explained kindly.

On one of these post-heart-attack walks, a morning on which we'd witnessed a rabbit have the nearest squeak of its life under the wheels of a jeep, I plucked up courage to ask about the anorexia. What was it like? How did she feel, looking back? I suppose I was trying to find out whether Hel was right, that Mum did believe it had been some kind of deliberate strategy.

'It's the worst thing I've ever been through,' she admitted, glancing round as if we might be overheard, even though we were on a deserted road between fields. 'There's nothing, *nothing* as bad as your child fading in front of you. Feeling as if you can't do anything, or you're making it worse. Just agony. I'd suffer a hundred heart attacks rather than it happen again. You see, when you're a mum it's your whole drive to nurture, so it's the cruellest blow to have someone you love refuse food in front of you. You search and search yourself for what you've done wrong as a parent. Was it because I dieted myself? Made her eat carrots even when I knew she hated them? Or because I shouted at her for outgrowing her school skirt within a month? Or was it because I spoiled her, or put too much pressure on her to do well? Or because we didn't teach her to stick up for herself at school? Did we raise her to be too polite? There were a million ways I could have failed. I should have made her move schools, I should have tackled the bullying better. I know I should never have talked about calories or my own weight in front of her.'

'That's mad. Loads of women diet and their kids end up fine. You can't blame yourself for that. The anorexia was an illness, it wasn't anyone's fault.'

Mum's face had gone tight. 'I'll tell you whose fault it was, if you really want to know. I curse her every night – that *awful girl*. Saskia Fox-Lawrence.'

And at last this hidden part of the past came pouring out, hot and angry.

Saskia had not been a friend, as Hel claimed, but an enemy of the worst kind. She had spotted Hel was struggling at school and pretended she was on her side. Inveigled herself into Hel's life. Then she'd taken her over. Nagged her to get slimmer at first, set her weight-loss targets which became increasingly harsh, turned nasty if she missed them. As time went on, she persuaded her to dodge meals and lie to her family, live a secret life. Had given her crazy exercise regimes to follow, some of which included getting up in the middle of the night. Called her Useless and Crap-Head and The Blob. Actually used those names in front of her. Systematically destroyed the little self-esteem she had left. Yet the meaner Saskia had been, the more tightly my sister had clung to her. The dynamic was twisted and powerful; it sounded like a true abusive relationship.

On and on my mother talked, unburdening herself. I listened with appalled fascination. 'I don't think I've ever hated anyone as much in my life as I hated that girl,' she finished. 'It's just as well she moved away or I don't know what your dad would have done with her.'

'My God. I had no idea. Why didn't you tell me this before?'

She looked away. 'Because I was ashamed.'

'Of what?'

'We should have worked out what was going on. I'm her mother, I should have picked it up. But *we* never saw this Saskia at all. They met in town or at school. And also our routine was upside-down, there was a crisis every day. We had health professionals coming in and out, hospital appointments, and I was missing days off work, and Helen stopped talking to me. By the time your dad and I understood what had been going on, Saskia had left the school and it was too late. The damage was done.'

Mum had paused by a farmer's gate to rest then.

'I do know I'm overanxious,' she said. 'I can't help it. The bad time might be years ago, but to me it feels like yesterday. She tells me she's better, and she is better than she was, obviously, but she's still not, she doesn't—'

'She doesn't run in the same groove as the rest of us.'

'No.' Mum looked relieved. 'You understand?'

'I'm not sure I'd go that far.' And I thought about how I'd caught Hel that very morning hiding her post under a magazine so I wouldn't see it; how the week before she'd slipped out into the garden to take some secret phone call. No, I would never understand the way she worked.

Afterwards Mum and I had walked slowly home, me picturing Hel as she'd been that night we nursed Pepper, when I'd naively believed she'd bared her soul to me. Saskia the friend. Saskia the enemy. Still we were mired in lies and secrets. Would my sister ever be able to open her mouth and just speak the truth?

Someone thudding up the office stairs made Gerry and me look up from our PCs. The door burst open and in came a delivery man staggering under the weight of a monster bunch of flowers.

'Is there a Rosa Heffer in here?' he said from behind a bank of lilies.

Gerry pointed with his pen.

'Cheers,' said the man and carried his swaying burden across the carpet towards her desk.

'Wow,' I said, turning in my seat to stare after him. 'Are those from Mr Lover-man? They must've cost an absolute bomb.'

'Nah, not from him. Oh, I forgot, you missed the drama yesterday.'

'I was out covering that demo in Frodsham till late. Why, what happened?'

'You didn't get to witness the dance of the dying swan.'

'Eh?'

'He's finished with her, Rosa's man-pal. Did it by text.'

'What?'

'I know, harsh. Alan went in to see her about four-ish to ask about photographs of the football stadium, and she's sitting there in floods of tears. It's all over.' Gerry pulled a heartbroken face.

'Why, though? Do we know?'

'No idea. I certainly shan't be asking.'

I took a moment to process the development. Well, well. Rosa dumped. Rosa brought low, shaken out of her insufferable smugness and discarded, just like a common person. Served her right. Except, to my surprise I found I actually felt sorry for her. The news seemed like another example of the meanness of fate. One more person floundering about with their dreams dashed. If glossy, confident Rosa had come a cropper, what hope was there for the rest of us?

'Bloody hell. So who are the flowers from?' I asked, as the delivery man backed out, shutting her door carefully behind him. He had a deflated air about him. I guessed his reception had not been as joyous as he'd been anticipating.

'Dunno. Most likely the Malloys, they've been phoning and sending cards the whole week.'

Donny Malloy had ended up overall winner of Take The Mike, with his cheeky comedic charm. Despite a tendency to veer towards adult double-entendre, he'd impressed the judges with his confidence, though the presence of his extensive and very vocal family in the audience probably helped too. I'd thought his mother was going to pass out with excitement. We'd had the St John's Ambulance on stand-by.

'Yeah, they've been pretty grateful, haven't they?'

'I'll say. It's what Mrs Malloy's lived her whole life for. And *you* made it happen. You. Who's the real star here?' Gerry made jazz hands at me.

For a moment I allowed myself to bask in his approval. The talent show had gone well overall, not counting some funny business with fake voting coupons in week eight. *The Messenger*'s circulation had been significantly boosted, and four other newspapers in the group were interested in the idea. Rosa had concluded it was a 'good job, Jen'.

I looked towards her office and saw, through the glass panel on the door, that she was sitting hunched right over, her brow resting on the desk top. That didn't look right. 'Think she's ill?'

He shrugged. 'Do you wanna go see?'

'Not especially.' But somehow I couldn't leave her there, forehead-down in her own pain.

I made my way over, trying not to catch the interest of Alan, and knocked very lightly.

'Yes?' came the peevish response.

I took it as permission to go in. Rosa was upright in her seat when I stepped across the threshold, but with a pink dent above her eyebrows. The magnificent bouquet sat in the corner, its message card torn out and discarded on the floor. I wasn't sure if she'd been crying but her make up was certainly blurry, her hair messy at the sides where it had slid free from the clips. It felt slightly shameful to see her without her usual poise, almost as if I'd caught her on the toilet. I'd watched her over the past months doing her strange facial exercises when she thought no one was looking, and practising smiles into the mirrored side of her pen pot. Stroking her parting into place, dabbing at her lipstick in a compact. Whoever the guy was, surgeon or lawyer or big-shot banker, he'd obviously meant a hell of a lot to her. She'd really been in love.

'I was wondering . . . if I could do anything?' I ventured.

'You can take those damn flowers away.'

'And do what with them?'

'I don't know.'

'Shall I bin them?'

'Whatever you think.'

'Can I – if you don't want them, would it be OK to take them home to my mum?'

She shrugged. 'Do what you like. I hope you've prepared adequately for this morning's interview.'

'Oh. Yeah, I have.'

At 10.30 I was scheduled to visit a Mr Luc Lambin, Canadian furniture designer to the stars, recently relocated to the Tallybridge area. He hadn't given an interview for a while but she'd managed to secure one, some deal struck in his cups over a fancy Chester Racecourse dinner. *The problem is, Jennifer,* she'd explained, *I can't go myself because I'm presenting certificates at Cestrian Academy and I'm the guest of honour. And Gerry has an appointment with the Mayor at twelve, and Alan's got to cover that meeting of the directors of Chester FC. But you should be capable of turning up at the studio and asking a few straightforward questions. There's nothing contentious here. Just for God's sake, don't do anything to mess up.* There's nothing like bolstering your employees' confidence.

'Well?' Rosa was waiting.

'Is there anything else I can do while I'm here? Anything to help, I mean? Only, you look upset.' I hoped she'd catch the genuine sympathy in my voice. I didn't much like the woman, but we're all sisters when it comes to being dumped. I could at least bring her a hot drink or do a chocolate run or lend her a clean hanky.

She dropped her face and looked at me from under her fringe, an unflattering angle that showed off the beginnings of jowls.

'Yes. You can get out and leave me alone,' she said.

I know when I'm beaten. I retrieved the ripped card, hoisted the bouquet and left her to it.

Afterwards, as I drove out of Chester, I found I couldn't stop replaying the scene. Witnessing Rosa in that state had rattled me because she was supposed to be invincible. Above your common-or-garden heartache. What had prompted the break-up? Had she fought, cajoled, begged? What answering forms of humiliation had he heaped upon her head? I was relieved I hadn't been in the office yesterday, when she was properly upset. The whole business, of course, made me think of Owen, and whether I'd been right to go back with him. In the end he'd said everything about Chelle I'd needed to hear: that he could now see she was selfish and calculating, and he'd been a fool to believe her spin. He was truly penitent about the things he'd said to me when we broke up. He loved me, he would try and make more time for me, and I could stay over whenever I wanted. So I ought to have been beside myself with joy. Yet something still wasn't sitting right. Three months ago I'd have given anything, anything to be his girlfriend again. But three months ago had been a very different place.

Before I could stop myself, an image of Ned popped into my mind: Ned as he'd been the last time I'd seen him, in the kitchen washing up alongside my sister, humming the theme tune to *Friends*. I'd announced I was staying at Owen's for a couple of days, and Hel had raised her eyebrows and Ned scowled at me. Then she'd passed the heavy pan to him and asked him to put it up on top of the cupboard for her where she couldn't reach, and the action had seemed so symbolic, so designed to press home the point that she *relied* on him, that I'd left the room immediately and gone to pack. He wasn't mine; Owen was mine and I needed to get a grip.

I slowed the car as the lanes narrowed. Now I was well into the countryside, driving past tastefully restored farm workers' cottages and barn conversions. The hedges were bulking out, the verges sprouting tall and, as the road climbed, the Cheshire Plain spread in front of me, rich and fertile. Here was a landscape well satisfied with itself. Before long, signs began appearing for Tallybridge and within another ten minutes I was pulling into Lambin's driveway.

The studio was housed in a series of converted farm buildings with solar panels on the roofs. In front of the biggest barn was a neat, sterile area of honey-coloured gravel chips with no flower beds or shrubs, only a couple of granite millstones propped against the wall. I parked the car, got out and crunched over to the door. Above me, perched along the roof line, fat pigeons called *You do, too; you do, too.*

I rang the bell and waited. Nothing. That was odd. I rang again. I checked my watch. I stepped back, as if any inhabitants might just need some space to encourage them out. I was thinking how Rosa especially wanted me to do this interview right because Lambin was a major name in design circles and it had been a coup to get him to speak to us at all. Briefly – madly – I wondered if it was worth a quick call to the office to check I'd got the correct day, but the thought withered at once as I imagined my boss's reaction when she heard. *Are you incapable of following instructions, Jennifer? See, I go out on a limb and give you a project of substance, and how long does it take you to mess up?*

I decided to take a slow stroll around the workshop, see if anyone arrived in the meantime. I could text Owen, maybe, or pop onto Twitter. But before I even got as far as the corner of the barn, there was a squeal of brakes in the lane and then a Lexus LS swung through the gateway and pulled up sharply on the gravel. The engine died, the door was flung open and an elegant blonde climbed out, waving.

'Are you the *Messenger* lady? Hi. I am so sorry. I'm Mrs Lambin. We got held up with a client and couldn't get away. My husband's coming, he'll be about another twenty minutes. He told me to go on ahead and keep you entertained.'

The accent was posh-English, with no hint of Canadian. She was tall and super-slim like a model, in a black polo neck and dark blue jeans. Her hair was short and textured, expensively cut. But her face was mobile and full of mischief. The mouth was too wide for a model's, and the brows too strong. Characterful, you might have said. She smiled easily, beckoned me towards the barn. 'Seriously, though, phew. I've been breaking land-speed records to get here in time. Mown down half a dozen pheasants at least. Come inside and I'll get us a drink.'

Their house was the most stylish place I'd ever set foot in. Everything was open-plan, or partitioned off with translucent panels. In front of me was a broad glass staircase, with brushed steel banisters and a circular skylight directly above. Some sort of mezzanine or gallery arrangement was going on at the far end of the building, and below it I could see a vertical metal tube, thick as a tree trunk, with a dramatic African-style rug laid in front of it suggestive of a hearth. The flooring throughout was some kind of very light wood. 'Should I remove my shoes?' I asked, because Mrs Lambin had peeled her ankle boots off straightaway.

'Only if you want to. There's no need. I got rid of mine because they pinch. Bloody things. Look fantastic, feel like instruments of torture. I'll have hammer-toes before I'm forty and serve me right. Now, what do you fancy? Luc has this whole fruit tea thing going, but I can do you normal, or I can make up some elder-flower cordial, or sparkling water, or something stronger if you're in the mood. No coffee about, I'm afraid, as it makes us both hyperactive.'

'I'll have a normal tea.'

'Excellent choice. Me too. Come into the kitchen and let's get that kettle on. God, and I tell you, as well as my feet being on fire for the last hour, I'm *bursting* for a pee – we were with the Duke of Westminster, have you met him? No? Nice guy – and he was having this intense discussion with Luc about the virtues of different woods and I didn't like to interrupt with, Excuse me, where's the loo, your Grace? So I'm bobbing about on one of his antique sofas, he must have thought I had ADD. And then we went outside and I tripped over one of his bloody stone lions.

Luc's signalling to me like, *What's the matter with you, woman?* She pulled an expression of fake-horror that made me laugh, and I thought how, if it had been Rosa who'd just visited a duke, she'd have been gliding about wearing an imaginary tiara and we wouldn't have been worthy to touch the hem of her garment.

The kitchen, as I'd have predicted, was stunning, all mini-malist chic and clever use of spotlights. What I guessed was a Lambin table graced the centre of the room, glossed ebony and breakfast bar height, resting on a twisted central pedestal. Our photographer was going to be in ecstasy.

I said, 'You do a lot of celebrity commissions?'

'We do. Luc's working on a piece for Brian May at the moment, a chair with adders twining up the sides. He'll show you when he gets here. I *love* your jacket, by the way. Is it velvet?'

'Brushed cotton.'

'Gorgeous. Red's your colour, isn't it? Makes me look a dog.'

I sincerely doubted that. The more I watched her as she moved around the kitchen, the more striking I found her. She glowed with health and energy. Her skin reminded me of adverts for spas and yoghurt and ski resorts. I liked her casual self-deprecation because it was funny and she wasn't fishing for compliments.

'Now,' she said, 'can I offer you a biscuit? We have some Belgian chocolate wafers, absolutely delicious. I'm on a stupid diet, but it would give me enormous pleasure to watch you eat one.'

'I'm fine.'

'OK. Let's get going, then. I appreciate you're on a tight schedule, it's very good of you to come out. I'll show you some of his work while we wait.'

Without a second's self-consciousness she took hold of my

hand to lead me through to the lounge. Oh! I nearly said, because it felt like such an intimate and unexpected gesture from someone I'd only just met. Her friendliness was warming, like standing in front of a fire on a cold day. You hear about these people who light up a room: Mrs Lambin was one of them. I bet her address book was bursting with friends, I bet the phone never stopped ringing with invitations. And I found myself recalling, of all things, a Welsh seaside holiday when I was eight, and a group of kids who were already at the hotel when I arrived. I remembered hanging about shyly in the foyer while Mum and Helen argued about rooms or meal times or the application of suncream, and then one of the gang, a stocky girl, had bounced over and asked if I wanted to play rounders with them. The rest of that week had been a blast. Danni, this girl was called. She'd been full of ideas and dares, a natural and likeable leader. Even on the days it rained and we'd been stuck in the hotel she'd organised us kids into games of hide and seek, or joke-telling competitions. Afterwards I'd meant to write but I'd lost her address. I wondered what had become of Danni, born as she was under a sparkling star.

Mrs Lambin guided me over to a tall, arched window in front of which sat a coffee table carved of golden brown wood and flecked with knots. I'm no design expert; to me, furniture's just something over which you drape your clothes or pile old magazines. Even I could see this was special, though. The top surface was beautiful, but what drew the eye even more was that the legs weren't symmetrical, they curved downwards via different routes, as if they'd grown by themselves. Branches, they might have been. Vine stalks. The polished lines called out to be stroked and followed with the fingers.

'Feel free,' said Mrs Lambin, reading my thoughts. 'He made them to be touched.'

So I squatted down on my haunches and examined the table more closely. From this level, the twisting grain of the wood reminded me of melting butter or syrup flowing out of a tin, or a golden scarf blowing in the wind. What type of wood was it? Did he know what the structure would be like inside when he began to carve out a block?

'This was actually his first commercial piece,' she was explaining, 'and the guy who commissioned it backed out of the deal – this is years ago, 2004 – so Luc kept it and it's worth a mint. Not that he'd ever sell it. He thinks it's his lucky charm.'

'Yeah? Wow.' I put my cup of tea carefully down on the slate windowsill where she'd rested hers, and reached into my pocket for my notepad. Might as well start the interview.

'How long have you two been together?'

She rolled her eyes. 'God. Too long! No, seriously, I left Cheshire in 2000 – I'd finished my GCSEs and my father got a job offer up in Edinburgh so we trailed up there, and then a year into my A levels I dropped out and started working in a gallery – I have no staying power, I'm totally bloody useless. And Luc was over in the UK on a kind of art exchange programme and we met and he just dismissed me as this jumped-up little schoolgirl – he's eight years older than me, he's forty. *Forty*! And I thought he was an arrogant tosser – he won't mind my telling you this, he thinks it's funny now – and basically he got me sacked from my job. Can you believe it? Mind you, I *was* totally arrogant. I needed taking down a peg or two. So then he felt sorry and he took me for a drink to apologise, and we had another huge row in the pub and then in the middle of it he fell in love with me. Well, there was a bit more to it but that is what happened.'

She took me over to look at a smooth-sided wall cupboard that seemed to have sprouted on its own from the bricks around it. I couldn't even see how it was held up.

'So you're originally from round here?'

'I am. An age ago. We had a house in Malpas.'

'Really? Which school did you go to? Not St Thom's?'

She laughed and pointed out a three-legged stool for me to admire. 'That's right. Old Thommy's. Though I didn't exactly have an illustrious career there. I'm sure the teachers were glad to see the back of me.'

'Oh my God, that's where I went.'

'No! Was old Mincing there in your time?'

'Do you mean Mr Minchin, the deputy? No, but my sister was always talking about him. He was there when she was. Camp as a boy scouts' convention. He wore cravats.'

'He did. With matching socks. The man was a legendary tool. Rang my parents to tell them I was a disgrace because I'd used a piece of his sheet music to blot my lipstick. And my father just laughed and told him I'd done much more disgraceful things than that. Who was your sister? Maybe I knew her.'

'Helen Crossley. She'd have been in the year below you, or maybe two years below. God, I'm so disorganised I haven't even got your forename down yet. You're still just "Mrs Lambin" in my notes. Sorry.'

'No probs. It's Sass.'

'Sass?'

'S-a-s-s. Sassy, if you like. That's what Luc calls me sometimes.'

Some dark anxiety plucked at my core. 'That's short for—'

'For Saskia. Yes, I was Saskia Fox-Lawrence at school, of all the bloody names to saddle a child with. Your sister might remember me because I was in a group that won Battle of the School Bands one year. Terminatrix. We were pretty bloody awful but then so was everyone else who took part. Actually, I say that but our bassist went on to become a session musician at Angelfish studios, so that wasn't entirely hopeless, although he kept falling out with the manager and I think nowadays he runs a travel agency in Manchester . . . Oh. Are you OK?'

There were no mirrors within my sight-line, but I could guess what had happened to my face. I knew my eyes were wide, my cheeks flushing with realisation.

'I think – I think you did know my sister,' I managed.

'Did I? Oh, OK. Let me think, then. And come and sit down. Here, I'll bring your drink for you. That's right. Mind the rug, I don't want you to trip. Would you be better with your jacket off? You seem awfully warm.'

On shaky legs I made my way to the Lambin sofa, a double-throne affair with gothic points at the headrests and green velvet upholstery. She lowered me into it, the way you might settle a poorly pensioner. 'Goodness. Are you having a dizzy do? You don't look very well,' she said.

'Having a dizzy do'? I could barely see straight. Dear God, right here in front of me was THE GIRL. The one who'd told my sister she was worthless and alone. Who'd programmed her to believe food was poison and that to eat was weak and disgusting. Who'd offered fake friendship which she threatened to withdraw whenever Helen didn't follow the rules. Who'd cajoled and bullied, set punishing weight-loss targets, urged her not to listen to her parents and to lie and cheat her way out of any real nourishment. This was the most evil schoolgirl in the world, grown up. How could she be here, living this wonderful life, after what she'd done to my sister? To our whole family. How dare she stand there and claim she didn't remember?

I said, 'You were her best friend. A huge part of her life for nearly a year.'

Sass put her fingertips to her mouth thoughtfully, then took them away again. Her brow was furrowed with concern. 'Look, I can see this is important to you, but I'm ever so sorry, I honestly don't recall her. Maybe if I saw a photo. That's it. Have you got a picture on your phone? My stupid old brain forgets all sorts these days. I'm probably on for an early menopause or something. And I had such an up-and-down sort of time at school I expect I've blanked quite a lot out. That's no reflection on your sister, obviously. What did you say her name was? Hannah?'

At that, hot outrage swelled up in me. I wanted to jump up and grab her cashmere sweater and shake her till her teeth rattled. OK, I would yell in her face, *you can stop this bloody pretence right now. Don't you understand what you did, Saskia bloody Fox-Lawrence? Do you know how much DAMAGE you caused? You bitch! You cold-hearted, manipulative bitch! Because I'll help you remember. I'll lay out the results of your twisted bloody experiment. Come home with me and see how you hollowed out my beautiful sister and left her stranded and ruined.*

'Her name is Helen,' I whispered.

'Helen. And which year did she leave?'

Again it was like a slap across the face. I pictured Hel slumped over the table, crying because she wanted to sit her final exams, and Mum arguing that she had to get better first, trying to use the situation as yet another bargaining chip, and each of us keenly aware that there was no way she'd be going back to school that year. There would be no prom for Hel, no shirt-signing and leavers' photo and super-soaker fights across the playing field. She'd slunk away from St Thom's prematurely, under a cloud of rumour and shame. A couple of half-hearted visits from the nicer girls in her class, a dribble of Get Well cards, and that was it. Game over. *Don't you know all this, Saskia? Don't you know?*

And then, like thunder breaking across the tension of the moment, the Lambins' front door banged opened and shut again, and there was the clatter of keys being thrown down.

'Sass? Sass, darling? You in there?'

She and I were just staring at each other. *What in God's name is going on with you?* said her expression. *What is the matter? Look, my husband is home and because I have excellent manners I am going to skate over the funny business by pretending you are normal and that this has been an ordinary, pleasant chat, the way it was at the start. Before you got your knickers in a twist about some vague school acquaintance who I can't even picture. So shall we buck up, eh? Do you want to do your job?*

'Yes, Luc,' she called brightly. 'The *Messenger* lady's arrived. We're sitting by the hearth. Come and say hello. She's a fan.'

A tanned, rangy man with a fine head of greying hair walked into the room. Like his wife, he wasn't conventionally good-looking, but there was an attractive air of confidence about him. They were a glossy, Sunday-supplement kind of couple. He wore a good-quality grey shirt and fitted jeans. His body language was easy.

'Well now,' he said. 'Jennifer, isn't it?'

I got to my feet, unsure what to do. I'd almost forgotten what I was there for.

Meanwhile Lambin crossed the floor and bent to kiss his wife. 'So how's it going? Has Sass been keeping you entertained?'

'Yes.'

'Excellent. She's good at that. And we're ready to roll, are we? You've got your notepad primed? OK, then. If Sass has shown you the pieces down here, you should come up to my study and take a look at my design notes. I'll talk you through some of the processes I use, and some of the inspirations. I want you to leave with a real understanding of the Lambin vision.'

He nodded his head towards the glass staircase and moved to usher me along. In a dream I did as I was told. And as I began to climb those transparent steps, my hand smoothing up the icy banister, it seemed to me that the place was unreal, a stage set. If I struck them, the walls would be revealed as cardboard, and the view through the window a painted screen. Nothing here was solid or sound. 'Hey, you should know, Jennifer,' he said, pausing mid-way and half raising the bottle, 'not everyone gets to come up here to see the inner sanctum. You're privileged. But it so happens you catch me in one hell of a good mood. For the next hour, I'm yours. You can go right ahead and ask me anything you want. I'm your scoop of the day.'

I took a deep breath, fighting to keep a grip on the situation, on my job, on Rosa's expectations.

In the space between my shoulder blades I could feel Saskia's eyes pricking curiously at the flesh.

When I got home that evening, Mum was sitting at the table with two tins of loose photographs and a pile of family albums.

'I thought this was a job I could be getting on with,' she said when she saw me. 'Come and see.'

The last thing I wanted to do was pore over old photos, not the way I was feeling. It had taken me all the energy I could muster to get through the afternoon. What I wanted to do was crawl upstairs and put my head under the duvet. But I laid my bag on the sofa and went and stood dutifully next to her.

This was an old album that she hadn't brought out for a while. One by one she turned the stiff pages, flipping backwards through time.

'When were these taken, Mum?'

'The Nineties. The years when I was useful.'

I ignored the maudlin comment and instead stared at the pictures. Mainly what we had was Helen at various ages feeding ducks, red squirrels, chaffinches, a lamb. And here was I, much younger, pretending to drip ice cream on Dad's head, balanced on a scooter, whacking a puddle with a stick. Because we were flipping from the end to the front, Helen got plumper and more normal-shaped as we went on, more relaxed about being in front of the camera. Her clothes were ordinary, not the bundles and layers she'd insisted on wearing at her most ill. There was one particularly striking shot of her embracing a standing stone, dressed in simple jeans and stripy T-shirt, with her russet hair blowing across the granite. She'd have been about thirteen then.

Mum, I imagined saying, *I met Saskia today*. Mum's face freezing in horror, her colour draining, her hand coming up to clutch her chest. Helen running in: *What have you done, Jen?* No, that was a meeting I wouldn't be sharing.

Instead I said, 'You've a lot more photos of Hel than you have of me.'

'She's been around longer. She had a seven-year start on you, remember.'

I sighed.

'What?' said Mum.

'I wish I looked like Helen.'

'Oh, don't say that. You're lovely as you are.' We gazed down at a photograph of me in a PGL canoe, an orange crash helmet jammed on my head. If that had been Helen in a boat, the picture would have shown a punt or a prettily painted rowing boat moving under willows, and she'd have been languishing in a white dress and sun hat. But that said, here she was at about ten with the guinea pig on her lap and laughing her head off, nothing serene or wistful about that.

'Wait a minute.' I took the thick edge of the page and lifted it over. 'Was that Norris?'

'It was.'

Norris was a three-foot resin garden gnome my dad had picked out of a hedge in a lay-by and brought home because he said he 'felt sorry for it'. Mum had wanted to put Norris straight in the bin, but I'd pleaded his case, so Dad had hosed him down with the pressure washer and we'd found a spot under the Leylandii, pretty much out of sight. Shortly afterwards, however, Norris moved, apparently under his own steam, to the edge of the patio. Mum accused me of shifting him – a daft suggestion as I was only six and not a lot taller than Norris himself – then she had a pop at Dad. Neither of us knew anything about it, though. She put Norris in his place again, and the next day he was back at the patio window, leering in. Every few days the gnome would travel some short distance, and I'd be beside myself with excitement to see where he'd got to. Indeed, as time passed, he got more daring and could be found balanced on neighbours' doorsteps, on top of walls or wedged in a tree.

Then one morning I came downstairs and he'd just disappeared. We searched and searched but no joy. Dad said he must have got lonely and gone to find some other gnomes to be with, and sure enough, a week or so later I had a card from Norris postmarked Llandudno saying he'd gone off to live with some mates, and not to miss him and to behave at school.

'God, I'd forgotten about him. What was the deal there? Was it you moving him about?'

Mum smiled. 'It was Helen. She'd get up especially early to do it. Only sometimes you were up before her and those mornings he had to stay where he was.'

'Helen? Oh! So why did she stop? I was gutted, you know, when it finished. I truly believed he was alive. I suppose she got bored with the game?'

'No, the bin men took him. She'd forgotten it was collection day, and she'd posed him on top of the wheelie bin. She was very upset when she realised. We even drove her to the municipal tip to see if she could get him back, but the manager said he thought everything would have gone in the crusher. Then, do you remember Norris writing to you? Dad had one of his drivers post the letter from Wales. It was her idea, though.'

My complicated sister. Just as you think you've got a handle on who she is, she morphs again.

'Look,' Mum went on, 'here you are at the Millennium scarecrow festival. That was a day. Half an hour before he took that photo, your dad had to rescue you.'

'From what?'

'Oh, you marched up to some teenage boys who were interfering with Dr Who's scarf and told them to leave it alone. Told them they were vandals and to go find something useful to do.'

'Did I?'

'You did, yes. They were much older than you but you weren't frightened. And then the woman whose scarecrow it was came out to say thank you. Don't you remember?'

'No. Nothing.' I racked my brains. 'Oh, unless – wasn't one of the scarecrows done up as a burglar climbing into an upstairs window? Because for a minute I thought it really was a burglar. And afterwards we went to a café where Dad sat on some chewing gum and you were furious with him because you'd only just had his trousers dry-cleaned?'

Mum looked doubtful. 'I don't know about that.'

Why did we all remember different versions of the same story? It was weird the way we each sifted the past.

At Mum's elbow was the tin of loose and jumbled snapshots. I could see a baby Helen in a highchair, Dad standing in front of one of his lorries, Mum twenty-something in a brown pinafore dress. I poked the top layer and a picture of my parents slid out, must have been from a time before us kids arrived. They were sitting on a low wall with a cold grey sea behind, Dad much slimmer and Mum much smilier, and they were holding hands.

There was a photo of Toffee inside his hutch where the wire mesh was in focus but the guinea pig behind it wasn't. There was a seaside hotel which I remembered specifically because Mum had left our swimming costumes to dry on the windowsill and they'd blown off onto the flat roof below and the manager had to send someone up on a ladder. There was a too-dark print of St Thom's school stage, with three spot-lit Year 12s performing a comedy routine written by me.

I fished out a snapshot and held it up so I could see better. 'I know where this is.'

Me, in junior school dress and cardigan, plasters on both my knees, walking along the top of a wall while Mum held my hand for safety. That wall no longer existed; it had been at the end of Mason's car park, but that store was gone and a B&Q in its place.

Mum leaned in to examine the detail. 'Oh, you were a devil for climbing. I had to watch you or you'd be up some tree before I could say Jack Robinson.'

'You're not watching me there, though. You're looking the other way.'

'Am I?'

It was plain her gaze was on something else, something not in shot. 'You're looking at Helen, aren't you?'

'I don't know how you can tell that.'

'Because you always were.'

'Don't be silly.'

'I'm not. I'm not getting at you, I'm just saying. People look at her and not me.'

'No.'

'Yes, Mum. You've always paid her more attention. It's OK, I don't mind because Dad pays *me* more. That's just the way this family works.'

Her mouth came open. She seemed genuinely shocked. Why? I wasn't telling her anything she didn't know.

'It's not like that at all, Jen. Oh, love, how could you think that way?'

'Because it's the truth.'

A clattering noise from the kitchen. I realised Helen was just the other side of the door, making our tea.

Mum said carefully, 'Listen, love, however it's come across, you've got it wrong. What it is, your sister's more . . . needy. And

I don't mean just the . . . the being ill. Even before. When she was little. She used to wait for me in the street, and stay close by my side as we walked, and ask me to help with getting dressed and, when she was older, with things like homework, everything. She needed the reassurance. And I was her mother so I was happy to give it. Then you came along and you were so different. So different. If you and I went out to the shops together, you wanted to walk ahead on your own. I had to shout at you to hold my hand when we were crossing the road. You wouldn't let me put on your coat for you or do up your toggles. I never even *saw* any of your homework. You wanted to be independent right from the word go. And you made friends at the drop of a hat, whereas Helen's always hung back. Everything that's come your way, you've jumped right in. Gosh, I remember when you were eleven and you went on that PGL trip to Menai, I worried myself stupid because Helen had been homesick and had a rotten stay there. But you loved every minute.'

'You make that sound like a bad thing.'

'No, *no*! I was proud of you. And it's been – ' she lowered her voice – 'a *relief* that you were able to manage the way you have. Do you understand? That you didn't need the same amount of support. At times it's been exhausting.' Her face was working as she tried to think how best to express herself.

'So by and large you left me to get on with it.'

'Because that was what you wanted, I thought! That was how you liked to run things. But just because I didn't go hovering around you, it doesn't mean I loved you any the less. You didn't really think that, did you? When you left to go to university, I sat on your bed and cried for a week. Don't look at me like that. I did. Ask your dad. Ask Helen.'

I didn't know what to say. From the kitchen came the muffled sound of the radio. Politicians and interviewers arguing; you could hear the indignant rise and fall of their sentences.

Mum touched my arm. 'I missed you so much. Silly, because I know you were happy in Manchester. But I felt redundant. Left behind, if you like.'

'You never told me.'

'What would have been the point? Make you guilty for wanting to go off and study? No, as I said, I was very proud of you. The problem with motherhood is that you want your children to grow up and away from you, but it hurts when they do . . . Anyway, you used to ring and text me. And I had Helen at home. I'm beginning to think I probably always will have.'

We both threw a glance at the door. It felt dangerous and disloyal to talk about Hel this way, though I couldn't deny it was a boost to hear Mum praise me against my sister. When did that ever normally happen?'

I stroked a photo with the tip of my finger: Helen, aged about six or seven, grasping a stick of candy floss, happy as you like.

The kitchen door opened without warning and the radio blared out. 'Oh,' said Hel when she saw me. 'You're back. I can't remember, do you like spinach?'

I moved away from Mum guiltily. 'Not much, no.'

'Bad luck, it's what we're having tonight. Get your dose of iron. You'll thank me in the end.'

There she stood against the jamb, the sleeves of her summer dress rolled up past her elbows. Round her waist she'd tied a blue silk scarf, and two or three daisies from the garden were tucked artfully into her buttonholes.

Pretty girl, big sis, troubled daughter, liar.

Who the hell are you? I thought.

After tea I texted Owen to alert him to a TV documentary he might like, then switched off my phone and went for a long bath while I tried to work up the courage to tackle Helen. Although where I was going to start, I had no idea.

'I've had a ponder,' Saskia had said as she walked me to the car. 'Because I could see it was important to you. While you were upstairs interviewing Luc, I actually dug out an old school photo, and I get now who you're talking about. I did know your sister by sight because of her hair, there was no missing that amazing mane. But I didn't ever speak to her. Not directly. She was younger than me, and the Year Ten form rooms were in the Science block whereas mine was in Arts, so we were on opposite sides of the building. We'd even have been on different dinner sittings. Our paths just never crossed. I mean, did you know the people in the year below you? So I think she must be getting me confused with someone else.'

'She must,' I mumbled, only because I couldn't think of any other response.

Then she said, 'I do remember this one incident. I don't know if I should tell you or not.'

'Tell me,' I said.

'It wasn't very nice. Quite sad, really.'

'Tell me. Please.'

'Well – a bunch of us were walking along the back of the building, along the path that runs down to the field; I suppose it would have been lunch break. And there was a group ahead, including this couple, him with his arm draped across her shoulders. I wasn't paying them much attention. And then, out of the blue, we heard the sash window above us thump open and someone calling from the top floor classroom. I assumed it was a teacher about to tell us off for some crime or other. But it wasn't. It was your sister – I can see her hair hanging down now – and she was yelling at the boy-half of the couple in front. She was going, "No, Joe. No, Joe." She kept shouting it. We were like, *Huh?* Anyway, he – Joe – just ignored her at first. Then he looked up and did this slow, mocking salute, and then he turned to the girl he was with and kissed her, full-on. It was really tacky. By then some people around were joining in and chanting, "No, Joe." Course, he was grinning and carrying on as if it was some big joke. I didn't join in. I thought it was horrible. Your poor sister. After a bit she disappeared inside and that should have been the last of it. But you know what school's like. Tiny little incidents get a momentum going, and for days afterwards I'd hear people in the corridors shouting out, "No, Joe." It was the catchphrase of the moment. You'd hear it echoing up the stair-well. It got changed to other things. Go, Joe; Yo, Joe; So, Joe. Hilarious. Not. And then, as the craze was dying down, the school got a visit in assembly from some kids' folk choir and they stood up on stage and sang this song with the chorus, "Oh, no, John, no John, no John, no." I mean, beyond stupid, but there was a riot. The Year Nines and Tens fell about sniggering, one entire row had to be sent out. I suppose your sister pretty much died of embarrassment. I felt sorry for the folk singers as well because they didn't have a clue what they'd done. Teenagers can be utter gits.'

We'd stood on the Lambins' driveway and I'd stared at the clouds racing by. I couldn't bring myself to meet Saskia's eye.

'I don't think she was very happy, your sister. You probably know, some people gave her a rough ride. I'd have spoken out against all the bollocks, only it's hard when there's a *wave* of feeling. Crowd mentality. You get laughed at, and nothing changes. I suppose I could have talked to her. Told her not to mind. But like I said, I didn't know her.'

'And then you left.'

'Yeah. Didn't keep in touch with anyone there. I wasn't that keen on St Thom's myself. I mean, everyone's on the receiving end at some time or other, aren't they? When I was in Year Seven, a Year Nine boy called Nikos Kukula took my sports bag and got his mates to play football with it. Kicked it till the zip split, then chucked it over the fence into the main road and I was too scared to go after it. Horrible. And I never told anyone, till you. Strange, isn't it? I don't know how we survive the cruelties of adolescence. Helen's OK now, is she? What's she up to? I bet she's an artist's model or something.'

'She works with abandoned pets.'

'Yeah? Wow. Good on her. That's brilliant. Look, I'm on Facebook. Get her to look me up sometime. It would be nice to chat. Swap old school gossip.'

Another of those moments where nothing seemed real. What was I missing? Which of them was lying?

I'd driven back to the office and spent the afternoon working on autopilot. Luckily Rosa's door was shut and her blinds drawn. She'd left at four o' clock, and I was two minutes behind her.

I sat in my room and told myself I'd tackle Helen as soon as she came up the stairs. When I heard her light tread, I stepped out onto the landing in front of her, blocking her way.

She blinked, looked me up and down. 'What?'

'We need to talk.'

A hunted expression crossed her face. She could tell I wasn't messing around. 'Do I have a choice?'

'Nope.'

Hel gave a shrug and turned towards my room, but I headed her off and pointed at her own bedroom.

'No. In here.' I pushed open the door. 'Come on.'

On the rare occasions I do enter Helen's domain, it always feels as if I'm crossing into a separate zone, one that's not part of the rest of the house. There's a hush in here that reminds me of the reading room at uni, and a sense of order that seems in direct contradiction to the everyday busy-ness of simply being alive. So the carpet's completely clear, magazine- and footwear-free. The windowsills are just windowsills and not home to books and CDs and ornaments and hair stylers and abandoned coffee mugs. Hel's beauty products are stored in a compartmentalised drawer, and not strewn across her dressing table like the aftermath of a riot at Boots. Her clothes wait patiently in the wardrobe on their colour-coded hangers, whereas mine lie draped about, ready for action. In here the walls are plain, light stretches broken only by a small cork notice board and her print of Waterhouse's 'The Lady of Shalott'. It's her place of sanctuary, and I understand why she generally keeps me out. I was mucking up the place just by being there. But for once I wanted to speak to her on her own territory. That felt important.

'OK, go on then,' said Helen. 'Let's get this over, whatever it is.'

'Sit down first.'

'God. What's with all the drama?' She hesitated, annoyed, then gave in and perched on the edge of the bed.

I said, 'This. I met Saskia Fox-Lawrence today.'

Hel's eyes widened and her mouth dropped open. I guess that was the very last bit of news she was expecting.

'No! *No*. How?'

'I was sent to interview her husband about his furniture design. They're back from Canada for a spell. He was late, so before he arrived I sat and chatted with her.'

'You *talked* to her?'

'At length.'

I waited, but she said nothing to that.

'It so happens that Saskia remembers her time at St Thom's pretty well.'

Again, no response.

'She remembers you. Not at first, but when I prompted her. After she'd checked an old school photograph. And what do you think she told me?'

'I have no idea.'

'Well, it was quite surprising because when I tried to find out about you and her, she reckoned she'd never even spoken to you. That, being in different years, you just never came across each other. She certainly wasn't your friend. Or your enemy, or anything. You didn't register in her life at all. Anyway, I thought she came across as pretty convincing. What do you make of it?'

Hel swallowed uncomfortably. 'So? It was an age ago. To be honest, Jen, it's got nothing to do with you. I told you before that I didn't want to talk about her.'

'It's got nothing to do with me? Oh no, except you're my sister, and I was ready to tear into this woman for ruining your life. I was completely fired up, and then it turns out I've been spun a lie. By somebody. I almost made an utter fool of myself. Almost put my job in jeopardy.'

'No one asked you to! What's Mum been saying? Has she been blabbing private stuff?'

'Never mind that. What's going on? Why did you tell me that Saskia was your best friend? And tell Mum that she made you anorexic?'

'I never did!'

'Mum said—'

'Well she shouldn't have!' My sister's face had grown dark with fury. 'I never breathed a word about Saskia to her! What actually happened was that Mum got hold of my diary and read some pages she shouldn't have, and made up her own ideas. Ah, see, you didn't know that, did you? Yes, she went snooping about and found my diary, with *private* written on the front, and just helped herself. Read some scribbled notes I'd made when I was feeling down, and assumed she knew everything about my anorexia off the back of them. Decided to go on a witch-hunt, instead of talking to me. Not that I'd have told her anything by then. Can you believe it? My diary!'

I was stunned. I couldn't picture my mother behaving so shabbily. Then again, hadn't I had a sneaky look myself through Hel's old school planner? But that wasn't like reading a private diary. A diary was a step too far. No wonder Mum had been cagey when she talked about Saskia.

'Fair enough, that's bad. That *is* bad. I had no idea. I'd have been pissed off, too.'

'*Such* a betrayal. I'd been trying to use the diary to keep on top of the shit in my head, and then she goes and stirs it up. Confronts me with stuff I couldn't begin to explain and didn't want to. I tell you, Jen, I was so livid I couldn't speak to her for days. I even threatened to report her to my counsellor at CAMHS. But she got into such a state . . .'

'When was this?'

'I don't know. About eight months, a year or so after I'd left school? Something like that.' She hung her head, picking at a fingernail.

I said, 'I know I'm probably being dense here, but I still don't get it. Was Saskia lying when she spoke to me? Were you mates or not?'

'Don't ask me, Jen.'

'I just want to understand. You're my sister. Honestly, I was ready to scratch the woman's eyes out for what I thought she'd done to you. It would have been a fight worth seeing. And I tell you something else: if it turns out she *was* stringing me along, I will go there tomorrow and finish the job.'

I tried a little laugh, but it came out as bitter and fake.

'What a fucking mess,' she muttered. 'All those years past, and it never seems to go away.'

'So talk to me. Please.'

On the notice board by her head I saw she'd pinned snapshots of the shelter dogs she was especially fond of, written their names below. There was one-eyed Isaac, and there was Pepper, much-grown. A sad-eyed Labrador, a Jack Russell-type, a foxhound, some shaggy-osity. Marlon, Chi-Chi, Amber, Pob. My sister loved them all.

'I don't suppose it matters any more,' she said at last, 'what you think of me.'

'How do you mean? I'm on your side.'

'Yeah, feels like it lately.'

'I am. Things have been difficult, you know, with Mum, and – well.' *Inviting dodgy men to the house behind our backs.* 'It's your life, I suppose. You're an adult. I just worry about what you've been doing.'

She sighed. 'You really want the truth?'

'About what?'

'Saskia.'

'Yeah. I do. And what's more, I think it would do you good to tell me. Get it off your chest. Come on. There've been enough secrets and lies lurking about this house and I don't think it's helped anyone. Explain to me how Mum got it wrong, what you were trying to say in your diary.'

Helen put her hands to the sides of her cheeks, dragging them down.

'OK. If you want. These are the plain, sad facts.' Her voice was so low it was barely audible. 'I made her up.'

'Huh?'

'I invented her. As a friend, I mean. She didn't even know I existed, so I imagined that she did and that she thought I was cool. My imaginary friend. At fifteen. Pathetic, isn't it? So now you know. Now you know how crap your sister truly was.'

It took some while to process. 'Was it a sort of crush?'

'If you like. She was popular and bold, couldn't-give-a-toss. I wanted to be that way, instead of some nervous little mouse.'

'You're not mousey.'

'I was in those days. Too nervous to speak up, wound tight the whole day, a target for anyone. I wanted to be sassy and funny and laid-back. Plus, she was incredibly pretty. She had this blonde razor cut, and she used to gel it up at the front like a Manga girl, so it came down over one eye. Just ice cool. Gorgeous.'

'Oh, but look at you. For God's sake, Hel, you're beautiful.'

'Not like that. You think – you've always thought – that the way I look is some magic charm which can get me whatever I want. The solution to everything. But it doesn't work that way. This – ' She flapped her hand in her face – 'is nothing. Nothing *lasting*. I make an initial impression with someone, and then it wears off and after that it's up to me, the inner-me, myself. And that's where things fall apart. I've never been good at making friends, not the way you are. God, you go into a room and people just warm up and chat to you. I've always envied you that.'

'You? Envy me?'

'God, yes. You make friends so easily you don't even realise it.'

'You said two women at work had asked you to go for lunch. Marnie and Niamh.'

'They have. They're nice, yes. But when I'm with strangers I don't seem to be able to do small talk, so I stay on the edge of a group and keep quiet, and people aren't comfortable with that. They think I'm being aloof. I'm not, it's just that my brain goes blank. Then I can see the disappointment as they get to know me and find there's not much going on after all. I'm too self-conscious and wary with strangers, and that makes them awkward in turn.'

'You quite like being by yourself. You've said to me you enjoy your own company.'

'I do, but that's because I've had to learn to. And then the other issue is, a lot of the types who do talk to me are actually trying to chat me up. They're not interested in me as a person. Never mind that sometimes I also manage to piss people off without even opening my mouth. You were there in the precinct last month when that woman strode over and told me I'd wear out my reflection if I stared at it too much. I mean, God! I wasn't even looking at myself, I was looking in a shop window.' Her tone was matter-of-fact, not self-pitying. And it was true what she said. Some people did take against her on sight through jealousy or resentment. Lucinda-Syndrome.

'Is that why you got picked on at school?'

'Oh, I don't know. Wrong place, wrong time, a couple of influential bitches casting about for their next project. I was a pretty visible target. You know, ginger nut. "Here I am! Come over here and bully me." Whereas Saskia was untouchable. She didn't get bitchy notes left daily in her locker, or her GCSE artwork defaced, or have everyone get up and move to a different table when she sat down in the dining hall. She didn't lose her virginity to a boy who broke her heart weeks later. She didn't mess up her own parents' marriage.'

'Don't say that—'

Hel carried on quickly, speaking over me: 'So Saskia became this symbol of a strong person and the kind of girl I wanted to be. I started thinking about her a lot, imagined her giving me advice and encouragement. And it helped. At first, anyway. But then, as the months went on, she sort of morphed into the voice of the anorexia. Because – and I do know how weird this sounds – sometimes anorexia *did* feel like my best friend and the only one who understood me. In my diary I began writing stuff down like, "Saskia says I should exercise more" or "Saskia says keep the faith" or "Saskia's disappointed in me, I've let her down". That's what Mum read. That's what had her charging up to the school to complain. Except by then, the real Saskia had left, thank God. It makes me feel sick to think about it. If she'd still been there . . .'

I could picture her, teen Helen, bent over her diary, scribbling away fearfully. Pouring out her darkest thoughts, searching for answers in her lonely, tangled mind. How horrible to then have your privacy invaded. She must've nearly died of shame.

'And you've never explained this to Mum?'

'How could I? I've never told anyone. Not even Ned. For weeks after she snooped I was too angry, and then, when that subsided, I was crippled with embarrassment. I mean, you would be, wouldn't you? Giving your mental illness its own name. Sheesh. Fucking cuckoo, I was.' She smiled ruefully, a shy curve of the lips.

A tension eased, a little flower of hope blossomed inside my chest.

I said, 'Were you loop-da-loop?'

'I was up the fucking pole, dear sister. Round the bend and coming back again. Nuts. Out of my tree.'

'Then – ' I groped around for the right words – 'then it wasn't really *you*, was it?'

'Huh?' Helen's head tilted to one side while she considered. Downstairs the TV blared briefly, then went to mute. Dad must have sat on the remote again.

I said, 'You know how you were saying you needed Mum to understand that when you were anorexic, you were properly ill? Well, telling her all this would nail it.'

She laughed.

'Yeah, it would, wouldn't it? I can't have that conversation, though, obviously.'

'Why not?'

'Because she's still recovering from the heart attack. The stress of bringing up the past again might be too much.'

'I think you're wrong. I think it would help.'

We stared at each other for a long moment. In The Lady of Shalott's glass I saw us both reflected, the russet-haired and the dark, frowning to understand. Two landless princesses trying to find their way through the midnight forest.

'Will you give it some thought at least, Hel?'

Her shoulders moved in the faintest of shrugs. 'You have to trust me. Trust that I'm working things out in my own way.'

Suddenly I felt exhausted with the intensity of the exchange. Once more the foundation blocks of what I thought I knew had shifted underfoot. Now I had to get to my own room and be alone, leave her to think. Again there was a family history to revise, a new narrative to work out. Those of us who'd been caught up in my sister's fantasy world would at some point need extricating from that illusion. Could my mother bear it? Was I right to push for revelation? In my mind I saw Saskia's broad, open smile, her square jaw and clean white teeth. I found myself edging towards the door, putting my fingers to the cold handle.

'Anyway,' said Hel soberly, 'we all have secrets, don't we, Jen? All of us. Sometimes that's how we survive.'

CHAPTER 11

Country Wise – Our weekly look at rural and folklore matters, by Briar Pipe

Around April, the landscape comes alive with birds. In one corner of my cottage garden, blue tits are busy inspecting the nest box, and a tiny wren flies in and out of the ivy all day long with his beak full of moss. The fields now are dotted with gulls and jackdaws, the rooflines with rows of starlings. It's a sign that spring has arrived.

But how many of us know the old stories and superstitions associated with some of our best-loved species?

The phone call came through at ten. Rosa's door was closed and she clearly wasn't picking up. Alan and Gerry had gone downstairs to help a driver unload a monster delivery of printer paper. I was the only one on the desks.

A Mrs Williams it was, angry and upset. She wanted us to come out and see the damage done to their property by the local hunt. Her village was a fair way off – Rewle, which was actually over the border – but she said she wasn't confident her small local paper would deal with the story properly, so that's why she was contacting us. Her logic was, we were bigger players, but we still knew the area.

Mrs Williams kept fancy chickens, plus some ex-battery hens, and she sold eggs at the roadside and supplied the little local grocery. She'd had some of these birds for ten years and they were more like pets. The previous week she'd been washing her hair, heard a racket at the rear of the house and come downstairs to find the garden packed with milling, hyper-excited foxhounds, and people on horseback trampling everything underfoot. She'd run out and shouted at them to get off her land, at which point one of the mounted men had turned and stuck two fingers up at her. Thoroughly frightened – their riverside cottage was out on its own and well away from near neighbours – she'd run inside to ring Mr Williams. By the time she got through and told him what was happening, the hunt had begun to disperse. She shooed the last of the dogs out, noting that her gate had been broken off its hinges and a hole smashed in the hedge, and went to survey the damage. That was when she saw the chickens.

Had the dogs eaten them? I asked in my ignorance. I wasn't sure whether foxhounds would do that.

No. What had happened was that the chickens were so distressed by the invasion, they'd taken fright and flown into the river where most of them had drowned. The brood she'd tended with such care had been virtually wiped out within the space of twenty minutes.

When her husband arrived shortly afterwards, he'd been livid and wanted to know which hunt it was, but she didn't know.

Because their smallholding was situated on the county border, it could conceivably have been one of three. So he'd jumped in his car, tracked them down just a few lanes away and, by pretending to be a follower, discovered it was the Glasington.

On appeal to the Master the next day, the Williams had been met first with a straight denial, then, when it was obvious the matter wasn't about to go away, hearty apologies. Later a hunt man had come to the door waving a cheque for two hundred pounds. They tore it up in his face, and he'd laughed and told them not to be such idiots. 'But the money wasn't the point,' the woman said to me. 'It was the invasion of our property, and the loss of the birds I loved, and those men's utter bloody rudeness. Everything. Scribbling your name on a cheque can't cancel that out. That's why I want you to print the story. Call them to account.'

I came off the phone all fired up. This could make a great piece, maybe even front page. Proper journalism, not the manufactured ramblings of Briar Pipe and his old country drivel. And it was mine, my scoop!

I tapped at Rosa's door and entered carefully. Since the break-up she'd been pricklier than ever, finding fault with me and my work on a microscopic level. She didn't like this semi colon here, these italics there. I shouldn't sound so cheerful when answering the phone. When did I last polish my shoes? I was slumping in my chair. It was 'common' to wink at your colleagues.

Today she had a face on her like a troll. 'Well, Jennifer? What's the problem now?'

'No problem. A great story,' I said, and proceeded to tell her about Mrs Williams.

She listened, frowning, cut me off before the end.

'Where did you say this was?'

'Rewle. Just outside there, really. Hartswell. I've looked it up on the map and it is within our range. Just.'

'No.'

'Sorry?'

'No it's not. It's out of county.'

'Yes, I know, but we covered that fire a month ago and that was Rewle. That was actually a mile further out.'

'That story was of some public interest.' Rosa flicked her attention back to her PC screen.

'So is this.'

She looked up. 'Oh, my goodness. You don't *believe* these Williams people, do you? A couple of anti-hunt chancers, that's what they are. Trust me.'

'You know them?'

'I know the type. Compensation-scroungers. Probably the sort who call Claims Direct every time they trip over a paving stone. Hunts are easy targets, high profile and wealthy. They get this kind of nonsense thrown at them continually, from locals hoping to make a fast buck. And The Messenger isn't going to give a platform to what's certainly a politically motivated scam. Call Mrs Williams and say we aren't coming.'

I was thrown. I'd thought the story had the hallmarks of a strong lead. 'Hang on. I could at least nip out there, get a few more facts. See if I thought it was bona fide.'

'You're not "nipping" anywhere. You've no vehicle, remember.'

That was true. My car had died and I'd had to scrounge a lift in that morning with one of Dad's drivers.

'And anyway,' she went on, 'there's no photographer availa-ble. Tam's out on the Wirral and Billy's covering the races all day. And you're supposed to be getting ahead with those Briar Pipe columns. I told you, I want three or four months in hand. Briar Pipe's a pinned feature.'

'But what if this is a story, Rosa? I mean, it could be the tip of the iceberg. Who knows how many landowners the hunt's ridden roughshod over? It could be a significant local problem.'

'I – told – you – no.'

'OK, well, if you don't want me to go, how about Gerry?'

She smacked her palm down on the desk, making me jump. 'For God's sake, Jennifer! How many times do you have to be told? There is NO story here, and we are NOT following it up. Can you grasp that? It's very simple, simple enough for even you to understand. Nod at me if you've got it. Yes? Can you do that?'

For a few seconds I stared her out, laser-beam style. I imagined striding forward, drawing her up from her seat by her chiffon scarf and flicking her hard on the end of her superior nose. *Oh, Rosa, Rosa, I'm so glad your heart got broken. May the same thing happen again and again. May you stew in your own bitter juice forever.*

Then I gave in, with a single jerk of my head. 'Right, then. If that's what you want. I'll go and write a piece about "hedgerow herbs", shall I? Since it's so very urgent?'

I waited for the nasty comeback, but more insultingly, she didn't even acknowledge me. She just returned to clicking her mouse and reading the screen in front of her. I was dismissed from her attention.

Closing the door behind me – by some miracle not slamming it so hard that the glass fell out and shattered on the floor – I trudged over to my desk. Was there really nothing worth investigating out in Rewle? How could Rosa be so sure? But that had been the judgement, no mistake. Instead, waiting for me on top of the cuttings and sheets of notes sat my antiquarian source text, *Down Honeysuckle Lanes* by Colonel Edward Smythe, 1929. *A Ramble through the Legends and Lore of the English Countryside.* Rosa had come across the dusty little guide at a book collectors' fair and had the idea of adapting chunks of it for the newspaper. Since then we'd all had a turn at being Briar Pipe, dispensing rural wisdom, although when Gerry did his stint he'd chosen to write about mole trapping which hadn't gone down well with everyone.

I opened a page at random. 'Comfrey', read the chapter heading. 'A Friend to Bees and Man.'

My phone bleeped with a text, and at the same time I was aware of Gerry and Alan clumping up the wooden stairs. When I opened my mobile, it showed a message from Owen: *Saleem wants to know if we're still up for trip to Wales on Saturday.*

I was. Keisha and Vikki had been hassling us to go out and see some friends of theirs on Lake Bala, and have a barbecue and some home-brewed wine and generally chill. Saleem was bringing a new girlfriend with him who we were gagging to see. Even the weather forecast looked hopeful. I was about to simply reply and confirm, when I had an idea.

Are you free right now? Have you still got keys to Saleem's van? I texted.

Yes and yes, came the answer a moment later.

I'll be with you in 10. Dig out your camera.

'Bloody hell, that was a job and a half, I tell you,' said Gerry, plonking himself down on his swivel chair next to me and wiping his brow with his shirt cuff. 'Still, we're stocked up with paper till about 2020. Have I missed anything?'

'Oh, only the start of the end of my career, probably. Listen, I'm ducking out for a bit. There's something important I have to do, and I won't be back before lunchtime. If Rosa asks where I am, tell her – tell her I've gone to cover an escaped giraffe on the A525.'

He let out a snort. 'Yeah?'

'Yeah.'

'OK. Will do. I'm sure you know what you're about and you're not headed full-on into any kind of shit-storm. 'Cause that wouldn't be like you at all, would it?'

I grinned, unhooked my bag from my chair, jumped to my feet and gave him the thumbs-up.

Owen parked the van round the corner, out of sight of the Williams' cottage, so no questions would be asked as to why *The Messenger* had sent their staff out in a vehicle marked 'Spice Delight'.

'Remember, as far as this woman's concerned, you're *The Messenger*'s official photographer,' I told him. 'That means no passing comment on the story, no engaging in debate. However strongly you feel. Basically, you need to take a ton of snaps and keep schtum.'

He nodded and mimed a zipping action across his mouth

It was Mr Williams who let us in through the newly patched-up gate. A wiry man of about fifty, wearing farmers' overalls and thick work boots, he walked with his shoulders hunched in a kind of glum resignation.

'I'll show you the coop first,' he said. 'Not that we've many girls left in it.'

There wasn't anything remarkable about the smallholding,

other than perhaps its proximity to the broad, slow-moving river. We'd arrived on a day of bright sunshine and the water glinted as it flowed between the grassy banks. The cottage itself was a pretty but modest two-bedroomed affair, in need of some renovation. The Williams also owned some outbuildings, and a paddock which they rented to a neighbouring farmer, and another field which they used themselves as an allotment. It was clear from the first, though, that the hens had been the big deal.

'We had some Silkies and Sussex and Faverolles, Orpingtons and a couple of ex-battery. My wife's pride and joy, they were. They had the run of the place and they loved it. Scratting about. Now we've just a handful left. About three-quarters of our stock gone, bff, just like that. Bodies piled up near the bend. Sal was very upset.'

The scene looked peaceful enough now. Leaving Owen on the river bank to take his photos, we went inside to sit in the low-ceilinged kitchen. And as Mr Williams spooned cheap coffee out of a catering pack, it struck me how different this room was from the glossy 'farmhouse-style kitchens' featured in Messenger Lifestyle. For a start, the quarry-tiled floor was scattered with seeds and chunks of mud. There was a tin of mite treatment on the drainer, a bucket of poultry grit on the doormat, a bottle of Verm-X by the soap dispenser. The table top was heaped with old newspapers and flyers. A battered gun cabinet took up the far corner, while the cupboard by the door looked as if it fastened with blue baler twine. Everything was scruffy, down-at-heel. None of your gingham ties, your Crabtree & Evelyn here.

First I had Mr Williams go through the events of the day again. Then I started to try and flesh the story out.

'Obviously you're angry with the hunt,' I said, 'but given you're a chicken farmer, isn't it a good thing to get rid of a few foxes?'

He shook his head. 'If you build a good, strong, hardwood coop and you lock it properly at night, foxes shouldn't be a problem. Our coop had an automatic timer controlling the doors – oh, aye, no expense spared for those girls. And you can see the fence round it. That's a six-foot heavy gauge mesh, buried a foot deep. Even a badger couldn't push through that. People use daft stuff like chicken wire and then they're surprised when a fox bites a hole in it. Chicken wire keeps chickens in but it dunt keep foxes out. Oh, and then we have an electric wire running about fox-nose height round the edge. That gives them a surprise; they don't come back after a zap from that.'

'I see. So you're telling me you've never had a fox take one of your fowl?'

'Nope. Safe as houses, our hens were. Well, I say that. Mink, you have to watch out for, and we lost some to a rat one time – accidentally shut it in with the chickens one night. That was nasty. So nowadays I always check. But you know, even if a fox was causing me trouble, I'd just get my gun and shoot it, easy and clean. The technology's so good it's a piece of cake to shoot something these days, long as you're using the proper calibre with a decent scope. A Bushnell, I use. And the point is, shooting would take out the actual fox that was causing bother. The trouble with hounds is, they flush out any old fox they come across, might not be the right one. There's no control. No control at all. As we found out.' He laughed bitterly.

Through the small cottage window I could see Owen crouching with his camera to get a low-angled shot of the coop. He was taking his role very seriously.

'I mean, don't get me wrong, I'm not one of these bunny-hugger types,' he went on. 'Pests are pests, sometimes they want sorting. But there are ways. Most foxes that need taking out get shot because it's quick and straightforward and it only involves one person and it doesn't damage anyone else's property. No need to assemble great crowds or special outfits or packs of animals to do it. You pull that trigger and the fox knows nothing about it. Just, bang bang, gone. You can bag several in a night if you have to. But the hounds, they kill, what, *tiny* numbers. Nothing that makes any sort of impact on the population. And that makes me laugh. Because what would you think if you had a nest of a hundred wasps and you called out a pest controller and he said to you, "Great, I've got this method where we'll just kill three or four of them and leave the rest unharmed." You'd think he was mad, wouldn't you? Same as, if you've got a fly in your bathroom, you just swat it with a paper. Job done. You don't get someone round to loose a pack of trained lizards onto your upstairs landing.'

I smiled at the image. 'When you put it like that.'

'I'm not anti-blood sports, Miss Crossley. I'm anti-palaver. I'm anti-bullshit. If anyone tells you hunting with dogs is necessary to keep fox numbers down, you know they're talking crap. It's just an excuse to thump about over other people's land and show who's boss.'

'OK. Interesting, though, because a lot of readers will assume that people who live in the country support the hunt automatically. That it's an urban–rural divide.'

'Don't know about that. Maybe once upon a time. Not now. You won't find much support for it round here, and most of us have lived in this hamlet our whole lives. In any case, the

Glasington's made up of city folk – bankers, estate agents, solicitors, corporate types. I think there's one or two you could just about call farmers, but they're really businessmen running food plants. Industrial-scale milking sheds, that kind of caper. They show up here in their great shiny vehicles, blocking the lanes and giving you filthy looks if you need to get past. We've tolerated them because we feel we've no choice. But then there's the broken fences and the mud trampled over your yard, your livestock upset – or worse. Oh, I've some tales I could tell you. But, see, you dare to make a complaint and then you're watching your back forever after . . .'

'How do you mean?'

'"Unfortunate things" happen. Never anything you can definitely pin on anyone, mind.' He was running his dirty nail up and down the Formica surface of the table, picking at the chips and cracks. 'Stuff like, your car tyres let down, silent phone calls, dog shit through your letter box. Oh yeah. Messages. And the people who send them have friends in high places. Rory Henscher up the road, he went for his usual summer job on the Langthorne estate clearing out rhodies, and he just got turned away; that was after he complained the hunt had smashed his gatepost with one of their 4x4s. And he'd been relying on that job. The loss of wages near-crippled him.'

'Did they tell him to his face? Did they say it was because he'd crossed the hunt?'

'Nothing so obvious. He knew, though. They stick together, hunt-folk. Thumb your nose at one and they all rear up. Chief auctioneer at Hardock's cattle market is a hunt member, and if you go against him or his mates then you find you can't sell your livestock, or it goes for next-to-nothing. Oh, we've had torch beams shone through our bedroom curtains at night. A dead cat left on someone's porch. And you get the impression that's only the thin end of the wedge. You've no idea what's coming next. They're not all thugs who go hunting, but some are. A few of these terrier-men are a law unto themselves. They have their own rules. Even the masters can't dictate what they get up to.'

'So are you worried about what might happen?'

Mr Williams pushed back his chair, which scraped with an evil noise across the tiles.

'I am, yes. The problem is, we're pretty remote out here. At night it's pitch dark. Your nearest police are a good forty minutes away, and that's if they come straight out, which they don't. But I've been taking precautions. I've nailed up our letter box. Postie leaves our letters in a tin by the gate these days. We're having a lurcher pup off Matty Higgins up the road, so that'll make Sal happier if I have to go out of an evening. And I've installed security lights. You remember the cheque the Glasington gave us? Well, I sellotaped it together and used it to buy a few useful bits and pieces. I thought it was, you know, appropriate.'

'It's going to cause trouble for you, then, if I print this.' I knew as a journalist that was the last point I should be making to him, but I didn't want to be responsible for harm coming his way.

He met my eyes with a defiant look.

'You know, I grew up on a farm, Miss Crossley. My father's farm, passed on to him by my granddad. It was going to be mine. Then, in the 1970s, we had to sell up and developers came and built a housing estate on top of it. Broke my dad's heart. So after that I worked hard and saved my money and had a bit of luck – Sal's luck, really – and eventually I was able to buy this little patch of land, and although it's not on the scale of my dad's, it's mine.

When I close the gate, I close it against the world. Some people might say, "Oh, it's only chickens, why are you bothering, you can soon get some more," but that's not the point. They were Sal's chickens, and she was heartbroken, and why should I stand by and watch bully-boys upset my wife? This isn't feudal times any more, we're not peasants beholden to a lord of the manor. This is my land and my property. I may yet go to the police – some of us round here want to but others aren't so convinced, because the hunt have these hot-shot lawyers and they can throw whatever money they want at the courts. But in the meantime I just want as many people to know as possible. Can you do that for me?'

'As long as you're sure.'

'I am.' He bent forward, placed his palms on the table and pushed himself to his feet. 'Now, let me get those photos I took last week, just after the Glasington had buggered off.'

By the time Owen and I climbed into the van, I was buzzing. Not only had Mr Williams given us an SD card of pictures – images of dead hens, feather-strewn grass, damage and mayhem – he'd passed on a list of contact details for other villagers who he maintained wanted to speak to me. What we had here was a damn good story, if I could get my sources straight first. Rosa would have to let it through. I'd go back this afternoon and give her the outline with a schedule for follow-ups, and she'd be gagging for me to get onto it. There were all sorts of leads to investigate, injustices to be aired. I would go among these people and give a voice to the oppressed. And through everything ran the sense that this one story could be the making of me, my scoop of the year, way above some stupid talent show, and never mind the usual brain-withering trivia I was asked to write.

'Happy with that?' said Owen, clipping his seat belt into place and firing up the engine.

I turned to him gratefully. 'I'll say. That was brilliant. Not brilliant for Mr Williams, obviously, but from a journalism perspective, a cracking interview. I got loads of stuff off him. And I have to say, you were great.'

'I only did what you told me.'

That's the point, I thought. I'd been worried he'd try to muscle in with his own thoughts on hunting or hierarchy. 'But I didn't half put you on the spot, phoning up this morning and just demanding you taxi me out here and then play photographer.'

'Yeah, well. It was important.'

He took his hand away from the wheel a moment to comb his fingers through his hair, and I thought I'd never seen him look so handsome. That sharp, stubbled jaw line, the fine nose, the beautiful, even teeth. Owen, my boyfriend. I was a lucky girl. I ought to be grateful.

The lanes round here were narrow and thick-hedged, so we had to go steadily. Twice we met tractors and had to reverse to a passing space, and on one stretch we came across a lone sheep which had got loose and ran about giddily till it blundered through a gap in the fencing. I enjoyed sitting high up in the van's cab. I could see into fields, glimpse strutting pheasants and lolloping rabbits and shimmering meres. On one gatepost we approached, a huge brown hawk-thing took off in front of us and flapped lazily over the valley. Summer was promised, you could see it in the land, and it made me think of other summers while I was growing up. The cherry tree in our front garden was in full flower now, and I remembered gathering bunches of the fat pink blossoms, and having a petal fight with Ned all over the drive. I remembered the three of us on a walk somewhere – had he taken us to a village carnival? – and as we were making our way along the public footpath he'd fallen behind Hel and me on the path, then taken a stalk of long grass and tickled us on the necks and claimed it was bees. Later we'd swapped round so we were walking behind and thrown burrs at his polo shirt.

I remembered him picking me up from school and having ash key competitions by the gates, throwing the helicopter seeds into the air and seeing whose took longer to spin to the ground. And there was another time when the three of us were mucking about on a canal bridge and he managed to kick his shoe right off so it landed in the water. Helen didn't half scold him for that. She and I had to get one on either side and support him, wounded soldier-style, as he limped along. Miles from the car, we were, and the ground was filthy-wet, and I ended up nipping into a newsagent's and begging a flap off a cardboard box to tie round his foot.

'We should go for walks in the countryside,' I said to Owen as the van crested a hill, opening up a stunning view of rolling farmland.

'Yeah,' he said non-committally.

'I mean, look at it round here. It's beautiful.'

'It might look nice, but the trouble with modern farming is that it's creating monoculture deserts. Industrial-scale crop production is death to the land. These spaces around us are actually sterile, it's deceptive. I was reading up about it last night.'

We slowed down for a blind bend, and at the same moment a mouse shot out of the verge and across the tarmac. It reached the far side and did an odd little dash backwards and forwards before finally flinging itself into a shallow ditch. 'Geronimo!' I imagined Ned narrating.

'Ha! Did you see that?' I said to Owen.

'No, what?'

'That mouse.'

'Where?'

'Down there. It's gone now. Only, it was funny, that scurrying way they move. Really intense and serious. Made me laugh.'

'I didn't see.'

'It doesn't matter.'

He shrugged and changed gear. I was trying to imagine us running through a field, waving grass stems and throwing sticky burrs at each other. It was no good, though, the picture wouldn't come. Besides, he was wearing a leather jacket; the burrs would just fall off.

I'd promised I'd treat Owen to a pub lunch as a thank you, and after the efforts of the morning we'd certainly both worked up an appetite. But it being Monday, everywhere we spotted was shut. We were coming into Chrishall before we saw somewhere that was serving food.

No. Drive on, I vibed.

'I'm gonna stop here, OK?' he said, slowing up the van and flicking on the indicator.

'Let's see if there's somewhere better further along.'

'Why?'

'I just don't like the look of this place.'

'Yeah, it's a bit nobby round here, I know, but I'm starving. Come on. It only has to be a quick bite.'

'We're not that far from Chester,' I argued. 'Another fifteen minutes.'

'Another fifteen minutes and I'll be forced to eat my own leg.

Sorry, Jen.' He pulled into the car park, switched off the engine, reached for the handle on the van's door. 'You owe me.'

He jumped out and I had no choice but to follow, even though every instinct told me to turn back. This was Joe Pascoe's territory.

'Can we hurry up at least?' I grumbled. Owen strode on ahead.

The Bridge Inn was definitely gastro-end, as pubs go. Outside the half-timbered building there were box trees in pots, and the inside of the porch had been painted that giveaway-middle-class pale green. The specials board was half in French: a cheese toastie here was 'croque monsieur'.

'Grab a menu and we'll get an order straight in,' said Owen. Swagged hops hung from the beam above his head.

There was a lot of noise coming from the other end of the bar, but we found ourselves a quieter corner. Immediately I got out my notebook so I could run over the main points. On top of the general hunt intimidation, there were two other lines of enquiry to follow up: the rumour of illegal artificial fox earths being built on the estate, and a possible tie-in between one of the terrier-men and a gang of badger-baiters. OK, there was nothing here that would make national news – no 'children savaged by hounds' – but we definitely had a story to make waves in the local area.

Owen peered over my shoulder at my scrawl.

'I was never going to wade in, you know. You didn't have to worry. This is yours, your first proper campaign. I wasn't going to mess with it. And I have to say, it's actually been great to see you working on something worthwhile instead of the usual mind-rot.'

'Gee, thanks. Could you say that again only slightly more patronisingly?'

From the far side of the bar came a deep male roar, and someone shouting that they had a Cunning Plan.

'I can't help it, Jen. You're better than *The Messenger*.'

'It's working for *The Messenger* that's given me the platform for this story.'

'Assuming you're allowed to print it. Have you thought about what you're going to do if Rosa still blocks you?'

'She won't do that. Not when she's seen the detail.'

'You said she goes to hunt balls.'

'It wasn't with the Glasington.'

'Well, I bet it wouldn't be the first time a hunt story's got hushed up. Didn't you say she has a *Boot the Ban* sticker on her car?'

I thought about that. A graphic of a wellington tilted as if it was in mid-kick. 'Yeah, but you see a few of those round here. There was some guy handing them out for free in the city centre. The pavements were littered with them for weeks after.'

A waitress came with an unasked-for dish of olives. Olives always made me think of Ned and the way he'd spear a couple on cocktail sticks to look like feet and then make them walk about and dance. I'd snorted a nose full of Ribena the first time he performed that trick.

Owen took a long drink, put down his glass. 'I reckon you should have a back-up plan, anyway. Hey, what's this here?'

There was an abandoned *Messenger* lying on the table next to ours and he reached across and picked it up. He made a mild show of reading the headlines, but I knew what was coming. He couldn't stop himself. Soon he was spreading the newspaper out on the table, flipping the pages till he found the Cream section and scanning for my by-line.

Over his arm I read: 'Seven Ways to Get that Golden Glow. Make bronzer your number-one friend!' And below it: 'Holiday Horrors – Your Must-Have Guide to a Summer First Aid Kit.' Pastel-coloured plasters and Evian Facial Mist, I remembered listing.

'Is that Friday's edition? Because you know I also did the coverage of the Flower Festival on page four.'

'I'm saying nothing.'

You don't need to, I thought. A script doesn't have to be spoken out loud for a partner to hear it.

'I'm learning, Owen, I'm an intern. I do a range of stuff on the paper and some of it's light, some of it's more meaty. That's how it should be. I've told you before, they don't let you loose on the major stories till you've learned how to produce decent, unfancy copy to a deadline. Anyway, in tomorrow's edition I've a double-page spread on keeping street-safe. That's not fluff. And what's more, I managed to sneak in a plug for the Revolution book-shop's self-defence classes. Rosa let it go through because it was just a tiny mention in a list, but even so, it was there. I did text Vikki to let her know it'd be in.'

'Oh, yes, she said. She was pretty pleased. Well, she'll tell you all about it on Saturday.'

'*Your father was a hamster and your mother smelt of elderberries!*' a man shouted from the other side of the bar.

'*Wrong way round. It was his MOTHER who was a hamster.*'

'*—Hung like a hamster—*'

'*Hamsters have massive balls—*'

Owen folded the newspaper away. 'Actually, there's something I need to tell you about Saturday.'

'The barbecue?'

'Yeah.'

'Sounds ominous.'

'Not really.'

'How do you mean, "not really"?'

'Well.' He leaned back in his chair. 'You haven't to let on I told you because it's supposed to be a secret, but Vikki and Keisha are getting engaged.'

'What? No. Wow! That's terrific! I had no idea.'

'Yeah, so when they announce it, you need to do a shocked face.'

'OK. And the reason you've told me in advance and so ruined my chance to be genuinely surprised is . . . ?'

'The wedding's booked for next April and they want you to be an usher. I thought you'd like a heads-up on that.'

'An *usher*?'

This was a bolt from the blue. Not the marriage bit – those two were practically married already – but that they wanted me involved. Me. In some sort of responsible role.

'Don't stress,' Owen went on. 'It's not like being a bridesmaid or a best man. You won't have to be frocked-up. I gather you just wear a buttonhole and show people to their seats and hand out service sheets, that kind of thing.'

Our dinner arrived and I took a moment to sort out my cutlery and think the news through.

'God, does this mean I have to organise a hen do?'

'Nah. Keisha's sister's doing all that. They might want you at a rehearsal the week before.'

'But why me?'

'Because they like you. They really do. Vikki especially. She was the one who gave me the worst ear-bashing when we split up.'

'Was she? You didn't tell me that. What did she say?'

'Basically what an idiot I was.'

'*Joe! Joe!*' a male voice was calling from somewhere on the far side of the pub. The name fell on my ears like an ugly, clanging bell. I whipped my head round to look, but the speaker was out of sight, round a corner. Oh, God, no, I thought, please don't let it be him. Not him. Please. How stupid had I been to risk coming here? Idiot-woman. I should have argued more, insisted we drove on past this danger zone. Joe Pascoe worked from home; it was highly likely he'd pop out for a bite at his local come lunchtime, wasn't it? Bloody hell, we might as well have set up a picnic table in his front garden. '*Joe! Hoy! Marky wants a packet of peanuts as well.*'

And yet, and yet, there were other Joes in the world. Why should it be him? There was no need to panic. It might be something and nothing. I'd watch the corner now and most likely a different man altogether would walk out.

The next moment he was there, standing at the bar. He had his back to me so I could only see his crew cut, his broad, confident shoulders under his red plaid shirt, his snug-fitting jeans. That was enough, though. My heart began to pound.

'Yeah,' Owen was saying. 'Viks is your biggest fan. And my biggest critic. She said there was very little chance you'd forgive me but that if I got a second chance then I had to grab it. And I'm so glad you came back. So glad.'

I watched, transfixed, as Joe leant on the bar top, bantered with the landlord and collected his drinks. I couldn't tear my eyes away from the detail of the transaction.

'And Keisha too. She rates you. Even Saleem told me I was a knob for finishing with you. Doesn't mince his words, our Saleem.'

The next moment, Joe had disappeared from view again. I could hear him, though, and his idiot mates. *'I'm a laydee. I'm a LAYdee.'*

For a minute or two I tried to carry on with my meal, but my mouth had dried up and my throat gone tight with hatred. Next to me, Owen tucked into his pie as if he hadn't eaten for days. Mostly he doesn't care much about food, his mind being on higher things, but when he gets ravenous he just wolfs whatever's around. I could see he was totally focussed on the plate in front of him. In fact he was so absorbed, he didn't notice at first when I stood up.

If destiny was going to torment me by dropping Joe into my path like this, then there must be a reason for it. This encounter was meant to be. I had an opportunity. It was up to me to act.

'Oh, you OK, Jen?'

'Need the loo.'

I set off after Joe. I didn't exactly know what I was going to do when I got there, I just knew I had to confront him. Inspiration would come.

As soon as I came round the corner I saw them. Four thirty-something men, flushed and happy with themselves, sitting at a large round table. The table top was strewn with balled-up serviettes and empty beer bottles and food that had spilled from their plates. I shrank back for a moment, out of sight, and listened in to their conversation.

'Do you remember when you nicked that charity bag off a woman's doorstep and brought the clothes into school?' one was saying.

'Aw, yeah. That was ace. And we all had a go at trying stuff on.'

'You had to stick your hand in blind and then whatever you pulled out, you had to wear.'

'Pair of pants, I ended up with, but I couldn't get into them.'

'Story of your life.'

'Didn't you have a bra, Maz?'

'That was deliberate. He was searching for one.'

'Suited him.'

'He's got the moobs for it.'

'And after, we threw the rest into the tree. I got the highest. I got a belt right up in the top branches.'

'Joe got a tie higher up than that. No one could reach it. It was still there when I left in Year Eleven.'

'Go, Joe!'

A roar of laughter.

Revulsion, as physical as nausea, overcame me. This was it. Time to act. Payback for my sister with her doodled page of hearts and moons; for Ned and his innocent loyalty; for my parents' grief in the years they watched their daughter shrink and pine. How dare Joe Pascoe sit there sniggering with his mates? Someone needed to show him for the git he was.

I took a deep breath, stiffened my shoulders and marched round the corner. They weren't even looking at me. I went right up to the table so I was practically touching it and, in one seamless movement, picked up Joe's nearly full pint and poured it over his head.

The effect was electric. All talk stopped at once as they stared, goggle-eyed. Joe himself I'd expected to splutter and flap about under the onslaught, to shout and protest, but instead he sat there, blinking in a comedy way as the fluid trickled over him and darkened his shirt. His cool reaction made him master of the moment, and I hated him even more. Only when the beer was finished did his hands come up to wipe his eyes and brow.

I made myself place the glass carefully down on the mat, and that simple gesture seemed to break the spell and reanimate the rest of them.

'*Fuck*-ing hell.'

'Woah!'

'Steady, Mrs.'

'Aye aye, what have you been up to, Joseph?'

'Who's this? Who've you been upsetting now?'

I swept my gaze round the table at them, at their wide grins and glittering eyes. This was proper entertainment, they were thinking. This was a floor show and a half. Aside from differences in skin shade and build, they were pretty much Joe-clones, with their plaid shirts and short haircuts. One guy had wire-framed glasses, but that was the only real distinguishing feature. His gang, they were. Like the one he'd probably had at school. Joe was making a big deal of licking his lips and fingers, trying to make out I'd done him a favour by delivering his drink that way.

'Can I help you?' he asked me, looking straight into my eyes. 'Do you need directing to the nearest psychiatric unit, love? Have I to give them a call?'

'Fuck you, Joe Pascoe,' I managed.

'Oooooh,' came the mocking chorus. *Go for it, darling*, I could hear them thinking. *Give us some more.*

There was so much I wanted to say that I found myself

speechless under their scrutiny. *Stay right away from my sister, you bastard. You've done enough damage. Leave her alone. Don't ever come round our house again, don't phone, don't write, don't text her, nothing. Just disappear off the face of the earth.*

'You, you . . .' I halted.

'You drive me crayayzee,' sang Joe.

Any power I'd had vanished in that second. My mouth worked but I couldn't get another word out. I'd failed. I was a useless sister who did nothing but harm.

'Seriously, love, what the fuck is the matter with you?'

All I could manage was to flinch out of the way as one of the Joe-clones fished out his mobile and began filming, making up a comedy commentary as he scanned the table.

'So what happens is, this nutter walks into a bar . . .'

'Get him a towel, Marky. Or some bog paper.'

'You gonna speak to us, sweetheart? You gonna tell us what's eating you?'

'She doesn't fucking know. Look in her eyes. She's not all there.'

They were sneering and slapping him on the back and joking and congratulating him for being a Lad. Oh, the fun they'd have retelling the incident, inventing various back-stories. Joe the ladykiller. Joe the Casanova. Women, they just couldn't help themselves when he was around. Even when he dicked about and it caught up with him, he was a hero. My sister's worst fears were correct and he was invulnerable.

'Honestly, guys,' he was protesting now, 'you have to believe me, I have no fucking idea what that was about. Not a clue. Never seen her before.'

'Like we fucking believe that.'

'My man!'

'I thought you'd sworn off mad bitches.'

'What are you like, mate?'

I left them in their smug tableau and ran to drag my boyfriend out of that hellish place.

A quarter to midnight and I was finally finished. Five hours I'd spent writing up the hunt story, shut inside my bedroom with a Do Not Disturb sign on the door. I was thirsty and my eyes were gritty and I'd barely spoken to my parents the entire evening. But this piece had to be right. Boy, did it have to be right.

Owen had prophesied correctly. Rosa had refused to let *The Messenger* criticise the Glasington in any way. In pursuing the story against her explicit instructions, I was stubborn, I was wilful, I was arrogant and stupid. I was not some kind of maverick reporter, I was a clumsy underling who couldn't even get the basics right. She'd already spelt it out to me. Mr Williams' claims were almost certainly provoked by envy. Or malice, or a personal grudge. He might even be a full-blown fantasist. If we printed the story, we'd be opening ourselves up to libel. I hadn't tried hard enough to get the Glasington's response (even though I'd been on the phone for an hour trying to track somebody down who would talk to me; even though I'd been misdirected by one person after another and eventually had some unidentified woman tell me to piss off). And no, I wasn't going to be calling anyone else, Rosa absolutely forbade it. I'd done enough damage to the paper by following up on this load of rubbish. Giving it credibility. I was completely unprofessional, dragging the name of *The Messenger* through the mud. I needed to get my head down and start bloody well doing as I was told or she wouldn't be answerable for the consequences.

I don't know what her motives were – fear of offending those people she'd spent months assiduously courting, I guessed, or a desire to protect friends of friends – but they clearly were more important to her than circulation figures. What was it Mr Williams had said? *Thumb your nose at one and they all rear up.* It didn't matter. This story was being published whatever.

So to my boss's face I pretended I was just a bit cheesed off. Rolled my eyes, sighed, glowered, settled down at my desk and began something else. The minute I was home, however, I logged into the newspaper's website and got busy. I rang the contacts given to me by Mr Williams and gathered some more examples of alleged hunt intimidation. The article I headlined *Hunt Mafia in Village Terror* – might as well go for it – and then I laid out the events in blunt, uncompromising detail. Mr Williams' and Owen's photos I uploaded next to the text. The one of the saturated dead chickens laid out in a row was particularly strong. Then, when the page looked the way I wanted, I sent out links to social media. As a very last stratagem I created a blog and reproduced the text and images on that, so that when Rosa spotted the story and removed it from the *Messenger* website, the article would still be accessible. I knew this was the end of my career at that newspaper, and maybe as a journalist full stop. I did consider the years I'd invested in getting my degree, and how lucky I'd been to land that internship against the competition, and about the money my parents had spent subbing me, but I truly felt I had no choice. If we weren't in business to print the truth, what were we there for? How, in all conscience, could I have called Mrs Williams back and told her the case was closed?

After I shut my laptop down I sat for a while on my bed. Then I decided I needed to get some fresh air, clear my racing brain.

I crept out onto the landing. Mum and Dad had gone to bed and the house was pretty much silent and dark, though there was a faint light showing from my sister's room. I made my way downstairs, groping through the gloom towards the kitchen, across the tiles, till I reached the door and turned the key. The door tended to jam in its frame during hot weather, but with careful tugging it eventually juddered open and I was able to step outside.

The air was warm and the sky a breathtaking dome of stars. I tiptoed across the patio, avoiding a fat frog which had appeared out of nowhere and was squatting by the steps. Then I walked to the centre of the lawn. Moths were circling the carriage lamps on the wall of the garage, white daffodils loomed out of the planters. I tipped back my head and took in the glory of the constellations. The vastness of the night was both reassuring and unsettling. So much sky and so little me. As I followed the familiar patterns with my eyes, I felt I was slipping out of my own life and out of time entirely.

I knelt, then lay down on the grass, flat like a sunbather. It was cooler down here and damper. Something rustled inside the bushes behind me, as if my presence had disturbed a small animal. Mouse? Rat? Hedgehog? I imagined the creatures of the night emerging, Bambi-style, to check out this prostrate stranger on their lawn. The next moment my mind skidded off heaven-wards, so I was convinced I could feel the earth revolving and wondered if I might get tipped off into the atmosphere to float around with space junk and satellites. Perhaps I'd become a constellation of my own. The Great Fool.

What have you done, girl?

You've jumped without checking where you'll land, that's what.

You've leapt out into the void and tomorrow you'll find yourself in free-fall. For God's sake, you can't bail out whenever you happen to disagree with your boss. This was my dad's voice, I realised. *I thought you had more backbone than that.*

Mum's face loomed in my imagination, anxious and exasperated. *But you were the independent one, Jen, the one who was going places. We had high hopes. What are you going to do now? We can't keep supporting you forever.*

I'll get another job, I'd tell them.

Oh yes? As what?

As what, as what.

Owen would be more sympathetic when I told him. *Well done, Jen!* he'd say. *That's so cool! And about time, too. I told you all along that place was bad for you.*

Like you'd know anything about the world of work, I'd snap at him. Rosa'll fill that position again before I can clear my desk. Essentially, with the click of a mouse, I've thrown away everything I've struggled for.

I recalled now his puzzled expression when I'd dragged him away from the middle of his pub lunch, no explanation. Pushed him through the door, jostled him into the van. 'What is it?' he'd asked in bewilderment. 'Someone I need to avoid, someone I did a story on,' I'd lied. 'No, don't go in and look. Just drive.' Running away from my own rash stupidity.

A clunk-thud from over the other side of the lawn brought me to myself. I blinked and sat up to see Hel, in bare feet and a long kimono, close the door behind her and begin picking her way towards me.

'Did you want something?' I asked irritably when she reached my side.

'To know if you're OK.'

'Not really, no.' I lay down again and fixed my sights on Orion. Odd how some of the stars that made him up were stronger than others. One was so faint it was hardly there. Disappeared altogether if you looked to the side.

'Can I do anything?'

'Nope.'

She sat down next to me, hugging her knees. 'Is it Owen again?'

'I've got myself sacked.'

'Oh. God.' Something that may have been the bat fluttered into the pool of garage light for a moment, then was lost in the dark. 'What happened? Did you finally tell Rosa where to get off?'

'In a manner of speaking. Don't ask me to give you the detail right now. I'm too tired.'

'OK. Well. Good for you.'

'Yes, good for jobless me.'

I was still absorbed in the sky, but I became aware of her stretching out next to me so that the crown of her head was close to mine but her feet were pointing away, towards the house. From above we must look like the hands on a clock. A soft tearing noise started up as she began to pluck at the grass by her sides.

'What am I going to tell Mum and Dad, Hel?'

'You definitely can't rewind here? You are officially unemployed?'

'Come tomorrow I will be.'

'Wow.' There was a silence between us, not unfriendly. 'Listen,' she said at last, 'I know you. Whatever it is you've done, there'll be a decent reason for it. You wouldn't jeopardise your career over nothing. So when it comes to explaining, just be straight with them, keep calm. Say you had to do what you had to do. There was no choice.'

'There wasn't.'

'Right, then. I'll back you up. Mum and Dad might be pissed off for a while but they'll get over it. Trust me, I've had plenty experience of that. Put your head down, insert your mental earphones and tough it out. For God's sake, Jen, you're twenty-three. You make your own decisions, remember?'

'My own cock-ups.'

'Sometimes you do have to upset a few people. You have to shake it up. Reach for what matters. Live a life less constrained.'

Ned's face rose before my eyes, imprinted against the stars. *Be careful what you advise, sister.*

I heard her sigh. Then she said, 'Anyway, at least you've got Owen. Things worked out for you there, didn't they?'

'Owen!'

'What?'

I remembered a summer evening when I was a kid and Dad had brought me out into the garden to look for a meteor shower that was scheduled. Normally with these events the weather turns cloudy at the crucial hour, but conditions for this one had been perfect and we'd seen loads of shooting stars, so many I'd lost count. I'd run out of wishes by the end, not that it made much difference as none of the things I wished for came true anyway. After the show was over, Dad had taken me inside, found Mum and Hel were in bed, and made me hot chocolate and let me stay up with him to watch an unsuitably violent thriller on TV. So, looking back, the wishes hadn't been the point. Most of them had been ridiculous anyway. Why did we get ourselves mired in unhappiness when the world was full of ordinary joy?

I said, 'I've been trying not to admit this to myself, but it isn't working between us.'

'Hey? I thought—'

'I know. When Owen and I broke up, I genuinely believed he was all I wanted in the world. But now I can see that what he said at the time was true: regardless of Chelle, we're just not a good fit. Each of us wants to change the other too much. He's right. He's always right about everything, and that's what makes him wrong.'

'I thought he'd been trying harder?'

'He has. That only shows it up more. It's a constant struggle to be what he wants me to be and somehow I've run out of energy. While we were apart – ' While we were apart, there was Ned – 'the spark died. Something fundamental changed. I tried to pretend it hadn't, tried talking myself round, but it's gone.'

'Does he know?'

'I don't think he has a clue.' Last Saturday night, sitting in Owen's window, sipping rum-laced hot chocolate together and gazing out over the weir. The place I'd thought I wanted to be. 'So there we are. You *and* me. Ironic, isn't it?'

'What is?'

'Both of us in the same boat. I mean, stuck with boyfriends we no longer love.'

She shifted, raised her hand as if to shade her eyes from the moonlight. She didn't deny it, though.

'You're going to have to straighten yourself out, Hel, same as I am.'

'Mm.'

'Whatever it is you're up to.'

'I know what you think—'

'Who was it, that day in the kitchen? When I heard that man's voice and he ran off and you were so weird after? If your conscience is clear, why can't you tell me?'

'I just can't. Please.'

'If it is Joe—' *He's too repulsive and I can't bear it.*

'It's not him.'

'Who, then?'

No answer.

'God, I don't know what to make of you. I never have done.'

Somewhere far off I could hear wind chimes tinkling.

'I promise you it'll come right,' she said.

'What will?'

'All of it. Everything.'

'Yeah?'

'Not for everyone. It won't come right for everyone. Just for us. The good guys.'

'You think the universe is that fair?'

She brought her hand down to her side, and where it fell there was the faintest contact between our knuckles.

'I think we make our own universes, in the end.'

CHAPTER 12

Four solid weeks of rain we'd had. The flooding was unprecedented. There'd actually been days when the main road to Chester was closed; I wouldn't have been able to get into work even if I'd had a job. Wouldn't have been able to meet Owen even if he'd wanted to see me.

In the meantime I'd attacked my bedroom, gutted it, set it up properly as a home office and then pursued the Glasington story with vigour. I'd met various dead ends: there were more people than Rosa didn't want this story out in the public domain. But there'd been one blinding breakthrough which had kept the momentum rolling. My investigations turned up one Launce Tart, ex-regional TV presenter from the 1980s, a local household name and the kind of guy who still opened supermarkets and fêtes. He'd been a member of the hunt for just two years, quitting in 2009 after a row with the Master. So keen was Tart to distance himself from any wrongdoing that he'd fallen over himself to help, giving me a long interview via Skype detailing some of the activities and attitudes he'd witnessed. 'I'm not into blood sports anyway. I only ever went for the social side, join in with the countryside, that sort of thing,' he told me. 'I rode at the rear. I never saw a kill.' Nevertheless, he was able to confirm some of what Mr Williams had said. 'A lot of the guys were OK, you know? Decent people. It was just this feeling one or two of them had that they could do what the hell they liked and get away with it. It gave me the spooks. Which is why I got out.' Now two high-profile animal charities were investigating, as well as the police. My blog post had received 150,000 hits.

I'd had offers off the back of it as well, but only from outfits who couldn't pay: fringe animal rights groups who wanted a volunteer press officer or web manager. So that was no go, because not only did I need a job with wages, career-wise I didn't want to tie myself down to a single-issue campaign. I watched from the sidelines as Launce Tart played the media; I observed how he moved from my blog interview to chats with local press, to a piece in the *Mirror*, to a profile in the *Guardian*. He spoke out against hunting with the zeal of the converted, rekindling his career in the process. Clever man. Apparently I'd had a national-interest story after all.

Other spin-offs had included messages from old college friends congratulating me on the piece, and a storm of pro-hunt abuse on Twitter, including a link to a field sports forum where members were discussing in robust terms what they'd do if they ever got their hands on me. The Glasington themselves had made a short statement denying everything, then withdrawn from the debate. Gerry had sent me a photo of a mug he'd started using in the office bearing the slogan *For Fox Sake Keep the Ban*.

'Well, I hope it was worth it,' had been Rosa's parting shot as she saw me sweep my neon paperclips into a cardboard box. Gerry had made himself scarce on the morning I left, but Alan had skulked around, rubbernecking, and Tam had given me a sad wave from over by the water cooler. That was a wobbly moment. Had it been worth it? Not in terms of financial gain, no. I hadn't made a penny out of the episode. My email to the *Guardian* enquiring about a follow-up piece or even some shift work had gone unanswered. I was earning pocket money by reorganising Dad's filing system at the haulage depot.

But in terms of my peace of mind, in terms of my sense that I'd done what was right and spoken out against bad behaviour, I was a winner. If I could go back in time I knew I'd have acted exactly the same. Only last week I'd had a card from Mrs Williams telling me how quiet everything had gone, how the intimidation seemed to have stopped for the moment, and expressing her heartfelt gratitude at what I'd done for them. The card contained a lucky cockerel tail feather. I stuck it in my pencil pot, on my revamped desk.

And today, the day of my sister's birthday, the skies had eventually cleared and we'd woken to mist rising off the grass under an already warm sun. I stood at my bedroom window and let my eyes follow a tatty crow which was stabbing its beak into the lawn over and over. Sometimes it froze like a statue and cocked its head, then it would jerk into life and jab downwards. I liked the way it walked about, this bird, with a jaunty, comical stride. Sometimes, when it paused, it seemed to be looking right at me, asking me what I thought I was doing.

'Clinging on,' I told it. 'Just about clinging on.'

I pulled on my trackie bottoms and a T-shirt, stuck a pair of trainers on my feet and made my way downstairs, in search of some coffee and toast.

In the kitchen I met Dad. He was coming in through the back door, laden with boxes.

'Are those Helen's presents?' I asked in surprise. As far as I knew, she'd only asked for a new laptop cover and a pair of Aztec-patterned slipper socks. She didn't like it when you bought too much, made a fuss.

He shook his head and put the boxes down on the floor. Now I could see they held a bottle of whisky, a collection of old, damp-swelled books, a bundled-up sheepskin coat. 'Mine,' he said.

And I understood what he was doing: dismantling his garage den. End of an era.

'Need a hand?' I asked.

'No. There wasn't much. It's all straight in there.'

'OK. Right.' I wondered if I should say something significant to mark the occasion. *Well done, welcome back into the family.* Instead I poured him a hot drink while he went to rehouse the whisky in the drinks cabinet and lose the books on the shelf.

A minute or two later and he reappeared, brushing garage dust off his sleeve. There was something determined but under-stated in the action. Suddenly I found myself rushing forward and giving him a fierce hug around his wide middle. He staggered slightly in surprise, then recovered himself.

'Hey up,' he said.

'I love you, Dad.'

'That's nice. I'm pretty fond of you, too.'

A beat.

'Are you OK, Jen? I mean, with everything that's gone on. Are you managing?'

'I'm sorry about my internship.'

His chest rose and fell with a sigh. 'Ah, well. You can't turn the clock back so there's no point fretting about it. You just need to crack on with the next phase, eh?'

'Yeah.' I broke the embrace. He was a good father. He was my father. Whatever he'd done, the past was the past.

'What have you bought your sister, anyway?' he said, rolling his bulk onto a kitchen chair. Helen's healthy eating programme really wasn't touching him.

'Earrings with little birds on them. Oh, and a zumba mix CD. It's one I've put together myself, of the best songs we're doing in my class. Because Hel goes to a different group now, I didn't want her to miss them. I thought I could teach her some of the steps. We could do the routines at home. And then if she ever does decide to come with me again, she'll know the moves so she can join in.'

'Sounds terrific. Will you do one for me?'

'Zumba to the sound of Mungo Jerry?'

'That's right. I bet I'd be red hot.'

'I bet you would.'

Dad had left the door ajar, and through it I thought I heard the sound of a car pulling up outside. When I put my head out to see, there was the rear end of Ned's Fiat tucked in against the kerb. I went to greet him.

'All right, shorty?' he said when he saw me.

'All right, scruff?'

We'd just about regained our equilibrium – I could sit in the same room as him and not feel gripped by an urge to get up and run away – but there was still a self-conscious edge to our banter. We didn't touch any more, no jokey wrestles or casual arm-linking. A nervous force-field surrounded each of us, keeping the other at bay. Our most intimate moment in the past month had been when he'd caught me on my own and told me he was proud of me for finishing things with Owen. 'Mind your own damn business,' I'd replied sweetly. He'd looked crestfallen.

I patted the roof of the Fiat. 'You're way early, you know. I'm not sure if Hel's even up yet. Her bedroom door was closed when I went past.'

'Good.'

'How so?'

'Because I don't want her to see her birthday present till it's set up.'

'Oh yeah? What've you got her?'

'This.' He opened the rear door and bent to slide out a large box. A blanket was draped over the top so I couldn't see the detail, but whatever it was it was a good size.

'Shall I take the other end for you?'

'Nah. It's not heavy. Just large.'

I followed him into the house where he nodded at me to clear the breakfast bar. I whisked away plates and cups so he could set the parcel down. Dad watched, his mouth full of toast.

For a while Ned faffed about, lining up the object so it was square with the edge of the work surface, then he took a corner of the blanket between his fingertips and drew it off with a flourish, like a magician. 'Ta daaah!'

What we had was a rodent cage, one of those multilevel deluxe ones with plastic pipes sticking out and pod-things and hammock-type arrangements. My first thought was, *He'll never squeeze a guinea pig through those tubes.* My second was, *If he's planning on installing that contraption here, however's Mum going to react?*

I moved forward and took a closer look. Inside the cage, propped against the wall, was a cut out of a hamster with a speech bubble emerging from its mouth. 'Hello! I'm Hammy!' it was apparently saying.

'Hammy?'

Ned pulled a sheepish face. 'Yeah, sorry. Not the most original of names, I grant you. Then again, creativity's not my area.'

Dad was lost. 'You're never giving her a cardboard hamster for her birthday, are you? Because I appreciate you know Helen best, but I can't see that going down well.'

I said, 'It's because he didn't want to stress out a real hamster by driving it over, is that right, Ned? But you're going to pick one up at the pet shop today?'

'Spot on.'

'Oh, right. And where's it going to live, this hamster-mansion?'

'Yes, where?' Mum had materialised, still in her dressing gown. Some sixth sense must have told her to hurry downstairs, that her domestic hygiene was under threat.

Ned held up his hand. 'Don't worry, Mrs Crossley. I've managed to sweet-talk my landlord into letting me keep a pet round at mine. As long as I don't allow it to damage the fabric of the property, it'll be OK, he says. I only brought the empty cage round to show you. To show Hel.'

Sighs of relief all round, though I found myself thinking how nice it would be if we did have a rodent on the premises again, a little fat hamster or a cheeky gerbil, maybe. I could have it in my room and teach it tricks. Toffee used to turn circles for Helen, and jump onto an upside-down shoebox to be fed.

'Right. And how long do they live?' asked Mum, ominously.

'A lot depends on how they're looked after, plus what species you get, because the Russian dwarf ones have a faster metabolism than the Syrian so that means—'

He never got to give us a definitive Hammy lifespan, though, because that's when Hel arrived on the scene.

She was dressed today in jeans and a floaty smock top, her hair taken up off her forehead with two enamel combs. She'd put on mascara and lip gloss and I thought I could detect a smudge of powder under her eyes, perhaps to hide the dark circles there. This last fortnight she'd been having difficulty sleeping, Mum had told me.

I went, 'Morning. I've put your present next door, on the sofa.'

Ned just grinned. I suppose he was feeling fairly confident about the reception he was going to get.

'Happy birthday,' said Mum, kissing her on the side of the head.

'Aye, happy birthday, love,' said Dad.

'What in God's name's that?' asked my sister, pointing at the cage.

'"Oh, darling, thank you so much for the amazing present."' Ned supplied a more appropriate response.

'Yeah, that. But what is it?'

'He's buying you a hamster, you ingrate,' I said, picking up my coffee again. 'And he's going to keep it at his flat for you so you won't have any bother. You won't even have to clean it out. Just play with it whenever you fancy. Isn't that nice of him?'

I suppose we were expecting too much. Hel was thirty-one, not six. She was hardly going to clasp her hands and skip round the kitchen, shrieking with glee. Still, a broad smile might have been reasonable. A few exclamations of mild delight.

She came forward and pinched open the wire hatch at the top of the cage, poked at the feeding tray, frowned.

Clearly time to leave them to it.

Dad poured Mum a coffee and handed it to her, and then they went outside to drink it on the patio. I could see them through the window, Mum scrubbing at something on the arm of the vinyl chair with her hanky. Meanwhile I folded my last piece of cold toast and stuffed it in my mouth. My fingers were greasy so I walked over to wipe my hands on the towel, passing Hel. She was still examining the hamster cage and fiddling with its various attachments. Her face looked knotted up with anxiety.

'This is a sleep pod,' Ned was saying. 'And this is his food bowl. And this here's a tiny litter tray. You can toilet-train them, the man in the shop said. Bet you didn't know that, did you?'

A run followed by a hot shower was what I needed to start this sunny Saturday. I was actually feeling fitter than I'd ever been, thanks to an extra zumba class and Hel's reduced-fat cooking regime. This hiatus, this period on stand-by while I reorientated myself and my career, I wasn't going to waste. I'd joined Revolution's online reading group, I'd caught up with Manchester friends, I'd even had a day shopping for wedding gear with Vikki. As well as reorganising my bedroom I'd streamlined my wardrobe, thrown out stuff I never wore, mended and altered the items that needed mending and altering. I'd taken my shoes to be reheeled, bought boot-trees and Scotchgard. Whatever was coming, however my future was going to pan out, I wanted to be ready for it.

I tightened the laces on my trainers and set off down the drive. A circuit of the estate would be enough to get my blood pumping. Best not to overdo these things.

It was still only mid-morning and the streets were quiet. I let myself move off the pavement and onto the road where I could run more freely and didn't have to watch out for dog mess. Some people were out washing cars. On one or two front steps small children played. It was nice to see the different families going about their daily routines. Round the corner I came across a house with a mesh-sided pen on the lawn and a small white bunny inside eating grass industriously. That made me remember Bersham Hall and their shed of giant freak-rabbits. Which made me think, inevitably, of the happy day we'd spent there – and of Owen. I imagined telling him about Hel's hamster, and what judgement he'd have passed on the matter. It wouldn't have been a positive one, I guessed. He worried that keeping pets was a waste of the earth's resources. *But Helen needs an animal of her own,* I argued silently. *She needs that focus. It's a safe attachment for her. It'll help boost her confidence and it won't demand too much in return. And hamsters are only small. They don't consume a lot, planet-wise.*

Then with a rush came the realisation, *I don't have to have those conversations any more.* All that was over. I no longer had to justify myself continually. I still missed Owen, but it was a dull, achy resignation rather than the keen pain of before. 'Please, Jen, no,' he'd said to me when I told him I was bailing out. 'I'm sorry. We've been through this. I was stupid over Chelle and stuff, I know that, and I'm trying to make it up to you. Don't give up. Not when we've come this far.' His face had been so pleading, so handsome, I'd almost given in. It would have been easier. But it would have been wrong. It wasn't fair to stay with someone if you didn't love them. However else my life was in flux, that much I was clear about.

My feet pounded the tarmac and I took in great lungfuls of air. I felt aware of the whole of the flesh of my body, my fingertips and scalp and pumping thighs, my dry lips, my wind-blown cheeks. I rejoiced in my working joints and the ligaments that strung my bones together. Over my head white clouds feathered across the blue. I was alive, I was healthy. The world was mine.

I ran on.

By the time I'd got home and showered, Hel was in the kitchen putting together some lunch. Ned hung about, nicking cherry tomatoes off the salad and casting unhappy looks towards the hamster cage. Whatever had been said on that topic, it obviously hadn't been what he'd anticipated. The air between them was chill and brittle. Like Ned, though, I had no idea why she wouldn't have been simply thrilled at the gift, unless it was because it had been sprung on her – not big on surprises, my sister – or because she was worried about getting too attached to something that probably wouldn't live that long. Who knew? Behind her long curtain of hair, her cheeks were flushed, and she was moving in a jerky, jittery way that made me think they must have had a full-blown argument.

'Stick that bowl on the table as you go past, will you?' she said to me.

I did as I was told. Mum and Dad were sitting on the sofa together, studying a book of crosswords.

'Is it foolishness, Don?' said Mum, sounding oddly plaintive and like a character from a Noël Coward film. When I glanced across, though, she was just talking about one of the clues.

'Not if coxswain's right,' said Dad.

I set up the pepper and salt pots and then returned to the kitchen. Ned was standing very close to Hel and whispering. They sprang apart when they saw me.

'Oh, Jen. We were wondering whether to do the cake for lunch or save it till tea, what do you think?' Hel nodded towards the fridge and the inevitable pavlova.

I said, 'It's your birthday. You get to choose.'

'OK, then. Let's have it now.' She gave a little grin, and for a moment she looked young and excited. I thought I saw her shiver. Then she came over all serious again. Something was going on with her and Ned, but I couldn't fathom what. He just avoided my gaze.

When lunch was ready, Hel sat at the end of the table to serve, as she regularly did these days, and we filled our plates with lean meat and wholemeal rolls and crispy vegetables. As we ate we talked, about Helen's presents, about where we were going to perform our home zumba practice, and whether she might like the bracelet that went with the earrings I'd bought her. Dad told us about the new driver he'd taken on last month, a guy who liked smelly garlic sausage on his sandwiches which stank out the office and the cabs. Mum related a story about a guest at the hotel who'd smashed a bottle of aftershave in the lift, with the result that you'd needed a hanky over your face before you could go in there. Ned was quiet, and I wondered whether to ask him when he was planning to go down the pet shop. Then I thought better of it and enquired instead how the renovations were going at Farhouses. So he described the upgraded French windows and how that was going to get more sun into the west lounge, and we listened politely, but my eyes kept lighting on Hel and the way she was pushing her food round her plate, sliding up her sleeve to check her watch. Two or three times I caught her eyeing the hallway. It was almost as if she was expecting someone. It crossed my mind that perhaps she'd invited a colleague from the kennels, and been too shy to mention it to us in case they didn't turn up.

At last it was time for the pavlova. Hel fetched it in and placed it in front of her, ready to slice. There was no birthday candle this year, but we still took a moment to wish her many happy returns. Her lovely face twitched and she blushed, self-conscious at the attention.

She said, 'Well, I wanted to make this special. I wanted, it's a special—'

And that's when the doorbell rang. Hel jumped in alarm and dropped the knife with a clatter. Her eyes were wide and fearful.

'Shall I get that? I'm nearest,' said Ned. But I was still out of my seat. I had this feeling – I think it had been niggling at me most of the morning – of foreboding, a sense that I ought to get out there into the hall and intercept whoever was trying to gain entrance.

It was a man who was standing on our doorstep. I could see that through the frosted glass. Tall, dark hair, a plaid shirt. A plaid shirt. I felt my breath leave my lungs and a crushing hopelessness descend. Even as my hand was half-raised to the latch I was still thinking, *If I was quick, could I nip through the house and round the back? What's the best way to head him off?* This stranger, who I believed was not a stranger.

'Who is it?' called Dad from the dining room.

It was no good, I was going to have to open the door. I grasped the handle and pulled.

For a few seconds we stared at each other. I was lost, wrongfooted; he was embarrassed. It was not Joe. It was *not* Joe. That was all my brain could manage.

'Jenny?' said the man. 'It is, isn't it? Don't tell me you've forgotten me already?'

Something shifted in my brain and the fog cleared. Since we'd last spoken – what, six years ago? Seven? – his hairline had receded and you could see his scalp showing at the front between the gel-spikes. He was thicker round the waist, too. His forties were catching up with him. But the eyes were the same, piercing and humorous.

I began to smile, I couldn't help it. His presence here was so absurd. He ought to be standing outside the school science labs, shouting at passing kids to do their ties up. 'Mr Wolski!'

'It is indeed. Though call me Tadek. Is Helen in? Could I see her?'

'Oh. Yes.' It was then I clocked the plastic bag he was carrying and the bunch of flowers poking out of the top. The delight at recognising him, at his not being Joe, drained away. What did he want? What was he here for?

'You'd better come inside,' I said.

I led him through and introduced him. And I knew, even as I watched everyone look up from their plates, that the scene would imprint itself on my mind forever. The last normal moments of the day. My parents' faces registered only total puzzlement, Ned was concentrating hard on his pudding, and Hel – Hel was a study in dread. Her whole body tautened and I wondered if she might get up and run to him, but in the end she stayed where she was. Next thing, she ordered me to get him a chair, which I thought was a bit rich. 'Oh, and another bowl while you're up, Jen.' I did as I was told because it was her birthday. Mr Wolski handed the flowers not to my sister but to Mum, who seemed both pleased and annoyed. I suppose she hadn't forgiven him for helping Hel find her kennels job.

'You've come to wish Helen a happy birthday?' she asked, trying, like the rest of us, to get her bearings.

'I have.'

'Well. That's nice. She didn't mention you'd be dropping by. Would you like a drink? Some pavlova?'

'Great, thanks.'

Hel was already passing some down. I tried to signal to her, to Ned, to ask them what was going on. Ned's shoulders were hunched defensively. Whatever it was, he had at least half an idea, I guessed.

'Have you come far?' said Dad.

'Churton.'

'Oh, Churton. Nice round there.'

'Yes.'

'Are you still at St Thom's?'

'I am.'

'Science, isn't it, you teach?'

'Biology mainly. My timetable's almost entirely A level these days. Some GCSE cover when I'm needed. I'm head of Sixth now, of course.'

'I see.'

'And I oversee curriculum development.'

'St Thom's, eh?'

'Anyway, it's nice of you to drive all the way out here,' said Mum, fingering the cellophane wrapper on her bouquet.

It was Ned who broke the small talk. 'Come on, Hel.'

My sister lowered her face.

'Helen has something she wants to tell you,' he continued,

pushing himself a little way from the table, as if to make a performance space for her.

Everything went quiet. Hel raised her head again, swallowed, glanced from Ned to Mr Wolski. Mr Wolski nodded encouragingly, and Ned reached out and took her hand.

'I . . . You need to know. I'm going away,' she said.

'Away?' said Mum at once. 'What do you mean? Where?'

'I'm going to college. Like Jen.'

'You mean Manchester?'

'No. Warwick. I'm going to train to be a veterinary nurse.'

'Bloody Norah,' said Dad.

'I got an offer a month ago, but I only formally accepted last week. I'm due to start in September.'

'*Warwick?*' repeated Mum.

'Well, the campus is actually in a village called Moreton Morrell. It's about an hour and a half away from here. Not too far.'

'And a fully accredited course,' Mr Wolski chipped in. 'At an RCVS Veterinary Nursing Approved Centre. We did our research, didn't we, Helen?'

'We did.'

Mum's face grew tight. 'Oh, you did? What about local colleges? Did you research those? What about Reaseheath and Harper Adams, places like that? They do animal courses. I've seen it in the paper. She could study there, no need to go away from home.'

'No, Mum. I have to go. I have to be far enough away so I can properly set up on my own.'

Now the news was finally out, I could see Helen's relief was giving her confidence. She sat up straighter, and though she was licking her lips continually and still grasping Ned's fingers, she was fired up with what she wanted to say.

'But how will you manage, love?'

'I'm thirty-one.'

'You know what I mean.'

We did, and what was there to say?

Mr Wolski shifted his chair round so he was facing my mother, and reached inside his plastic bag. He drew out a glossy brochure and some web page printouts which he laid in front of her. Then he began to turn the pages and take her through them, describing in positive terms the town, the campus, the course outline, the pastoral tutor system and the medical access available to students. He spoke calmly and with authority, and I thought, Yes, this is his job, isn't it? I bet he handles such situations all the time, reassuring worried parents that their kids have made the right choices and will survive away from the nest. Maybe not in such charged circumstances, but he'd know the kind of concerns they had, and how to allay them. It would be a very familiar script. How would Helen fund a degree, Dad was able to ask, and Mr Wolski told him about the loan application process and the rates of repayment. Did you assist her with the forms? Mum wanted to know. Of course he had. He'd sat with her at our kitchen table and gone through every section; later on, he'd helped her arrange a fortnight off from the kennels so she could get some hands-on experience at a vet's. He'd even, it transpired, taken her down to an interview, on a day we'd assumed she was at work.

That stung. That smarted. It all did. Because she could have confided in me, for God's sake. Those months leaving me to stress about what was really troubling her, what was going on in her head – shutting out Ned as well – when we could have helped and encouraged. The nights she and I had sat together and talked, when she'd given out so much of herself. Would it have killed her to confide that extra step? Why hang on to one key secret? Why not share with her sister? There'd been so many opportunities. Had we made any progress over this last year?

I looked up and she was watching me. She knew what I was thinking.

'I *couldn't* tell you,' she burst out. 'I'm sorry. I wanted to. But if I'd failed – I mean, if the college had rejected me and I hadn't got a place – it would have been so much worse if you'd been in the loop. I thought, at least if I do it on my own and it comes to nothing, I can squash everything down and pretend it never happened. I'd prepared myself for that, I could cope. But not if you'd all been in on it. If you'd been commiserating and blaming the admissions tutor and asking if I was going to try again. Or saying it was for the best anyway and I'd never have stayed the course. I couldn't have borne that. Jen, I almost told you. A couple of times I was so close. I *wanted* to.'

She was racked, I could see it. And I understood that was the way her mind worked, although it didn't instantly cool my resentment. I said, 'You're going to have to stop thinking like that. There are going to be failures. You'll have to learn to handle them.'

'I know.'

Dad picked up the brochure and studied the centre pages. Mum started spindling the paper napkin on her plate. 'So what's going to happen with Ned, Helen? Will he be going down there too?'

Helen's eyes swivelled to her boyfriend.

'We'll work something out,' he said. I noticed he'd let go of her fingers, or she'd withdrawn them. How did he feel about her plans? At what point had she broken them to him?

I found myself picturing my sister in scenes from my own university life: crossing St Ann's Square, sitting in my old tutor's study, buying stationery in the Student Union shop; I saw her in some science lab, dripping something from a pipette into a test tube; in a white coat, filling up a needle so she could give an injection; bending over a poorly cat, examining a guinea pig. No, not a guinea pig, a hamster. A fat orange hamster. Terrible timing, Ned. No wonder she hadn't wanted his birthday present. Hammy would be staying in the pet shop for sure.

And here came the second blow, and a sense of what Mum must be feeling: *Helen was leaving us.* Finally my sister was going away, breaking up the family. We would never be the same again. This year had been our last together. I was surprised at how much that hurt. I glanced over at Mum and she was looking scared and lost. Dad had his arm round her.

'Come on,' I said to Hel. 'Mum's upset.'

She nodded and got up from the table, squeezing past Ned. We flanked my mother and coaxed her out of her chair, led her over to the sofa. Then we sat on either side of her, hip to hip. Mr Wolski spotted his cue and asked Ned if he could have a cup of tea, which meant both of them disappeared into the kitchen. Dad stayed where he was, poring over the brochure.

'OK?' asked Hel.

'No,' said Mum. 'No.'

I sighed and squeezed her arm. 'Don't you want Hel to get a degree? Use those A levels she's accrued? It's the opportunity she's been waiting for, that course has got her name written all over it. And isn't it great that she's feeling confident enough to take such a step forward?'

'I can see that.'

'Well.'

'But she could do the degree and stay here. She'd be happier. She doesn't like being away from her things, does she?'

'I'll have to learn to cope,' said Hel. 'I need to stand on my own two feet. Like Jen did.'

'You're not the same as Jen, though.'

I said, 'No. Helen's a lot braver than me.'

She shot me a grateful look. 'Thanks, sis.' Then she adjusted her hair comb, and addressed Mum directly. 'Come on, let's get this out in the open. Say it. The anorexia.'

I saw Dad's head come up, heard the far-off chink of mugs from the kitchen.

Mum took a deep breath. 'All right. I'm worried that if you go away and you're not happy, you'll start again.'

'Even though I've been OK for years.'

'You can't guarantee the future.'

'Oh, come on. No one can. *You* can't guarantee you won't have another heart attack.'

'Hel!' I said.

'It's true, though, sis. None of us knows what's ahead, especially health-wise.'

My mother was frowning, trying to process her thoughts and get them into order. 'A heart condition, though – it isn't the same as anorexia. I've no control over it.'

There was a long silence after that. Mum's hand came up to her mouth, showing she was aware that what she'd said should probably not have slipped out.

Helen waited to see if she'd elaborate. Eventually she said, 'You think I can control my anorexia?'

'I don't know,' said Mum in a small voice. 'Yes. A little bit.'

'You think what happened was that I decided to become ill and then I decided to recover?'

This time there was no answer. *I knew it*, said Hel's expression. *Didn't I tell you this was what she secretly thought?*

'Listen, Mum. Your heart attack seemed to come out of the blue, didn't it? Well, it's like that with anorexia. It just lands, boom. Nobody knows why it strikes some people and not others, although there is a professor somewhere I read about recently who reckons it might be to do with brain development in the womb. Which is a bit like you being predisposed to heart disease. Maybe. I don't know, they're still doing research. Anyway, think about how, when you'd got over your heart attack, you did those things to help you get better, like the walking and the support sessions and changing your diet. And that's like me, when I started to get better and I was able to take charge of myself and try to eat more. But when we were in the middle of the worst of it, at the critical point, neither of us could do anything. We were too ill. Do you see what I'm saying? Mine was a mental illness and yours was physical, but they're both still diseases. Anorexia's a full-blown mental health disorder, not an exercise in family-hating bloody-mindedness. Don't ever think it had anything to do with you. The counsellor told you that. What happened was no one's fault. No one's fault.'

Dad was sitting like a statue. I noticed Mum had her hands clasped in her lap and she was stroking one of her thumbs with the other.

Hel laid her palm over them, to still the nervous action. 'We should have talked about it more.'

'I never knew what to do for the best.'

'Do you understand what I'm saying, though? Do you believe me?'

'Mm.'

'*Do* you believe me, Mum? It's only what the doctors told you. And you, Dad? What do you say?'

Dad shook his head. 'It's above me. I'll be honest, I've never understood. Which is my failing, I know. All I want is for you to keep well. And your mother not to be sad.'

'Hel's trying to make you understand,' I said.

'But if what she says is right,' said Mum, 'then how is that any better? It means the anorexia could strike again. Like lightning.'

'No, because she'll do what you're doing: she'll take care of herself. She'll let the college medical centre know, and she'll talk to her tutors.'

'That's right,' said Hel. 'And I'll let you know if I'm having problems. Any problems. And I'll email you every week, and we can phone whenever you want. You can visit. I can pop home sometimes. I'll keep in touch. More than Jen did when she was away.'

I pulled a face at her.

'I have strategies in place these days,' she continued. 'And in any case, the bad time feels such a long way away. I've sorted out so much stuff this year to get my head straight. Jen's helped me. I'm as ready as I'll ever be to face the world. And yes, I'm scared, I'm terrified, actually, but I'm going to go and at least have a try.'

'You can always come home if it doesn't work out,' said Mum, a note of hope in her voice.

'I know that.'

'I still don't like the idea.'

'No.'

Hel and I cuddled into her protectively. I said, 'Hey, do you remember when I was little and you used to tell me that "life was made up of pie crusts as well as filling"? And that I "had to eat the crusts up as well" because that was how life was?'

'Did I?' Mum wiped her eyes.

'Uh huh. You'd recite it before we went to the dentist's, and if I had a test or exam coming up, anything that I didn't want to face. But you'd tell me to focus on the pie filling that was coming up in the future. That would get me through the crusty times.'

'To tell you the truth, it was one of my mother's sayings.'

'Well, it helped. So now I'm saying it back to you. The wisdom of Grandma Lyons, eh?'

Mum exhaled crossly. 'Oh, when she said it, she never meant it as a consolation. She said it to spread the misery. What she meant was, "Life's grim, girl, toughen up." Nearly all pie crusts, my childhood was. Hard work and not a lot of fun, and the strap if you were what she called cheeky.'

'I can't imagine you being a cheeky child.'

'I wasn't. I wouldn't have said boo to a goose. She only meant if you were making too much noise playing with your friends outside the window, or if you left crumbs on the tablecloth. Once she slapped my face till my ears rang because I accidentally dropped a dish on the hearth and it broke.'

Hel and I exchanged glances. We'd known Grandma Lyons was a sourpuss, but not that she'd been such a cow. Mum never talked about her life pre-marriage. It had never occurred to me to ask, either.

'She hit you?' asked Hel.

'She was just a very strict woman. It wasn't unusual for those days. And I thought, from being tiny, if I grow up to have children of my own, I'll make it really lovely for them . . . You know, the only thing I *ever* wanted was for you two to be happy girls, and us to be a happy family.'

'We are, Mum. We *are*.'

I leaned right forward and stretched out my hand to my father. He dithered, embarrassed, then reached over and gave my fingers a quick squeeze before letting go. Poor man, he's not one for group hugs.

Then I said, 'Hel, do you remember that Christmas when Dad dressed up as Santa to creep past the window, but I spotted he was wearing his old slippers?'

She laughed. 'Oh, yeah. God, and you were only about five. You and your damned observational skills. You were such a pain. It was supposed to be a magical moment, and all you could do was bang on about how come they both had the exact same footwear.'

'Yeah, sorry about that.'

'You were rubbish, little sis. Do you remember that chrysalis hatching out in the shed? How we'd go and visit it every day, and then when it did break open it turned out to be a huge pink moth and you were freaked out by it.'

'It was a monster, though. Size of a table mat.'

'What about when you spread glitter glue over your pumps after you'd watched *The Wizard of Oz*?'

'Ha, yes. I thought they looked ace. Except I walked on the lawn before they'd dried and picked up a load of grass clippings.'

'And then Mum rushed out and got you a pair of sparkly pumps to make up for it. Spoilt, you were.'

'I was.'

'Here's a good one. Do you remember when Mum tricked those Jehovah's Witnesses into taking a great lump of treacle toffee each, and afterwards they couldn't speak? The Lord's words were all gummed up. Were you there?'

'I was sitting on the stairs, watching.'

'And there was a really hot summer one year when Mum taught me how to make ice cubes with edible flowers in them. So pretty. I remember her showing me how to hem trousers, too. And a trick to tell if an egg was rotten or not.'

'Dad helped me learn the Highway Code. Sat testing me night after night, so I'd pass first time. Which I did. Not that I'm showing off or anything.'

'Mum once made me a birthday cake with ballet shoes iced on the top of it, and real ribbons trailing down the sides.'

One after another we threw these memories out, hardly pausing for breath. 'My God,' said Helen when we ran out of steam. 'It's almost as if we had a great childhood, isn't it?'

Mum said, 'We made a lot of mistakes, though.'

'Show me a parent who hasn't.'

I suddenly thought of Tadek Wolski, wondered what he was doing in our kitchen right now, and the things he might be saying. Who did he think he was, sneaking around the edges of our family? Last year I'd thought my mother's indignation at his providing Hel with a reference had been overreacting. Now I got it. What business was it of his to interfere, above the people who were closest to her? And yet, almost as soon as the thought formed, I realised it was wrong to be angry with him. He was a decent bloke. Always had been. One of the few teachers who let you get away with make up in class, and who

didn't blow a gasket if you handed in your homework late. The reason Helen had chosen to confide in him was because he knew what he was doing. He was an expert on university and college submissions. That was his job. Ned and I might have backed her in her application, but we wouldn't have been able to guide and advise her the way he obviously had. And aside from all that, he was her friend. Hel had few enough of those. I had no right to feel resentful.

My mother lifted her finger and stroked my sister's hair. 'Tell me you're not running away from me?'

'I'm not running away. I'm setting out. I have to *do* something.'

'You've done a lot!'

Hel sighed. 'Yeah. Mostly I've sat at home collecting exam passes. You know, Mum, there was this woman I happened to meet last year who'd cycled the entire length of the country to raise money for charity. All that way, and she was just ordinary, not an athlete or anything. But she'd collected thousands. Organised herself, and then got on with it. I've not been able to stop thinking about her. To be that determined, that useful. I want to make *my* mark.'

'Not by cycling, love?'

'Not by cycling.'

'Well, thank God for that at least.'

'I mean, we have to . . . *engage* with life, or what are we?'

For a few moments Mum struggled. 'Promise me you'll look after yourself when you get there. Promise.'

'I promise.'

'You'll let us know if you get into difficulties?'

'Straightaway.'

This same conversation we were going to have a dozen times

or more before September came. My mother was going to need endless reassurances, endless encouragement before she felt Hel was safe to go.

Subtly I shifted my position on the sofa away from them and got to my feet. I needed some time alone to process my own thoughts on the situation.

'And is there a canteen, or do you cook for yourself? Don, what does it say in the brochure?' Mum was asking.

I said, 'OK, look. Since the drama's over, I'm going to have a stroll up to Spar if anyone wants anything?'

No one took any notice.

I slipped out into the hall and picked up my purse.

Don't ask me what I bought in the mini mart. On the walk up there I'd had a vague idea about getting my mother a small gift, but she already had Tadek's flowers, and anyway I didn't know if that was overdoing it. Instead I wandered up and down the aisles, sticking random stuff in my basket and finally exiting in a whirl of thoughts and voices.

A hell of a risk you took dropping that revelation, I rehearsed saying to my sister. *It's only four months since she came out of hospital.*

We can't base the entire rest of our lives around not ruffling Mum, came the immediate response. I could hear Helen saying it. *Look, Jen, I applied for that course before she got ill. Even if I deferred my place, it wouldn't make any difference to the way she feels about me leaving, would it?*

I tried to picture how the next few months would pan out, how the dynamics of the house would change when I was the only daughter there. Hel's room shut up, her food cupboard untouched. Mum constantly needy and near the edge, Dad and me attempting to keep her spirits up. No Ned for me to go to and let off steam because he'd be down in Warwick, visiting at least.

No Ned.

I stopped short on the pavement and pressed my hand hard against my temple to quell a wave of panicky sorrow. What bleakness this autumn promised: no job, no Owen, the family disjointed and subdued. I was going to have to fight hard to keep on top of myself.

But I would. I'd find employment somewhere. I'd make an effort to build up my social life too. See more of Vikki and Keisha, drag Vikki along to a film now and again, because she liked going to the cinema and Keisha didn't. And some people from St Thom's still met up at the Crown on Friday nights, so it might be worth dropping in there. I was getting more into my running, so I could hook up with a harriers club, maybe. Or I could investigate evening classes. I'd seen a poster in the library advertising creative writing sessions, and another for a photography course, both of which I'd always fancied trying. However wobbly I felt, I certainly wasn't going to sit in my room and mope. That wasn't me. As for Ned, Hel taking him away was a sign; that really was a chapter closed. Time to move on. Blimey, I knew plenty of people who'd had to start again – like Mum after Dad's affair, and Hel after she came out of hospital. They'd managed and I would too. So much of what I'd thought was important to me had been stripped away lately, and yet – to my surprise – I was still OK. Even if the thought of Ned departing was like a rip across my heart.

Then, as I was thinking about him, there he was, a hundred yards away and sitting on a garden wall just up from our house, kicking his legs against the bricks. His head was cocked, watching the road. When he saw me he jumped down and hurried towards me.

'I needed to speak to you, alone,' he said as soon as he got close enough. He held out his arms but I dodged them. I felt too raw for a hug.

'What's everyone else doing?'

Ned dropped his hands to his sides. 'Your dad and Helen are still propping up your mother. Tadek's gone.'

'Has he? Having dropped his bombshell, he's buggered off?'

'There wasn't a lot more he could do, he was a bit redundant. But I had a good chat with him and he's OK, actually. I liked him. His wife's a Macmillan nurse, did you know?'

I shook my head.

'Don't have a downer on him, Jen. He does feel bad about the way Hel set things up. He tried a few times before to get her to share.'

I allowed Ned to take my bag off me. He winced at the weight. 'Bloody hell, what have you got in here?'

'Dunno.'

'Windscreen wash and a set of Tupperware boxes, I can see poking out. And is that a pineapple?'

I said, 'When did she tell you?'

He closed the bag again. 'This morning. After the hamster debacle. She took me upstairs, out of the way, and I asked her what on earth was going on, because I knew how badly she wanted a pet, and that's when she explained. That's when I got the full confession.'

'So you didn't get much warning either.'

'Nope. You honestly had no idea?'

'Not a clue. Although some things make sense now, like the way she was last autumn, extra secretive and cagey. Around that period you thought she was getting ill again, do you remember? She'd be hiding web printouts from me, and slamming down her laptop lid when I came near. Snatching up the post before anyone else could see it. I suppose she must have had a lot of admin to sort out behind our backs. You know, once I came home early from work and almost caught Mr Wolski in our kitchen. He nipped out of the door just in time.'

'What? Bloody hell, Jen. You never mentioned that.'

'Oh, well, I didn't know it was him, did I? Hel swore blind there was no one and it was the radio I'd heard. And of course I had no idea what was really going on, so it was hard to challenge.' I paused, recalling my fury at what I'd thought was the bastard Joe Pascoe invited into our house. Not that I'd be sharing that particular detail with Ned.

I shook the image out of my head. It was never real anyway. For all my past frettings, and the hideous, scalding embarrassment I'd put myself through when I'd confronted the man directly, I now understood that Helen had never wanted to meet up with Joe in the flesh. It had been his ghost she wanted exorcised, not the living man.

'So what did you say to her when she told you about Warwick?'

Ned raised his eyebrows. 'What could I say? It took me a while to get my bearings. But when I did, I told her I was proud of her, that I supported her if that's what she wanted to do. I said it was good she was feeling so confident. I said I was sorry she felt she couldn't confide in me – she did apologise for that. But she's made up her mind, Jen, there's no negotiating to be done.'

'Yes, but what are *you* going to do?'

'How do you mean?'

'What's going to happen? Are you moving down there with her? Will you just see her weekends?'

He let out a tight laugh. 'Neither. She doesn't want me any more.'

'Huh?'

'She's finished it.'

'*No.*'

'She says she doesn't want a boyfriend for a while. She needs to focus on making a new beginning for herself.'

'Oh. God.' The pavement seemed to pitch under my feet.

'That's why I came out here, to get you on your own. I thought you should know.'

'But when we were sitting at the table, you never said anything. I assumed you'd just stay together. You implied—'

'What I said was, we'd *work something out.* I didn't want to blurt the news out in front of your mum, not yet. Give her time to get used to the college business first. I knew she'd go into meltdown if she thought Hel was going to be completely on her own down there.'

'You're going to have to tell her at some point.'

'We will. Let the dust settle first. For now, it's between you, me and Hel.'

'Oh, Ned. I'm sorry.'

'Why?'

'I don't know. It's what you say when someone tells you their relationship's broken up.'

Carefully he set the shopping bag down on the pavement. I noticed the pineapple had pierced a hole in the plastic and one of the spiky leaves was poking through.

'You're not sorry really, are you, Jen?'

'I don't know. I daren't think what it means. I feel – I feel as if someone's taken a photo of our family, torn it up and thrown the pieces high into the air. They're all falling round me and I don't know where any of them are going to land. I've no points of orientation any more.'

'Yes you have. You have me.'

'Do I?'

We stared at one another. Then, very slowly, as if to give me chance to duck away, he stepped forward and put his arms around me.

I said, 'Hang on. No. We can't. It's too soon.'

'Don't you think we've waited long enough already?' His voice was soft, reassuring.

'We're going to have to wait a while longer. There's too much going on. Well, isn't there? Surely you can see? The bed's not cold.'

'The bed's been cold for a long time. I told you that last year.'

Half of me wanted to draw him to me and hug him tight; half of me wanted to push him away. I felt overwhelmed by the rush of changes, and by my own dizzying emotions when I thought of the possibilities opening up for us. 'I need space to adjust, Ned.'

'Soon, though.'

'I think so.'

'That's good enough for me.' And he lowered his lips to mine, and we kissed. Kissed and kissed, and kissed again, and I let myself stop thinking and went with it, lost myself in his soft skin, the taste of him, his familiar scent and contours. I heard the faint whine of a lawnmower somewhere, and the cheeping of the birds in the trees behind us. Cars passed. A child cried, *Mum! Mum!* The sun was warm on my back.

At last he pulled away to look at me. 'Oh, Jen.'

Inside me I imagined a bank of flowers flushing into bloom. Clouds broke, knots of tension eased, pain I'd been clenched against for so long now dissolved away. This was right. This was what I'd not dared let myself want.

'Will it be OK?' I said.

'It will.'

I remembered what Hel had said that night in the garden about the good guys, about making our own universe. Ned was mine; all I had to do was reach out and take him.

'Kiss me again,' I said.

But at that same moment I spotted over his shoulder something bright, someone with a flash of orange hair standing way off down the street, watching us. A jolt of recognition. Of horror. My sister. I took in her tall, still figure as embarrassment flared up through my body.

In a panic I stepped backwards, pushing him off.

No, God, no, you've got it wrong, I wanted to call out to her. *This isn't how it looks. Truly! I haven't been circling, plotting to nab your boyfriend at the first opportunity. I would never do that. HE would never do that. I'm your ally. I've been good! I've been level! After everything we've been through this year, please don't let this one crazy moment spoil it.*

Hel gave nothing away. She remained where she was, her face a blank. Then her arm came up and she waved. Waved at me, kept her palm raised in what almost looked like a salute, then turned and walked away from us both.

I hardly knew what to expect as I went into the house. Ned and I came in separately, him via the front door, and me through the back on the pretext of unloading the shopping. Ridiculous. We couldn't have looked more guilty if we'd tried. The pineapple had stabbed me in the thumb, too, which served me right.

When I dared to come through, Ned was nowhere to be seen, but Dad had moved to the sofa with Mum while Hel was arranging flowers in a vase on the dining table.

'Nice walk?' she said when she saw me.

I blushed to the roots of my scalp. If my parents hadn't been there, I'd probably have thrown myself at her feet and begged forgiveness, Victorian-melodrama-style. Such shoddy, devious behaviour from the one person I'd assured her she could trust. The moment she'd seen us, she must have guessed there'd already been something between us for me to be flinging myself into his arms. I had no defence. Not one. I couldn't even plead that it was the first time we'd kissed.

Before I could formulate any kind of response, though, Mum piped up on the subject of student accommodation. Was there any kind of doorman on the flats, she wanted to know. Or a caretaker? Someone you'd contact in an emergency? Was the outside area well lit? Where would Helen keep her car? Would her insurance premiums shoot up?

Calmly Helen carried on snipping the ends off flower stems. 'I don't know. Why don't you make a list of questions and we'll research the answers together?'

But what kind of a place was Warwick? Mum persisted. Were there gangs? Was it wild, like parts of Manchester? She'd worried when I was there about me going out in the evenings.

I said, 'I was in a major city for three years and I never had any bother.'

'I'm sure I'll be fine,' said Hel.

She took a rose and split the stalk about an inch of the way up from the bottom, like a professional.

Ned reappeared and went to sit by my mother.

One by one my sister placed the flowers in their vase, tweaking them into place. I concentrated on her actions and tried not to stoke my guilt by replaying the scene in the street. A white rose, a pink rose, a spray of fern, two lilies. 'Anyway, Jen,' she said, 'while I've got you here, while Ned's here, there's something I need to ask you both. It's been bothering me and I want to get it sorted.'

'Oh?'

Quickly I pulled out a dining chair and sat down. Then I held my breath and waited for the worst.

She began, 'This hamster . . .'

'Huh?'

'I've been thinking about him. Now, I can't take him with me. Pets aren't allowed. But I don't feel I can just leave him in the shop. The idea of that makes me very unhappy. I've seen too many animals stuck in the kennels, waiting and waiting. He needs an owner as soon as possible. Space to stretch his legs and explore, stimulation, a human to bond with.'

'OK.'

'Someone to *take care of him*, Jen. What I'm saying is, I hate to think of him *left on his own with no one to love him*.'

'How do you know he's a he?' interrupted Dad.

'Because he is.' She widened her eyes at me. 'So anyway, I've considered this carefully and I've decided *I want you to take him*.'

'Don't they smell, though?' asked Mum.

'No, they don't. Jen, will you do this for me? Will you *keep him safe* and look after him? It's important for me to know.'

'I've heard they bath in sand,' said Mum.

'That's chinchillas,' said Dad.

'I don't want sand all over the house.'

'Or is it gerbils? Which is it has legs like a kangaroo?'

Hel addressed our parents. 'Listen, will you? I've given it some thought, weighed up the pros and cons and it would put my mind at rest if the hamster was here, with Jen. I don't want to be worrying about him while I'm away. I don't want that extra stress. I need to be free from distractions and focussed on the course. Yes?'

They sagged, helpless. She knows what buttons to push, does my sister.

'And I know Jen'll appreciate him. *I know she'll love him.*'

How I longed for the power of telepathy. Are you getting this? I vibed at Ned. Can you hear her? Is she talking about a pet rodent or is she trying to say something else?

My mother's expression was still doubtful. 'Couldn't Ned keep it round at his? That was the original plan.'

I said, 'If I've understood, I think it's important for Hel that I have him, and here, where I can keep an eye on him.' Helen nodded theatrically. 'I could put the cage in my room, out of the way. I'll do everything, cleaning and feeding. I'll keep it super-tidy. There won't be so much as a flake of sawdust on your carpet.'

Mum turned to Ned, who was huddled in the corner of the sofa. 'But is that OK with you? Altering your arrangements. It seems wrong. All of it.'

He cleared his throat.

'Of course it's OK,' said Hel. 'Ned just wants the best for everyone, don't you?'

'I do.'

'Well, he's a very kind boy,' said Mum.

Hel bundled the clipped-off ends of flower stems into the wrapping from the bouquet and scrunched up the cellophane into a ball. Her arrangement looked lovely, stalks and colours balanced in natural harmony. She'd made a perfect job.

'I think he's the kindest man I know,' she said.

There was no chance to get Hel alone, no space for anything except family talk and the endless rehashing of the afternoon's events. So it wasn't till nearly 11 p.m. that I realised my phone was dead. I took it up to my bedroom so I could plug it in to charge, and straightaway an email pinged through. When I opened up the message it was from someone at the *Guardian*.

Dear Jenny

Sorry I haven't replied earlier to your offering. I've been snowed under with this MPs' scandal-thing. Loving your blog! Please give me a ring on 020 3151 4227 and we can have a chat.

Regards

Julia Marcus-Pieterson

God. God! I read and reread it. Looked away, looked back and it was still there. A chat. A 'chat'. She 'loved' the blog! Oh, bloody hell. I stood there, staring at the screen, while the implications ricocheted around my head. The thunderclap ending to a tumultuous day.

It was too late to call there and then, obviously. Too late even to alert the household; Dad had taken Mum to bed and Hel had retired to her room with her prospectuses. Ned had gone home before tea (to lie down in a darkened room, I suspected).

I started to text him, then immediately took fright and deleted what I'd written before sending. No. That was silly of me. It would be best to find out what this woman wanted before I went spreading the news around. For goodness' sake, she might only be calling to say, 'Sorry, you're not for us, but keep up the good work.' She might just want to know if there'd been any developments in the story that she could turn into column inches herself. Or it might be a one-off commission. Or none of the above.

I paced round the bed for a while, rehearsing some of the things I might say to this Julia. I smoothed my hair and buttoned up the neck of my blouse as if I were actually at an interview. When I did speak to her I'd have to find a space where I wouldn't be interrupted. Stick a notice on my door, switch off my laptop. No, I'd have my laptop open so I could reference the blog, but I'd switch off the sound and alerts. My full focus would be crucial. I'd make some notes in advance. Whatever she was after, I'd be on the ball.

One last read of the email – it was true! It existed! – and I replaced the phone on its charger. I thought I'd go downstairs and brew myself a cup of coffee, jot some thoughts down while my head was still busy.

The landing was dim, but my parents' light was still on because I could see the glow round the edges of the door. I hesitated at the threshold, listening to Dad's low mumble, then Mum's anxiously pitched responses. You didn't have to hear the detail to work out the conversation that was passing between them.

Hel's room was dark as I passed on by.

Even in the hall I could smell the lilies that Mr Wolski had brought. The scent hung around the whole of the downstairs, and I knew for me it would always be the signature of that afternoon, of that moment when Hel told us she was leaving. I tiptoed into the lounge and switched on the standard lamp, then carried on into the kitchen. The radiance coming off the cooker's digital display, together with the moon shining through the window, was enough to navigate by. My mind was churning with incisive comment and brilliant ideas I might lay before Julia, and I worried that flicking on the harsh central light would send them fleeing.

So I didn't see Helen till I'd filled the kettle and was slotting it back onto its stand. She'd taken one of the tall stools and tucked it into the corner, where Pepper's basket once sat.

'Christ almighty!' I said, sloshing water over my hand. 'What on earth are you doing? Are you OK?'

She was wearing a fleece over her nightie, plus her new Aztec socks. 'I'm fine. Having some thinking time.'

'But why here, in the dark and the cold?'

'I came in to get a drink and then I got playing with the hamster cage. I wanted to see if the wheel squeaked.'

The cage still sat on the kitchen top, triggering the events of the day to replay themselves on fast-forward: Ned struggling in with his blanket-covered surprise, Mr Wolksi standing uncertainly in the hall, Hel's announcement, Mum's dismay. Me kissing my sister's boyfriend in the street, in full view of the world. The kiss she saw and which I had not yet explained.

'Oh, God, Hel. Look, I hardly know what to say. I'm so, so sorry, I was going to come to you first thing tomorrow and apologise—'

'There's nothing to apologise for.'

'Yes, there is. What you must have thought! Let me tell you how it happened. Please. Because I don't want you to think anything dodgy was going on behind your back. You're my sister. I would never do that to you. *Ned* would never—'

'Stop.'

'But you need to know. It wasn't that we'd—'

'Jen, I've known for ages that he loved you.'

'What?'

The plastic casing of the cage glinted between us.

'I'm not stupid. When you've been with someone that long, you know how they tick. I saw where his heart lay. I knew why he stayed with me. I should have let him go sooner, but I wasn't quite ready. I am now.'

'He does love you.'

'In his way.'

'He does, lots. Neither of us would ever hurt you. If you said—'

'It's all right. I promise. Shush, now.'

She slid down off the stool and came towards me. When she reached me, she took my hand and led me so we were standing next to the cage. Then she placed my palm on the top.

I said, 'You *knew*, then.'

'Yes.'

'I'm not sure what to say, Hel.'

'Don't say anything. Just – take care of my hamster. Take good care of him. That's all I ask.'

Intense sadness welled up and broke over me. 'Helen!'

'Sshh.'

'I don't want you to go!'

'Well, that's tough, kid. We Crossleys have got to strike out for ourselves. You too. Your time will come. And I'll be cheering.'

'It's frightening, though. So much change.'

'It is, but it's going to happen anyway. Might as well flow with it.'

I thought of Mum and Dad in bed above us, navigating the ship of our family through the rockiest seas for years and years. When love's so freely given, you don't even notice it.

I said, 'Are we OK, you and me? Tell me that and, whatever happens, I'll be fine.'

She touched a slender finger to the corner of my eye where a tear was forming.

'More than OK, little sis. More than.'

AFTERWARDS

We're only a week into November but The Poacher's already decked out with Christmas gear. Even as we crossed the footbridge over the canal we could see the MERRY XMAS banner tacked across the slate roof, and when we entered the threshold, the inner porch door was stapled all over with festive menus. Now we're in the saloon, with tinsel snaking along the bar top and draped untidily across the door lintels. Someone has tied a plastic Santa mask to the front of the fruit machine, which just looks weird.

Mum tuts at this brash consumerism, but it's a half-hearted effort on her part. She's too happy to be annoyed. She's happy it's her birthday, of course; she's very happy with the eternity ring Dad has bought her in a gesture of rash romanticism never before witnessed. Mainly she's happy because I'm home for the weekend and we're out together as a family, which is what she loves best. Or perhaps not quite a family, because for today we have Ned with us and not Helen (although I have a surprise in store there for later which should go down well).

We pick a table, sit, and I lay my tote bag carefully down on the floor, tucked out of the way. Dad flaps his hand at the menu. 'Have whatever you want,' he says. 'Whatever you want.'

I've got everything I want, I think to myself. Underneath the table, Ned and I are holding hands. It's daft of us but I don't care.

While we're waiting for someone to take our order, Mum points to an ornamental teapot on the windowsill next to my elbow. It's *Alice in Wonderland* themed, and poking out of the lid is what I assume must be a dormouse.

'It looks like our friend,' she says.

It does, too. Hammy is exactly that shade of orange – though he's no longer called Hammy. That was the only condition I imposed, the dropping of the naff name. Ned said how about we called him 'Johannes Cabal' after a book he was reading, and I said you can't call a hamster Johannes Cabal. So we shortened it to Yo-Yo, which suits him perfectly as he's forever up and down, climbing his cage, the sofa-back, your arm, the curtains. Once Mum left him unsupervised for ten seconds and he made it right the way up to the curtain rail and had to be rescued. She's moved the cage into the lounge, I noticed; it sits on a plastic table cloth near the window. Dad's told me she likes to talk to Yo-Yo while she's dusting. It's the turn-around to end all turn-arounds.

'Yes, whoever thought we'd have a pet in the house again,' she says, revealing that her thoughts were running along the same lines as mine. 'What a strange year it's been.' And she starts straightening the cutlery and the table mat, and nudging the salt and pepper pots into their proper place.

When the waitress comes over, we give our order promptly and without fuss. Beef in beer for Dad and Ned, rustic pork casserole for Mum, and I plump for the salmon.

'That's what Helen used to pick,' says Mum wistfully. Perhaps she thinks I'm choosing it as some kind of tribute. But the reason Hel always went for fish when we made her dine out was because it was a low-calorie option, whereas I'm having it because it's simply what I fancy today. To be honest, Dad could do with a bit of poached salmon in him rather than the beef. He's been told by the doctor to shave two stone off. Mum has this campaign to get him out walking with her in the spring.

At the table on our left a teenage boy sits opposite his parents and glowers. He did try earlier to sneak his phone and do a bit of texting, only his mother put a stop to that. To relieve the boredom he's currently spinning his butter knife on its axis. You can guess how this is going to end. Like every other bloody male on the planet this autumn, Ned included, he is wearing a plaid shirt, and that makes me remember Joe Pascoe and the last contact I had there. I was on Crewe Station, waiting for the London train, and for no reason I could justify I found myself checking out Ellie's Facebook page. This time I found the settings changed to public, and I could see her profile had undergone a makeover. For a start, she didn't describe herself as 'married' any longer; her Relationship Status was a blank. Divorced or separated? In a sense it didn't matter. Joe was clearly gone. Her photos of him had been deleted, and there were lots of new ones of her out with girlfriends, partying and enjoying herself. Stacks of supportive messages on her wall, too, and cartoons about the failings of men and how life was too short to put up with bastards. The message was clear: Look how well I'm doing now he's out of my life. Look, Joe, at what you threw away. Look, everyone, look.

Joe's own page had vanished.

I thought about his little girls, and how, if I ever got married, I'd make damn sure I gave it my best shot. I would not muck about and spoil things. When life was so full of tragedy, what madness was it made people throw away their own hard-won happiness?

'Are we ready yet?' murmurs Ned, breaking into my thoughts.

'Oh! Nearly. Yes.'

I push back my chair and hook my fingers through the handles of my tote bag so I can pull it up onto the table. Mum frowns as I slide out my laptop and switch it on.

'Not while we're eating, Jenny, surely?'

'I won't be long. There's something I need to show you. Something you're going to be very impressed by.'

The teen across the way eyes me enviously. I click and type. The wi fi connects. We are live.

'You've not told us what sort of a week you've had, anyway,' Dad's saying. 'Have you interviewed anyone famous yet? Any politicians? Bigwigs?'

'I don't do that, I've told you. Politicians come in and do these little speeches sometimes to the whole office, and I catch a few of those. We had that spying bloke on Tuesday. But it's the website I work on at the moment. Behind the scenes. It's not like when I was on *The Messenger*, out and about. Not yet.'

'I see.'

He doesn't, though. I swear he switches on the news every night expecting me to be on the screen, standing outside Downing Street with a mike or something. I'm a journalist working in London for a national newspaper, his reasoning goes. Therefore I must have hit the big time. But the reality is that I'm just doing shifts, I'm not on a permanent contract. The whole set-up's day-to-day, a leap of faith. A toe, I hope, in the door.

Ned reaches across and clicks the mouse a few times. A window appears on the screen and my mother cranes to see. Then she cries, 'Oh! Oh! Oh!' because my sister is in the centre of it, grinning.

I twist the laptop round so we can all see her, and she can see us.

'Helen?' says Mum. She sounds shocked, and I think, Come on, you've seen webcams before, they had one on *Holby City* last week. I angle the screen to get a better view and that's when I understand why she's so fazed. My sister's cut her hair off.

'You've cut your hair,' I say like a div.

'Have I? God, no, where's it gone?' Hel mimes amazement, claps her hand to her scalp.

'I mean, it's nice. It was a surprise.'

'Yeah, well. I was having to tie it up for lab work anyway, and I can't be bothered messing about with hot oil and conditioner any more.'

Although it's a radical change, it does actually suit her. She's gone for a short, feathered style, slightly 1970s, and it frames her cheekbones and makes her eyes seem wider. Not everyone could get away with it but my sister's beautiful, so she can.

'Cool. Where did you have it done?'

'Some place up by the castle. Can we talk about something other than my hair? Happy birthday, Mother.'

'Thank you,' says Mum, struggling to pull herself together. 'And thank you for my card and the music box. Gorgeous.'

'No probs. What are you having to eat?'

Dad takes over here. He gives her a full run-down of what's on the menu, and they exchange a few jokes about there being a thing called 'fat-immunity' on birthdays, which means you can eat whatever you want for twenty-four hours and not put on any weight. In the middle of this, our order arrives and we lose a minute or so to the handing round of plates and passing about of vegetables. Of course, none of us feels we can start eating while the conversation's going on, but Hel urges us to tuck in.

'It's quite like old times,' I say wryly. I kind of mean with my sister watching us distantly, from inside her own space. She gets the reference – I can tell by the face she pulls.

'Give us a taste, then,' she says to me. 'You know how I love my salmon.'

'OK. Open wide.'

She does as she's told and I scoop of a fork-full of fish and hold it to her onscreen image, as if I'm feeding a baby. I'm aware people in the room are watching us, but then they always did when Hel was around.

'Yum yum,' she says.

'So what have you got on for the rest of the day?' asks Ned. He's a little bit shy, I can see. A little bit awkward in her company still.

'I've an essay to finish this evening. Oh, and Tadek and Gill are dropping by tomorrow on their way to Oxford. And there's a quiz night I might go to on Sunday, this mature students' group I'm in – depends how tired I am and whether I managed to nail my assignment.'

'You must pace yourself,' says Mum.

'I will.'

I can see my mother's eyes searching the screen, looking for signs she's lost or gained weight. Secretly I've been doing the same. As far as I can judge, though, Hel's just Hel, as ever.

It doesn't take long till we run out of news. It's less than a

fortnight since my parents went down to visit, and I was texting her the previous night. So we say our goodbyes, and Skype's switched off, the window vanishes and the laptop goes away. Only then does Mum droop and grow tearful. But after a minute or so she's back on track.

'Well, that was nice,' she says, 'and very kind of you to set it up, Jen. Very thoughtful.'

I shrug, embarrassed. I'm thinking how tough she is, tougher than any of us thought, and how well she's doing generally. She's had such a lot of adjustments to make. When I'd first confided to Hel about the *Guardian*'s offer, and how I didn't dare leave our mother so soon after the last upheaval, she'd dismissed my worries at once. 'You can't spend the rest of your days trying not to upset her, Jen. You have your own life to live. So does she, actually. She just hasn't realised it yet.'

But I thought perhaps she was starting to. As well as the walking regime, there'd been mention of a Pilates class, and maybe signing up as a Friend of Hawkstone Follies. She and Dad had even been out together to see a play at our small local theatre, something I don't remember them doing before, ever. It was a brave new world, all right.

'And has that flatmate of yours sorted out some window locks yet?' Mum's asking me now. 'Because if she hasn't, your dad's going to come down and install some, aren't you, Don?'

He nods. 'I am. You can't stint on home security. Especially not in London.'

Criminal hub that it is. I could point out that someone had the wing mirrors off their next-door neighbour's Megane last week, but I don't.

Instead I attempt to reroute the conversation by fishing out my phone so I can take a photo of Mum showing off her birthday ring. This works. I take four good, flattering snaps, one of which I'll send to Hel for her family photos wall. I'm admiring them and not really paying attention to my dad when Ned asks, 'What's up, Mr Crossley?'

'I think I've left my camera in the car. I wanted to take some pictures on that.'

He makes to lever himself off his seat.

Ned leaps up at once. 'No, I'll get it for you. Give me your keys.'

'Yeah, I'll go too,' I add.

I don't hang about to look, but I know Mum and Dad will be exchanging glances. It's been hard for them to absorb this whole boyfriend-switch situation. They're still getting used to the idea, still needing reassurance that it's above board, and that makes Ned and me self-conscious about public displays of affection. Though to be honest, I suspect my mother's main emotion is relief that we're not losing Ned from the family – this polite, well-mannered, helpful young man, so much woven into our history from its darkest time onwards; the son she never had. He'll win her round. He'll win them both round.

Until then, it's best to be discreet. As soon as we get outside, he pulls me into a huge bear-hug and starts kissing my face and neck.

'Come here, you.'

I'm laughing and protesting and kissing him right back all at once. 'Stop it, you loon.'

'You love it.'

And it's true, I do. It's bliss to be physically close like this. I've missed him like hell these last months. Skyping and texting and meeting up at weekends makes it bearable, but only just.

'Listen,' he says. 'I've been dying to get you on your own. There's something I want to tell you.'

'That you adore me and worship me and the sight of my body is more than mortal flesh can stand?'

'That as well. Obviously. But something else.'

'What?'

Instead of answering, he kisses me again, and for several long moments I'm lost. I can hear the sounds of clashing metal and voices coming from the kitchen window. I can smell cooking in the air. Are those spots of rain on my cheeks and hands?

At last he breaks free. 'I've been speaking to my boss.'

'Old Randolph?' I begin to smile because lately Randolph's a bit of a joke between us. Ned does impressions of him searching for his glasses when they're on his head, and chewing the end of his pen till the cap comes off in his mouth. It's very funny. But then I consider what my boyfriend's just said and experience a shoot of alarm. 'Hang on. You've not done anything mad like hand in your notice?'

'Calm down. No, I've asked him about a transfer.'

'Transfer?'

'Down to their London place.'

'What?'

'Don't look at me like that. I've put in an application to the Bedevere group care home in Enfield. Royal Meadow, I think it's called. I mean, I could have applied to the one in Berwick or Lincoln but I didn't think that'd be much use to us.'

I'm blinking, trying to take in what he's just said. 'You're saying you'd move?'

'It would be a hell of a commute otherwise.'

'And Randolph's OK with that?'

'He's fine. He rang me this morning to tell me it's in motion. I've been dying to get you on your own and share the news.'

I'm searching for obstacles because fate can't be this kind. 'Are there other applicants for the post?'

'Don't know yet. Maybe some internal ones. But Randolph'll give me an excellent reference. He'll tell them how good I am at removing squirrels, for starters.'

'How will you afford to live down there? It's insanely expensive, you know. Even renting a tiny room like mine.'

He taps the side of his nose and does a shy little smile. 'Ah.'

'Never mind "ah". Address the question.'

'The job comes with accommodation. It's so I can be onsite more. Do long hours for not-great pay. But the point is, we can be together. Together, Jen. At long last.'

He reaches for my fingers, gazes into my eyes, and for one mad moment I wonder if he's about to propose. The moment has that degree of piercing intensity about it. Would it be so rash if he did? One day, I think, he will. And I know what I'll say.

'But even if you get this job,' (I can't stop myself) 'what happens if the journalism doesn't work out and I have to come back here? Or I need to move to another job somewhere else?'

'Have some faith. Stop being so negative.'

'I'm being realistic.'

'There's a time for being realistic and a time for leaping outwards hopefully. Leap, Jen.'

'There's been a whole lot of leaping recently—'

He stops me again with another kiss. My head's in chaos. What comes next? What else is going to loom up on the horizon, unpredicted? I daren't speculate.

'Right,' he says, smoothing my hair where his passion has

ruffled it. 'We'd better go get that camera. Otherwise your dad'll think I've abducted you.'

'I can't keep up with you today. It's like you're rocket-powered.'

'Powered by something. Not rockets.'

I start towards the footbridge but he tugs me in the other direction. What's he doing? Where does he want me to go? It's just narrowboat mooring up there. Then I understand. He's after running across the top of the lock gates.

I shake my head because I'm grown up, and a sensible journalist working on a national newspaper, and it's the route Hel and I took when we were kids. That kind of silliness is in the past.

He only pulls harder. I resist, laughing.

Finally he breaks free and strides off. He jumps lightly onto the narrow wooden beam, not even bothering to hold onto the metal guard rail. The surface looks slippery and worn. If he fell, he'd plummet into brown water and smash his head on the brick bed below. Look, now he's swaying about, standing on one leg, pretending to lose his balance. Basically he's so full of joyous energy he doesn't know what to do with himself. Annoying as he is, I don't believe I've ever loved him so much.

'Come on, Jen,' he says, stretching out his hand for me. 'Let yourself go. Follow me.'

And I do.

ACKNOWLEDGEMENTS

Thanks to: Sue Blower, Janet Jones, Kathryn Lester, Tracy Hartshorn, Joyce Carter, Louise Rodge, Hilary Lloyd, Pauline Higginson, Bethan Cole, Jill Finlay, Gill Broad, Anna Wild, Susan Percival, Emma Woolf, Richard Tyrone Jones, Alison Winward, Betsy Powell, James Gilbert, Alex Varley-Winter, Tom Morton, Hugh Warwick, Joshua Philpott, Frederika Whitehead, Vikki Broughton, @Psychedgirl @racheltoal @mapex_mustard @FiserableMucker @kirstendeanne @DanPurdue @TeresaStenson @ilovealcopop @Grufflock @Mister_Snoops @mumoss @Smokesniper @rainedonparade @sketXIII @bromleyoo1 @benwahwah @godigumdrop @gspro15198 @EmpJNorton @ianfarrington @RetroWench @IkklesaTwit @Retro_Review @KellyTcroft @nicoleharris @pablo_0151 @woulf_howl @campbellhowes @jodiebird22 , Clare Hey and all at Simon & Schuster, Peter Straus and the team at Rogers, Coleridge and White.

NB: the best zumba classes can be found in Bangor-on-Dee village hall at 6.30 p.m., Wednesday nights.